The Web and the Wing is a Part One of a Trilogy covering the period from The Declaration of Peace, the Armistice November 1918, until The Declaration of War, September 1939

Volume One:

November 1918 to Christmas 1930.

THE
WEB
AND THE
WING

Teresa Raftery

Matador
9 Priory Business Park
Kibworth Beauchamp
Leicestershire LE8 0RX, UK
Tel: (+44) 116 279 2299
Fax: (+44) 116 279 2277
Email: books@troubador.co.uk
Web: www.troubador.co.uk/matador

ISBN 978 1780885 612

British Library Cataloguing in Publication Data.
A catalogue record for this book is available from the British Library.

Typeset in Aldine by Troubador Publishing Ltd
Printed and bound in the UK by TJ International, Padstow, Cornwall

Matador is an imprint of Troubador Publishing Ltd

With love
To my children
Katherine, Robert, Susan, Richard, Fiona,
and to my parents
Thomas and Margaret Raftery

LIST OF MAIN CHARACTERS

Claire.   Born 1900. Daughter of a miner killed in a disaster in one of the Earl's mines in 1908. The tragedy orphaned Claire, her mother having died when she was three.

Anna.   Claire's aunt. A servant in charge of the laundry rooms at Ardleagh Hall, who was granted permission to take Claire in, to live with her.

Frederick.   The Earl of Eglinton.

Margaret.   Wife of the Earl.

James.   Born 1900. Second son of Frederick and Margaret, whose elder brother Austen was killed at Easter 1918, in France during the First World War.

Martin.   Born 1895. A mining engineer working in the Earl's mines.

Ralph.   Born 1898. Son of Albert Rawlinson, a successful, Lancashire cotton-mill owner.

Alva.   Duke of Arradova. A wealthy, Andalucian estate owner, Cordoba, Spain.

Amelia.   Wife of Alva and sister of the Earl of Eglinton.

Leonora.   Born 1904. The Anglo/Spanish daughter of Alva and Amelia.

Raimundo.   A General in the Spanish Army and close friend of Alva.

Georgio.   Nephew of Raimundo, also in the Spanish Army.

Bude.   Rumanian. A successful photographer, in exile, his family having lost title to their lands in the aftermath of the Balkan wars.

Johanna.   German, Born 1910. Daughter of Hans von Cours, a German banker, a man of influence.

Kurt.   German. Born 1906. Ambitious son of an impoverished, lower middleclass, factory foreman, Kurt gains a first class degree as an economist and later becomes a member of Hitler's S.S., the Schutz Staffel, (Protection Squad).

When certain conditions pertain, certain things appear,
just as violets do in early spring.

CHAPTER ONE

The Armistice, 11th November 1918

An uncontained excitement quickened the village. It heightened the expectations and hastened the pace of all, save the sluggish waters that continued to slop themselves sulkily against the grimy mill wall. The thick, dark smoke that usually poured from the mill's tall, soot-blackened, brick chimney was now only a grey trickle. There was to be no work this day. Siren and hooter from coal mine and mill had added to the clamour of the Church and Chapel bells since eleven that morning, proclaiming the anticipated, longed for and eagerly welcomed news that it was over. The war, the Great War, "the war to end all wars", that had taken its toll of every town and village in England was itself finally ended and the oft repeated promise of the last four years, "It will be over by Christmas", was at last true.

Making her way up the hillside, Claire left the village behind. She turned and looked down on the grey, damp, little boxes of houses, cramped row upon row upon the mill, where the river slackened its pace to a slow flow across the valley floor. One by one the hooters and sirens were ceasing now, but she could still hear the bells, both distant and near, as she continued her climb and followed the lane that skirted the woods before leading across the rise of rich pasture land that stretched towards the Hall. 'Soon,' she told herself, 'it would come into view, just around the next bend.'

There, there it was, Ardleagh Hall. Seeing it again was always like a first time. She stopped walking and pushed a rain-wet lock of black hair back under her damp scarf. 'It is as lovely as ever,' she thought, 'timeless, never changing.' Behind the outline of its gables and fine stone walls, on the reaches beyond, the bracken rusted against the scattered, grey moorland rocks, its auburn coloured ferns glistening luminous in the rain. Claire walked more slowly now, cherishing the view, for these were the moments when it belonged to her, as do all things belong, at least a little in some strange way, to those who love them. But such sentiments were pushed firmly aside as she drew close to its entrance. Hastening her pace she turned away from the grand, front gates and followed the lesser approach that took her along the tall, enclosing walls to the servants' access.

Already, the delivery carts and drays were arriving in the rear yard. Drawn by heavy horses straining into their collars, they were trundling forwards across the cobbles, their axles turning as large, iron-shod hooves, overhung by tousled fetlocks, scraped gratingly against the hard stones. The place was a hub of activity as drivers' mates began unloading even while the wheels still turned, but busy and bustling as it was, there was no confusion as everything was moved quickly and unerringly to its appointed place.

Not wanting to be in the way, Claire slipped through the yard and headed towards the market garden where seemingly endless, neat plots of vegetables stretched out on either side as she passed along the narrow path between. Yet, despite the regulations that had given such priority to food production during the war, there had been no changes elsewhere in the extensive gardens. The beautiful trees, ornamental shrubs and topiary work, the manicured lawns, immaculate flower beds and well-tended paths, were as cared for as ever. Passing the greenhouses and the tool and potting sheds, Claire now arrived at the rear extensions of the Hall. Here she regarded herself as being on home ground for this was where the washhouse, her Aunt Anna's domain, was situated.

Anna, a tall, seemingly tireless woman in her fifties, was in charge of all the laundering. Her duties now were mainly supervisory and from the smallest napkin to the heaviest of curtain drapes, nothing escaped her vigilance. She had worked at the Hall for over forty years and during that time her diligence and eye for fine detail, together with her trustworthiness and total discretion, had placed her not only high in the esteem of the Earl of Eglinton and his family, but had resulted in a measure of independence being bestowed on her.

Claire pushed open the small, green painted door that gave access to the drying yard. Stone flagged and partly covered in, it was here that the long, damask table cloths and fine, linen sheets were hoisted aloft by the clothes-line pulley to drip disconsolately, or on a good drying day to billow in the wind like sails before being taken in to be ironed. Today however, the yard was empty except for a few rows of smalls hanging damp and listless under the half-roof shielding them from the steadily drizzling rain. The laundry door was tightly closed. The place seemed deserted and the only sign of normality was the couple of bicycles belonging to the maids who came in each day from the village. But the scene belied the celebratory bustle going on inside.

On wet days such as this, ideas of washing were usually abandoned and all efforts concentrated on catching up with the ironing and mending. Inside the big, copper boilers, that on better days bubbled soapy water and steamed condensation onto the windows and tiled walls, the washing was left to simply steep waiting for the fires to be lit once more. In the pressing room next door the maids would be busy, leaning over large ironing-boards, pushing their weight onto the ember-heated flat irons to smooth away the crumples from the crisply starched, white linens.

Claire hesitated, but decided against going in search of her aunt and leaving the drying-yard, pulled its narrow door closed again. Her aunt's duties took her throughout the Hall and she would surely see her in the kitchens later in the day, especially since it was at her bidding that she was coming back to work here again after an absence of over six months. She had left with several other servants, after last Easter. The government had asked owners of large houses to help with the war effort and ease the labour shortage by employing fewer domestic staff. Since then the family had been living in their London townhouse in Park Lane.

Glancing around on her way to the kitchen, Claire could not help noticing how nothing ever seemed to change. But then, why should it? Life at Ardleagh Hall had run on timeworn wheels for generations of the Eglinton family and their expectations and attitudes emanated an air of confidence that this would naturally continue to be so for generations yet to come. 'All the same,' thought Claire, 'there must be some changes, considering that much of the Hall has been dust-sheeted and shuttered these last six months.'

She had first come to the Hall ten years ago at the age of eight, when her father was killed at Brackworth Colliery, one of the Earl's mines, in the worst pit disaster the village had ever known. Sixty-seven men, the whole of the night-shift except three, had lost their lives trapped below ground. Claire's mother had died a few days after Claire's birth and Anna had been allowed to take in her orphaned niece to live with her.

Attached to the laundry building, Anna's living quarters were far to the back of the Hall, well away from the main body of the house and none of the family had much noticed the presence of one little girl, none that is except James, the younger of the Earl's two sons, who was the same age as her. Later, when she became old enough, Claire also had gone into service, like Anna.

Since leaving the Hall, Claire has been lodging with the Pendle family who owned the village bakery and main stores, earning her keep by helping out in the evenings or before setting out in the mornings for the village school, where she had been lucky enough to find work helping with the little ones. Despite the war, the government, Lloyd George's coalition was changing the school leaving age and on March 13th, when the Education Bill had its second reading the M.P.s had voted to raise the age to fourteen. With more men leaving for the front, the school was under pressure and the headmistress, a spinster sister of Mrs Pendle, had readily accepted Claire's offer of help knowing her to be not only intelligent and a willing worker, but also an avid reader and very literate.

It was at the Pendles that Anna had found her niece only a few hours ago when she had come at the housekeeper's request to ask her to return to work.

"We were short staffed already," said Anna, "and now two of the maids have come down with 'flu and all of a sudden we get word from the Earl that he and the family are about to arrive. We don't know just when, but the Earl wants everything put back to rights. He wants Victory celebrations and the housekeeper's been told to organise for a full staff again and have everything back like normal by Christmas, the way it always was."

"But it can't be, can it?" Claire had said flatly, her dark gray eyes full of the candour of youth. "Nothing can ever be the same again."

"No," replied her aunt thoughtfully. "No, of course...it can't."

They were referring of course to the death of Austen, the Earl's elder son, who had been killed last Easter at Arras in France, during Ludendorff's offensive against the British lines.

Thinking of Austen, Anna had continued.

"It's going to hit the mistress hard all over again come Christmas, when the festivities really start an' there's big welcome parties for those who'll be coming home. We'll all have to be 'specially thoughtful for Lady Margaret and tell the new staff to be so as well."

"Yes." Claire had agreed absently, but she was really thinking of James who, now eighteen, had received his papers and would soon have had to leave had the war not ended. Her gladness today at the Armistice was due more to relief about James, than other concerns or the fate of the nation.

As if reading her thoughts Anna had spoken again.

"And Claire...about James...you must remember now..." But under her niece's full enquiring gaze, Anna's words had tailed away and she had paused, uncertain how to proceed. Her lips were pressed together as she searched for words...words to define...but it was no use and Anna realised that what she wanted to say was virtually indefinable.

Still, she tried again, in a different way.

"Claire, as I was saying…about James, you must understand, it's different now. He's different, older and…" At last and with relief, Anna found something definite to say.

"Well, he's Lord James now. He's next in line to the title, to the Earldom."

Claire had watched Anna struggling but had said nothing. She knew full well what the older woman was trying to tell her and it would have been easy to simply reply,

"Yes Aunt Anna, I understand." But she could not, for it would no longer have been true.

'The truth is,' thought Claire, 'it's Anna who doesn't understand, but how can she? She doesn't know how James thinks and feels, doesn't know his innermost thoughts like I do, but I can't tell her even that.'

Nor had Claire been able to find the words to tell her aunt that much as she loved the Hall, she did not want to return to work there, that being in service was not what she now wanted for herself, that she wanted something different, that she was studying to educate herself. Most of all, she could not tell Anna why her life was easier if she did not think of James. She needed an excuse so that she could refuse, but there was none.

The school was closed because of the virulent Spanish 'flu epidemic that was sweeping the country. There was no evidence to connect it with Spain, but that was the name given to it. Throughout the autumn it had raged across Europe without abating, killing more trench-weakened troops than the guns and the gas, so the newspapers said. Now the sickness had reached Lancashire and was adding to the hardship and absenteeism. With the school shut and the children sent home, Claire had time on her hands. No, she could not refuse. So it was that reluctantly she had told her aunt she would come later in the day.

But now that she was actually here, her misgivings were returning in full force. Having arrived at the kitchen side-door she put out her hand to the latch, but she did not lift it. Memories she had been keeping at bay were rushing back, flooding her mind and letting go of the door handle, she stepped aside. She needed time to think, to sort out her thoughts and she knew just where to go. When they were children, she and James had known all the hidden places.

As she entered the stable-yard Claire glanced around, but saw no-one. Almost all the looseboxes and stalls were empty. The horses had been requisitioned long ago and, like many of the grooms, sent to the war. Having reached the hayloft without encountering anyone, Claire carefully climbed the rickety steps of the ancient tower to the little garret behind the clock. It was as cobwebby dusty as it had always been but like so much else, was unchanged. She crossed the old boards to the wall where long ago she and James had scratched their names with horseshoe nails. Yes, they were still there and she touched them, tracing the 'J' and the 'C' with her finger, but the brickwork was very old, the plaster loose and flaky, and little bits crumbled away leaving the letters less distinct. She moved towards the air-vents from where they used to look down into the yard, seeing but not being seen. Far below a solitary stable-lad was sweeping soggy, fallen leaves into a heap before shovelling them into a cart.

A few weeks more and the stables would be full of bustle again the way they used to be. Hunters and hurdlers would fill the boxes. Grooms and handlers would return to their old jobs and new staff would be taken on to replace those who would not be coming back and life would go on. Leaning against the wall, Claire let the memories she had been keeping pushed away, return. She was older than James by just a few weeks and had known him more than half her life. They were close. They trusted each other. As children, they had played together, shared their thoughts, talked endlessly for hours in unmeasured, un-weighed words until... until when? She cast her mind back...to the day of his sixteenth birthday, more than two years ago.

The celebrations that marked it also marked the first time she had waited upon the Earl and his guests. It was just another job and it was not the serving itself that she minded. In any case, no one had much noticed her, but it was this very lack of awareness of her presence that had afforded her the insights into their 'other' world, a different world, one shaped by attitudes and expectations of people who were other than herself and who looked on her as different also.

Even now Claire's recollections of that day were as sharp and as painful as thorns in her mind, for that was when the many little incidents and confusions of which she had already been gradually becoming aware had crystallised into realisations and become clear and had fitted together like the pieces in one of those small box-puzzles which when shaken a certain way, fall into their intended places and a picture can at last be seen.

She should have seen it before and of course, in a sort of way, she had. At least, that is to say, she had recognised there were big distinctions between their circumstances, between hers and those of James. How could she not? But that day, the day of his sixteenth birthday, that was the first time it dawned upon her that these distinctions did not only exist between circumstances, but between people themselves, that they put barriers between them, barriers that could not be crossed and that was when she had started erecting barriers of her own and avoiding James, though none of it was his fault.

Yes, she remembered it, James' sixteenth birthday, a day packed with happenings and people, when the Hall had been crowded with the gentry from both near and far. It had gone endlessly on, culminating in the evening in a Grand Ball. The place was thronged and the occasion had developed into what society would politely term 'a crush'. There was so much going on, in so many crowded rooms. Was it really that as time went by, more and more people arrived? Or was it that she had just become more and more tired? Whichever, as the evening wore on and the Ball wheeled into full spin, it seemed the pace of the dancing became ever faster and faster, to music ever louder and more jarring.

Garbed in her maid's dark, long-sleeved heavy uniform she felt hot and conspicuous against the bare, bejewelled and perfumed shoulders of the many beautiful, young women gowned in bright velvets and swirling silks, who were thronging around James. As the wine and champagne continued to flow, there were too many raised voices, too many raised glasses and a brittle excitement in the air, echoing artificial laughter.

The long, glittering mirrors in the gilded ballroom reflected in kaleidoscopic fashion the radiant colours that eddied and changed as the merrymakers turned and circled and glided away. She had tried not to notice James, but now and then, glimpses of him, tall, suave and handsome, laughing and dancing with one lovely partner after another had flashed across them, bringing him into her view once more. But he was far removed from her, belonging to that world that was different, that had begun to seem no more than a dream to the one she lived in. Drab-dressed and dowdy, she was as miserably swathed in self-consciousness as a Cinderella still at the ball after the midnight hour had struck. How she had wished she could leave so as not to be seen by him, but that could not be and the festivities had dragged on.

Finally, when the dancing stopped and the guests had gone, she went to bed, but not to sleep. Her life, her world, the one in which she had grown up, had changed. For a long, long time she had lain awake, thinking, but at last the understanding came to her that in fact, nothing had changed, not really, not out there in the world.

The world out there was just the same as it had always been. These barriers, these differences, they had always existed, component parts of a social framework that gave the grownup world its order. No-one was suddenly imposing them upon her. It was just that she and James, in growing up were growing into them, were becoming part of an unalterable structure that had been in place for decades, long before they had reached it.

All the same, even if nothing out there had changed, something had inside her and over the next few weeks, James realised that there was something wrong but knew not what. He had tried hard to find out but, for the first time, she could not share her thoughts with him.

Other events had also occurred shortly after James' sixteenth birthday, that brought their own changes and she and James saw little of each other for several months. Earlier in that year, the rules regarding conscription into the armed forces had been extended and preferring to be a volunteer, Austen had left for the Army. In his absence, the Earl began to focus much more on his younger son. Clearly he considered a sixteenth birthday to be that which should mark a boy's initiation into the world of men and he began to organise his son's life for him. James disliked this. He found it restricting. His own personality was emerging and there were many issues on which he did not see eye to eye with his father. His opinions and viewpoints were turning out to be very different from those expected of him and he stayed with friends as often as possible.

Claire's thoughts were interrupted by the old clock in the tower grumbling its protest at the approaching hour, its ancient wheels jerking into readiness to strike. Roused from her reverie, she moved over to the opposite wall that afforded a view of the woods where they sloped down to the river's edge. There they had played and nobody had asked her then to understand, but then again, nobody had much noticed. She smiled at the thought, remembering how skilled James had been at avoiding supervision and escaping the confines of his regulated life and how, with her, had gone to places and done things just not a possibility for him otherwise for she was streetwise, knew how to get around the countryside, knew the shortcuts through the alleys of the small nearby town, knew which of the tradesmen would give them rides to get there.

She could pass unnoticed and with her, so too could he provided he ruffled up his appearance. She knew the best jumps across the fast-running brook, knew the best escape routes to outwit irate farmers, which bridges could be safely under-climbed to avoid being seen, which culverts could be passed through, which to avoid and the times when they were flooded and unsafe. She knew where the best blackberries grew and which of the old ladies in the village would return the kindness of a basketful, with big pieces of homemade treacle toffee or slices of cake. At harvest time she could wander far afield, knowing which of the drivers drawing in the hay could be relied upon to let them scramble up the back of the wagon for the ride home. Cushioned in the sweet smelling softness they could see for miles from the top of the creaking, swaying load.

On these escapades with Claire, James tagged along keeping his mouth shut and letting her do the talking. It was a source of merriment to them both that whilst Claire could switch with fluent ease from a local dialect to an accent and grammar exactly like his own, he found himself quite unable to do the reverse despite her best endeavours to teach him.

There was also much he taught her that otherwise she would have never known, music she would not have heard and more literature than she would have ever read. He told her about his lessons at school, often lending her his books. There was a library at the Hall with beautifully illustrated books that must not be removed. He would tell her the times when nobody would be there, which the best books were and where to find them on the shelves. It was when he played the piano that she heard for the first time, the lovely music by Mozart and Chopin and was entranced by the latter's Nocturne in E flat.

When he practised she listened from outside the music room's open window and he played the pieces she loved the most. One day she found a book about Chopin and Aurore Dupin, daughter of a prostitute and an aristocrat. Acutely aware of social injustice and prejudice, she had become a famous writer. She was a socialist and went by her pen name, George Sand. Flouting all convention she left her family to live with Chopin and according to Chopin himself, it was she who inspired his finest music. Claire learned how intertwined music is with literature and history and poetry and her interest in these subjects widened.

But those times were now past and Claire turned away from the view of the river where they had played in the days when there were no divisions, no divides, and brought her mind back to her present worries and concerns.

After his sixteenth birthday she had continued working at the Hall and, until last Easter, she had managed very well. She had read the score and understood. In fact, if Anna had spoken to her last Good Friday, about James, her answer would have been simple.

"Yes, I understand. We were children and we could be friends. Now we're grownup and we can't. That's the way the world is."

But Austen had been killed last Easter and what had happened in the days that followed, had changed her mind around, swirling her thoughts and emotions with questions she must sort out for herself and she could no longer say,

"Yes, I understand. That's the way the world is."

The old clock ceased its rumbling. It had readied its ancient levers. Poised on the silence they were about to fall and sound the hour. It was too late for further reminiscing. There was too much to be done and lifting the trap door, Claire began her descent.

The old clock's reverberations died away. Claire left the tower and skirting the vegetable gardens, took the path towards the kitchens. She entered by the side-door that opened into what she called the nether-regions, a continuity of sculleries, cold-rooms, larders, vegetable pantries and other small, cellar-like chambers, where silver was polished, knives sharpened and all manner of paraphernalia was cleaned and cared for. They were unoccupied and she saw nobody as she passed along the corridor.

At its end, on either side of the archway that led into the main kitchen, were two further extensions. One was equipped with sinks, one of which was a large, wooden one for the finer things, glasses, crystal and delicate, eggshell china. The other was the pastry pantry, with a cold, marble-topped table to keep the pastry cool when being rolled. Claire glanced inside. Cook can't be far away, she thought, looking at the mound of soft, white dough beside a large rolling-pin and baking dish.

She went through the arch into the kitchen. At its far end, a couple of steps led down into the back entrance porch. Beyond it was the cobbled yard she had passed through earlier. The heavy, oaken door stood ajar and Cook's voice could be heard, sternly raised in remonstration. Claire smiled to herself, pitying the unfortunate who had not toed the line. The stream of light was suddenly cut off by Cook's bulk. Throwing words over her shoulder and fiercely wiping her hands on a tea towel, she heaved herself up the steps.

"...an' just you mek good an' sure you do," she threatened.

Sharper ears than Cook's would have caught the muttered, grumbling back answer that came from the disgruntled maid who was following behind.

Cook suddenly caught sight of the young woman waiting for her. Her voice rang out again, this time in pleasure.

"Oh Claire, you're back, thanks be," and the over-plump, old woman lifted her eyes heavenward, as if this unannounced presence in her kitchen was due to direct intervention from on high.

"Oh, you don't know 'ow good it is t' see you. I 'aven't found 'a good un' since you left," she added, shooting well aimed, dark looks at the sullen Millie. The maid clattered her metal bucket far more than necessary and muttered about the delivery men who, in addition to several stacks of crates, had left a mess in the back porch.

"So, tell me 'ow you've bin?" asked Cook. "How's things bin fo' you since you went?" She focussed afresh on the slender, young girl, noting the subtle changes since she last saw her.

'Er's goin' t' be a beauty,' she thought, but her liking for the girl had little to do with her looks. It was Cook's firm belief that, 'Handsome is, as handsome does.' and it was Claire's temperament and manner that counted most with her.

'Still, where'd you see another t' match?' she wondered, stealing another look at her, at the expression in the dark gray eyes, the glossy, shoulder length, black hair. 'Yet for all o' that, there's summat more, a sort o' calm…' but before Cook could give it more thought, there was a loud crash in the porch followed by a piercing squeal. Cook spun round, ready to make off in the direction from which it came. Claire touched her arm.

"No, you go ahead with what else you have to do. I'll give her a hand."

A hefty, corner crate had brought upon itself the brunt of Millie's resentment by its refusal to move at the shove of her broom. Its comeback to her final clout had been to tipple down a box of bottles that had been balancing on its top. Fortunately, or otherwise according to one's viewpoint, Millie had broken its fall and only one bottle was smashed. But its landing had certainly shattered what remained of the maid's brittle-thin patience.

"Right stupid it is, way yon lot 're all piled up. Jus' look at 'em," she grumbled, her mouth set in self-justification as she thought of another accusatory remark.

"Look at' em, will yer. Yer wouldn't think as 'ow there's rationin' still goin' on, but then agen…" she added in an unpleasant tone, "that's cos there ain't any, leastways not 'ere any-road, an' never 'as bin, not fo' the likes o' them as can afford to…"

She got no further.

Cook had appeared at the top of the two short steps that led to her kitchen and with what would be best described as a bellow, obliterated Millie's bleat.

"There'll be non' o' that kind o' talk, not 'ere, not in my kitchen an' jus' you remember my girl where yer wages comes from or the'll not be comin' at all come Friday next."

The thought was sufficiently chastening to silence Millie and having dispatched her to dispose of the broken glass, Cook shook her head. Despite the display of robust energy she had just exhibited, she suddenly looked drained and tired.

"We're so short 'anded, but 'er'll 'ave t' go, 'er's more hindrance than 'elp an' cheeky wi' it. If I thought 'er'd e'er mek good I'd try trimmin' 'er to size, but it's no use, 'er's all wrong." Cook sighed wearily as she fretted. "It's this war…made proper 'elp so 'ard to get. Young uns today know as 'ow they can mek more money in that 'munitions factory an' they shows yer such a different attitude to 'ow it wer' in my young days."

"Well, now think," said Claire trying to cheer her, "the war's over. The bells and sirens were sounding as I left the village. The armament factory 'll be closing soon and anyway, I'm sure, given a few more rounds like that, Millie will shape up."

"No," replied Cook despairingly, "...not that one. I should 'ave known. 'What's bred in the bone yer can't tek out o' the flesh', an' 'er mother wer' one o' them forever handin' out pamphlets for them suffragettes as marched round wavin' banners, chainin' 'emsells to railings, meking a right nuisance o' themsells."

About to reply, Claire bit her lip. She knew of old that it did no good to argue with Cook. Her ideas were as fixed, rigid and as permanently in place as the solid, cast iron cooking range that took up almost the whole of one wall. In any case, this would be a particularly ill-chosen moment to cross her.

Cook took advantage of the silence.

"That Millie...'er's like a lot o' others...'er don't listen...'er don't know 'er place...an' 'as no respect for 'er betters."

This, Claire decided, she could not let pass and her words blurted out.

"Maybe like a lot of others, she doesn't believe they are our betters."

Cook's expression turned suspicious.

"Now don't you be tekin' up them new-fangled ideas as 'ow, 'Jack's as good as 'is master.' Way I see it, God made everyone t' their place…an' it's where they should stay. This war's giv'n a lot o' folks ideas above their station. I don't hold wi' it. It's not right an' it won't work, you'll see."

"Well it worked for the suffragettes," said Claire. "They've made the government give them what they fought for and next month in the December elections, for the first time ever, women will be able to cast their votes."

Despite her best endeavours, triumph sounded in Claire's voice, but never lost for an answer Cook retorted.

"Not all of 'em they won't, on'y women o'er the age o' thirty an' there's many a one as won't be votin' on account of 'aving to admit to that. Politics...waste o' time botherin' wi' 'em when there's work t' be done," she countered. "Th' Earl and Lady Margaret 'll be back soon. an' th' House still isn't open proper an' afore we know, it'll be Celebrations an' Christmas. Oh, but it'll be good t' be gettin' back t' normal," she added, her face beaming in anticipation.

Claire was wondering if James would be returning with his parents. She wanted to ask but the thought of betraying her interest was more discomforting than the effort of containing it. She ventured instead, a question about Lady Margaret's return and tagged "and James?" onto the end of it.

"Well he's 'Lord James' now, bein' as 'ow he's next in line t' inherit...so Elliott keeps tellin' us," said Cook tartly. The relationship between her and Elliott the butler was an on-going jostle for the upper hand and she was more concerned with Elliott's remembered rebuke than with Claire's question.

Irritation at Cook having muffed her cue swept over Claire. She was tossing up whether to just ask bluntly, when 'Lord James' was coming back when Cook, as though she had only just heard, replied.

"Well, th' Earl an' Lady Margaret arrive on Sunday, that much is now fo' sure, but I can't say if James 'll be comin' wi' them, though instructions were to 'ave 'is room ready an' Madge was in there all mornin', airin' it an' seein' to 'ave a fire lit in the grate, an' Anna 'ad one of 'er maids sortin' out pillows and linens for his bed an' layin' out his things."

Claire winced inwardly. The intimacy of images conjured up by talk of pillows for his bed and all the personal things he used, gave her a swift twist of torment that left her with an almost physically nauseous ache. She grappled with it, struggling to smother it and wishing she had never asked.

"You've gone all pale dear," said Cook, in concern. "...you've bin on the go too long, an' in all th' excitement it's bin too much."

"No, no, I'm fine," protested Claire hurrying off to the pastry pantry. Her thoughts were in turmoil. She was unsettled about so many things. The title to which James had succeeded on the death of his elder brother was just one more symbol of her inequality, one more mark of his increasing status and stature, one more remove that life was placing between them.

It was all these things, but it was more. To Claire it was one more dig of the spur into the flank of her fierce determination to make something of herself, one more prod to her pride, a pride that had made her vow to herself that she was going to become everything she wanted herself to be.

Standing before the marble slab, she took the soft dough and began to mould and shape it. As she did, she tried to put away distractions of the future. Better just to live the moment, arrest all thought, stay conscious only of the present. It was a technique that worked for her, putting her in touch with some calm, creative force that welled up from her awareness of her own autonomy and gathered strength from her resolve.

The last pie decorated and the chore complete, she returned to the kitchen and Cook set about updating her on the latest gossip, much to the annoyance of Millie on whom Cook took reprisal by maintaining an obvious silence whenever she appeared.

"Jus' let 'er wait 'till next time 'er's tellin' us off for idle chatter - talk o' 'Don't do as I do. Do as I says'," she bitterly complained to Claire later.

Idle chatter it may be, but it was informative and Claire had learned that the relationship between James and his father had not improved. As Cook put it, "They don't get on at all, they don't."

The Earl had brought James with him on a recent trip to Lancashire to check on the estate and liaise with the mine managers and overseers. Coal being vital to the war effort, the mines had been kept working at full production. The exigencies of war had put a stop to the accusations of exploitation, low wages and dangerous working conditions that had provided the Trade Unions with ammunition against the pit owners and all rules and regulations had been rigidly enforced, making the mines easier to manage.

Usually during these visits from London it was from Eric the chauffeur, that Cook got most of the gossip, but during this last one she had been able to see for herself the trouble between father and son. Now that James was heir to all the properties, the Earl was determined his son would follow the course he had mapped out for him and he had been insistent he accompany him on this particular round of colliery inspections. On the day in question, the meeting of managers and foremen had been held at the Hall.

"T'wer jus' like in th' old days, when they came," said Cook nostalgically, "...everythin' dusted an' polished, wi' fires burnin' in't grates. But after the others had gone I went to clear away, bein' as 'ow we wer' short o' maids, an' it wer' then as I heard 'em. It didn't sound right, sort o' too serious I suppose, so I waited. Well, their voices wer' low to begin with an' I couldn't rightly hear, but there wer' no doubt they wer' arguin' an' then I heard James sayin' it wer no use blamin' the miners all the time. A different look 'ad to be taken at what they wer' bein' asked to do, an' the conditions they 'ad to do it in an' listenin' to 'im, I couldn't but agree, but the Earl, he got cross and vexed, raisin' his voice an' sayin' as 'ow he'd best do as he's bin told an' learn more on management, then he'd know 'ow 'ard it is to mek th' pits pay.

"Well, that got it goin' an' James asks 'ow much profit it'd lose t' buy new ropes 'stead o' waitin' till the frayed ones snapped, puttin' lives at stake, an' after that it got so bad I wer' feared the door'd open an' one or other come burstin' out an' I'd be caught alistenin' so I didn't get t' hear the end of it, but Eric tells me there wer' a dreadful, frosty atmosphere on the way back an' he reckons they've still not rightly made up an' he'd know, seein' as 'ow he gets t' talk to staff at the Park Lane house.

"...an' Lady Margaret's still not well an' Lord Frederick's specialists 'aven't helped, but what else t' expect when she's grievin' o'er one son, an' bin worrying 'bout 'er other one 'aving' t' fight as she's 'ad cause to till this mornin'. He should've let 'er come round in 'er own time 'stead o' keep insistin' she pull 'erself together an' get out an' about. Well that's 'ow it is, wife an' son an' th' Earl not best pleased wi' either o' 'em. Lord alone knows how it'll be when they gets back 'ere, an wi' this Celebration an' kitchens not sorted an' this flu epidemic..."

Unable to keep track of Cook's harassment, Claire interrupted.

"I'm surprised he wants to celebrate, given what happened to Austen."

"Well, we won an' the Celebration's t'show it wasn't, well...all...fo' nothin'..." Cook trailed off lamely, frowning as if puzzling over what she had just said. "Don't you see?" she asked, her brow still puckered.

"No I don't," said Claire bluntly. "I can better see what we've lost. What have we won when we're worse off than we were before?" she stopped abruptly.

Her outburst had been a case of, 'How do I know what I feel, till I hear what I say?' and in an effort to redeem the moment, she added, "Of course, it's right to be glad we won. So tell me, when's this big put-the-clock-back Celebration going to be?"

Millie's timing was perfection. Her entry was superb. Before Cook could answer, she swept through the kitchen bearing before her the big, mopping up bucket full of dirty water that she was on her way to empty down the outside drain. Her presence had been forgotten by the other two, for she had been a long time in the pastry pantry on her hands and knees quietly scrubbing the floor and listening to Cook's every word and Millie now reckoned it was her turn to speak.

"Oh, 'aven't you 'eard...?" she asked in feigned surprise, raising her eyebrows and turning to Claire. "This Celebration's not goin' to be on'y one big occasion, so to speak, like, 'just-one-day-of-a-do'. No, this Celebration's goin' to be an whole three days of it, an house party wi' dancin', an' big dinners an' folks stayin' 'ere at th' Hall, an' a pheasant shoot, wi' them big 'ampers stuffed full o' food so folks won't be going 'ungry while they're 'manning the guns'. Oh...an' there's goin' t' be huntin' as well, a big day's huntin' wi' a lawn meet, 'ere in the grounds so they can all sup o' 'The Stirrup Cup'. So, if I wer' you," said Millie, darting a mean and meaningful glance at Cook, "I'd no' be worryin' an' wunderin' if the three o' them's goin' t' be happy when they gets back, cos if folks can't be 'appy wi' all that lot an' all their money, they don't deserve t' be. It's other folks as we should be feeling sorry for."

Claire turned away to conceal the merriment creasing her face at the sight of the vehemence creasing Cook's. And Millie, with an aplomb that would have won applause on a London stage, timed her exit as beautifully as her entrance and disappeared from view letting the slam of the heavy, back door proclaim for her, the futility of reply.

"No, don't, don't," cried Claire as she tried to prevent a choleric Cook from setting off in pursuit. "Don't go after her. She has to come back."

Cook stopped in her tracks. The satisfaction of vengeance could be heard in her voice.

"An' this time when 'er comes...er's goin'."

CHAPTER TWO

Cordoba, Andalucia, Southern Spain
December 1918

*T*he hot sun that had furnaced the land all summer long had relented and the days were shorter now. An evening breeze stirred among the dry leafstalks. All colour, all moisture drained, they had silvered the earth, but now the sun, molten on its downward path, spilt streaks of roseate gold that tinged them pink and flamed the sky beyond the hills.

Leonora waited. A little while and reflections from its burnt orange embers would bring all the lands, mountains and plain, valley and river and far off glimpses of Cordoba's roofs within its glow. She relaxed in the cool, dry air and leaned back against the smooth rock that out-cropped from the escarpment where the plateau ended and there began the long sweep of descent that evened out only as it reached the valley floor and levelled with the river, the Guadalquiver.

Far below it meandered, westwards, southwards, curving easily on a course the road could not always follow.

'Will its waters be in Cordoba by nightfall?' she mused and let her memory fill with images of it in the darkness, lapping the stone embankments and towers, glinting the lights of the old Roman bridge, flowing past riverside walks and fountained gardens where lanterns cast shadows that danced in their light, timelessly evoking spirits from the legacy of the ancient city's Moorish past.

Cordoba, she missed its loveliness, missed visiting her grandmother in her exquisite and well ordered, riverside home, with its trees and flowers and hallowed sense of safety behind its high walls and elegantly wrought iron gates. Its calm and peaceful atmosphere made the sounds of violence and anger that had intruded from outside of late, seem to belong to another world, a world that Leonora had pieced together from snatches of grownups' conversations.

She knew that the Anarchists had been making trouble in the country, on and off, for many years and that the rioting had intensified anew in that dreadful August of 1917, the summer before last. That was the time of the all-out strike that had gripped and so disastrously paralysed many parts of Spain. It was also the time when for weeks on end, she had scarcely been allowed beyond the doors of her parents' home in the city centre. Her father, Alva, Duke of Arradova, said that the insurrections had flared afresh because the agitators had taken heart from the success of the workers' revolution that year, in a far off country called Russia and that much more should be done to stop the unrest.

But in all of her fourteen years, the troubles had not really intruded into Leonora's sheltered life any more than that dreadful war in Europe that had just ended, except that these days news of every fresh disturbance was followed by long drawn-out meetings held behind the tall doors of her father's private study, meetings from which he would emerge looking pale and tense and angry.

Otherwise life had gone on just the same until that dreadful morning three weeks ago when she and her grandmother were returning in their carriage, having attended Mass in Cordoba's great Cathedral.

It was then, without warning, that the measured pattern of Leonora's ordered life had been blown apart and all that hitherto had been nothing more than impressions left on her mind from the half-overheard, horror stories of others, became a raw reality exploding in screams and crushed by the deafening noise of heavily falling masonry. A bomb had exploded and people were pushing and fighting their way through the confusion to which they were adding. A rising flood of hysteria filled the cramped space between the high buildings as the clamour was compacted and then splintered apart by the crack and flash of gunfire coming from no-one knew where.

Caught in the confines of the narrow street, the bomb blast had ripped away their carriage door and hurled Leonora and her grandmother to the floor between its leathered seats. The road before them was blocked with rubble and Leonora had watched terrified as the crowd grew rapidly in number and began to close in tightly around their conveyance. Its ostentatious, well-kept appearance made it a target for their hostility and the torn off carriage door was being held jeeringly aloft and passed around. Their family crest, proud proclamation of their nobility, was battered but still brilliant against the shiny black of its panel and was serving to incite still further their mockery and threatening taunts.

Having regained her seat, her grandmother was sitting upright and motionless, close to the gaping space where the door had been. Her face was impassive and she seemed impervious to both the danger and the derision, but Leonora, numb with fear, was pressing herself as far back as she could into the thickly padded upholstery, bracing herself as the mob began to rock the vehicle violently from side to side.

Artura, their driver, was still struggling with the frightened, sweating horses as obediently they twisted and strained, slipping and scraping their iron shoes on the cobbles as they tried and tried again to turn the carriage round.

Never before had Leonora seen people such as these, so many and so near and nothing like the peasants who worked for her father on his huge estates. This was a mob, angry and threatening and out of control. She looked around wildly but on both sides was confronted with faces close to her own, faces filled with rancour as acrid as the smoke that was swirling in the dust and the noise and confusion on the suffocating air. Her grandmother's gaze never wavered but remained steadfastly fixed upon Artura, as though the force of will could ensure the success of his efforts. Intent on his task, he also seemed not to be hearing the jeers and the threats that were filling Leonora with mounting panic.

But the mob was not to be ignored. They were retaliating against a Civil Guard atrocity carried out earlier in their area and were now intent on making trouble in this usually quiet part of the town. Violence had broken out and when shots were fired, rioting began.

In spite of the jostling and their fright, the horses had almost succeeded in dragging the carriage around, when suddenly a man at the front leapt forward grabbing the reins of the one nearest to him. As if at an awaited signal, Arturo sprang into action. For a few brief moments he wielded his whip with devastating effect. As the man fell backwards, Artura urged the already frantic animals on again. It was all that was needed. They made a last, wild lunge, checked momentarily as their trappings took up the strain and then plunged powerfully forward once more. The carriage lurched dangerously, scattering the mob, and then it was free, rattling and careering in breakneck manner, leaving the rabble behind.

In the annals of the ongoing battles between Spain's Left and Right wings, it was a very minor incident, a mere nothing compared with the street killings, the assassinations of leading figures, the rampaging of the rioters and the terrorizing of individuals that had bedevilled the country since the closing decades of the last century. But for Leonora it was a horrendous happening, far outside anything that her sheltered life could have helped her to imagine. Why should these total strangers and so many of them, hate her father and her family so? Their coarse threats and insults kept echoing in her mind frightening her afresh and for the rest of the afternoon after reaching home, she was sick and wretched and hung around the house not knowing what to do, quite unlike her grandmother who was continuing calmly with her normal activities seemingly none the worse for what she dismissively referred to as 'the incident'.

Leonora's grandmother was of Castilian descent and showed as little of her emotions as appeared on the faces of her ancestors in the large portraits that lined the hall of her family's ancestral home. In keeping with the traditions of her lineage, the old lady placed her duties, as dictated by family honour and The Church, and in that order, above all other considerations. The unalterability of these guidelines afforded her a fatalistic serenity not shared by her granddaughter. Arturo also appeared unperturbed and spent the rest of the afternoon quietly, taking careful stock of the damage to the vehicle and making arrangements for its repair.

There was however, a marked change in this routine-like atmosphere with the arrival home of Leonora's father, the Duke of Arradova and her mother, Amelia. Her mother's voice could be heard coming from the hall, soon followed by the sound of her quick footsteps on the stairs and the closing of her bedroom door. Grimfaced after talking to Artura, her father went upstairs to join her. Within a short while, Leonora heard the sharp exchange taking place between them.

Amelia was not Spanish. She was English, very English, the sister of the Earl of Eglinton. For years she had argued with her husband that their lives would be easier if they lived abroad. The morning's events were grist to her mill. Going downstairs Leonora found her grandmother even more rigidly serene than usual and later that evening her father announced his decision.

He told his wife and daughter that he had arranged for them to stay with friends in their country home some miles outside Sevilla, temporarily of course. There, they would be quite safe until the disturbances ceased. Meanwhile, he would spend time at the castle on the estate.

Centuries old, the castle stood some miles outside Cordoba city. Although the family had not lived there for generations it still filled a purpose as a useful outpost for the running of the estate and part of it was kept in service. Whilst there, Alva would confer with his overseer, Bastanta, and finalise long term plans for even stricter security of the olive groves, vineyards and plantations. Bastanta, who lived on the estate, would see to it that his orders were duly carried out. As he spoke, Alva exuded confidence, assuring his wife that there was no cause for worry. The estates would continue to produce. This turbulent period would pass.

He had managed so far, to keep from Amelia the alarming news that only a few days ago, a neighbouring estate had been raided, its crops destroyed and outbuildings burned. In the fighting that followed, the estate manager had been savagely beaten. Some landowners, wanting strong measures, were now liaising with the Army and the Civil Guard. This also was something best kept from Amelia. She could be sensitive about such matters and argumentative. She did not understand that there really was no choice, that here in Spain certain things had to be done, a certain way.

Hoping to allay any misgivings she may have, he reminded her that there had been trouble before, but the unrest had always settled down and would do so again. They simply had to stand firm. For her part, Amelia needed no reminding that there had been bad times before. Working her tapestry, she listened to her husband's dictates on what was to be, and what was not, listened very attentively, not only to his words, but to the sound of his voice. It was, she concluded, his authoritative tone, the one with the ring of finality to it.

'Hmm, a pity,' she thought, '...sounds as though he means what he says.' The pity was that she had no intention of staying with the friends he had chosen, in their country home outside Sevilla, especially not at this time of the year. The very idea of being incarcerated there, surrounded by dull people, scarcely ever out of Church all through Christmas and the New Year and for Heavens only knew how long thereafter, had already thrown her into a peculiar imbalance, somewhere between boredom and alarm.

It was more the pity, because for years she had been hoping that things might improve, but now she could see that they had already gone way beyond, what was way too far. She had tried to adapt to life in her husband's country, to adopt its customs, but had finally grown sick of it and was tired of living in a land that kept its women cooped up and she did not want her young daughter Leonora to continue being brought up in it. It would, she believed, be far better for her to continue her education in England.

Prior to coming to live here, Amelia's images of Spain had been of flamenco dancers, clicking castanets, colour, vivacity and fun...flowers, spirited horses, handsome men, the warm air of evening and strummed guitars and what had she got?, the reality of life with Alva.

'No, no,' she silently strictured herself, '...let's not dwell on that...not just now.'

She had watched her husband, especially in recent months, involved in intrigues and power struggles, using his political pull and his high up friends in the Army and the Church and she was tired of the way he lived his life, and hers. She had had enough of Spain and its unmanageable problems, of his worries and his estates and his pestering her for a son. She did not want to bring a son into this, to inherit all this anxiety, to have to wade through all this ghastly mess.

Furthermore, having a son would really put paid to any chance of escape. She might get away with a daughter but never with a son, for Alva would root a son of his very deeply in this Spanish soil and she could never leave a child of hers behind, certainly not in a situation in which he would be weighed down with the baggage of his forebears, tied to tradition, lumbered with his heritage, in a role predetermined for him before he was born. Oh no, she could see it coming from afar. Even as she went into labour Alva would be waiting and the ball and shackles that came with his great grandfather's crib, yes the very one, would be ready to be fastened round her little baby's ankles...well, that was how she saw it.

And what if it were not a boy, what then... Alva pestering for repeat performances, Lord alone knew how many, until she finally produced a male heir? She would not have minded so much if his fixation sprang from natural, paternal instinct, or love. "But I know it doesn't," she murmured. "It's all to do with precious pride, his macho ego, reproducing himself and the blood of his illustrious lineage...well, so-called."

Moreover, Amelia loathed Bastanta. He was hard and crude and his methods were brutal. Most of the time she feigned not to know what went on, but she was well aware of how he kept control over the peasants and their vast lands, he and the other caciques.

'Cacique', the word stemmed from the chiefs of the aboriginal tribes inhabiting those parts of the 'The Indies' that the Spanish had conquered many years ago. It was through these chiefs that the Spanish had maintained control of their colonies. Bastanta's methods were as cold and cruel as those employed then, but they worked and his efficiency and thoroughness and the contacts he had with others as ruthless as himself, had served Alva well in the past. Even Alva aimed to know only as much as was necessary and took care not to ask too many questions.

Amelia shuddered and pushed such thoughts away, concentrating her mind on the delicate flower in her tapestry. As she drew the pale, silken thread through the frame, she comforted herself that she need not think of such things any more. She had made up her mind.

So it was that on the following day, Amelia had added her own particular explosive charge to Cordoba's already unstable situation. She had appeared on the main stairway, elegant as always and dressed for departure. At the same time, the carriage appeared at the front of the house and her luggage began to pile up in the hall. Continuing her descent she called over her shoulder to her maid, giving her some last minute instruction and then, in a continuation of the same sentence, informed her husband who had just appeared on the scene that she was leaving for a sojourn in Biarritz.

Her demeanour was as usual, but her words, like Alva's of the night before, meant what they said. With a sweetness of manner but somewhat tart tone, she told her husband she was not going to bury herself miles outside of Sevilla, that if she had to be buried she would prefer it to be when she was dead rather than alive and whilst she did not relish the prospect of either, it was now clear to her that life in this fanatically religious, seemingly godless, bomb-throwing country of his, was a constant toss up between the two and she did not believe that Sevilla was any safer than here.

She added that she had made the necessary arrangements and would be sending for Leonora within the week. Moving to the cold comfort of the castle was his free choice. Hers was to spend Christmas with her daughter in more amenable surroundings.

There had been another hug and kiss for Leonora whom she had promised would join her shortly and then on the shock wave she had created, she swept out, leaving her husband no time to gather his wits to prevent her.

The next several days had been difficult for Leonora. Believing that the best way to ensure his wife's return was to refuse to let her daughter join her, her father had sent word to his wife that Leonora would be accompanying him to the castle.

A week of upheaval had followed. Porters were ordered about. Workmen were harried and retainers were sent on to the castle in advance. There was much closing down, lifting, carrying, locking up, loading, carting and counting - a great deal of counting. Wagons were burdened to axle breaking limit. His mother, not partial to commotion or taking instructions, wisely withdrew to stay with the paternal side of her family in Castille where they owned a great deal of property and the Duke and his daughter were now ensconced in the castle. A measure of routine had been established, but not normality. Amelia had not returned and Alva had not got over his vexation.

With typical perspicacity, Amelia had foreseen the very problems now besetting him. The castle had never been designed for comfort and the boredom she had envisaged for herself, was hanging like a grey pall before her daughter who was making no attempt to conceal her preference to be with her mother. It was doubly irritating for Alva to have Amelia's absence prove her point. His daughter's waywardness was of course, due to her mother's influence and made him all the more determined not to let her go. Leonora responded by being alternately sulky or defiant. She did not accept his contention that joining her mother was scarcely worthwhile because Amelia would soon be back.

That Amelia was making problems was nothing new, but her increasingly frequent absences were becoming difficult to conceal. Alva's excuses were wearing thin. How was he to explain a wife who kept taking off alone? A wife's place was with her husband, not gallivanting whenever she felt upset or the mood took her. It was intolerable. Man was head of the house. The laws of the land, social customs, all declared so and, as Holy Mother Church decreed, "A woman must obey her husband in all that is not sin." It was a lesson every child at school was taught.

But by far the worst of all Amelia's defects was her failure whether by misfortune or design, and Alva was beginning to suspect the latter, to provide him with an heir. Other women wanted babies, why not her, and why could she not just settle down instead of wanting to be abroad most of the year?

"Other landowning families live abroad. Why not us?" she argued, pointing out that many latifundia owners were absentee landlords. He could not deny it. The latifundia, those great tracts of land that made up the greater part of Andalucia often belonged to families who lived, not on their estates, but spent most of their time abroad in capital cities or fashionable resorts. It was what Amelia wanted him to do and judging by his daughter's difficult attitude she was getting the same idea.

But Leonora was not just being difficult. True, she was bored but she was also lonely and unsettled, uncertain about her future and afraid of the revolutionaries. She was sure her father was doing his best, but he never told her his plans. There was Bastanta, who knew everything, at least it seemed he did, but she never talked to him.

Leonora had watched him and her father, deep in discussion that morning. Oh, how she had wanted to know what was being said, for she knew nothing of what was going on. It was Letitia, her elderly nurse, one of their old retainers who had come to the castle with them, who kept Leonora informed, passing on all that she gleaned from the messengers who often called.

The old woman would send them down to the kitchens for refreshment whilst their errands were being dealt with. She would then follow and, as they sat at the large, wooden table, hungrily pick up every crumb of news that they let fall. Rumour was rife, but what was certain was that the violence in Cordoba had escalated since their departure and several more deaths had been reported. Alva had been right. The bomb explosion in that part of the town by the Cathedral had signalled an increase in the revolutionists' audacity.

Clashes and explosions were now commonplace in the city. Almost everyone seemed to be on strike because even those wanting to work stayed at home for fear of reprisals. Services were disrupted, shops raided and many were boarded up. Shortages led to looting and despite the patrols of the dreaded Civil Guard, even the wealthy residential areas were no longer safe. Public transport had almost stopped and those that kept going were sometimes overturned and set alight. Old scores were being settled under cover of the disorder and it was next to impossible to find the criminals.

The gossip blamed the anarchists, but the word 'anarchist' was all too often used to simply mean troublemaker, whereas the real Anarchists were members of a properly ordered, recognised political party and adhered to an austere code of conduct and a strict set of rules. It was true that they used violence but their supporters maintained they were nonetheless still good people because they were doing it to help the poor and held classes to educate them when nobody else was doing anything for them, least of all the politicians.

Leonora found it all terribly confusing. It was all too mixed up, too full of contradictions. There were too many different groups of people, many of whom were fighting against each other. There were the Communists, the Marxists, the poor farmers, the workers in the factories, the braceros, the Anarchists and the Extremists. She found this last group the most baffling, because although they shared the same name, it seemed that they often believed in totally different things.

There were also the Liberals, the Socialists, the Conservatives, the Monarchists, the Moderates, the Right Wing, the Left Wing, the bourgeoisie and over it all the Army and the Civil Guard, who were not really meant to sort it out, at least not in the way the Cortes, the Spanish Parliament, was supposed to but who had a great deal of say-so in everything and frequently stepped in to stop the fighting and all too often made it worse. There was too much arguing, too many conflicting opinions and try as she would, Leonora could make no sense of it.

The riots sparked by the Russian revolution persisted and by late 1918, Andalucia was in the middle of what historians termed, The Triennio Bolshevique, The Three Bolshevic Years from 1917 to 1920. Cordoba had long been a centre for the Anarchists and this was the chance they had awaited. Anarchy, an offshoot of the Communist creed, proclaimed the overriding rights of the individual and preached that no man owed any allegiance to any central authority whatever, not even to "A Government for the People, by the People" such as the Communists wanted.

Having unnerved her charge with news of the latest unrest, Letitia comfortingly assured her,

"But never mind my dove, my little one your father knows what's best to do. He wll make everything alright." Letitia had also looked after Alva as a small boy and now, as then, he could do no wrong.

Thoughts of Letitia brought Leonora sharply back to the present. The day was drawing to a close and the air was cooler now. It was almost two hours since she had made an excuse to her old nurse and slipped out unseen. She was forbidden to leave the castle unaccompanied, but she had managed to sneak her mare out of the stables and ride away unnoticed. There would be trouble if her absence were discovered. Reluctantly she rose to her feet, brushing the dust and dry stalks from her skirt. She was tall, slim and mature for her age. The rich, silken hair she tossed over her shoulders was a burnished auburn, her complexion clear and her eyes a dark amber in her grave, young face.

Far away, in a sky from which the sunset glow was fading, an eagle turned in wide and graceful sweep, curving the fine, smooth line of its downward arc against the broken ruggedness of the mountains beyond.

"So free," the girl whispered longingly to herself as she watched it soar, "so free."

She had spoken softly, but there was a whinnied response from a chestnut mare, tethered to the stump of a long dead tree. The animal had been standing quietly, waiting under the withered cork-oak with patience not part of its young mistress's nature. Now, it sidestepped in expectation, raising small eddies of dust from the hard ground. The shrivelled tree marked the furthermost point of their rides, the limit which even Leonora had managed to agree with herself, should not be transgressed.

With the obedience of long training, her mount stood statuesque as she took up the reins and with a movement that was both an instruction and a caress, smoothed her fingers down the length of its well groomed neck and grasped the pommel of an old fashioned side-saddle. The ornately tooled leather was soft and pliant and finding the stirrup, Leonora swung herself gracefully upwards, then urged the horse forward and moved as one with its rhythmic pace.

Turning in the direction of the castle, she cast a backward glance at the well loved scene. When may she see it again…not for…how long a time…if her truancy had been discovered or family plans should change once more?

At fourteen she herself was changing and she missed her mother very much. Life was so much easier when Amelia was around. Spirited and astute, she never failed to find ways of softening the inflexible corners of Alva's rigid regime. She was also pretty and persuasive, good at securing remedies for life's ills. Leonora envied her ability to conjure from her doctor, cures and prescriptions concurring exactly with what she wished for herself. When seemingly suffering one of her 'bouts of indisposition', he had recommended, "…a change of air, ideally abroad and not to travel alone," and so Leonora had been allowed to go with her.

This time however when Amelia left taking with her all the distractions her presence never failed to provide, Alva's attention turned to Leonora. She found his strictness demoralizing. She was growing up, becoming a woman, yet inexplicably as she matured he seemed to consider her more of a liability rather than less.

'He would treat me differently if I were a boy,' she told herself. 'But then everything would be different if I were a boy. He would pay me attention, but in a different way, for as a son I would be being taught to manage the estates.' She drew rein and looked across the magnificent view before her.

Seen from high on the escarpment, the lovely lands of Cordoba, bathed in the evening light, gave no glimmer of the turbulence tearing the province apart. They showed no sign of the distinction they created between those who held title to them and those who did not. Here, as in other parts of southern Spain, possession of the land marked the stark divide between modes of existence. It determined one's manner of being. It meant the difference between affluence and the misery of poverty and the gulf between was as wide and deep as the river valley that separated the escarpment from the distant, purple hills beyond.

Immense, like an endless carpet, the vast expanse of the Arradova estates stretched out across the lowlands and the olive groves and Leonora felt pride. Her life had taught her nothing of hardship. She was unaware of the kind of destitution that her family's inheritance of so much land bequeathed to those who had none, the braceros, the landless peasants who worked on them and nothing in the beauty of the scene disclosed the legacy of vicious hopelessness that was their birth-right.

Yes, of course she had heard of 'land deprivation' and 'social injustice', who in Andalucia had not? But for Leonora they were mere words, words that scattered the endless talk of which she heard so much. There were other words too, like 'insurrection' and 'insurgency', but they were used to describe what the braceros and others like them caused, not what they suffered, and did not explain what their lives were like. She knew nothing of their homes, or families. They came from, who knew where, at harvest time and lived together in a big, communal barn on the estate until the crops were gathered and then they disappeared offstage again, like so many extras with no further role to play and she had never questioned to where, or to what.

But although the braceros left, the problem remained. It was referred to as the 'Land Question' or, the 'Agrarian Problem' and had been debated on and off for many years in the Cortes. The degree of urgency the debate merited rose and fell as on a seesaw, according to the ratio of revolt on the other end. The need for change was frequently raised, only to sink again under the cost of reform, which was unacceptable to those with the power to bring it about.

But Leonora had worries enough of her own, of her future and what lay ahead and as shadows started to slant across the contours of the valley below, she turned and cantered away. Towards the end of the escarpment, the path curved. The terrain was rugged, steeper now. Drawing closer Leonora slowed her pace for soon the scene would change and the castle itself be seen. Suddenly, beyond the next crag, the bulk of its dark silhouette soared upwards. Bold as the prow of some proud ship it arose piercing into the mauve-daubed sky, its walls and gables seemingly a continuity of the promontory itself, barely distinguishable from the rock cliff out of which they grew.

Knowing Amelia's dread of seclusion, Leonora could understand her adamant refusal to stay there. Unlike her father, her mother saw it only as it was now, cold, gaunt and uncomfortable. Not so her husband for whom it proclaimed the part his ancestors had played in driving the Moors, the so-called Infidels, from Spain, back in the late fifteenth century, in the reign of Ferdinand and Isabella. For Alva, the castle stood as a monument to glories past, a bulwark against change.

Unapproachable from the rock defences behind, access was from one side only. On others, the terrain fell precipitously away. The towering masonry of sculptured stone, of turrets and ramparts, reared above the young girl as she rode into the deep shade of a huge, high arch. She did not see from where Bastanta came but, without warning, he was there standing before her blocking her way. Horse and rider halted and for a few frozen moments, all three were motionless.

Then, overbearingly, he raised a hand to the bridle. The mare stiffened jerking her head, but sensing the man's unyielding rigidity, knew better than to resist. Leonora was angry, angry as Bastanta, but neither betrayed their feelings. Unable to ride on she turned to face him.

The dark eyes holding her own were as stone-like as the hand that held her mount. Neither spoke, but each read the other and both understood. Her defiance of her father's instructions could make trouble for her. But his failure to prevent it could make trouble for him, trouble he needed no more than she did.

He extended his hand to assist her. It was a cold courtesy, but one it was wisest to accept. Matching his manners, she prepared to dismount. Still neither spoke. It was better for both that the incident remain unacknowledged, that it pass unnoticed, a non-event.

Moving easily she slipped from the saddle, aware of his grim attention full upon her. As her feet touched the ground he towered above her, but as she handed him the reins she barely acknowledged his presence and with the merest inclination of her head in his direction, she turned her back on him and walked away.

Crossing the courtyard, a small smile of triumph twisted her pretty mouth. She need not worry. She would hear nothing further about her escapade. It was not in Bastanta's interest to inform her father. No, he would not tell, not this time and...but there would be no next time.

Bastanta was not a man one fooled twice.

CHAPTER THREE

Ardleagh Hall. December 1918.

*I*nside the old mansion, transformation was taking place. The Earl and his retinue had arrived. Lady Margaret would be arriving soon and the Earl's sister, Lady Amelia, was also expected. Although there was still much to be done, a pattern of work had been organised and the rooms were coming back to life as staff took up their old positions and new ones settled in.

An enormous floor to ceiling Christmas tree now stood in the centre of the inner hall's black and white marble floor. Its wooden barrel tub and lower branches were already gaily decorated with baubles and bright ribbons and workmen were ascending ladders, trailing festooning streamers with which to bedeck not only its upper reaches, but every surrounding picture rail, chandelier, window pelmet and other, as yet unadorned protuberance.

Claire had finished work earlier than usual and was making her way up the narrow, back stairs to the attic room she shared with one of the other maids. The winter evening was closing in on the big house, coaxing the lamplight to brighten the windows in its darkening walls. On reaching her room, high under the eaves, she crossed to its far side and entered a curtained alcove. This was her private domain. From here she could see most of one side of the Hall's lovely gardens. Here, she could be alone, as she wanted to be for she had heard only moments ago that James would be returning tomorrow. It was months since they had seen each other.

She picked up her book and curled in the seat of the small dormer-window by her bed. For a while she remained as she was as the shadows in the garden deepened and the swiftly falling night, stealing their outlines, merged them into itself until they disappeared and there was nothing more to see. Her book was open before her, but she was not reading. She was filled with anticipations of the coming day and, unable to concentrate, she laid the book aside.

In the two years since James' sixteenth birthday, difficult though it had been, she had made reason prevail. She had been sensible and throughout the months that followed, any caution that Anna may have given her, would simply have served as affirmation of her own decision. But then...that was before last Easter.

Last Easter, how well she remembered it.

It was early, at the end of March. They had been looking forward to Austen's arrival, to the break in routine and to hearing the latest news. When word came that all leave had been cancelled, everything seemed dull and cold. It had been a miserable weekend. In addition to their disappointment, fears were confirmed that the war was going badly and the worry had resulted in a lot of edginess and hanging around.

There was talk of a massive German offensive, stories that Erich von Ludendorff had joined his troops with those from Germany's eastern front to create a force of some three million men and had launched an all-out assault on the Allied lines in France.

The reports proved true and as information about heavy Allied losses filtered in, Lady Margaret had confined herself to her room. The Earl spent most of his time in his study, shuffling his papers and James, who had just returned from school, had gone away again to stay with friends for a few days.

It was on Easter Sunday, at Arras in France that Austen was killed, the very time he should have been at home on leave. Communications were badly disrupted and uncertain and the news when it came was conveyed directly to his father by phone.

The following day, without any forewarning of what had occurred, the servants had been summoned to take their places in the large, front hall. As they entered, James was already by his father's side. She had not seen him for several weeks. He was taller. His expression had changed and he looked older and tired.

The Earl delivered the announcement about Austen bluntly, without preliminary, as though it could be done no other way and continued with whatever else he had to say, but Claire was no longer listening. Further words could neither lessen nor add to the misery of what they had been told. James already knew, but seeing his colour drain as the words were spoken she lowered her eyes, staring despairingly at the floor.

In that strange way that in moments of dread or crisis, the most insignificant and unimportant details stand out in glaring clarity, so the geometric pattern of the Persian carpet imprinted itself indelibly on her vision as though her mind, swimming in its disbelief at the awful enormity of what her senses were saying, must fasten itself upon something fixed and real and small enough to be within its scope.

She longed for the truth not to be what it was, for the dreadfulness to end. The priceless rug at which she was staring, how utterly worthless it had suddenly become. With an effort she stopped looking down and raised her eyes. She wanted to close them, to shut out everything but she could not and her gaze was drawn ineluctably, as if by some powerfully magnetic force towards James. She saw he was already looking steadily at her. His face was immobile but his gaze conveyed an intensity willing her to understand and somehow, she did. Across the distance of the hall she knew what he was silently asking.

His father had finished speaking. There was utter stillness in the air, no sound, just nothingness as though time was no more. And then, in an inexplicably hypnotic fashion that was never later to make sense, the space between her and James perished too so that she could see his face, close and clear in minute detail, the look in those expressive eyes, no further than a breath away, the long lashes and fine brows, each facet of his features, as if a mirage before her, the graining of his skin and yes, the small mole that marked his left upper lip, so close. By what trick, of what compelling, psychic force were they mirrored, magnified as by a lens in the tension of their gaze? And then, abruptly...the spell broke.

She leaned against the heavy table behind her. The moment passed. Space separated them once more and time also was moving again to the tick of the great, grandfather clock as the swing of its pendulum pushed out the seconds, first to one side, then the other.

James gave her one last look, then turned and followed his father from the hall. The servants left in one long file, passing through the door before breaking up into small clusters of two's or three's, standing silently, or talking softly. Not wanting to be delayed, Claire passed them by. She must find some excuse to slip away, for she knew that James was waiting for her and without a doubt she knew where he would be.

As soon as she could, she had hurried through the grounds. The light was fading, but on reaching the shrubbery she soon found the narrow, disused path that led to the old, ornamental Japanese garden. It was a forgotten corner, neglected for years and overgrown, but a few fragile, white crocus flowers still survived, standing stiff and chill against the cold. Drawing near, she saw again the miniature, sculpted figurines and carved stone lanterns that marked the way to a flight of small steps cut into the side of the sunken garden.

Descending, Claire came to where the moss-covered rocks, overhung by ferns, surrounded the quiet pool nestling in its depths. Here and there a willow brushed the paving as it trailed from steep slope and curtained the inner places from intrusion.

The place had seemed deserted, but was not. He was there, shadowed by the boulders where the waterfall once splashed. He turned and came towards her. They did not speak. There was no need. As his hands touched her, they had looked full upon each other and the awkwardness of recent months fell away. The wordless understanding of their childhood, their intuitive knowing of each other, the way that it had always been, carried them across the barriers that had kept them apart and they moved into each other's arms. A long while passed as they held each other close and when he slipped his cloak around them both, their tears were on each other's face and they found shelter from the wind.

A glance, a movement, a touch...and both knew how the other thought and felt. Tightening his arms around her he drew her yet more closely to him and his lips, searching hers, moved gently across her cheek. The sky was darkening now and the pool was barely visible save for the breeze ruffling its surface into corrugated crinkles of water, breaking them unevenly into splinters of reflected light. Softly, he spoke.

"Thank you for being here. How did you know?"

Her voice was little more than a whisper. "The way we always do."

"...and you knew where I would be."

Claire nodded, before adding, "It was here we first met. You found me crying."

"...a few days after Anna brought you to live with her, when your father and all the night shift...."

Claire put her finger to her lips. "Shh. Stop, it haunts you, I know. It was a long time ago. It's past. It's what's happening now that counts, to you and about Austen...and your mother? How is she?"

For some time James did not reply. Once or twice, he appeared to be on the verge of doing so, but strain flickered on his features and he remained silent. When at last he spoke it was to tell her haltingly, that his mother was under sedation, that she had been so for the last twenty-four hours and he had argued with his father about it.

"He summoned the doctor within hours of giving her the news. He gave her no chance to come to terms with what has happened…as though he cannot bear a show of emotion, especially an expression of grief."

Night was falling. Against the skyline, the gabled silhouette of the Hall could be seen behind the trees. Along its walls, a few squares of light had appeared as rooms were lit within. James looked towards it.

"The house seems so big and empty, with no-one knowing what to do, except father. He always knows what to do."

Concerned, Claire looked at him for his words were touched with bitterness she had not heard before.

"He's doing it now, just as he has since he heard about Austen. He calls it, getting organised, making the necessary arrangements, his stock response to emotional situations. When mother continued to cry he called the doctor to tranquilise her, not for her sake, but for his."

Claire listened, understanding his feelings were about Austen, as well as his father.

"Shutting out feelings allows him to stop seeing things he can't afford to see," she said softly, "...things that would get in the way of his keeping control, managing everything as he does. It's the way of the world he was born into and...I think he cannot help himself."

"…a world in which shedding tears is seen as giving way...and fear, even when it's overcome is looked on as a flaw in one's character, a lack of moral fibre, instead of a healthy response to danger," said James, "...it's irrational, for how can you come to terms and deal with emotions you can't even admit you have?

"And Austen was afraid. He told me so when last on leave, what it was really like at the front, in the trenches, things that have never appeared in the papers and never will. How men who'd been in the worst of the fighting and shown great courage, sometimes cracked up, suffering shellshock from the constant bombardment. They were given no chance to recover before being put on a charge and without a court martial or even a proper hearing, were shot, executed ignominiously for cowardice. When some of the officers complained, the top brass said it was, to encourage the others. Austen tried to tell father, but all he got was a lot of talk about doing one's duty and not being found wanting."

Again, James hesitated.

"It's what our row was about last night. Last night was unreal...we should have been trying to console mother and one another, instead of which mother was lying down upstairs, passed out, and father and son were standing up downstairs, arguing...

"Claire, I shouldn't be talking about this."

"No, it's better this way. I want to hear." But as Claire spoke, she shivered, for the war was far from over and soon James would have to fight and she was afraid.

Their arms around each other they stayed long into the night. The moon's rays lustrous as the wing of a young dove shone through the web of black and tangled branches and in the gardens of Ardleagh the darkness softened and all was at peace.

In the days that followed they had been unable to meet. Lady Margaret was far from well and the Earl continually wanted James to be present in her stead. There could be no funeral for Austen, no grave, as there had been none for Claire's father but the Earl had insisted the memorial service was to be held without delay and making the arrangements had taken precedence above all else. Details of time and place, the arrival of cars, the order of seating in the Church were planned, with all formalities observed.

The day of the service had been wet and blustery. Delays and disruptions occurred for which no allowance could have been made and with no leavening of the strained atmosphere, the tension combined with the sadness to overstretch everyone's nerves.

On entering the Church, Claire was crowded into the allotted space near the back, along with the other servants. Through the huge congregation, she caught glimpses of James, standing between his parents at the front. During the service the vicar spoke many words, of valour, sacrifice, duty. They rang out briefly and then were no more than echoes. Finally it was over.

The last guest, climbed into the last car. It scrunched over the gravel and was gone. Everything that should be done had been done, yet still it seemed something had been missing. Was it, as Anna said, because the emphasis had been on the wrong things?

A change of air had been recommended for Lady Margaret and the family went to stay at their waterside retreat in the Lake District. On their return James had left for what would be his last term at school and his parents had moved to their Park Lane house in London.

As was customary, the servants were informed of the change by Elliott, the butler, at breakfast time. It was, so they were told, because being in different surroundings would help to take Lady Margaret's mind off her distress. She would be less likely to be reminded.

"Reminded! Huh," Cook had exclaimed with what was almost a snort, "as if she can ever forget."

There was silence until one of the maids ventured, "yes, I dare say it'll tek more'n different surroundings to get 'er Ladyship's mind off what's 'appened. It would me, an' I reckon as 'ow they're no different."

Elliott, unwilling to concede any similarity between Lady Margaret and the recently arrived dishwasher, had been equally unable to produce a suitable reply. He had been spared further effort by the housekeeper.

"Oh I'm sure while they're in London, their Harley Street specialist will discover what it is that's ailing Lady Margaret," she remarked.

"Needs no 'arley Street specialist to discover what's troublin' Lady Margaret," asserted Cook, "...'er's grievin'. Leastways 'er would be if on'y he'd let 'er...grievin' an' worryin' as well, 'bout her other son James who'll be 'aving to go an' fight."

"Lord James." Elliott had corrected her.

"Meks no difference," Cook had retorted acidly, "...his title won't save him. It didn't save his brother."

It had been shortly after that morning that the Earl had returned to tell them he was closing down part of the Hall in response to the Government's appeal to those with large establishments to help with the war effort and reduce their number of servants. A small skeleton staff including Anna and Cook were to stay on in a caretaking capacity. The rest were to be let go. He and Lady Margaret would stay at their Park Lane house for the duration of the war.

Eric the chauffeur however, who had driven the Earl from London, had told Cook it was his belief, that the Earl's decision had little to do with the war effort but was because, with her Ladyship in poor spirits, the social life in London was more to his liking.

"He makes arrangements, tells me to bring the car round and when the mistress doesn't want to go, he says she's not helping herself and if she makes an excuse, saying she's not feeling well, has a headache or suchlike, he has his doctors call on her and they've said she should visit this special Clinic and from what I can see, they're making her worse 'stead of better, because they now want her to stay in this Clinic for a few weeks."

After listening to Eric, Cook and Anna had been concerned for Lady Margaret, agreeing that home was the best place for her, not some strange Clinic.

Claire's dismissal notice had put an end to the indecision tormenting her since the memorial service. During that long drawn out ceremony, cold truths about James' life and hers had made themselves felt. The very scene in the Church had been as one of those tableaux in which everything is symbolic of a deeper reality, James at the front with his back to her and she crammed in at the rear. Even the way he was flanked by his parents, one on either side, had signified the forces that would control his future, his father and the dictates of circumstance on one hand, the pull of his mother's emotions and needs on the other. Their very expectations of him underlined the disparity between their situations and Claire was well aware hers would not change unless she herself changed it.

While living at the Pendle's, Cook had brought Claire a small package James had posted to her. It contained a book and a letter he had written while in the Lakes, in which he described the moonlight reflecting the mountains in the water at night, pure and still, and the beauty of a countryside Claire had never seen. The book was of Wordsworth's poetry, much of which had been written in the Lake District and James had marked certain poems and meaningful passages he wanted her to read. Fearful that if she wrote to him, her letter may fall into other hands, she had not replied.

The war news had remained depressing until, later in the summer, the tide had turned. The Allies had succeeded in breaking Ludendorff's offensive and, as a morale booster to all who came into the shop, Mrs Pendle had pinned up her war map, bristling with the little pin and paper flags that marked the military advances and retreats. The Union Jack flags were seen to have moved steadily away from those places like Arras, over which they had passed backwards and forwards, fraying the paper.

November, and the Armistice had come quickly after that.

It was all over and against her expectations, she was back at the Hall and tomorrow, James, who was now at Cambridge University and whom she had not seen for months, would be returning too.

CHAPTER FOUR

Cordoba, Andalucia. December, 1918.

Raimundo de Conde strode purposefully across the flagged floor of the Castle's great hall. As he went he dropped his hat and gloves onto the seat of a tall, oak chair, one of many that stood in line against a heavy table. The crossed swords on his epaulettes, dusty after his long ride, designated his General's rank, a position he had held for several years and which determined his whole way of life. But it was on matters other than military that he had come to the Arradova castle this morning, although given his friend Alva's current obsession with the re-establishment of law and order in the land, no doubt the subject would soon arise.

The two men had been close friends since boyhood. They came from similar backgrounds and their families had been friends for generations. Raimundo however, had not been heir to a family fortune as Alva had, but his ability and influential connections had brought him high office and at forty-eight he had no complaints. He was also one of the few men with whom Alva was on familiar terms.

But the intimacy had its price and Alva could expect that one of Raimundo's first questions would concern Amelia. Never having liked her, he had warned Alva against her from the beginning. It added to Alva's irritation that there was now no concealing that Amelia was beyond his control and although his friend had never actually said, "I told you so," the thought was there in both their minds.

Alva could not even appeal to Raimundo's understanding of the difficulties of handling a wife, for Raimundo, never having seen any necessity to marry had never done so, although he had not allowed this omission to deprive him of the unquestionable, or indeed the questionable, pleasures an attractive woman could offer. He had always unswervingly adhered to the principle that every act be performed for a purpose and with a satisfactory outcome in mind. Even as a 'young blood' he had adroitly managed, by a careful observation of the socially prescribed discretions, to remain above reproach whilst gathering his worldly experience.

Alva's youth had been less exciting. He was much more serious due to his awareness that as the only son, he would inherit the vast Arradova estates and, in the fullness of time, must hand on to his own son and heir, all he himself had received. It was therefore a foregone conclusion that Alva would marry one day. Raimundo however was unencumbered by such considerations. The friends had known their lives would diverge as they gravitated towards their preordained spheres, Alva's, towards the marital, Raimundo's towards the martial. In dealing with Amelia lately, Alva deemed his friend had chosen the less belligerent of the two.

Although unburdened by either wife or offspring, Raimundo did have a nephew, Georgio, of whom he was extremely fond. The young man's father, also an Army officer, had been killed fighting in the Rif in Morocco and Raimundo had, in many respects, taken over the paternal role. His discussion with Alva this morning would, if successfully concluded, greatly enhance Georgio's future social and financial prospects and for a man of his girth and bulk, he ascended the wide, stone stairs in an energetic fashion.

Leonora had been studying in her room and was bored. Wondering who had arrived she went to find out. Nearing the stairway she heard voices. There was no mistaking who was with her father. It was the General. Leonora had known him since she was small but now avoided him, taking exception to the way he treated her as if she were still a child, while appraising her with eyes that knew she was not. Too late to retreat she stepped quickly into the stone recess of a narrow archway that opened off the upstairs gallery. In slow, ambulatory fashion the men approached until close to where Leonora was hidden. They then paused, as though wishing to finalise an understanding of importance. Their close proximity was unnerving. Afraid she would be discovered she could think of nothing save the awkwardness of her situation until the mention of her name gripped her attention. Such snatches of conversation as she could hear however seemed disconnected and it was difficult to trace a meaningful thread.

In fact, her eavesdropping was posing more puzzlement than information. Why did they keep mentioning Georgio, the General's nephew, and what was the arrangement that kept cropping up seemingly concerning him. She gathered he had just received a commission in the Army. She already knew he had succeeded brilliantly whilst attending the Officer Academy and if his uncle was to be believed, was destined for a promising career.

She was still straining her ears when, interrupting their discussion to light their cigars, they drifted out of earshot. When she heard them again, they were discussing the Left Wing affiliations of Alva's cousin Luis, a politician in the Cortes. He was the nearest male in line to the Arradova inheritance and Alva regarded his Socialist leanings dangerous to the future of the estate, especially at this time of anarchic violence.

"Yes, I know your cousin Luis is getting older," said Raimundo, "but we must take into account that he may have sons one day. We must be cautious, consider the legalities. For generations your family has observed the Salic Law, excluding females from succession and now, by planning to exclude Luis..."

But Alva did not let him finish. The very suggestion that Luis, whom he had always considered weak and ineffectual may have sons when he himself had none, pricked his pride and he cut his friend short.

"I'm well aware the Arradovas have observed the Salic Law for generations," he blurted out irritably, "that's because for generations there's always been a male in direct line of descent, but that's not now the case. That's why our arrangement must stand. Don't worry we're not going to be thwarted by any so called legality. Nothing is going to get in the way of my making Leonora my successor, so put your mind at rest. The documents have already been drawn up."

Leonora almost gasped, but caught her breath. Could she believe what she had heard? No, she must be mistaken. Slowly she inched along the cold stone of the recess to where an ornamental grating was letting in spears of light and the aroma of the men's cigars. Her father was speaking again.

"Have no concern about the Salic Law Raimundo. You know it was not part of our ancient Spanish Law. It came about after Spain's King Carlos11 died without heirs in November 1700. The War of the Spanish Succession was fought and Philip, a French Bourbon, the grandson of Louis X1V of France and of Carlos11's sister, Marie Therese, ascended the Spanish throne. But the 1789 French Revolution brought many changes. The French King, Louis XV1, was guillotined. Napoleon came to power and invaded Spain, with more changes again when he was defeated...and, as you know, when Spain's King Ferdinand V11 was without a male heir, he renounced the Salic Law, and in 1833, his infant daughter became Queen of Spain. She became Queen Isabella11 at only three years of age...you remember?"

"Indeed I do, and with her mother as Regent," responded Raimundo. "But if you're trying to reassure me, you'd have done better not to speak of it, for look at the grief that caused. When Isabella ascended the throne instead of Ferdinand's brother Carlos, all hell let loose. That's what started the Carlist Wars, causing trouble that bedevils our country to this day."

Through the grating Leonora watched the General emphasize his words, throwing up his hands as if in despair, at each fresh point he made.

"The Carlist Wars," he continued, "...they not only split the country they split families too, caused factions and divisions in the Government and in the Army itself. Why...even the Church became involved. The Church backed the Carlists in trying to put Carlos on the throne and suffered for it when the Carlists lost."

But her father made no attempt to argue. In fact, as he turned to face his friend he was smiling, showing no trace of his former annoyance.

"Raimundo, how right you are. But look at the end result. Look how advantageous it is to us now in our hour of need. And how did that come about? Well, you know as well as I do. When the Carlists tried to seize the throne from the young Queen, the Regency was very vulnerable and needed all the strength and backing the military could give. The result was that the Monarchy became dependent on the Army and that gave the Army a very strong and powerful say in the running of the country. It sanctioned the right of the military to take a hand in the political and internal affairs of Government and the Army has never let go of that power. In fact, it has taken advantage of every opportunity since to strengthen it still further.

"So think about it Raimundo," continued Alva , "with so many Communist and Liberal ideas of democracy spreading across Europe and threatening to take root, aren't we fortunate indeed to have an Army that's not only politically influential and powerful, but also Right Wing? And with you yourself, so highly placed in that Army and with Georgio following in your footsteps, rest assured my dear friend, you need have no worries about cousin Luis or any little Luis he may have. He has no influence, scarcely any money and he's unpopular. The Establishment is very set against liberal do-gooders like Luis. Georgio on the other hand, is acceptable on all counts. He's tailor-made for our agreement."

"And Leonora…?" Raimundo asked.

"…and Leonora also," replied her father with assurance. "You'll see. When the time comes, Leonora will fit in just as nicely. Now come my friend, let us drink to it."

The two men drifted slowly to where the flight of stone steps descended to the flags of the great hall below, their voices growing fainter until fading into silence.

Leonora was elated, but still a little puzzled. How was Georgio perfect for their arrangement...whatever it was? Oh well, no matter, he was a tedious, pink faced, young man with well combed-back hair and of no concern to her. She had seen him a few times since he had left the Officer Academy and on each occasion he had been wearing an impeccably well cut, neatly pressed uniform, shiny, polished knee boots and a general air of readiness to please and at the moment, she was much too delighted at becoming an heiress to bother about him.

What gladdened her most was the sense of importance it gave her. Her father's dissatisfaction at having only a daughter instead of a son had always disturbed her, fraying her self-esteem whenever it came to mind. Now it seemed all would be different. He was including her in his plans and she was happy.

Alva, however, was not happy. His expectation that he would one day have a son had borne the same degree of certainty that night would follow day. The realisation Amelia had forced upon him, that this was not the case, rankled deeply. The less he concealed it, the more Amelia made it clear that, for her, one offspring was quite enough.

Alva no longer looked upon his wife as light hearted and vivacious. She was, as Raimundo had always said, frivolous. It was also unfortunate that she was younger than Alva and instead of settling down had adopted a very modern attitude.

Obviously, this had not escaped Raimundo's attention and to Alva's further chagrin, he raised the topic of Amelia as they descended the stairs. It became evident as he spoke that his concern was now focussed on Amelia-as-mother, rather than Amelia-as-wife. Presumably, he now regarded the latter as a lost cause.

Raimundo began tactfully, praising Leonora, saying,

"She is developing beautifully and I assure you, nobody is happier with our agreement than I am myself, except of course, Georgio," he added, with a knowing little smile. "He will be delighted to hear all is settled and I trust Alva that as Leonora matures you'll ensure she doesn't come too much under the influence of her mother. She has formative years ahead of her and it's a pity when a young woman develops too much of a mind of her own."

Alva's reply was sharp edged. For years Raimundo had been offering advice regarding his wife. Now he was extending it to guidance about his daughter. To add to Alva's irritation, he had just received an infuriating letter from Amelia and needed no further reminder of her obduracy.

'The trouble with Raimundo,' he thought, as he watched his friend ride away, 'is that all too often, he's right.' Amelia's ability to evade the obstacles and strictures placed in her path was infuriating. Her appearance of feminine fragility was devastatingly attractive, but maddeningly deceptive, for it concealed an equally devastating strength of will.

Amelia loved Biarritz, a favourite resort of the English for many years. When Alva refused to live anywhere except his beloved Spain, she became adept at finding excuses to spend time abroad. She was making a fool of him. He had decided to go to Biarritz and make her come back. He had written to her and very promptly, she had replied.

The stiff, square of white vellum, now lying starkly on the dark wood of his desk, could not be ignored. In her neat handwriting, she expressed with hypocritical regret, her disappointment that by the time he arrived in Biarritz she would already be on her way to Ardleagh Hall, where she intended to spend the forthcoming Christmas.

He knew what she was up to. She was, he was sure, planning to have Frederick and Margaret invite Leonora also to spend Christmas at Ardleagh and then to suggest they stay a little while longer, 'for just as long as the violence rages', and a refusal from him to allow it would appear boorish and, even worse, unconcerned for his wife's and daughter's safety, which was nonsense. They would have been perfectly safe in Sevilla if he had been obeyed.

Oh yes, he knew what she was manoeuvring towards. Once ensconced at Ardleagh with Leonora, Amelia's next move would be back to Biarritz with her, for 'just as long as the violence rages'. He knew Amelia. He could picture her now, sitting innocently in the drawing room of Arleagh Hall, all sweetness and light and feigned surprise at his attitude, her lovely, long legs crossed elegantly as they emerged from the hemline of fashion's latest length. He could scarcely arrive and demand that she get up and leave, not when, more than likely, Margaret had already extended a welcome to both her and their daughter.

He fumed inwardly. The English do everything differently. The atmosphere there is all ordered and calm. They take their tea and their time, discuss everything thoroughly, compromise, adapt, and with a discreet nod here, and the right touch there, make felt their expectations that if dealt with correctly, matters will sort themselves out.

No doubt Amelia had their full sympathy, having told them about the bomb blasting off the door of their carriage with his mother and Leonora in it.

"I can't go for her now...walk in and insist she comes home," he muttered.

Incensed, he tore up her letter and dropped it into the wastepaper basket. 'Amelia', he thought angrily, 'will come home, only when Amelia is ready.'

Crossing the room he tugged on the bell pull. When Virgo appeared he asked him to send word for the carriage to be brought round. If he could not deal with Amelia there were other concerns with which he could.

There was to be a meeting of several estate owners in Cordoba in a few weeks' time. Raimundo had pressed him to be there. He had told Alva the Army was poised to strike against the Anarchists and wanted to know the extent of support it could expect from the core of influential, large estate owners whose families had held the upper hand in the province for generations and who had a vested interest in maintaining stability.

It was such a man, Rodrigo, Alva now wanted to meet. He intended to give him the General's message and ask him to pass on the word to the other landowners prior to the meeting, so they could glean information from their caciques who always knew what was happening in their vicinity and also knew how to ensure their orders were heeded.

Alva could not but brood on the present situation. The conflict triggered by the Russian revolution and the unrest from Spain's massive General strike in the summer of 1917, continued. Unlike other European countries that had been at war, the men of neutral Spain had been at home and the antagonism had not ceased. When, just a few months ago, the entire Russian royal family, the Czar, his wife, their four daughters, their only son and some servants, had been cold-bloodedly murdered by their Bolshevist gaolers in the cellar of the house where they were being held, alarm had spread like wildfire amongst Europe's ruling class.

With the end of the war, demobilised men across Europe were out on the streets. The Communists were well organised. Their marching song was, 'The International'. Their cry was, 'Workers of the World Unite'. Even in Germany, a country long considered a bastion of order, the Kaiser had fled only days before the Armistice and the monarchy had collapsed.

Once again, here in Spain there were demands for reform, many of which vociferously targeted the owners of the vast estates that covered much of Andalucia, threatening them to concede tracts of their land to the peasants. The situation was one of concern but now was not the time to show it for if the upper classes weakened and the rabble gained control, all hope of restoring order would be lost.

Journeying home after his evening out, Alva relaxed. His friend Rodrigo's self-assurance had restored his confidence, but then Rodrigo was like that, a tall, broadly built, well-adjusted, affable man. As the carriage rocked rhythmically from the horses' steady pace, Alva decided to give things more time to settle, even perhaps, to be more understanding of Amelia, but not too much. She had no right to refuse him another child. The thought afforded no consolation. Being right availed him nothing when arguing with Amelia.

She had scant time for his Church, its rules, regulations and threats of everlasting damnation and her husband's total obedience to it was yet another bone of contention between them. She did admit some of its festivals were colourful, but that the processions at Easter had the dampers put on them by endless lines of miserable looking penitents in long, black robes and pointed conical hats, looking as if they were members of the Ku Klux Klan and she simply would not accept his reasons for not living abroad, that the safeguarding of the estate came first and that he owed it to his family.

"But which family Alva, you, me, Leonora and your mother, or this other family that no longer exists, that's only a list of beautifully scripted names in a book in the archives? Why sacrifice ourselves for a family that's nothing more than bones in a family crypt?"

Alva was reassured that his arrangement with Raimundo added extra security to the estate. It was not long to wait. In a few years, Leonora would be of marriageable age and Georgio had agreed to all the clauses specified, including retention of her family name.

He must keep faith. This dreadful phase would pass. Backed by the Army and the Church, the Right would prevail. They would win.

As Rodrigo had pointed out, in the end, they always did.

CHAPTER FIVE

26th December. Boxing Day, 1918.
Ardleagh Hall, Lancashire.

*T*he long, strident call of the hunting horn pierced the wintry, morning mist. The fanfare of its high, shrill pitch shattered the cold, frosted air, cutting as the splintered ice crystals that scattered the hard ground. Across the hillside, all nature startled, listened, and was still. Alerted, the wild life tensed, whiskers quivered and on lifted heads, ears pricked. Resonant with the sound, rock and stone, bare tree and leafless branch, echoed the warning. Only the birds chattered, flapping their indignation. All else waited.

In the foreground of the Hall, the hunt was gathering. For some time now, horseboxes had been arriving in the stable-yard, while horses being ridden to the meet were coming up the drive, some frisking with arched neck, others walking quietly on loose rein, but all with plaited mane and braided tail, oiled hoof and gleaming, well groomed coat, bearing a rider, resplendent in hunting pink or black jacket with, at the throat, a snow-white, silk stock secured by golden pin.

Some had come early and, handing over the reins to the waiting grooms, had left their whips and crops at the entrance and gone indoors to warm themselves. Others, whose horses were being brought for them, were arriving by carriage, or by car.

The Hall was welcoming. The spread branches of the Christmas tree were burdened with glittering knick-knacks. Log fires blazed in open hearths. Holly, mistletoe and Christmas decorations of all kinds, bright ribbons and tinsel, festooned the ornate, plaster mouldings and dangled from on high. The atmosphere befitted the festive season and new arrivals were quickly caught up in the gaiety of the scene. The merriment prevailing was ,without a doubt, due in no small measure to the steaming contents of a punchbowl prettily hung around with little, silver drinking vessels and to the frequent dipping of its matching silver ladle. It was set in the centre of a large, oval table and surrounded by trays of delicious, bite-sized delicacies. In addition to the just mentioned heady brew, there were drinks of a less concocted nature for those who, not knowing what the day may bring, wished to keep a check on what they drank.

After a while, with nerves steadied or inflamed by what they had imbibed, those who were to join the hunt readied themselves to leave and asked for their mounts to be brought round. The horses, sensing what awaited and eager for the chase, pranced and cavorted as grooms, holding firmly to their bridles, manoeuvred them towards the mounting blocks.

Gallantly cupped hands took hold of dainty feet and lifted pretty ladies to their saddles. Some men, with dash and style, vaulted with apparent ease onto their steeds. Others, disinclined or less able, mounted more mundanely, foot in stirrup. Soon, one way or another, all were settled in their saddles and gathering up their reins.

Once the hunt started, there would be no stopping, no turning back and in these last moments tension mounted. Gloved hands made reassuring, once-again-last-minute checks, touching buckles, tucking straps into their keepers. There was skittish behaviour as mares objected to their saddle-flaps being lifted and their girths hitched one more notch. Stirrup lengths were adjusted, martingales inspected and steeds tossed their heads as bridles were tested and curb chains checked twice.

For many of the riders, weighing their chances of crossing wide ditches, clearing stone walls and making it safely down many a bank, all these precautions were simply a matter of reducing the risks, but for some it was a ritual, almost religiously carried out, taking the edge off their nerves while they waited.

Claire was waiting too. She was standing with several other servants on the side lawn of the Hall. Sheltered from the wind by the shrubbery thicket, they were watching the goings on. She was wondering if James would be joining the hunt for she had heard he had returned but had seen no sign of him as yet.

She had managed to be off duty on the afternoon of his and Lady Margaret's expected arrival and when their car swept to a standstill outside the front portico had been well placed to see without being seen. But Lady Margaret had arrived alone. With the anti-climax however had come an unsought easing of disquiet for despite all her imagining, or possibly because of it, she could no longer gauge what James' attitude to her might be. It was a long time since they had last been together and given the many changes and the new friends he must have made now he was at the university in Cambridge, she wondered would he notice her at all.

'He will, no probably not.' The two thoughts circled. Which to believe and she very much wished she had answered his letter when he had written?

Hearing the chatter of the other maids nearby, Claire pushed her thoughts aside and joined in. The scene was gay and colourful. Horses with riders mounted were milling around, frisking, sidestepping off the paths, and the hounds were adding an extra spice of excitement, relishing their freedom and bounding about.

Several of the guests who were not hunting, intended to foot follow, which was a misnomer because for the most part they would be in their cars. Ready and well wrapped they were entering into the spirit, calling out comments and wry warnings to their mounted friends.

At the end of the drive, beyond the massive, stone pillars and decoratively crested gates that gave onto the road, clusters of villagers were waiting to see the spectacle that soon would leave the grounds. It was a sight worth the seeing, a traditional picture that had changed little down the years. The attire was the same, the crisp tailoring of the men's jackets contrasting with the flowing lines of the ladies' riding habits.

It was partly the timeless nature of the scene and the well observed etiquette of dress that rendered two of the ladies there on horseback, very noticeable indeed. They were modern and proving it by riding astride. One was Amelia, younger sister of the Earl, who was on a visit from Spain where she now lived having married a handsome Andalucian nobleman many years ago. The other was a good friend from the days of her youth, still living in the county. They were causing stares and more than one whisper, from behind a raised hand.

One of the maids standing close to Claire spoke up. "Will yer jus' look at 'em, will yer, wi' them breeches an' on'y them short pelmet-looking things as they's passin' off as skirts."

"Allus was a wild un," said one of the older servants, who remembered Amelia from years ago. "When I thinks on some o' things as yon youn' Lady used t' be up to, afor they married 'er off."

She had spoken softly, but not softly enough.

"She was not 'married off' as you so rudely put it and don't you say that again." The rebuke came from the housekeeper, self-appointed guardian of family honour.

"Well...no I don't suppose 'er wer'...well, not that like that any road," conceded the older maid before murmuring under her breath, "but I still say as 'ow the Earl wer' right glad to see her go...'er wer' an' andful an' no mistake, though, mind you," she added, the softening of a smile touching her face, " 'er wer' the prettiest thing you'd ever see an' allus the centre o' attraction."

Although they were speaking of times past, it was evident Amelia had lost none of her touch. She was in the midst of a group, all eagerly laughing and chatting to her. Claire glanced across and James was there too.

Caught unawares, her attention taken by Amelia, Claire's heart skipped a beat. She was assailed by the same, all too familiar, hard hitting, sinking sensation that was far from pleasant and difficult to overcome.

She forgot Amelia. The surroundings blotted out. All she could see was James seated on a large, grey hunter, some yards away.

"You O.K. yer don't look it?" said the maid standing next to her. Claire murmured her thanks, saying she was fine, but she was not. The moment passed. The feeling remained. But it was alright. She could look at him now.

He looked leaner, harder more mature. Chatting to his aunt, he appeared relaxed, very much at ease. Switching her gaze to Amelia, Claire could only admire her. She was elegant and slim, graceful and very feminine and although no longer in the first flush of youth, was very attractive indeed. Her dark red hair was cut in a long bob, drawn back into a fine net and shining with lustre beneath the black velvet of her hat. Her features were delicate and fine. Her close fitting jacket revealed her figure and neatly nipped-in waist and the long line of her thighs was shown to advantage by riding astride.

" 'As 'er come 'ere for long?" asked another.

"No," replied the housekeeper, who was the authority on family matters. "She'll be returning to Spain shortly."

It was said with a certainty that would have gladdened Alva's heart, had he been around to hear.

"But I did hear 'er may be comin' back an bringin' 'er daughter wi' 'er," chipped in the parlour maid. "Supposin' to be for 'er education but it's more to do wi' all that trouble they're 'aving in Spain, wi' them anarchists an' communists, whate'er it is they calls 'emselves."

The housekeeper did not respond and the informant, unsure of whether to reveal the full fruits of her eavesdropping, paused, but restraint was not one of her strong points and she blurted out the rest.

"…but then I 'erd as 'ow she's o'er 'ere, cos things ain't what they should be 'tween 'er an 'er 'usband."

The housekeeper had heard much the same, but rounded on the miscreant nonetheless.

"That's wicked tittle-tattle. You are not to repeat it."

"It don't be wicked tittle-tattle when it be no more 'n I 'eard," retorted the girl stoutly in her own defence.

" 'An I reckon 'er's right," whispered another grudgingly, " 'cos 'er listens when 'ers passin' doors, well...more like when 'er stops passin' 'em...an' I'll tell yer more..."

But she never did, for at that moment the hunting horn brought the waiting to an end.

Its notes had carried far afield earlier in the day when it had sounded the traditional summoning of the meet and anticipation had been rising since those first, clear notes had died away. Now, its tones bore different tidings and anyone still not ready knew they were too late, for this time it signalled that the hunt was moving off.

Claire's attention was again taken by Amelia. She had ridden up to James to give his mare a good luck pat. Keeping her balance, she leaned out of her saddle and in response to some quip he had made, laughingly gave him a pretend push. There was something indefinably lovely about her, an essence, an aura that conveyed ease and enjoyment to whoever was with her and James looked happy in her company. The hunt was now on the move and he took up a place beside her in the procession of riders heading towards the front gates.

Of good physique, James sat his mount well. Still paying attention to his aunt, he was oblivious of the admiring glances from the many young ladies present. The war had caused a serious dearth of eligible men, resulting in a quite desperate shortage of escorts and prospective marriage partners and James was very eligible indeed.

As the hunt continued down the drive, it began to sort itself out and an amount of jostling was taking place as favoured positions were sought. Riders on young, less experienced horses were trying to tuck in behind more reliable ones known to be good at giving a lead. Others were endeavouring to stop horses with a reputation for refusing or falling at fences, from taking a space ahead of them. There was crowding and bunching as riders quickened their pace, or fell back a stride on finding themselves within range of notorious kickers, not all of which had the customary, red ribbon woven into their tail-braiding to give warning of such a dangerous trait.

Some horses, pulling and hard to restrain, crammed against others as they pressed through the stone portals of the entrance but, once outside, the cavalcade quickened and turning onto the road, broke into a canter and began to disperse. Soon they were out of sight and the onlookers at the Hall turned away.

Those of the Earl's guests, intent on seeing more of the fun, piled into the waiting cars and carriages and tucked their knee rugs round them. There would now be debate and argument about the line the hunt would take. Once decided, they would be driven from one vantage point, so it was hoped, to the next. At each of these they would climb onto the bonnets of their cars, stone walls and stiles or whatever gave the best grandstand view and with field glasses raised, join vicariously in the hunt.

Villagers ran hurriedly across fields, up slopes and hillocks, the fitter ones who got there first, shouting encouragement to the less robust, panting and straggling in their wake. With luck they would catch sight of the galloping column, probably fewer in number than when they set out. Whenever the hunt disappeared for some time, an exaggerated sense of mystery surrounded its whereabouts, to be followed by heightened excitement when sighted again, be it as tiny dots on a far panorama, or splurging suddenly, larger than life through the thickets of a nearby field.

None of this hunt spotting was idle exercise. It was vital to see all that was to be seen, or how could one join in the endless discussions, asking others, "Did you see...?" or "Do you remember...?" and so add to the stories that would grow with the telling to become legends relived as one passed round the port or sat over a beer, on winter evenings yet to come.

As a way of passing an afternoon it held no attraction for Claire. She could see the appeal of riding in the hunt, or being in a fine carriage with one's friends, but none whatsoever in running around the open country or standing in the cold beside a muddy ditch or boundary hedge. When given the choice she had opted to stay and help Cook. It was warm in the kitchen, pleasant with the aroma of cinnamon spice and mulled wine, whisky and lemons for hot toddies, all of which were in preparation for The Stirrup Cup, to be served to the hunt while on horseback, should they pass this way.

If they doubled back through Ladies Wood, as Charlie the retired head forester had prophesied, one would catch sight of them from behind the Hall as they headed for the river bank.

Charlie had worked on the estate for years and knew everything there was to know of the surrounding countryside, including the age, cunning and earth location of every fox around.

"If they teks a run up thro' Gorsefields an' comes round by Moorland rock as whar they'll be hopin' on pickin' up scent, there's a crafty youn' divil of a dog fox up thar, jus' comin' into 'is own. If they gets onto 'im, he'll lead 'em on, give 'em a right run for thar money a'for he runs 'em into Ladies Wood. Lots o' low branches thar be in that wood an' that'll slow 'em up. Then he'll giv 'em th' slip proper, for he'll 'ead 'em straight on for the river an' yon big drop-bank."

Charlie had chuckled and slapped his thigh in relish. "Muddle the scent right proper he will, for he'll cross the river, run aroun' for a bit an' then slip back in the wather an' away off downstream."

"Jus' listen out," he had advised Claire, "for the Master soundin' 'is horn, an' the hounds 'giving tongue'...an' you'll get a good view if you gets yersell t' the back of th' house. An' I'll gi' you another good reason for tekin' a look. Youn' Rawlinson'll be out wi' 'em on his latest buy, a fine beast, a big, showy black, an' he don't know it yet, but that's whar he'll get 'is 'come-u-pence'," and once again Charlie had laughed, until a fit of coughing stopped him.

Claire had no reason either to like Ralph Rawlinson, the mill-owner's son, but why should Charlie dislike him and relish the thought of him coming unstuck. At first, the canny, old forester refused to be drawn, but Claire was not only intrigued, she was persuasive.

"Why don' I like 'im?" he finally responded. "Well shall us jus' say as I'm mekin' up for someone as liked 'im a bit too much...a youn' girl, workin' at 'is father's mill, daughter of someone I know." Charlie had paused, silent and serious for a moment before adding in an acerbic, bitter tone.

"Them Rawlinsons, they thinks as 'ow money can buy 'owt, an' mek up for 'owt. Well it can't and that thar 'orse as he'll be on, knows now't about pound notes." Again he paused and then his face began to lighten.

"An' I c'n tell yer. When that 'orse says "No", it means No, an' no amount o' bullyin' or persuadin' 'll mek it change it's mind. When that 'orse sees wather, that'll be it. There be no way it'll drop itsell down that bank. Not for 'im, not fo' nobody, no matter 'ow much money they 'ave in thar back pocket."

Despite her sympathy with his earlier sentiments, Claire was amused.

"But Charlie, how do you know all this? How do you know his horse won't jump the water?" she asked, amazed at the confidence with which Charlie had delivered his forecast.

"Cos' I knows th' chap as sold it to 'im, an' he don't like youn' Rawlinson, no mor'n me. You watch out an' you'll see what I means, for when they be comin' up to yon drop-bank, youn' Rawlinson'll be thar, all showy an' shove o'er like, an' pushin' 'is road to th' front but when that black brute as 'e'll be on, gets ev'n as much as a sniff o' th' wather it'll stop, an' the big laugh'll be, that lad Rawlinson won't be able to stop 'imsell tryin' an' a'tryin' to mek it go. Likes 'is own way does that youn' man wi' ev'ryone an' ev'rythin' he comes up agin."

Claire could not disagree. Ralph was too big for his boots. His father, Albert Rawlinson owned a few cotton mills, including the one in the village which Ralph was now helping to manage. It was also rumoured that by means of a couple of astute land deals, Albert had succeeded in buying or leasing property bordering the Eglinton estate.

In addition to being a shrewd businessman, Albert Rawlinson was also socially ambitious. He was best described as a self-made man and, as if in compensation for his own deprived childhood, he bestowed on Ralph every material advantage that money could buy. In the father's eyes, the son could do no wrong.

In fairness, it must be said that the twenty year old Ralph was very good looking. He was possessed of handsome features, black hair, deep blue eyes and a naturally beguiling charm which he frequently enhanced by a display of impeccably good manners. The result of all this advantage, plus his father's adulation, was that Ralph held a very high opinion of himself and as Charlie had said, was used to getting his own way. He had been entered into the same school as the Earl's two sons and being the same age as Austen, the two boys had been in the same class. They had shared a common interest in sport and had become friends. Although it was difficult to actually fault Ralph, Claire did not like him.

Shortly after Austen had joined the Army, Ralph had been conscripted, but within weeks had suffered an injury to his hand, which although not serious in itself, had resulted in his discharge from armed service.

On the day of the hunt Claire was busy in the kitchen. There was no mistaking the horn's clear call. She paused and listened and having found a pair of field glasses left by some absentminded guest, decided to take Charlie's advice. Pulling on her coat, she hurried outside.

As the hunt plunged into Ladies Wood, seeing the branches and briars and pitfalls before them, the riders endeavoured to steady their mounts. Checking and weaving and searching a way, they sidestepped the hazards or stretched for the jump, clearing the obstacles strewn in their paths. Balanced precariously on the stone balustrade that encircled the terrace where the land fell away, Claire was afforded a view of the far countryside and was able to see the leaders as they emerged from the trees. Scratched and scathed with some a little torn, they were collecting their horses and putting them to the gallop once more.

Holding with one hand to the Virginia creeper, she steadied herself and focussed the field glasses. Viewed through the powerful lens, the big drop-bank of which Charlie had spoken looked incredibly close and she could pick out in amazing detail, even the stones embedded in its almost vertical, sheer face. The gusts of wind ruffling her hair and tugging her skirts brought more sounds now, the sharp yipping of the hounds, the warning shouts and staccato commands as the leading riders approached the river. Loose horses in nearby fields raced to the fences, whinnying shrill greetings to their fellow creatures in the hunt. By now the hounds had arrived at the water and flopping splashily, had reached the far side. Panting and confused they were circling madly and sniffing the ground, for as Charlie had said, the fox in his cunning had indeed muddled his scent trails by running in rings before doubling back to the river.

In the background the last of the stragglers were emerging from the shadowy curtain of the wood, but those in the lead were now on the steep drop. With fingers white with cold, Claire focussed the glasses again. The Master was first, then the field-master, the huntsman, the whipper-in and those whose pride was to be at the front. The leaders never faltered, keeping their stride to the last before making the leap.

The graceful curve of their flight was broken rudely and abruptly by the heavy, jarring impact of their landing in the waters below. Cumbersomely then, they fought for their footing. Slowed by the flow they made their way across, moving more quickly as they came to the shallower reaches of the far bank. The Earl was amongst them, riding in a movement-to-minimum manner astride his well-muscled bay.

Then, in steady, rhythmic pace came James. He brought his mare to the brink without fuss and with weight well forward and keeping contact on long rein urged her on. Amelia was there too. She came at a dash, in quick and edgy movement on her pretty, finely built cob. It rushed to the very edge and for the merest blink of its rider's long lashes hung poised until a flurry of her reins and flourish of her whip released some spring of animation and it dropped itself into the river below.

Regaining dry land the riders endured the juddering they had come to expect as their horses shook water from their coats. Knowing full well what the fox had done, the Master summoned the hounds and wheeled swiftly away to the right.

A haze now obscured the few riders bunched together, still on the take-off side. Steam, rising from the sweat on the horses' flanks, heaving from resisting all attempts to make them jump, mingled with the condensation of warm breath on frosty air. Stirred by the continuous activity, it swirled around in the weak rays of the sun. Gradually the numbers diminished as would-be refusers succumbed to the pressure of pelting or persuading and complied, whilst other riders pocketed their pride, gave up and rode away. The excitement died down. The turbulence in the river subsided and it was then, through the dissipating veils of mist that Claire saw Charlie's prophecy had taken solid form.

Immobile and statuesque with Ralph straddled in the saddle, the stolid, black gelding was resolutely withstanding his every effort to make it budge. True to form, it had rooted itself the instant it sensed the proximity of water and there it remained seemingly cemented to the earth, possessed of a rigidity deemed only possible if each one of its legs had been screwed to the ground where its hooves had landed.

The creature moved not an inch, not a muscle. Totally devoid of any sign of life or sense, it neither reared, nor bucked, nor plunged, any one of which activity, would at least have given the unfortunate, young man the opportunity to salvage some pride by an exhibition of bravado and ability to stay aboard. But no, the stubborn, black beast was giving him nothing. In marked contrast to his normal nonchalance and usually splendid seat, Ralph's wild walloping and desperate swinging of both his booted legs were causing great hilarity among the spectators. Ralph was stranded with no way to save his face, now reddened with embarrassment.

It was, when it occurred, without the least vestige of warning that the animal sprang to life, spun round, seemingly on one leg, and with the speed of light itself took off in the direction from which it had come, carrying its hapless passenger with it.

And there, had Ralph been wiser, he would have let the chapter close, but Charlie's assessment of him was as accurate as his prediction of the horse. Young Rawlinson was no man to suffer defeat and leave it at that.

With the aid of the borrowed field glasses, Claire finally spotted him against a green background, a couple of fields away. He was galloping the animal madly round and round in diminishing circles. It was the old equestrian trick of deploying the horse's speed against itself to which Ralph was about to add a new dimension. Ralph's idea was, that having built up a good head of steam, he would bring the horse out of orbit and still in its dizzied and disorientated state, fire it at the bank. It was a wild chance that could only have succeeded, if the animal's furious pace and confusion were sufficiently long lasting to carry it by the sheer momentum of a blind and headlong rush, up to the water's edge and over.

The tactic could scarcely be credited as horsemanship, but it might have worked, on another. On the water-phobic gelding, it was preordained to fail. Once launched on a straight course the creature got a fix on its bearings and on reaching the river, weighed anchor once more and, as before, its moorings held. A cheer went up from the onlookers. Those amongst them who worked at the mill were finding the incident particularly entertaining.

But Claire dared wait no longer. Jumping from the balustrade, on feet numb with cold, she ran back to the kitchen. Cook was fussed. The Stirrup Cup was a pet hate of hers and with the hunt in the vicinity, serving it was almost a certainty.

"It wer' allus the same in the days a'for the war put a stop to it," she grumbled. "They goes a'clatterin' off down that drive, an' ne'er a body knows whether or when they'll come a'clatterin' back wantin' it all-ready an' waitin', an' me wi' no way o' knowin' afore-hand, if or when, that'll be."

Cook paused, seemingly dwelling on the sheer folly of it all, "...an' when they does come back, it's muck an' mud ev'rywhere, dirtyin' the drive, tramplin' its edges an' churnin' up the gravel 'cos they says they 'ave to keep them 'orses movin', wi' 'em bein' all damp and sweatin' after the gollopin'...great lumpin' things."

"Gets hersell in as big a lather as th' horses, she does," commented one of the maids to Claire. "Mind you, I do say as 'ow I see 'er point, an' it's not as simple as yer'd think, servin' drinks an' things to folks on 'orses, dodgin' round 'em, watchin' yer don't get yersell tramped on cos of 'em not keepin' still, or gettin' yersell kicked, wi' 'em bein' all worked up from the chasin'. It ain't easy I c'n tell you."

"No," Claire replied, "...it doesn't sound so."

But it was not the thought of the horses that was upsetting her. It was the prospect of having to dance attendance on the bevy of beautiful, young huntswomen who, if this morning's performance was anything to go by, would be thronging round James. The picture did not make much call on the imagination. She could see them already in her mind's eye, elegant in their riding habits, flushed with excitement and exercise in the fresh air, perfumed, wearing makeup, flawlessly groomed, even if a little mud-splashed or dishevelled, and manoeuvring their mounts close to his while darting him glances with come-hither eyes.

'Oh stop, stop thinking this way,' she screamed inwardly at the scourge of envy down-dragging at her heart. 'You can't blame them. It's what their upbringing's befitted them for, what all the schooling and grooming and Coming Out was about... the marriage market, it's a gamble, like playing roulette. Until they win for themselves a husband no lower on society's ladder than themselves, essential if they're to keep their present friends and status, their futures are hanging in the balance for not even the most fiercely independent of them could, of her own endeavour, retain her social standing, recreate for herself the circumstances into which she was born.'

'It's a raw view, even callow,' she mused, '...but it's true. The system snares them also and time isn't on their side. A dozen more years or so and any one of them still a spinster, will be deemed to have failed, an old maid, on the shelf, at home with her parents, or living the life of a maiden aunt in the house of a married sister, caring for her children instead of for her own.'

The deaths of so many young men killed or maimed in the war had increased this possibility and the competition was heightened by another throng of beautiful, young debutantes coming fresh upon the scene each year.

'Yes, life's tough for them too,' Claire told herself.

It was a brave attempt at self-consolation but afforded no cheer and proved a pitiable defence against the covetous emotions now threatening to hold sway.

"They're 'ere," the announcement came from the garden boy, suddenly thrusting his head round the kitchen door.

"Right," said Cook, wiping her hands on her pinafore before taking it off, "… them trays are all ready, an' y' all know yer places an' what yer to do…an' remember," she added, "like the housekeeper told you, smile nicely…an' try t' look like yer glad they've stopped by."

Shuffling into line with the others, Claire took a last minute check on herself. Mercifully her shoes, too well worn, were mostly hidden beneath the long, crisply clean over-apron she had just put on, but her hands, continually in and out of water, were rough and chapped and her nails, constantly splitting and breaking were cut to the quick. 'No way to hide them,' she thought miserably as she stood, waiting the signal to go.

"Oh come on, cheer up, them 'orses ain't that bad," said the maid who had spoken earlier.

"Thank you," said Claire, aiming to smile.

'It's not the horses,' she thought, looking steadily ahead but seeing only the alluring young women from whom James could choose and abruptly, with no further thinking, her decision was made.

No of course she could not just hang up her pinafore and walk out on Cook, not with the extra houseguests and the New Year celebrations still to be held, but come Twelfth Night, the formal close of the Yuletide Season, the date the festivities ended, she would leave. It was only a matter of days.

The doors were opened. The riders were waiting. Smiling, Claire walked boldly forward and lifted her tray to the prettiest young lady in the hunt.

CHAPTER SIX

Ardleagh Hall. Twelfth Night. 6th January 1919

*I*t was a bitterly cold day. Gusts of damp air driven down from the moors by the biting wind, scudded against the stable walls and spattered the pools in the yard. The temperamental grey mare, petulant in bad weather, had proved a rough ride. Now that she was back in her box and well bedded down, James was more than happy to close the stable door on her and get back to the house.

Taking the short cut behind the shrubbery he caught the fragrant scent of burning pine and holly leaves. It seemed an odd time for a bonfire, but then he remembered which day it was. Today marked the traditional finish to the Christmas Season, the end of the Old, the beginning of the New. He stopped, turned aside and took the rhododendron path towards the clearing. Seeing Claire, he stopped again. So there she was. This time he would make no mistake.

Watched by a small group of servants and attended by the gardeners, a great pyre of tinder-dry evergreen leaves, coloured streamers and fancy paper trimmings, torn wrappings and ribbons, was swiftly succumbing to the bright, yellow tongues of flame being whipped around it by the wind. In the midst of the haphazard heap the Christmas tree, stripped of its baubles but with tatters of tinsel and gilded fir cones still clinging to its branches, was slowly charring to a skeletal stump.

Twelfth Night, the day when every last vestige of Yuletide adornment must be taken down or, as the superstition of ill omen decreed, be left hanging until Christmas next year. Well, so the housekeeper insisted, but Claire was convinced she had just made it up as an excuse for a good sort out and clean sweep. A stickler for routine, she strongly disapproved of the additional work and waste of the Christmas disruption. As more bags and barrow loads were brought to the blaze, the clearing out continued.

Stripped of their festoons, the bare look in the rooms created an air of finality. It was in keeping with Claire's mood as she stood with her hands in her pockets, staring at a cluster of red berried twigs. The fire caught and consumed them, turning them into little black bits for the flames to play with before breathing them upwards on curls of its smoke. Lost in her thoughts, her gaze stayed centred on the space where they had been. She did not see James appear at the far end of the path, then turn and go back.

She had remained resolute in her decision, said good-bye to Anna, packed her bags and Jimmy, the carter, had promised to take her to the village station.

Changes of kitchen staff were the province of Cook and the housekeeper. Lady Margaret did not trouble herself with such matters. Cook was upset but, like Anna, had kept her word and told nobody. James did not know Claire was leaving. Cook and Anna did not understand and Claire could not explain, but it was something she knew she had to do. 'I've got to change my life,' she told herself, 'be better, become...more than I am and becoming so, make my life different and nobody can do this for me, only I myself.'

On finding Claire by the bonfire, James had pulled back. He would wait. He had to talk to her on her own and was not going to miss this chance. He was certain she had been avoiding him since his return from Cambridge. He had caught one brief glimpse of her just before the hunt moved off and had not seen her since except two days ago when she was passing the end of a corridor, but by the time he had raced to the corner she had disappeared. He had even made excuses to go down to the kitchen but to no avail, not that there would have been much point if she had been there, not under Cook's eagle eye.

He had been puzzled by her never being where he expected her to be. It seemed uncanny until it dawned on him. Of course, that was the answer. Given the way they knew each other it was easy to guess where the other would be and it was then that he realised she was deliberately eluding him. Now that he had spotted her, he would wait and catch her on her own.

Amelia was also leaving today. Alva had made his annoyance fully felt at her move to Ardleagh. Taking its measure Amelia had realised that if she wanted to achieve her long term goal, she would have to tread very carefully. She had therefore for the time being, conceded to his wishes regarding her return to Spain.

It was a small price to pay for her daughter's ultimate greater advantage, a mere sprat to catch a mackerel. As she had intended, Alva had looked upon her promise as a conciliatory gesture on her part and had been disarmed.

Amelia could be seen now, crossing the front lawn, her light step and graceful movement making her easily recognisable from afar.

"They c'n say all they likes 'bout Lady Amelia," said Aggie, "but 'er fair cheers a body up."

She had passed the same remark a couple of evenings ago after Amelia, without warning, had descended to the kitchen while they were preparing dinner. Having congratulated them on the delicious dishes they were cooking, she then generously spread her appreciation around in more tangible form before taking her leave.

"Meks thee feel as 'ow thar be at least one body tekin' note o' all thee does for 'em an' I'll be right sorry when 'er's gone."

There was truth in what Aggie said and all agreed Lady Amelia had brightened the atmosphere and the mistress seemed better when she was around. Even so, Lady Margaret had not joined in the festivities.

Amelia was walking the grounds looking for James. She spotted him, half-hidden by the wall on the far side of the shrubbery waiting his chance to talk to Claire.

"Ah, there you are," she called quickening her step.

"Found you at last. Your mother thought you were still on your ride, but I was sure you'd be back by now."

"Amelia..." he exclaimed. Seeing Claire, he had completely forgotten his aunt's departure.

"I'm leaving in a few moments. Come and join the rest of us for a last drink before Eric brings the car round."

"But..." he began.

Amelia linked her arm in his.

"Please, no buts, I'll be gone in a few minutes," she said almost plaintively, guiding their steps towards the front door.

As he passed through into the entrance, James cast a backward glance towards the spirals of smoke rising above the rhododendrons.

"Just a few minutes," his aunt had said. He hoped so. Any longer and he would need to make some excuse.

The last of the Christmas tree, its branches burned through, slipped further into the ashes, sending up a shower of shining sparks and ending Claire's abstraction. There was nothing to keep her now. The time had come, but with it had also come regrets, perversely too late, at not having told James she was leaving. Was it that she could not bear to say "Good-bye"? Had she been avoiding him, creating difficulties in the desperate hope of finding what she longed for in their being overcome? No, that was silly, for with things the way they were it could not be…not in the way she truly wanted it to be, between her and James.

Well, whatever, it was too late now. Jimmy, the carter, was walking up the path towards her.

"I'm on my way back t' th' village Claire, so I can giv' thee a ride on th' wagon now."

She thanked him. Yes, she was ready.

"I'll be sorry t' see thee go. Why is thee goin'?"

Claire made a brave attempt at a smile. "Oh, let's just say Jimmy, I'm not keen on traipsing around with trays."

"Aye, but these days a job's a job for all o' that, an' with all o' the men comin' home from the fightin', thar aren't goin' to be too many jobs aroun'. What'll thee do?"

"I'm going to Manchester," she answered and in reply to his comment that it was a big city for young girl, she replied that the bigger it was the more likely she was to find work.

She and Jimmy had left by the servants' entrance. As they passed the tall, front gates, Claire stole a last glance up the main drive. She could see Eric by the car drawn up to the front portico. Everything looked just the same. Quickly she turned her head away. Her optimism and confidence were a sham. Her eyes were stinging. She had a lump in her throat and not much idea where the road stretching out ahead was leading.

The engine of the large, polished automobile was running smoothly. Eric, his uniform immaculate as always, was standing beside it. The wide, front doors stood open. Last goodbyes were being said and the Earl was soon helping his sister into the back seat. There were repeated last minute reminders, much waving and promises to write. The throb from the engine increased and the car began to move. The family waved their last farewells and then turned back towards the house. James was relieved. It had been, as Amelia had promised, a matter of minutes, not long at all.

His father had asked him to wait behind. He wanted to talk to him, but James walked away while his attention was still on the departing car. Hastening towards the garden he heard his father's voice, but feigning deafness he kept walking. 'He probably suspects I've heard,' he thought, 'but he won't make a fuss, too many servants around.'

When he got to the fire, the small group had broken up and in answer to his questions the gardeners could only answer.

"Don't know Sir. Don't know where she is."

She must have gone back indoors but he could not keep hanging around the kitchen like some lovesick swain. He had done that already this week and had run out of excuses. Cook had a nose for these things and Anna looked askance at him enough already. Better just to keep a sharp lookout and choose his moment.

Leaving the Hall behind, the car picked up speed. Amelia reclined into the comfort of the back seat. She glanced at her watch and checked again the time on her first class, rail ticket from Manchester. Yes, all was in order. Her trunks had already gone on ahead. She could relax, no rush, there was plenty of time. She closed her eyes, peace perfect peace.

She had found it a strain coping with her brother. Usually it was just a bit of a pain, but this time she had to engineer him and that had definitely been a strain. Frederick was older than her by several years and had been appointed her guardian when their father died. As head of the family, he had charge of the family trust. Habit dies hard and he never seemed to have thought to relinquish his role as guardian. She loved him, but really he could be dreadfully bossy if let be, a trait she usually countered by playing a straight bat, but not this time.

This time she had had to be biddable, constantly, for he would be no use at all if he got upset. To have him listen to her she had to catch him in receptive mood, for only then could she prime him to carry out her plan, without him knowing what it was, or even that she had one.

It had not been easy, far from it. It had seriously taxed her diplomatic skills. Not for ages had she had to work so hard, not even on Alva, not since…she could not remember when.

But it had been worth it. Remembering, she felt again the glow of satisfaction, the quiver of relief at having finally obtained her husband's consent about their daughter.

Having lulled Alva into a less guarded attitude by not arguing with him about Leonora over Christmas, she had then needed to get Frederick to talk to him, but without Frederick realising that she wanted him to, or just what it was she wanted him to say, which meant getting Frederick himself to want it, for Alva's suspicions would be immediately aroused if he sensed any hint from Frederick that she was behind it.

She could only bless her luck. The gods had favoured her. Her chance had come after dinner, late on Boxing Day, the day of the hunt. They were in fine spirits, having imbibed before the hunt, sipped from the hip flasks passed around as they rode, supped of the Stirrup Cup later and enjoyed the jubilation so often felt after a good hunt, thanks to the exercise, the relaxation of nerves strung taut before starting and, last but not least, the giddy relief at having survived the chase, its thrills and its spills, without harm.

It was late in the day, very late. They had dined well and she and Frederick were sitting in front of the fire. Margaret had already retired. James was, Heaven knew where, and she was about to go to bed when Frederick suddenly announced, as though he had only just found out, "This is Christmas. We must celebrate," and had ordered a bottle of rare vintage to be brought from the cellar.

Actually they were both quite exhausted but somehow, after that, she could not leave him drinking alone and she had opened a box of the crystallized fruit liqueurs she had brought from Spain, his favourites, delicious, but as she realised later, very thirst making.

So he drank, and some more, and she talked, and she talked of the violence in Spain, of its disruption to Leonora's education and of the riot the child had been in and how it had frightened her and how she herself did not feel safe in Spain anymore and how she really wanted Leonora to go to boarding school here in England but no, it could not be. No, Alva would never agree, no never. But if only he would and if her daughter were safely settled in school here, she could perhaps face returning to Spain.

Frederick awoke the next morning with a throbbing head. He remembered dozing the night before in front of the fire after dinner, but nothing more, nothing to cause this. He must have over-exerted himself during the hunt. He was getting older. He should go easier on himself.

It was later in the day that the idea came to him. He really did not know why, nor where it had come from, but suddenly the notion of Leonora going to boarding school occurred to him and once it occurred, it seemed like divine inspiration, for ever since Amelia had arrived at Ardleagh, he had been worrying she might not go back. Worse still, he kept getting an awful foreboding that to escape the riots in Spain she might want to bring her daughter here to live with her, to stay, indefinitely. Oh Lord no, the days of his guardianship coming back to haunt him. He still had bad dreams about that time and just when he was telling himself he should start easing up and this time there would be two of them, not just the one, but he did have a duty, the child was his niece and Margaret was very fond of her.

All the same he was not happy and was sure his fears were justified for Amelia had told Margaret she did not like Spain and was nervous about staying there and now he was nervous too. He knew his sister.

But, thought Frederick, his heart lifting, if Leonora were safely tucked up in boarding school, he could practically insist, family values and such like, that his sister return to her husband.

Alva read and re-read Frederick's letter and had pondered. In truth, he found supervision of his adolescent daughter somewhat trying in her mother's absence. Although still totally opposed to her joining her mother abroad, he could almost approve of an English boarding school. It would be disciplined, structured, and above all, would remove Leonora from Amelia's influence and when she left at eighteen, she would be of marriageable age and his responsibilities would become her husband's. In fact, he wondered why he had not thought of it himself.

But, for Amelia, that was not the end of it for there still remained the question of which school. She had already selected the one she wished her daughter to attend and so, the task of nudging and influencing her brother's thinking began all over again. Finally, guided by Frederick whom Alva believed to know best in these matters, he made up his mind and informed his wife of his choice.

On learning of her husband's decision, a wily smile of relief played on Amelia's lips. How very fortuitous, Alva had opted for the very school she wanted. It had all worked out nicely.

James knew his father was waiting, but he needed time to think before facing him. He could guess what was coming. It had been on the cards since he discussed his application to change courses with his tutor, just before Christmas. Since then, James had been fostering a faint, unrealistic hope that some administrative error or oversight may leave his father unaware, but his optimism had been extinguished on seeing the letter arrive from Cambridge.

Since Austen's death, his father had taken it for granted that James would one day take over the running of the estate and the mines and despite his son's protests, had arranged his studies to befit him for the task. James however, had no intention of letting his father mould him to his expectations.

Close to Claire, he knew the hardships and dangers the miners faced every day. He saw their situation from a viewpoint totally different to that of his father and could not adopt the same hard attitude. All this, he could argue about and did, but what he could not tell his father was that his aversion to the mines and the way they were run, went much deeper than that. Nor could he tell him why.

It was rooted in his suspicions that the Brackworth colliery disaster and the loss of the entire night shift of miners, including Claire's father, could have been avoided. When the disaster struck, fire and a roof collapse had thwarted all rescue attempts to save the men. The general opinion was that the explosions had been caused by gas and hearsay was that the suspected presence of gas had been reported some days before the disaster. It had long been believed in the village that the Enquiry, set up to examine the circumstances surrounding the tragedy, had been less than straightforward. Its report was published but certain aspects of the catastrophe were never ascertained and its findings were indeterminate.

Subsequent to the explosions, the mine had flooded, but the suggestion of draining it had been dismissed. The mine had been declared unsafe and quickly sealed. Many said too quickly. Nothing further was attempted and that was how it had remained. But whatever the Enquiry's conclusion, there was nothing vague about James' memories of that night. They were still vividly etched on his mind. He had been eight years old.

The terrible, steel-edged lament of the pithead siren's long, compelling, keening whine had seared the valley. Its mourning was heard on the moorlands and reached to the hills beyond. In the darkness James awoke and listened and heard the other sounds, of voices in the hall below, of doors opening and being closed. Word of the calamity had broken and the sleeping house was roused to the urgency of comings and goings. Below the window of his room a car scrunched the gravel and then another as his father's men, the mine manager and others, gripped by fear and desperation came with frantic messages and looking for advice. As the enormity of the disaster was realized there was shock, then panic and alarm and in the frenzy of confusion, instructions were being given and orders issued or countermanded and withdrawn.

James strained to hear, then pulled on his dressing gown and crept downstairs. Unnoticed in the shadows and the press of others' needs, he had watched and listened, taking in all that was happening and being said.

What was it he had heard? What was it in the hoarse words stumblingly stammered by the ashen faced and almost incoherent man who had suddenly forced his way in and pushed his way through to get to the Earl, or in the harsh insistence with which he had been quickly pulled aside and roughly shoved into the privacy of the small office in the rear hall, the door of which his father then firmly closed… and later, when the handle turned and the door opened and he heard his father speaking in low, intimidating tones, warnings intended only for the pale faced man's ears but which he also could hear, but hearing did not understand for though he understood the words he could not grasp why they were being said, not in the way they were, not then. He had not gone back to bed that night but stayed, a hidden, unsuspected witness, listening to what was going on and that was when his doubts began and then came guilt, making him want to have nothing to do with the mines.

Since becoming heir to the title and estate, his father's determination to force him in that direction had caused many rows between them, rows aggravated by James' suspicions. Equally determined to choose his own future and not wanting to waste time studying for qualifications he did not intend to use, James had applied to change his courses and the recently arrived, Cambridge crested envelope gave warning of trouble in store.

To his surprise however, his father did not appear to be annoyed when he entered his study. Laying aside his newspaper, he expressed his disappointment that his son had not kept him informed of what he unfairly termed, was this change of mind. Then, with what appeared to be a genuine interest, he asked him what his preferences were. To James it seemed the opportunity he had hoped for and he fell into the trap. Of course his real love was music as it had always been, but first he needed to know what standard he might achieve and so decided not to mention it yet, but to wait and see how the conversation went, for if he failed in the assessment regarding music, Cambridge offered many different studies.

He spoke of his interest in aviation, communications and radio, but that he needed to get more advice. His father remained attentive and James spoke of the other opportunities he was considering, scientific research and physics, telling his father of a lecture he had attended at Manchester University, given by a Professor Ernest Rutherford who was doing work on atoms, a field of study still in its infancy.

"The world's changing father. It's an exciting time. Now the war's ended, improvements in technology will encourage commercial flights. Sooner or later, it will bring travel within reach of the masses, lessening the divide between rich and poor. It will no longer be the privilege of just a wealthy few. Avenues are opening in the arts as well, especially music, particularly now with Marconi's new invention. These innovations will help blur out the distinctions between those with wealth and those without. Recordings that can be heard in one's own home will bring music within the scope of people who've been unable to attend concerts," said James, full of enthusiasm.

His father was listening, not interrupting. Maybe this was the moment to talk about music as a career. It was still in his curriculum. He practised every available moment and his tutor had said he considered him gifted.

James waited, then took the plunge, telling his father that the other possibilities were really, well, no more than second strings to his bow.

James' chosen instrument was the piano not the violin, but it was an unfortunate choice of metaphor and his father promptly dashed the suggestion.

"Music, fiddle-playing, what sort of a career do you call that? Travel for the masses, getting rid of the divides between rich and poor. Where do you get these notions? You've been listening to too much socialist clap-trap. You'd do well to consider how and by whom, your education's financed. I do not intend to have you waste it chasing airy ideas, Rutherford and his atoms indeed, too small to even see the darn things. Tell me - what conceivable impact do you think they could have on this new world you talk about?"

Having put down most of what his son had said, Frederick discarded his irritation and adopted a quieter tone.

"Your duty, James, is to build on what's being handed on to you, onto what's solid and tangible. If you dislike the mines, learn how to put the right men in, men who know how to turn in a profit. That's what good management is about. I've already written my reply regarding your wish to change courses. I want to hear no more about it and by the way, don't think you can leave and get a job as you suggested some weeks ago. Anything worthwhile and you're going to need references. Prospective employers will want to know about you and when they learn who you are, they'll feel it wise to get in touch with me. So you won't find getting employment as easy as you might think."

The meeting dragged to an end. As far as Cambridge and a career of his own choosing were concerned, James realised that for the time being, short of embarking on something drastic, there was little he could do. It was one of those moments he really longed for Claire. As always, she would understand. He had to find her. He wanted to talk to her. He had to know why she was behaving as she was.

CHAPTER SEVEN

January 1919. Cordoba. Spain.

Leonora had not been sure just what was in store for her but, at last, word had arrived. She was to attend an English boarding school and she and her mother were to leave for London. There was a great deal of shopping to be done, clothes to be bought, fitted and altered, if need be. All these preparations had to be attended to quickly for her father was anxious that she be there for the beginning of term. From what he had said, it seemed the idea and choice of school had been his, but surprisingly it was her mother who had all the answers to her questions. It was she who filled in the picture of what the school was like and what she could expect.

After listening to her father, she had been a little daunted. 'All in Correct Order', very 'By the Book', was how he had described it. But after talking to her mother she was excited, for her mother had said that while in London, she would take her, not only to the school outfitters, but to a boutique for a fashionable outfit and to the theatre as well. All travel arrangements had been made and she was to leave Cordoba early in the morning. For the last two hours Letitia had been helping her to pack. The old nurse had been given her orders and was sticking to them rigidly.

"No," said Letitia, taking from the travel trunk, items Leonora had just put in. "Your father said, 'only what is needed for school'."

Leonora pursed her lips in irritation. She had been on the point of asking if she could look through the old chest full of family photos and souvenirs that she had come across in the room where the travel trunks were stored. 'Better not,' she thought. 'She'll only say,' "Wait until I ask your father," or "No, no, there isn't time."

She wanted to go through them again, to take something with her to England for she had the same, strange last time feeling, as when returning from her ride some weeks ago.

After Letitia had closed the last case and left, Leonora made her way to the chest.

Kneeling on the hard, boarded floor, she pulled out its contents, spreading them around. Sorting through the various boxes and albums she came across one, quite old and ornately bound. It must have been pretty once, but its ruche of frilled ribbon and lace trim were now crushed flat with the weight of all that had been put upon it. The silver stencilled roses and the lettering on the cover had faded, but she could just make out the date, 1902.

It was her parents' wedding album and with it was another marked with the same date, of photographs taken in that same summer seventeen years ago, the year when they had met and married, the century just two years old and she herself not even born.

Slowly she opened the pressed together pages and saw pictures, long unlooked upon, sepia tinted slivers of life, framed fragments of light and shade showing instants of social occasions and joyous events, in which they were both happy and smiling.

She gazed at them and tried hard, but found it impossible to imagine the vivacity and movement that must have taken place in the interims between each of those forever frozen moments in which they had posed and smiled for the camera. She tried to conjure up the love and the laughter, the continuity of warmth and colour that must have animated the happenings linking one, 'Watch the birdie,' session to the next, but she could not.

Leonora looked long upon the pages of photos in which they appeared so much in love, so delighted with each other and could only wonder, 'If it were like that then, how has it come to be as it is now?'

She had spent longer than she intended and it was late when she heard Letitia opening and closing doors, searching for her. Knowing she would be told to put back the photos she had chosen, she quickly gathered the ones she wanted, pushed the boxes to one side and trying not to look flustered hurried to the door.

"Leonora, well you know the carriage will be at the door at dawn's first light and…" Seeing the untidy piles scattered across the floor, Letitia's voice trailed away.

"Oh, look at the mess," she admonished, shaking her head, "…but leave it now," she insisted, ushering her charge out of the room. "It's too late to attend to it now. I'll see to it in the morning."

But it was Alva who later that night noticed the door ajar and seeing the room had been disturbed, went in. Wondering at the clutter, he pushed the nearest object with his foot, then stooped and picked it up. His wedding album, he had not looked at it in years. Holding it to the lamp, he gazed at it and turned the pages as his daughter had done, but unlike his daughter, he did not have to wonder…he knew…and the memories returned…

Summer 1902…only months after his father's death. His father had died without warning, an unthinkable occurrence, sudden and catastrophic for the whole family, a terrible shock. They had all put on mourning clothes and cloaked themselves in grief. The funereal gloom that hung like a dark miasma in the cold, vaulted crypt had clung to them to be borne back to the house by the long procession in which they were carried, seated behind the black-draped windows of the heavy carriages dragged by black horses, with sombre trappings and black plumes.

It had continued to hover like the doom of some as yet unfulfilled threat, over the entire household. His dutiful sisters had seated themselves day after day around the disconsolate widow as though waiting for a non-existent someone to tell them they may do otherwise. The weeks passed.

Never given to the expression of emotion, his mother became ever more withdrawn, clinging to her stone-like sorrow as if it were a rock, the only abiding and constant feature in the sea of discontinuity that had become her world. Increased liabilities and family demands descended upon Alva, now head of the household and bearing his father's mantle as his only son. Initially he had supposed that as the sudden shock of loss subsided, such pressures would ease, but this had not come to be and what he had hoped was a passing phase, began to fossilize into established habit.

The attorneys arrived. All the family gathered. The atmosphere was stressful as the Last Will and Testament was read out. Whether from intent, oversight, or simply the untimeliness of the deceased's demise, the expectations of certain members of the family had not been met and had become issues of dispute. This, in turn, further distressed his mother Elvira who as always, was most concerned, overly so, thought Alva, with family wellbeing. But her position had changed. The reins were now in his hands and her endeavours to settle the situation in her way, were making matters worse.

The worries of the estate, the olive-growing, the vineyards, the harvesting and marketing, all were now in Alva's charge and he resented the family's interference, the continuing calls on his time and attention, the constant queries and unfair demands. The doleful atmosphere pervading the house weighed down on him. Added to his other newly acquired responsibilities, it was irksome and as time went by with no sign of improvement, he had become irritable and depressed. Miserably he cast around for an escape that could not be classified as evasion of duty.

It was while in this downcast mental frame that he conceived the idea of a trip to England. An important part of the estate management was the exportation of wine and sherry. 'It was,' he told himself, 'his duty to familiarise and update himself, to learn more about such matters.' Yes, he would go to England, on business. His mind made up, Alva informed his mother and after enduring a difficult couple of weeks, finished his preparations and left for London.

The city was vibrant, shaking off the dust of the Victorian era and throbbing with excitement at the forthcoming Coronation of King Edward V11. Alva enjoyed the congenial hospitality bestowed on him, once he had presented his letters of introduction. Most of all he was impressed with the dependability and working order that here in London, underlay the energy of everyday pursuits. The pace at which the English conducted their business was to his liking. Activity at the financial centres, the banks and seats of commerce he had visited was lively but unhurried, vigorous but devoid of haste. It disturbed him to compare it with the troubled state of affairs in his own country, continually being reported in the international press.

Sitting in the lounge of the Savoy Hotel one morning enjoying an excellent cup of coffee, Alva's eye was caught by an item in The Times newspaper, an article on the closing of the Cortes and the declaration of martial law by Spain's boy King, the sixteen year old Alphonse X111, who had only recently ascended the throne and was trying out his newly acquired monarchical powers. The King's action was in response to the strike of workers in Madrid and was deemed most unwise, for only three months earlier in Barcelona, one of Spain's most important cities five hundred had been killed in violent clashes with striking workers in street battles that were far from being isolated incidents.

Alva laid the paper aside. How stark was the contrast of events in his own country with the order and reliability in England. How did the English manage it? He would very much like to know. In the centre of London and in the cosy, agricultural counties, such stability could be expected, but how was it in the poor and deprived industrial regions he had been reading about?

He had heard that in some of the working class areas, living standards were desperate with wages barely at subsistence level, particularly in the industrial heart of the North, the coalmining and cotton spinning regions of Lancashire. Yet even so, there was none of the type of vicious rioting, bloodletting and killing, currently happening in Spain.

He had come to the end of his stay but decided not to return home just yet. He had been making enquiries and had been surprised to learn that a considerable quantity of the produce he exported to England, particularly his fine sherry, was subsequently transported to the industrial North, something his father seemed not to have realised. Direct importation would surely result in higher profit. It was an avenue worth exploring.

Lancashire's damp climate suited the cotton spinning industry. The moisture in the air helped to prevent the snapping of the newly spun, delicate threads and several of its towns and villages were forested with the smoke-belching chimneys of many mills. It was also the main coal producing area and the plight of the workers in its mines and mills was said to be appalling. There were strikes and industrial unrest, but they were settled without the shocking atrocities perpetrated in his country. So how did the English manage their labour problems?

It would be interesting to see first-hand how the British capitalist system worked in the North. It was, after all, the terrible conditions in Lancashire's mills and mines in the last century, that had inspired Karl Marx when writing his Communist Manifesto. Marx had spent time in Lancashire thanks to his friend Friedrich Engles, who helped him financially. Engles' father, a Prussian textile manufacturer, had a branch of his business in Manchester and his son, who worked for him, was based there. Alva reasoned that if conditions were as bad as he had heard and order was still maintained, there were lessons to be learned.

So it was that he booked a suite at one of Manchester's best hotels, and travelled north. Boarding the train, he warned himself he did not know what to expect, never a truer word. It was not so much the events that were to happen when he got there that would change his life, as the outcome to which they would ultimately lead.

Naturally, his main concerns on arrival were to learn the final destination of his produce and to assess the size of the market. He made a few contacts and dined with one or two potential customers in the hope of their signing contracts, but the possibilities were not as promising as he had hoped. Lacking the letters of introduction that had made his stay in London so enjoyable, the results were disappointing. In truth, Lancashire did nothing to cheer him.

Being on business, he did not travel to the beautiful moorlands. He did not see the rivers coursing through the tree clad valleys, nor the fine country houses on the hillsides overlooking them. He had stayed within the built up areas and was unaware of the loveliness of land unscarred by industry.

The deprivation in some of the regions he had seen was quite appalling. It was a poverty bereft of promise, barely sufficing a hand to mouth existence. Men in worn raincoats and cloth caps, women huddled in their shawls, back and forth they went to work each day, clattering the pavements with their wooden soled, iron-shod clogs, their lives marked out by the treadmill of the morning, noon, and night shifts.

'What hope of what unattainable purpose,' pondered Alva, 'keeps them moving in the mechanistic round of toil that marks the cycle of their lives?'

He did not, could not know of the decades of drudgery that had hardened the spirit of these workers to dogged resolution. They had learned how to survive, but their round of constant daily toil left them little by means of which they might improve their lot. They knew from long experience the limits their conditions had created, the barriers built by lack of opportunity, the boundaries they could not get beyond nor rise above. The employers, the mill and mine owners, also knew the limits, knew the cutting to the bone margin, they could impose.

Technology was improving. Return on capital was profitable and Alva saw the use industrialists made of both man and machine. Neither was ever idle. Shift work continued day and night. Alva witnessed a great deal of this, but saw nothing of the workers' living conditions and after two weeks in the North he had no wish to. He had not enjoyed his time there. The soot-laden air blackened the buildings and although it was summer, his stay had coincided with a bout of dull, damp weather.

On rising one morning, he looked out of the window at the grimy walls of the building opposite, at the dull sky, promising to drop more rain and felt again the emptiness occasioned by his father's death, his awareness of his own mortality, its seeming lack of meaning.

Quickly he summoned attention and ordered his bath to be run, his breakfast tray to be brought and arrangements made for his return. But as he packed and prepared to leave, thoughts of the situation awaiting him made him think again. Alva was not an impulsive man, but on the spur of the moment he decided to break his return journey. A few days of sun and relaxation would afford him the opportunity to reflect on ways of improving his future, to mull over the possibilities his new contacts might open up.

The rain now spitting at his bedroom window settled the matter and the place that sprang to mind was Biarritz. It had been in the newspapers a great deal lately owing to the patronage of the English King Edward V11 and as a result had become a most popular resort with his subjects. Yes, why not, a diversion, Biarritz.

He had given no particular thought to the choice. He had never been there, but he was sure to find it agreeable or it would never have become one of the King's favourite haunts. Yes, Biarritz. The King's royal approval had bestowed an unimpeachable respectability on the place that was not in the least diminished by his dalliances there with one or other of his mistresses. In fact, for those in the know, it lent an additional frisson of delicious permissiveness. For those not in the know, Biarritz retained its longstanding reputation as a decorous, sun-blessed retreat.

For Alva however, after his forthcoming sojourn in Biarritz, its reputation would never be the same. It was there, he would meet Amelia.

It had been a chance encounter with her brother, the Earl of Eglinton that brought them together. The Earl's estate was close to the part of the world Alva had just visited and in the course of conversation, they learned to their amusement that their paths had almost crossed during Alva's recent visit to Manchester. The Earl was a connoisseur of fine wines and the possibility of importing sherry directly, interested him. They agreed to meet again the following evening to discuss matters further.

They had already dined and were enjoying a postprandial brandy when Amelia made her entrance, unannounced. Her sudden appearance through the haze of cigar smoke was theatrical, its effect upon Alva, electrifying.

It could be said that he was never to fully recover from that first impact. He was galvanised by the very chemistry of her presence. At her approach he reflexed upright to his feet. Amelia did not bat an eye. She was well aware of the reaction she could produce, when she chose and this was an occasion when, she chose.

She had been watching the dark, good looking man with her brother for some time from across the room and being bored with the company she was in, had decided to join them and satisfy her curiosity. She responded to Alva's over precipitate courtesy with a practised graciousness that swirled his inner turmoil anew. Seated beside him, her light, almost teasing manner quite masked her discernment as she assessed, not only her effect on him, but Alva himself.

In the days that followed, getting to know Amelia had proved an exciting experience. Her attitude to life was utterly unlike anything Alva's upbringing had induced in him. Amelia saw the world around her as an offering from which she took only that which was pleasing. Like a butterfly that chooses to alight on only the fairest of flowers and never waste a flutter of bright wing on any prospect in the garden that offers no advantage and promises no pleasure, Amelia opted to settle upon Alva. Not that he could be described as a fair flower, but with his aura of breeding and his fascinatingly mysterious air of melancholy, he could certainly be judged a rare bloom.

Had Amelia been challenged on this her life's guiding principle she would have regarded such illogicality as sheer nonsense. Alva however was not challenging. He was being challenged. He found her direct and irreverent manner, her audaciously inviting gaiety, refreshing. It was certainly the very antithesis of all that the demureness of Spanish femininity had taught him to expect from a woman and was not at all the deportment usually displayed by one still unmarried, looking for a husband and therefore anxious to portray herself as a suitable bride.

But then, Amelia was not looking for a husband. Her brother however was, needless to say, not for himself, but for her. To this end he had for some time now, been scanning Burke's Peerage, 'Who's Who' and of late, even the horizon, but so far his quest had met with no success. Amelia was simply not prepared to join herself in matrimony with any of the possible suitors he had put forward.

"Nevertheless," as the Earl kept saying to his wife after listening to his sister's cutting comments on his latest suitable find, "Amelia simply has to be made to realise she must marry soon. She's twenty-two already and she's wasting her good years. Every season, yet another bevy of lovelies sally forth to be presented at Court and launched upon the social scene and I don't care what she says, getting older lessens her chances of making a good match."

So far, she had given her brother no serious cause for concern, but she was unnervingly attractive to the opposite sex and he regarded her as far too fun-loving. It irritated and tired him to have to keep monitoring her movements whenever she was out of sight. She was beginning to set him on edge.

Tuned as he was therefore to Amelia's overtures and responses in such matters, the Earl was well aware of the emanations passing between her and the handsome Spaniard. At first, he considered that the situation merited little more than a wary eye, but as certain aspects of the Andalucian's hitherto obscure background began to emerge, most notably his affluence and aristocratic lineage, the Earl deemed him worthy of more attention. In discussing the matter with his wife, he learned that she had already enquired into the Spaniard's suitability.

Meanwhile Amelia had continued to open up for Alva a whole new way of being. Fascinated, he watched her float her way through life. Amelia could brush aside irritation and annoyance as easily as crumbs from her lap. She did not actually flout the social mores of the day, she was much too clever to create difficulties for herself, but she did resent the restrictions they imposed and her sharp wit often found ways of making them appear ridiculous and turning them to her advantage.

Alongside such light heartedness Alva looked upon his troubles as nothing more than a burden of relics left over from a stultifying past and with Amelia showing him how, he was confident it was a burden he could shed. Always in the midst of gaiety she drew him into her circle and infused in him a joie de vivre he had never before known. The world in which he had left his sisters, garbed in mourning, sitting in self-denying solemnity around the grieving widow was dark years away from the one to which Amelia had brought him. He was now afraid of losing her. He must therefore look seriously at the realities. Would she, would her family, accept him? Indeed, who were they? What was her family history?

He learned that the family to which his beloved belonged was influential in social and financial spheres. Alva's motives were not mercenary. Nonetheless, he was sufficiently commercially minded to realise that membership by marriage to a family with such connections could prove remunerative in many ways. He himself came from a society that understood this, for these are things that differ little from country to country.

Whilst in England and taking advantage of the hospitality extended to him, he had listened to conversations in the various clubs and drawing rooms and had learned a great deal about the workings of England's successfully dominant economy. Imperialist Britain boasted an Empire on which the sun never set. It provided her with an unfailing supply of low priced, raw materials, cheap labour and an easy market for her manufactured goods.

The resultant import and export trade created much mercantile activity, which fostered further industry in her shipbuilding yards, which in turn increased the demand for coal and steel. This furtherance of Britain's maritime interests had also made London a centre for insurance and world banking.

On the other hand, Spain's sphere of influence had dramatically decreased during the Napoleonic era and again, later in 1898, when she had lost virtually the last of her remaining colonies abroad, Cuba and Puerto Rica near South America and others in the Philippines. The loss had diminished the authority of the government and at the time, the King was still a minor.

Alva envied England's political and economic stability in which he would have liked to have some share and had tried while in London, to enter into negotiation on certain schemes only to be met with a subtle cooling off, as a tightly knit coterie safeguarded its own interests and closed ranks,

It was therefore most heartening now to find that every door the lovely Amelia opened for him was seemingly being kept wedged ajar by the Earl himself. He would have been less surprised had he been aware that his social and financial status had been subjected to Lady Margaret's scrutiny and had satisfied the specifications on the list.

The list was exactly what its name implied. It itemised the prerequisites essential for entry into the Eglinton family. It was a handy yardstick by which to measure a prospective candidate for Amelia's hand and unless a suitor passed muster in this regard, her brother could refuse his approval, without which Amelia would not receive the considerable funds otherwise due to her on marriage.

Keeping in mind the maxim, "Wise alliance is the corner stone of a stable society," the Earl had decided that possibilities between Alva and Amelia were to be encouraged. Even the Spaniard's un-Englishness could be overlooked for reasons which the Earl would deny even to himself, but which had certainly influenced his thinking, which ran along these lines.

Being an Andalucian of lineage deeply embedded in his own culture, Alva would, if he married his impulsive and unpredictable sister, be taking her with him to live in a society well known to hold very traditional attitudes to women, one which had the reputation of keeping its wives and daughters not locked up exactly but, speaking metaphorically, somewhat behind bars, albeit of a decorative design.

The anxieties that Amelia had already occasioned him had led him to look warmly on such practices. Of course, he told himself, such notions about Spanish tradition were fanciful and he had no wish whatever to see his sister incarcerated, but there was no denying that an Amelia, married and settled, was a big responsibility less and would put an end to all the vetting and vigilance that had been plaguing him these last years. The pleasure of this prospect was such, that the Earl deemed it worth his while to sacrifice time and attention to ease Amelia's path in Alva's direction.

The little party was in hopeful spirits and when Alva heard Frederick express an interest in seeing for himself the fertile vineyards that produced the sherry he exported, he was quick to encourage the idea.

"Particularly," Frederick continued, "now that we're about to do business together and given that we're almost in Spain already."

Both men smiled. Ulterior motives were far from their minds. Both believed in the sincerity of the suggestion and were happy to ignore the geographical fact that, with the French/Spanish border being not far away, they were indeed almost in Spain already, but that the whole of the Spain's considerable length still lay between them and the fertile vineyards.

Alva quickly picked up the hint and readily extended an invitation to the Earl, his wife and his sister. Amelia was enchanted with the idea of seeing Sevilla and Cordoba. Alva was enchanted with Amelia. The Earl was enchanted at the furtherance of his plans. Margaret expressed her regret that she was needed at home, at the Hall, thus relieving herself from acting as chaperone and the game promised to go beautifully.

The Hall, even as her sister-in-law uttered the words, Amelia was reminded of how dull she found life there, the monotony of the social round, her brother's tedious watchfulness, his constant disapproval of all she found fun and his nipping in the bud every relationship he considered undesirable, in short, his continual wet-blanketing of her life. Set against that, how inviting and full of promise was the prospect of Andalucia in the company of this dark-eyed, enigmatic Spaniard, who could be passionate and gentle, courtly and ever attentive and whose silences were not the boredom of someone with nothing to say, but bespoke hidden depths.

During the visit to Andalucia, all had gone as hoped. The days he had spent with Amelia, had lifted Alva's spirits. All hint of despondency had evaporated and she had breathed pure magic in its place. Her ability to enhance his wellbeing was part of the spell, but it had nothing to do with magic. Her sorcery owed nothing to a witch's brew. Neither was it accidental, or innate. It was due to qualities much more mundane, dedication and common sense.

Years before, while growing up in the 'naughty nineties' of Victorian England, Amelia had looked upon the world into which she had been born and, with the awesome clarity of youth, had observed how very unfairly different was the world of man, to that of woman. By the time she reached adolescence, she had also realised how impotent she was to change it and the futility of letting this upset her. It was in her nature to make the best of things and she figured there was nothing for it but to adapt, for which it was essential to see things as they truly were, to accept her weaknesses and use her wiles.

By now she had her rules worked out, most important of which was an absolute refusal to be dragged down by matters disagreeable that could not be changed. She treated obstructive people to doses of her considerable charm, the efficacy of money, or the influence of social standing. Really stubborn cases merited an application of all three.

Her modus operandi served her well. It freed her from the clutter of pointless care. It was however, one of which Alva was never to get the measure.

Not surprisingly her brother knew her somewhat better and despite having come to genuinely like Alva in the few weeks of their acquaintance, self-preservation prevented him from suffering any compunction in wishing his sister upon him. Accordingly, as Frederick's hopes took on definitive form, he applied himself even more assiduously to presenting Amelia as a desirable bride.

Despite her power to dazzle having been well demonstrated, her brother decided to enhance its brilliance by increasing the funds attached to her dowry. He realised this was an expense he could probably have spared himself for Alva appeared as enthusiastic as ever, but experience of Amelia had taught him to anticipate the untoward and in the event of her radiance inexplicably waning, a reflection from the financial advantage attaching to it may help to sustain a residual glow. All went well and before long, the marriage was arranged.

Both parties considered it a most advantageous match and when the time arrived for Frederick to give his sister away, his pronouncement on the happiness the day brought him, was both heartfelt and sincere. To Alva, his bride could not have appeared in a more favourable light than when, in the luminous rays of stained glass windows, adorned in orange blossom and robed in purest white, she took her vows and changed her name and title unto his.

In the years that followed when her buoyancy of spirit was to prove unequal to its double load and he foundered in the depths of their wrecked relationship, Alva was never able to fathom just how she had kept them both so miraculously afloat in those delicious, early days, but somehow she had, steering them past the submerged hazards on which they were later to come to grief.

With the passing of time, the dreams had cruelly dimmed. It was not so much that things had changed, as evolved along the lines of progression laid down by the natures of those taking part. The present reality therefore, although vastly different from their expectations, nevertheless conformed exactly to what the seeds sown by their temperaments and nurtured by their intentions, had destined it to become and the differences between them now were as manifest as those between the raptures of that long ago summer and the dried out relics and faded photographs scattered at his feet.

Wearied, he looked down at the album he had dropped, its once pretty, silvered lettering and ruche of ribbon, as colourless and crumpled as his visions of what might have been.

But it was late, too late now and it was better not to think.

CHAPTER EIGHT

Ardleagh Hall. Late March 1919.

*T*he decorative, dead leaf arrangement on the corner table of the main hall had been there throughout the long winter. Lady Margaret laid the bright yellow daffodils she was carrying down beside it.

"There, the first real flowers of the spring," she said.

She stepped back, admired them and felt cheered She had not bothered with flowers for...a whole year? Yes, the end of March, one whole year. There had seemed no point. She had been so tired since leaving the Clinic and had spent a great deal of her time in her room.

Not surprisingly, few of her friends now called. Only James had persisted with her. He had come to her room again this morning as he always did when at home, to see how she was faring and to tell her the latest happenings. After his visit, she had remained staring down into the garden as she so often did, but today even she could see that it was different. It was coming to life. Some of the almond and the cherry blossoms had opened and the daffodils had sprung from nowhere. She had just looked at them making no effort to be pleased, but as she gazed she had been drawn to them and her listlessness felt less and for no real reason she had left her room and gone outside.

Once in the garden she noticed many other little messengers of life, small promises of beauty yet to come. The flowers, the birdsong, all that used to give her so much pleasure, how strange she thought that at her lowest ebb she had simply turned away from them, deprived herself, but they were still there, still being brought into being by that mysterious force she knew about, but knew not what.

Best of all she had really enjoyed herself. For the first time in months she had felt a touch of joy and William, the head gardener, had been so genuinely pleased to see her, so appreciative of the attention she was giving to what he had been doing in the months she had been away.

When she returned to the house, the luminous golden trumpets, the daffo-down-dillies as her father used to call them were in her hands, although she had not meant to pick them. But a glance at the great grandfather clock told her that she had no time for flower arranging now. It was almost eleven, the hour at which her husband wanted to see her and James in his study. She really must not be late. She would have no excuse for heaven knows it was little enough she had to do these days, as he often pointed out.

She sighed at the truth of it, being only too aware that his valet, his butler, the housekeeper, Anna, Cook and the many maids at their disposal had everything under their control. Increasingly it came to her attention that as the Earl's wife she was required only to fill a role, not serve a purpose. With Austen gone and James almost always away, what sphere was there that she could call her own? What was there she could do that some paid professional would not do better?

Was there anything at all that would make a real difference whether she did it or not? No nothing, came the answer. Even so, it would make a difference if she were late. Quickly she spiked the long stemmed blooms amongst the dried leaves with a promise to their beauty to rescue and arrange them later.

On her way to the study she wondered what it could possibly be that Frederick wished to see her about. It was unusual for him to consult her these days. In fact they scarcely talked. Although everything was supposed to be as normal, Margaret had to admit that her marriage scarcely existed anymore, not as a marriage should. Its structure was still in place but it was sadly lacking in content. In truth it had been slowly withering for years, even before the terrible happening of a year ago had sounded its death-knell by putting it to the test, a test it had miserably failed.

That fateful day when Frederick had walked into her room and delivered the brutal news, she had, as he later informed various doctors, nurses and specialists, "given way", "not reacted well", as though there were a good way, a right way.

If there were she still did not know to this day what it was. Certainly she had not behaved as he had. How quickly he had buckled on his own armour, his hard-edged protection, as if grief were an enemy to which one must not yield, a foe that must be kept at bay. But, in hardening his heart against his own pain, he had hardened it against her also, for in failing to erect defences of her own she had become the traitor on the gate of his and, like the grief itself, needs must be stopped.

And she had been put into that awful Clinic where everything had gone from bad to worse and she became a problem to which the specialists were paid to find an answer. But as she herself found out, they had no answers, only questions. She was questioned and questioned again and when, unable to enlighten them she kept her silence she was labelled uncooperative and was expected to tell them why she was behaving so.

They needed explanations but she had none to give, only anger at the futility of war and grief at what it had taken from her and in the months before it ended, fear at what it might yet take and when one day, sick of being called to account, she had let them have the only thing she had to give, an outburst of raw, unprocessed, gut emotion, they knew not what to do. So they had pinned on her another label. It read 'hysterical' and Frederick had been sent for and it was agreed that until such time as the label no longer applied, it was best she remain where she was.

It was then she knew how very, very careful, she would have to be. So she worked out what it was they wanted and pre-shaped her explanations in the hope that they would fit into the rigid spaces in their minds that they were meant to fill, explanations as clinical and sterile and sanitised as they were themselves and as the long weeks of summer had dragged by, she had walked in their tidy garden, along the straight and narrow paths with trimmed, straight edges, and sat beside the formal, flower beds and behaved in the required way, possessing her soul in patience, concealing all she really felt and wondering all the while if she would ever be let go.

And when finally the label was removed, stuck to it was every last shred of tender feeling she had once had for Frederick. Even on her way home she knew she was not wholly out of the wood for Frederick, as her husband and with the agreement of the doctors, had the power to legally arrange for her to be put back there and if she were, everything at the Hall would still run as normal in her absence.

The study clock chimed eleven and Frederick entered. Margaret was already seated, waiting for him. He had brought with him several folders and brochures which he put down on the table before turning to greet her. He took a cigar from his case and concentrated on lighting it. The seconds ticked by and James arrived, followed by Alice the maid bearing a tray of coffee. She set it down and departed. They were ready to begin.

He had, so he informed them, planned a trip abroad. Margaret watched him as, almost detachedly with his back to her, he spread out the various pamphlets and papers. He was a large man, not overly heavy, but tall and broad. His movements were as always, slow and deliberate. His hair was neatly trimmed and evenly combed above the stiff collar of his well-starched shirt. It had thinned considerably over the years and what remained had gradually greyed to a pepper and salt mingling. She remembered the blonde, unruly waves she used to ruffle in their early days. Then, like a young Adonis, the youth so beloved by Venus, his behaviour towards her had been one of gentleness. The hair, she could live without. The loss of gentleness, she lamented. She sighed and turned to look through the mullioned windows, watching the cherry blossoms tousling in the wind.

He might at least have told her he was arranging this trip. Judging from the number of leaflets and tickets, preparations were well advanced. She would have liked to have had some input and felt like saying so, but there was nothing to be gained by making a fuss and she let it pass. She had, on occasions before her so-called illness, asked to be consulted and for a little while thereafter, he had gone through the motions. That was all. It was demoralising but arguments were more unpleasant and she went to lengths to avoid them, a self defeating exercise that had served to increase the imbalance between them, putting him in the driving seat of her life as well as of his own. Too late Margaret realised she had let it happen and now lacked the experience to deal with it.

He had finished shuffling his papers and was arguing with James. Nothing unusual in that, the two of them rarely saw eye to eye. She poured the coffee into the fine, bone china cups and tuned into what was being said.

James was objecting strongly, "...the Grand Tour, six whole weeks of it and Ralph Rawlinson!" She rose, taking her husband's cup to him and as she set it down, glanced at the brochures on the table, pictures of Italy, Venice, Florence, Rome, Pompeii, and of Greece, Athens, the Parthenon, all the places she had visited on the Grand Tour of her own youth and on so many holidays since.

Thoughts of all the preparations that would have to be made, the innumerable changes of dress, the dictates that etiquette demanded, the long, interminable lists of all that must be taken, a menial task until she forgot something, whereupon it promptly acquired a rise in status and became a matter of real consequence. All those travelling trunks to be packed and crates of possessions to be loaded and carted about, all the touring and trotting round Europe and the endless talking about it afterwards, she was averse to the whole idea. She would be more than happy to take it as read, along with the literature he had collected.

Two lines of Wordsworth's poetry came to mind.

"The world is too much with us, late and soon,

Getting and spending, we lay waste our powers..."

'How true.' she thought. The last thing she wanted at this juncture was a lot of pointless activity and moving around just when she was picking up the threads of her life and hoping to be able to put her returning energies into something creative, like her plans for the garden. She sat down again, sipped her coffee and tried to calculate her chances of making her voice heard and of opting out. Certainly not at the moment, father and son were still arguing and James was protesting, not about the Tour itself, but about the inclusion of Ralph, the mill owner's son.

The mill owner was how Margaret still thought of Albert Rawlinson, but in recent years he had become more than just that. Hard working and astute he now owned, in addition to his cotton mills, tracts of valuable land some of which verged on their own property and contained extensive coal deposits, so she had heard. Indeed, it seemed he could even be on his way to becoming a mine owner himself.

The original plan had been to take Ralph with them on the Grand Tour, as Austen's friend, when the war ended. They had been in the same class at school and had shared a keen interest in sport. Being in the same teams, an easy comradeship had developed between them and although Margaret did not care for Ralph, she had kept her opinion to herself. But the war had dragged on, putting everything on hold and after Austen had been killed, nothing further had been planned.

When Ralph had begun calling on them again she had been surprised, all the more so now she realised James liked him no better than she did. It struck her as odd that Frederick was planning to include him in their travelling party, especially when in the past she had heard him describe Albert Rawlinson as, 'a man one would not invite to one's club'.

The Grand Tour, it was de rigueur for young people of their social standing. Becoming familiar with the culture and the capitals of Europe, the famous sights of other lands, was an essential part of their education. Being well travelled was generally regarded as important as being well read. But at the moment, with Europe suffering the effects of war, with turmoil on the continent, bitter wrangling over the Peace Treaties, Capitalism battling against Communism, the forces of order fighting to put down the insurrectionists, running battles in the street, was it wise, she asked Frederick? He told her they were not going on the full Tour, only parts of Italy and Greece and they were going by sea, not overland.

"The sooner we take up the old ways, the sooner we'll get back to how things were," he asserted.

She sighed. Could he still not see, there was no 'getting back'? All was different now. Gone was the atmosphere and style of yesteryears. She particularly noticed it when friends came to dine. The conversation, if you could still call it that, invariably turned to politics, to talk of Trade Unionists, radicals and reactionaries, the growth of the Communist Party and all too often became overheated. It was in such bad form. Everything had speeded up. The old graciousness had gone...along with the leisure and social certainty they had always looked upon as theirs by right.

James' voice cut in on her thoughts.

"I don't enjoy his company. He's not my friend, never was, so why does he have to come and have you spoken to mother about it? In fact, have you spoken to mother at all about this trip?"

"This tour is mainly for your mother's benefit, for her health. Her doctor advised it. Why fuss her with details of bookings and reservations?"

"But does mother even want to go? And anyway...why take Ralph?"

"Because my time will be taken with seeing to her, so it's best you have a companion."

Margaret got to her feet in protest. She wanted to say she did not need nannying but before she could speak, Frederick used her reaction to reinforce his point.

"There, you see. Now she's upset. You're distressing her with your arguing."

"That's not true..." began Margaret then bit her lip. An outburst of vexation may be put down to nervous disposition and reported to her doctor. But James was also on his feet, gripping the edge of the table as he leaned across it facing his father.

"Please answer my question. Why Ralph?"

"Because I promised his father and my word is my bond."

"I don't believe that's the reason. Yes, Ralph was to have been invited, but that was before..." James stopped abruptly then started again. "What happened to Austen has changed all that."

Riled by his son's stance, his father snapped.

"It has not changed..." but before he could say more James cut him off.

"No it hasn't, has it? Not for you but it's changed everything for mother and for me."

Even as he spoke James realised that by not letting his father finish his sentence and in taking the words out of whatever context they may otherwise have had, he was being unfair. He felt a pang of guilt, but angry as he was he ignored it.

"How dare you?" His father's tone was ice-cold. "This is something I will not let pass but to spare your mother further unpleasantness, I will speak to you after she has left. Open the door for her."

Catching James' eye Margaret indicated otherwise. She moved to the fireside chair and settled herself comfortably, adjusting the cushions behind her back. It was clear she did not intend to move. She nodded towards her husband.

"Thank you Frederick, but I'll stay. You see, I also would like to know, why Ralph?" Taken aback, her husband looked at her. It occurred to Margaret it was the first time she had properly merited his attention that morning.

His stare was impassive. He turned back to the table and with his usual, self assured movements, began collecting the papers, taking his time as he replaced them in their respective folders. When he had finished, he spoke.

"Clearly in this atmosphere there is nothing to be gained by further discussion." He crossed towards the door and half glancing in his wife's direction, he added, "Perhaps I will see you at dinner."

"And you," he said, turning to James, "come to the library at four."

Needing a breath of fresh air and wanting time to think, James was walking in the rose garden, not that it offered much inspiration. The sifted soil was black and weed free, but the bushes were nothing more than clumps of cutback stems. The air was damp and chilly, a typical March day, wet and uninviting. He would be glad to get back to Cambridge. It was one of those moments, and there were many of them, when he deeply missed Claire.

When he heard she had left the Hall he had hung around the village like a fool in the hope of seeing her, only to finally learn she had gone to Manchester. Anna had been no help. He had not even got an address from her. He was right. She did regard him dubiously. He understood, of course. He was not so dumb he could not see why. Claire was very lovely. Her aunt was being protective, or was it that Claire really did not want to see him?

Had she been a young woman of his own social circle, he would have known exactly what to do. It was precisely because she was not, that Anna's attitude was as it was and why he had to be so circumspect.

James got the picture. He was not naive, nor was Anna. Marriage prospects for young women in Claire's circumstances were largely determined by their respectability, reputation, call it what you will. It served in much the same way as wealth and social status did in his milieu. For young women in Claire's situation it were as though, lacking material goods, the measure of their virtue was the yardstick of their worth.

Mercenary, yes maybe, cynical, perhaps, but there it was. Did not the Bible say? A virtuous woman has a price above rubies and naturally Anna did not want Claire hurt in any way.

The old tower clock sounded the hour, better go to the library and get it over with. He knocked and hearing his father answer, pushed open the door. He glanced around and it struck him forcibly how nothing in this room had changed, the same faint smell of wood panelling and polish, his father already seated behind his desk his clasped hands resting on the large, leather bound blotter in front of him, all as it had been when he had been summoned to it as a child and the memories provoked an awareness of his defiance.

Seeing James enter, Frederick nodded in the direction of a small, strategically placed chair and began without preliminary. He spoke incisively, carving each word with care.

"Your remarks this morning were inexcusable. They call for a retraction and an apology."

Ignoring the chair, James walked slowly towards the fireplace. He rested one arm along the mantle-piece. He was taller than his father and, still standing, looked across at him. He saw a man, set and unbending in his expression. James took his time. Without replying he let his gaze wander, finally focussing on a heavy brass poker dangling from its keeper in its ornate, marble niche.

He had known what was coming, had known he would be asked to apologise. It was the usual procedure. He had already thought about it and decided not to, not this time, at least not yet. He had however not decided what he would say, except that it would be the truth. He was sick of duplicity and artifice. The silence hung. His father asked again.

James drew a deep breath and let his gaze travel from the poker to his father's face and the first words that came to mind came out.

"About this morning...and Ralph, I know why Albert Rawlinson wants his son taken on this trip. It puts polish on him, helps him climb the social ladder. What I don't understand is why, when Austen's no longer here, it's still important he comes," James paused, his eyes remaining fixed on his father's face. "It has nothing to do with mother, or me, or your word being your bond, has it? So tell me. Why?"

There was a force in James' tone Frederick had not heard before.

They were looking across at each other, a strange, palpable uncertainty between them. James was never sure later how it came about, but suddenly in the heightened tension, his probing thoughts triggered some impulse in his brain, connecting them to something he may have already sensed but had not recognised...and the realisation struck.

"It is..." he said, slowly. "It's tied in with the Brackworth."

Was it, as he later asked himself, a statement, a question, or no more than a shot in the dark? Whichever, it caught his father off balance. Watching him intently, James saw, for the briefest of a fleeting instant, almost imperceptibly, deep behind the eyes, the merest flicker of...he could not say exactly for it vanished almost instantaneously, but it vanished too late.

For one split second the veil had fallen, the truth had been exposed and what had been a supposition...was knowledge now.

He looked away. Already his father was expressing outrage, demanding answers, but James had too many unanswered questions of his own hammering him.

Why had he not realised it earlier? Although the Brackworth still haunted him, he had supposed it long gone from his father's mind, was in the past, buried as were the men who had worked that fateful shift. But was it?

He looked down again at the readied fire in the grate, at the grease soaked paper, the dry kindling waiting for the flame...and the dangling poker, like the sword of Damocles, waiting to be put to use.

His father was driving questions at him.

James snapped. "I don't know. I don't have the answers," he flung the words across the room, surprised at the strength of his defiance. "So why don't you tell me why you don't want to upset Albert Rawlinson?"

His father had never before been opposed by him like this and he was incensed. He also was now on his feet, pacing the floor, his voice raised and angry in his attempt to overcome his son's.

But James' sense of injustice was blazing forth. It had been fuelling for years and was not to be quelled now. With each of them intent on having his say, neither was listening to the other, but the servants were listening to them both.

Facing each other and with neither showing sign of backing down, they did not hear the rapid spattering of footsteps coming to the door that was suddenly flung open and swung wide. Breathlessly, Margaret, burst in the room. Swiftly she spun round, deftly closing the door behind her.

"You can be heard from the top of the stairs and at least two of the servants are listening at the back hall door." She turned and saw her husband almost quivering with rage.

"Oh dear, you do look upset. Shall I call your doctor?" she asked, her voice sounding full of concern. Whilst at the clinic, Margaret had learned the art of self-control, but this remark had been more than she could resist.

Frederick glared at her for some seconds. Her irony was not lost on him, but he made no reply. He turned to his son, his voice little more than a hoarse whisper. "Go. Just go. Get out."

James turned on his heel, paused, inclined his head to his mother and left the room.

He headed through the hall towards the stairs. 'I was right. He would never have reacted so strongly had I been wrong,' he thought. 'There has to be more to it for him to get into the state he did. I know I was angry, the way he is with mother, his attitude towards…Austen, with nobody being allowed to say what they feel, everything being acted out on one level when it's really happening on another…and now, this pretext about Ralph, when it's really about the Brackworth. Why now after eleven years?'

The answer to James' question lay in the safe, concealed in the panels of the library bookcase. It was contained in a letter bearing a government seal that had arrived a few weeks ago from one of Frederick's friends at Westminster, telling him that the newly formed Coal Commission was considering Trade Union demands to nationalise the coal industry, a development that would result in control of the mines being taken out of the hands of the present owners.

After the door had closed on James and Margaret, Frederick seated himself at his desk. The dullness of the afternoon hung heavily against the rain spattered windows. That business with James just now, how much had the servants heard? His insubordination was intolerable. Had he just guessed? There was no way Frederick could know.

He crossed the room and took the letter from the safe along with a thick, manila envelope marked, 'Ref: Brackworth Mine'. It contained a recent report, some drawings, designs, maps dated 1908 and even earlier over which he ruminated for several minutes.

He was worried. Nothing was going right. The wretched war was over but instead of getting better, things were getting worse and those in charge were tackling them in totally the wrong way.

Worried by the increasing strength of the Trade Unions and afraid that a major industrial crisis was looming, the Government was listening to the Labour Party leaders and in January, an Industrial Conference had been formed. The setting up of this Coal Commission with its talk of Nationalisation was one of the results. At first Frederick had tried to disregard their proposals. But the talk was persisting, reactivating his anxieties of years ago. Quietly he had called in mining-engineering experts to investigate the feasibility of reopening the Brackworth. Privately he had been hoping the report would confirm it was not possible thus putting his mind at rest, safe in the knowledge that any evidence in its depths was beyond reach. The report disappointed him, for although it stated that the accumulation of water in the years since the disaster, together with the lie of the land and nature of the surrounding strata, presented serious difficulties, it was not considered that the problems outlined were insurmountable. The solutions put forward, recommended the construction of an adit and a change in the direction of the Sough. This however would require the purchase of adjoining land.

What Frederick read made him anxious. What if the Commission did put its seal on Nationalisation? What if with new technology, modern methods and the sort of funding the Government could provide, the mine were reopened...others poking about down there. No, he would not contemplate it. There was still deep bitterness in the village and the talk that the Enquiry had been a cover-up had never ceased. He had decided therefore, to buy the land outlined in the report and take whatever safeguards he could. Then, if Nationalisation seriously threatened, he would, hopefully, be able to deal with the situation before his fears became facts.

He had given instructions therefore for the land in question to be bought and had been assured the contract would soon be signed. He was then told that Duckworth, the vendor, was stalling. It finally turned out that Albert Rawlinson had stolen the deal from under his nose. Rawlinson was a shrewd operator. What was he up to? Frederick had to find out, but in a friendly, casual way, without being obvious. What he needed was easy access to him, without arousing suspicion. The inclusion of Ralph on the tour was ideal. Keeping Rawlinson informed of the itinerary, finalising his son's travel arrangements, would provide ample occasion to be in touch. Furthermore he would be giving Rawlinson something he dearly wanted, thus allowing Frederick to tactfully indicate his own expectation of a quid pro quo. Every man has his price, reflected Frederick and Rawlinson would go to any lengths to give his son the advantages he himself had lacked.

Once the tour was over and he had got what he wanted, he would simply let their association die a death. He had not expected Margaret to be awkward, but he was sure she could be persuaded, talked to, shown a firm hand if need be. But James had become insufferable. However, first things first, get his wife on board, then deal with the son.

Gathering up the papers, Frederick returned them to the safe. He alone had the combination. No-one else could open it.

Would it were the same with the Brackworth.

CHAPTER NINE

Ardleagh Hall. Late March 1919.

After leaving the library, James went to his room. He was standing, with his hands in his pockets, staring out of the window, wondering precisely why his father was getting involved with the Rawlinsons and what, if anything, he could do to get his future onto a better path.

His own aspirations were blocked and the tracks his father had laid down for him pointed in directions he did not want to go. Being the younger son had been an advantage. It had given him the possibility of choice. Now, if his father had his way his life would be mapped out for him. He would have no more choice than a wound up mechanical toy about to be set down on the rails that had come with the game.

Everything had been so different when Austen was around. James missed him terribly, and Claire. There was no-one to talk to any more, except, there is Martin, he thought.

Martin was a young engineer working in his father's mines. James decided to try to get in touch with him. What he needed was a quiet chat in private, but he was always recognised these days when out locally. Ruefully he smiled, remembering his forays with Claire, when incognito he had rambled far and wide.

Had his father, James asked himself, ever wandered round the village, through the rows of back-to-back houses where his workers lived? Had he ever looked down into the squalid, flagged backyards where babies in their prams and dustbins and the family's one and only lavatory, and no room for anything more, were crammed, or walked on a hot summer day down the airless, high bricked alleys dividing them, so narrow that men and women could hardly pass?

My father talks about conditions, but he never sees them. He seldom goes down the pits and never when work is in progress, only on Sundays and even then, not to the coalface. He stays in the main galleries. He doesn't see the danger, feel the heat, or taste the coal dust.

James had only recently got to know Martin. He had come from Ireland with his uncles and grandfather thirteen years ago when he was eleven and like many working class boys of that age, had been put to work in the mines straightaway. He was bright and intelligent and as soon as he was old enough he had enrolled at night school. From that time on whenever he was not working he was studying. Now, at twenty four, he gave the impression of a man who knew what he was working towards.

There was no doubting Martin's astuteness. When underground, he had an almost uncanny sixth sense, an intuitive feel for what the situation was at any given time, a gift which he himself dismissed but which those around him had come to trust. He had been working elsewhere, when Lord Frederick heard of him and signed him on with a contract.

He was different from the other workers, keeping to himself and very much his own man. Martin would be easy to talk to. He still spoke with a soft brogue and structured his sentences in the Gaelic fashion, often giving you an answer, if he wanted you to have it, without your having to ask the question outright.

He was typically Irish with an infectious wit and his way of communicating was one in which words were more of an accompaniment to what he was saying, rather than containing the whole meaning within themselves. Was it because of this that James had a greater certitude and trust in what Martin told him, than when spoken to in language so exact it seemed riveted to rigid structure?

James' opportunity came some days later. He was in the stable yard saddling his mare when Martin came to speak to the head man. A young filly being broken in, had just thrown her handler and Martin had stayed to give a hand. When James complimented him on his horsemanship, he had replied.

"My pleasure, as with most things, they just need understanding."

He had been reared on a farm in Ireland and prior to taking up his studies had often helped in the stables of a nearby stud. Fearless and effective, he had a keen eye for conformation, was able to sum up temperament and potential and had a way with horses that seemed to make them want to do his bidding, James told him he was welcome to exercise the horses if he wished and invited him to ride out one day.

It was a sunny spring morning and the two young men were galloping their mounts up the rocky, steeply inclined track between the trees. On reaching the top they reined in. James confessed himself breathless.

"She's fitter than I am. How do you find her?" he asked, nodding towards the large, grey mare Martin was riding.

"She pulls, fights for her head, but nothing that won't come right with schooling," came the answer.

"Then you should take her out more often," suggested James.

"Well, I'd love to, but are you sure? Isn't this White Witch, your own, the one you hunt?"

"So, you've noticed her already?"

"Oh yes, I've noticed her. I notice all horses, can't help doing," Martin admitted.

"Actually I'd be glad if you would take her out," said James. "It's the end of the hunting season but she didn't get out as much as I'd have liked and it would do her good to get some extra schooling. In truth, I find her rather, well...strong," he confided.

Martin nodded. "I know what you're saying," he agreed with a wry smile, "...took quite a hold with me back there, but there's nothing mean about her. She just takes a bit of settling, so if you're sure about your offer, I'd love to take it up."

"Good. We'll get out together again before I leave and you're welcome to ride her while I'm away."

James was pleased. The grey was not a ride many would favour. She had a brilliant jump, but was more than a handful at times, far too wayward when the mood took her but Martin had got the better of her and would put manners on her. The mare sensed this too and had stopped fighting. They rode on in companionable silence for a while.

The subject James wanted to discuss had already been broached. Whilst talking in a general way about conditions underground, James had raised the question of the Brackworth mine without revealing his real interest.

"If it's the Brackworth you're interested in," Martin had said as they set out, "...we'd best go up to The Ridge."

James had agreed and so their choice of route had been decided and had brought them to the track they were now following along the high ground. Presently they came to a clearing which afforded a good view.

"Here we are," said Martin, glancing across at James as he spoke. He rode on another few paces before coming to a halt and pointing ahead. "Over there...the site of the Brackworth's old workings."

"...and of questions that never got an answer," James replied.

The engineer shot a quick look in his direction. "Thinking of the Enquiry?" he asked.

"A lot of talk without hard facts," ventured James.

"No definitive answer regarding the cause," responded Martin, "...simply concluded no cause could be determined without access to the mine and that conditions made that impossible." He was thoughtful for a while before adding, "It made for a lot of anger among the miners, the mine being sealed so quickly...and the bodies not being brought out. Despite the danger, they'd wanted to make some attempt, at least make some exploration."

"Yes, I remember the Memorial Service, the scene later, outside the Church. It has also been said the Enquiry was a cover up."

His companion looked concerned, but did not answer, then, "...give the horses a breather?" he suggested.

James nodded. "Good idea."

They dismounted. Martin took the reins, loosened the horses' girths and having tethered them joined James sitting on a nearby boulder.

"Ironic, isn't it?" said James, his lips twisting unhappily. "Sealing the mine, the very thing that was meant to close the case, is exactly what's left it open to question. Resentment still simmers and the talk's never stopped."

"Well you'll never stop that," answered Martin, ever the pragmatist, "...not without facts and with no chance of finding any."

"But, if the mine were reopened?"

Martin took time to answer. When he did it was the engineer in him that spoke.

"Look, I don't want to speak out of turn, but it's my belief the Brackworth's a mine that should never have been opened, not where and as it is, but the seams were good and rich, considered too good not to be exploited, but some things are like that. No matter how tempting, they're best left alone."

They sat in silence for a while, each in their own thoughts.

Above the far horizon, as if a smudge from some careless artist's brush, a haze of smoke daubed the distant sky. It was the give-away, tell-tale sign of the industrial workings of Manchester that lay beneath. Beyond the sprawling city, were the lowlands of the Cheshire plain.

Manchester, it was the mecca towards which all and everything from these parts sooner or later seemed to make their way, raw materials, migrant workers, the mined coal and given the lie of the land, water also. This was facilitated by a network of several interconnecting canals that provided an economical and useful means of transport in the area through which they flowed. It was into these canals that the waters from the Navigable Level ultimately emptied.

The Navigable Level, it was the name given to the complex system of subterranean canals that existed in some of the mines.

Although referred to as canals, the underground waterways of The Level were in fact nothing more than long, water-filled tunnels, rarely more than eight feet wide and hewn to a rough arch overhead, in some places only about four feet above the water's surface. They were navigable only by the narrowest of boats. But what the boats lacked in width they made up for in length and had both ends shaped as prows for once in these underground tunnels they were unable to turn round. They were known as Starvationers, a name derived from their appearance, long and thin and showing their ribs.

The Navigable Level, the entire plan was the brain child of Francis Egerton, the third Duke of Bridgewater. It dated back to the mid-seventeen hundreds and was an engineering masterpiece of renown that had been visited and studied by engineers from many other lands, even from as far away as Russia where it had attracted the attention of Catherine the Great.

Deep in the heart of the mines, these interconnecting, subterranean waterways formed an intricate system of more than fifty miles. They reached to some of the coal seams themselves, to the very levels below ground at which the excavation of the coal took place. Their various water levels and flows were regulated by devices that were the result of complex feats of engineering.

It was a hard and dangerous life for the miners who worked in The Level, for the narrow, rock tunnels had no banks. The men hauled the boats along by wearing belts attached to chains with hooked ends which they hitched to staples secured in the low ceiling of rock overhead. Cramped in their positions they then pulled on the chains attached to them, whilst shoving the boats forward beneath their bodies.

At times when the water levels rose, they lay on their backs in the boats and propelled the craft forwards by 'walking the roof', which meant pushing the boats onward by lying on their backs in the boats and walking their feet on the rock ceiling close above.

The boatmen's only guiding light through this claustrophobic, tunnel world of weird, shadow shapes and ominous, echoing sound, was the flame of a guttering candle-lantern in the prow, small ally against the impenetrable blackness that in the recessed darkness of deep mines, presses cruelly against the eyes. It is blackness of a kind never known above ground where however black and dark a place may be, vestigial residues of daylight frequency remain. Not so in these deeply buried regions of the earth where no glimmer of the sun's natural light has ever reached.

The whole system was one of economy. Not only did it provide a means of transporting the mined coal, but the narrow canals through which the Starvationers passed, afforded the additional advantage of draining the waters from the workings of the mines they served and with them the otherwise ever present danger of flooding. This was made possible by the falling away of the surface level of the land towards the south, thus allowing an outlet for the waters. From there on, having left the mines, the waters flowed on into the much larger, open-air, ground level canals which ultimately fed into the Manchester Ship Canal, the largest of them all.

The exit into daylight from this Hades web of dripping channels was a cave-like opening in the side of what looked like an old, water-filled, deep quarry situated in the beautiful, Tudor village of Worsley. The deep pool into which the narrow boats then floated was picturesque, surrounded by tall cliffs of rock on three sides, shaded by trees only a mile or so from the magnificent gated entrance to the Duke of Bridgewater's one-time mansion and estate.

From here the waters flowed into the Bridgewater Canal and the narrow boats went into the unloading yard, before returning to enter the Level again through a smaller aperture, close by and similar to the exit one. The coal they left behind was then carried by much larger barges to be hauled along the surface canals by carthorses plodding the canal banks.

As a child, James had heard about The Navigable Level. At first it fascinated him, but later on learning about the men who worked out their days in that way, he was appalled and was glad it was no longer used as it had been. It was however, still maintained as a vital, drainage facility, channelling mine waters from the workings.

"...miles away?" asked Martin. His voice brought James back to the present.

"I was thinking about The Level, how useful it was to the mines it served," answered James.

"It was, but it's of no use to us. The ground levels in these parts don't allow it."

"But to get back to the question of reopening the Brackworth, could it be done?" queried James again.

"Not without a different drainage system. It's the lie of the land that made problems for the Brackworth." Martin got to his feet. "You see the gully over there," he pointed across the valley. "You wouldn't think it, just by looking, but it's not as deep as the Delph used by the Brackworth. It was the mistake made right at the start. It meant the sough couldn't properly serve its purpose. I've seen the old records, well parts of them, certain sections are missing. The other readings taken when the mine was sunk are fine, but that false one caused drainage difficulties that were never properly overcome. They worked on it later, tried to find other ways, but were too hampered by the land contours. It would have meant tunnelling through them in places, tricky in this area, too many faults in the strata. It's what gives the district its character, pretty and picturesque, outcrops of rock, wooded ravines and the like, but it's unpredictable."

"Are you saying it can't be done?"

"Not necessarily, technology's improving all the time. If we could get as far as the Dudley collieries, they'd facilitate us, at a price. Drainage isn't a problem for them. Our difficulty's reaching them. We own, or have permissions for underground working on the properties in between, barring Duckworth's land. The question was whether he would sell. Then out of the blue, I hear it's sold."

"I see," said James, "but water's one thing, the explosions are another and they're what caused the roof fall. There was no mistaking them. They were felt above ground," insisted James, hoping to learn more about the cause of the disaster.

"True," the engineer replied, "...but one thing can cause another. The records give little away but enough to show some of the trouble. Down the years, water seeping from higher levels caused collapses in the ventilation shafts. They were poorly located anyway and should have been re-bored, not patched up and made-do a case of new cloth on old garments. When the air shafts are not in proper fettle, poor ventilation, insufficient air circulation...given the conditions..." Martin paused and looked across, his dark eyes steadily holding James', "gas soon accumulates." he added.

The look, the words, hanging heavy with significance in the quiet of the moment...

'He knows, he damn well knows,' and James was in no doubt that Martin knew exactly and conclusively what had caused the Brackworth tragedy.

Martin remained silent and James was appreciative that, sensing the situation, the engineer had given him his answer without his having had to ask.

James sat quietly weighing up what he had been told. No wonder the mention of the Brackworth unnerves my father, he reflected. With gas suspected, all work should have been stopped until the investigation was complete and James felt guilty at his further thought that his father's angst was due in the main, to the smear on his reputation, the sheer odium of it, if one day the truth should come out.

"I wouldn't worry about the talk of a cover-up," said Martin after a while. "In the absence of shift reports and the like, there was no hard proof and verbal evidence was disregarded. Access was declared impossible and the Enquiry ground to a halt."

"Your uncles, did they hear of any specific reason?"

Martin was slow to answer, "...simply that it was what those in charge had decided. It made for a lot of anger as you know, but even those who disagreed with the Enquiry, when they saw the way it was going knew the situation was hopeless. There was nothing they could do. They couldn't defeat the Powers that Be."

"So all that's left is ill-feeling and suspicion. What are your thoughts Martin?"

"That some things are best let go," he answered, "...and to my mind the Brackworth's such a one, full of potential but also of trouble. Times change though and with modern methods, better technology and machines, who can tell? I still don't like it...leaves me with a feeling it bodes no good, funny how a place can sometimes seem to have a personality."

"And if it were opened, do you think there'd be any answers, any evidence found?"

"You mean any natural evidence?" asked Martin. "I'd think not, not after all this time. The earth's a living entity, constantly shifting, healing itself, closing the voids we make in it. It's one of the main causes of roof falls. It's possible some places escaped unscathed, air pockets where the flood water couldn't rise, or where the fire possibly died out, starved of oxygen. It depends where the explosions were. If the little stock office or safety officer's locker stayed intact, there could be reports there, day memos, shift instructions that could serve as evidence, who knows? Why do you ask? Is it a concern with you?"

"At times...yes," confessed James. "It would be good to lay the ghosts."

"I doubt you'll ever do that. It's not what's buried in the mine...it's what buried in people's minds. That's where the ghosts are, not at the bottom of the Brackworth shaft." Martin paused before continuing. "The past belongs to the past. You can't live the Then in the Now. No good comes from poking at old wounds and if any evidence were found of the kind that could cause trouble, I'd say to get rid of it before anyone with a mind to mischief could get to it." He was thoughtful awhile. "The way I see the Brackworth, there's something about it that just can't be put to rest."

He stood up abruptly.

"Pity though, about the Duckworth land," he added, practicality asserting itself. "It's unlikely to come on the market again. I must find out who's bought it."

Back in the saddles, the two men began their descent letting their horses ease their way down the stony track. James felt better about the problem, having aired it with Martin. The engineer was right. Let it go. Let his father handle it as best he could. For James, this meant putting up with Ralph as graciously as he could during the coming tour. Ralph's company was not a pleasant prospect and the possibility that Claire may end up working for him if she could not find work in Manchester, was worse, but at least he would know where she was. Meanwhile he was working on another idea.

It involved Leonora. It had been decided she spend her week-ends and holidays from school, at the Hall. Alva, knowing Frederick's strict views on what was best for young women, had agreed that the ordered routine at Ardleagh was suitable and that Amelia would visit her there.

James was trying to persuade his mother that Leonora was reaching an age at which she would soon require a personal maid of her own. He had put it to her, that his cousin's wardrobe with its frocks and foll-de-rolls would need attention, that she would want to play croquet and tennis, take walks and whatever, none of which she could do alone. It would, he suggested, make things easier if she had a maid-cum-companion, someone sensible, responsible, a little older but still young and energetic enough to join in the things Leonora would enjoy.

The idea left his mother wondering where to find such a girl, of good speech and suitable manners and she accepted James' suggestion regarding the thoughtful, dark haired girl who had helped out over the Christmas period. Was she still here, she asked? James said he thought not but being Anna's niece, Anna was sure to know how to contact her.

Feeling devious, he was hoping his mother would not mention it was his idea, for then Anna may not reveal her niece's whereabouts. Anna's suspicions were unpleasant enough, but if his mother were even to guess his feelings for Claire, obstacles would be put in the way.

Just in case his ploy did not work, it seemed worthwhile to try other means and he wondered if Martin may know.

The horses were striding out on the lane's wide, grass verge. Relaxed after their exercise, they were stretching forward rhythmically on loose rein, onward in their eagerness to reach home and their feed of oats.

"You haven't seen Claire Mulvern lately, have you Martin?" he asked, trying to give a casual tone to his question.

"I haven't, haven't seen her for some time," came the disappointing reply.

"If you do, would you ask her to get in touch. There's a vacancy at the Hall."

"Sure, and don't worry. If she's around I'll notice her," said Martin raising an eyebrow.

James was quick to return the banter.

"I see, like that is it, horses and women?" he asked, stressing the 'and'.

"Anyone would notice Claire Mulvern." Martin gave a soft, low whistle as if in awe.

"She's a beauty, but horses and women, you ask. Horses yes, but women...?" He raised a hand trembling it as if nervous. "In any case, right now I have my work to think about and I remember my Grandfather's advice, marry if you must but never fall in love."

"Do I take it you've never been in love?" James questioned.

"Never," came the quick response, the Irish twinkling in him. "It's a sickness I'm told."

James did not reply and as they strode on for home, he heard the soft lilt of Martin's voice singing an old Irish ditty, almost inaudibly under his breath,

"Oh, have you been in love my boy and have you felt the pain?

I'd rather be in gaol, my boy, than be in love again.

For the girl I love is beautiful, but I'll have you all to know

That I met her in the garden where the tatties grow."

No, Martin hadn't guessed. He was far too tactful to be singing a song like that if he had. 'Not that it would matter anyway,' thought James, 'anything private is safe enough with Martin.'

CHAPTER TEN

Cordoba, Andalulcia. April 1919.

*A*lva's mood was black as the darkness around him when he returned to the castle, late into the night. His day had been arduous and dispiriting, but the anger that had flared in him at the meeting energised him still and barely had the carriage wheels stopped turning, when he swung its door open and quickly crossed the castle yard.

It fuelled his movements as, two at a time, he mounted the cut-stone spiral back stairs that gave added access to his rooms and sharpened his command to Virgo, his old retainer, as he flung open the door and passed through into an inner chamber. The servant was aged, but still erect. He had served his master for many years past and as he approached, he gave the impression of having acquired immunity to both rebuke and praise.

Alva tossed in disgust the newspaper he was carrying onto the heavily carved four poster bed. Already Virgo was engaging himself in the duties customary to his master's return. He reached for the paper to tidy it away. His master's reaction was too sharp.

"Leave it," but even as his voice cut the air Alva stopped himself. Virgo's wordless equanimity calmed him as always, levelling the edge off his temper, easing the pressure behind his eyes. He continued more evenly. "There's something in there I wish to go through again."

Silently Virgo replaced it, but not before he had taken careful note of the headline. Whatever was contained therein was of more than usual significance if tonight's display was anything to go by. The servant knew his master well and could read even the most subtle of his moods. That, however, was not all that Virgo could read. Unlike almost all of his station and unknown to his master, Virgo could read the printed word. It was an ability he considered best to keep to himself, since it was the Anarchists who had taught him, as they had many others. He did not follow their ways, but he had listened to and learned from them.

It was good to be literate, to be able to find out what was happening, to be aware, to think. But it was wiser in these turbulent times not to show it, especially when your son had been your tutor, when he was still active with the Anarchists and when you loved him very, very deeply, even if you did not hold with all of his beliefs.

Quietly Virgo crossed the room, picked up Alva's cloak, shook the creases from its folds and hung it behind the tall doors of a darkly polished wardrobe. He then went to a small adjacent room, where steam was rising steadily from a large, iron bath. The cauldrons had been ready these two hours past.

The meeting that had delayed Alva had been a stormy one. There had been one or two with military connections present and a couple of politicians, but they lacked the rank or influence to give the reassurance Alva sought. Most of those attending were wealthy land owners, drawn together by a mutual need to protect their own interests. As the meeting wore on however, it became apparent that they differed widely on the question of how those interests would best be served.

What had made matters worse, was the continual passing round of the newspaper, El Correo de Andalucia, The Andalucian Courier, in which was an article, containing the emotive threat that if the Andalucian landowners did not change their ways, they would end up being 'drowned in their own blood'. Clearly it was an attempt to intimidate them into hastening the reform process, by parting with some of their lands. What gave the words their particular import and intensified the alarm they were calculated to inflame, was that the newspaper was regarded as Right Wing and was the voice of the A.C.N.P. the Asociacion Catolica Nacional de Propagandistas, a conservative Catholic organisation formed a decade ago in 1909, intended to assist the landowners in countering the influence of the revolutionary agitators. Over the years, the landowners, Alva amongst them, had given the A.C.N.P considerable financial support.

The article had caused controversy at the meeting, provoking the diehards and panicking the fearful. Tempers frayed and voices were raised until it became impossible to be heard and this, at a time that called for unity and strong nerves, not confusion and alarm. The force and violence of the uprisings in Andalucia, flaring anew in the spring of 1919, had already driven some estate owners from their lands and here and there along the table's length, the emptiness of high-backed chairs bespoke their fear for them.

Alva had wanted an agreement that strong action would be taken against the agitators but Raimundo had been unable to attend and the military who had been there had been somewhat guarded. The politicians present kept arguing about workers' rights and looking at both sides, exactly the sort of claptrap his cousin Luis preached. Others, like Alva, were demanding to know what was being done about the attacks on their estates, the buildings set alight, the crops destroyed and those parts of their lands taken over by groups calling themselves small soviets, but which were nothing more than unruly mobs. They wanted assurances that the Army and Civil Guard would intervene and they pledged to give their full backing to such action, organising their caciques, their hirelings and strong men in support and had warned that unless such measures were taken, the present violence could escalate into the long dreaded, civil war.

At this there had been a welter of protest as the more moderate elements insisted that military intervention would aggravate the explosive situation further and the resultant backlash would cause civil war. In the wrangling that followed, arguments had raged with everyone speaking at once. Interruptions degenerated into acrimony and with his patience played out and nerves raw with frustration, Alva had risen, pushed back his chair and walked from the chamber.

But far from calming down as he journeyed home, his agitation had gnawed him anew.

The comforting sounds of splashing water and the scented warmth of steam, told him that his tub was waiting and pulling on a towelling robe, he went next door.

His bath relaxed him and returning to his room he picked up the paper from where he had thrown it. It was particularly worrying, coming from a newspaper that usually spoke in the landowners' interests, but Alva was sure he knew what was at the root of it.

Formed at a time of unrest, the A.C.N.P., generally known as the Propagandistas, aimed to win over the workers and peasants by offering cheap fertilizers, agricultural advice and credit to buy machinery, build barns and enable them to become self-supporting. In return the beneficiaries must pledge not to take part in Left Wing activities. The Church, with its detestation of Communism, had given its support to the scheme and a Jesuit, Angel Ayala, had been one of the founder members. The Andalucian land-owners however, gained little benefit because their workers, the braceros, were landless peasants unable to avail of the offers.

After the insurrections erupted in 1917, many smallholders further north with a few acres of their own, became fearful of the Communists and their schemes of collectivisation. Anxious not to lose the little they had, they became increasingly Right Wing, banded together into small groups, and joined the Propagandists. With its numbers increased, the much larger organisation became known as the C.N.C.A. Confederacion Nacional Catolico Agraria. The Propagandistas however, still retained its identity and the A.C.N.P remained the largest syndicate within the C.N.C.A.

Owing to the varying conditions in the areas from which these small farmers came, their needs and expectations differed, causing conflict about what should be done. Many wanted reform by way of land concessions and claimed that the intransigence of the Andalucian estate-owners was a stumbling block to the organisation's success. In the hope of raising the support they needed, a group of the most vehement of them had been touring Andalucia since January, attempting to pressurise the estate-holders into handing over some of their land to the peasants. At the time of the scheme's formation there had been no mention of concession of land and this was a reversal of the scheme's original objective.

Alva knew who was to blame - those groups of trouble-making, come-lately, small-holding farmers who had swollen their ranks. Since Cordoba was the centre of Anarchic activity, they were concentrating their efforts on the province. Provoked by the continuing refusal of the Andalucian landowners to succumb to their demands, they had labelled them as 'men whose obduracy would bring about their own destruction,' and 'intransigent, blind egoists, loud in their charity and yet paying wages so low, they would not dare admit to their confessor'.

Alva was furious at such short sightedness, when only last month martial law had been declared again in an attempt to stop the looting, killings and riots over food shortages. Had they forgotten it was the riots in the bakeries that had sparked the Russian Revolution?

The A.C.N.P. carried weight in political and legal spheres and Alva regretted not having kept in touch with its founder members, Antonio Martin Mondero, a Palacian land owner, the Jesuit Angel Ayala, whose liaison with the bishops and their pulpit-power could prove useful and Angel Herrera, who had connections in both political and ecclesiastical circles.

Mondero was now tipped to become the next Director General of Agriculture and Alva was optimistic that being a large land owner and a founder member of the A.C.N.P. he would undoubtedly share the same objectives as himself. Angel Herrera had close links with the Vatican and its Hierarchy. Passionately dedicated to law and order, his ambitions were well known. Alva was annoyed with himself for not having maintained contact with these men for they had risen to prominence, were influential and it would have served his interests well to have done so.

Until 1909 all had been relatively stable in Alva's life, even his marriage, so he had believed. Leonora was five and he expected Amelia to be with child again soon. In the country at large, there had been flare-ups and the Anarchists still battled with the authorities as they had since arriving in Spain and settling in Cordoba forty years before, but Alva was confident order could be maintained and so his life had continued, until that week of May1909, known ever after as 'La Semana Tragica', 'The Tragic Week', when atrocities of such ferocity occurred that the country was rocked with panic and fear.

The trouble had started in Barcelona, the capital city of Catalonia, sometimes called the city of bombs due to its reputation for violence. Many of its workers were peasants from Andalucia, forced by poverty to leave their homes. In the latter part of the last century the exodus was so great that the train carrying them became known as the Transmiseriano. They found work in Barcelona's sprawling factories and production plants where their revolutionary fervour and anarchic doctrines received a ready hearing. Catalonia, Spain's main industrial and productive province, was deeply resentful of Madrid's centralisation policies. With the loss of Cuba in 1898, the province had suffered a decline in its textile trade and believing they had cause for grievance, its citizens wanted their independence. Its pot of anger boiled over in May 1909 when the government in Madrid, more anxious than ever to preserve Morocco, now its last remaining colony abroad, ordered the call up of many Army reservists from Catalonia.

The flame touched the fuse as the men were being taken under guard to be loaded onto the waiting ships. Fierce fighting broke out releasing pent up bitterness. There were vicious reprisals and countless tragedies. Anguish welled up and in the week that followed, hatred overflowed. On both sides, restraint was lost. Old scores were settled. Revenge was wreaked even on the dead as graves were desecrated, corpses disinterred and one even danced with in the street. News of the appalling brutalities shattered the complacency of the ruling classes, leaving them unnerved and on edge.

Finally, when some sort of order was restored, vengeance in the name of Justice was extorted. Retaliation worsened the situation. Executions, ordered by peremptory trials, were swiftly carried out. The extreme injustice shocked the civilised world, provoking an international outcry. In what was seen as appeasement to foreign opinion, the young King Alphonse X111 sacked his Prime Minister,

Maura. Respect for the monarchy suffered and the government fell, creating further instability. The country was leaderless, in a state of shock with no-one certain of what to do.

Not so Amelia; the confusion she felt did not extend to looking for an answer. Reading reports of the atrocities and seeing the pictures of death and destruction, of corpses lying in debris littered streets, she had been appalled and when disturbances occurred, a few streets from their home, she had packed what she needed and left, taking Leonora with her. She had already threatened to do so, but Alva had not taken her warning seriously, not until he arrived home to find the house empty except for the servants.

To be fair, she was not alone in being alarmed. So was the Establishment and in Churches throughout the land, the famous encyclicals of Pope Leo X111 were being recycled and preached again. They had been written several years earlier, but were regularly taken off the shelves and dusted whenever the resentment of the disgruntled masses threatened to reach danger point. The encyclicals appealed to employers to give the labourer a better deal and spoke of his right to a fair wage. It was hoped that the repetitious reading of them would mollify the working man, applauding as they did, the dignity of work and thus by extension, that of the worker himself.

Theoretically they made excellent hearing. In practice they were ineffective. Such sermonising came ill from a Church whose religious orders were said to own one third of the country's capital wealth and people had ceased to listen. In the wake of La Semana Tragica, it was going to take more than hollow phrases resounding from pulpits and resonating in the empty spaces of Church roofs to disperse the tension in the air.

At first, Amelia's conduct seemed so unreasonable it did not register at an emotional level. Her husband saw it simply as a practical difficulty. She was a woman, frightened by violence, but she was his wife, subject to him and must be made to realise she had to return. He would be kind, overlook the incident, but he would be firm, very firm. He had therefore made the necessary travel arrangements and sent them to her along with his instructions.

Amelia's response on receiving them was so unexpected its recollection caused him, even now, to stir uncomfortably in his chair. He reached for the brandy and carefully holding it in his hands watched the glint in the liquid amber, sparkling in the glass. Appreciatively, he inhaled the throat-catching fumes and drank. There were many un-pleasantries he preferred to forget. That was decidedly one. Her defiance had come as a bolt from the blue and proved far more difficult than anticipated. At a loss and not knowing how to cope he had confided in Raimundo, who had advised him that if Amelia would not come, Alva must go and fetch her. This sounded simple, said by someone who had not undergone his recent experience.

It was at this juncture in Alva's life that Angel Herrera's emissary had arrived seeking support for his and Angel Ayala's newly formed association, A.C.N.P. the Propagandistas. They were contacting prominent people of whom Alva was one. Their proposals could not be said to promise Utopia itself, but they appeared to be on the right lines and it had occurred to Alva, that if Amelia could be persuaded reform was taking place, she would return. Alva's eye was very much on the future. He wanted a son.

On reaching her side, he had been gentle and understanding. Over a romantic dinner they had shared a bottle of her favourite champagne, Veuve Cliquot, La Grande Dame, and talked long into the night. He spoke of the improvements in conditions that Herrera's measures would bring about and had made pledges and promises assuring her the agitation would quieten down. Amelia had listened and relaxed. Determined to win her over he had stayed with her in Biarritz, giving her his full attention. They had danced, made love and a few days later she returned home with him.

Now, ten years later, Alva could not but admit that the picture he had painted had been too rosy. But...Amelia had believed it.

Looking back, he had to ask himself, in all honesty, had he? In fairness, it was not the estate owners' fault that all was at its present pass. Back in 1909, they had had no crystal ball. They could not have foreseen how five years later, Europe would be in the throes of a bloody, long drawn-out war at the end of which, most of Europe would be in revolt. The Czar of Russia, the Austro-Hungarian Emperor, the Kaiser of Germany and other less notable rulers, all had gone from the scene, murdered, banished or in exile, their thrones toppled, their empires divided and the rabble running around in the ruins trying to seize power.

Sadly, but not surprisingly, Amelia no longer listened to his schemes and his dreams.

She was away again at the moment, having gone to England to be with Leonora during her Easter, school holiday. More than likely she would be returning via Biarritz. Alva was correct in his assumption. At this moment, as he sat brooding over his brandy in his gaunt castle, she was enjoying a pleasant evening on the French coast. No idealism burned in Amelia's breast to preserve tradition, especially when it served her husband far more satisfactorily than her. Succession for succession's sake she deemed unfair, for her husband had the right to all of his wealth and possessions all his life, regardless of whether she lived or died. She, on the other hand, if she outlived him, would as his widow, be required to hand over her home to his successor and move into some dower house, with such modicum of means as she was allocated, thus preserving her late husband's estate to be handed on to his heir.

Amelia no longer looked on life as a continuity in which the past must be preserved and dragged forward to be hooked onto the present, which must then be spent planning the creation of some imaginary better future, stretching out indefinitely ahead and never reached. Amelia saw life as concentrated in the living moment and belonging, most emphatically, to herself.

She also saw that it was short, too short and as the old adage tells, "Time and tide, wait for no man." They ebbed and flowed according to the immutable laws that governed them. That was their nature. She had hers and it did not incline to sitting around waiting for what was unlikely ever to arrive. Amelia lived in the present, leaving her husband to shape his future from the shadows of his past. That was what Alva was trying to do, but the future promised no new dawn. The old order, the ancient alliance of Throne, Church and rule of Law, that complex weave of political, psychological and physical forces that had once supported his secure world was now under threat. What would his grandfather have made of it?

He thought back to the first grand ball he had attended as a child. Hundreds of wax-dripping candles, ensconced in the iron chandeliers, huge as chariot wheels, had cast their light upon the gay and dancing throng below. How proud he had been when his grandfather, the family patriarch, a tall and stalwart man, had lifted him onto his shoulders and danced around the floor with him and though only a small boy, how much a part of it he had felt himself to be.

But that world…the world as he had known it was endangered by previously unimagined forces. A new Liberalism was tipping long-held values upside down, twisting old ideals inside out, distorting them until they appeared as the phantasmagoric images that result when slides in magic lanterns are put in two together or the wrong way round…and he could lose all that he held dear, all he had inherited, all that he must hand on to his son…his son, what son?

Oh, damn Amelia's behaviour, her forever going away. He needed her, needed not to be alone in his desolation. Frivolous she may be, but when she was around he never sank into the depths he had sunk into now. He had accused her of being selfish, inconsiderate, of not thinking and there was truth in what he said, but tonight even her selfishness he could deem an asset, a touch-stone of sanity that ensured one's own well-being. The very common sense of it appeared wholesome in this cold, dark hour, a small, hard rock of cheerful practicality jutting above the brooding sea now breaking over him. At this moment Alva even envied her capacity not to think, her talent to select just what she would or would not entertain and her ability to cease doing so, whenever she chose. Amelia could switch off her mind as easily as switching off a light and just as easily go to sleep.

Tonight his mind had taken leave of him, was running away beyond his control. Weary and exhausted, he drained the contents of his glass and sank deeper into the recesses of his chair.

In his dozing, part sleeping, semi-conscious state, thoughts of Amelia stirred. She must come back, she must or....and out of the capricious, shifting shapes and images of his dreaming brain, she took form and answered him.

"So, I must come back…I must, or..." She was laughing, her infectious laughter so full of merriment, "...or what Alva?" Quickly her expression changed to one of teasing, mock concern. "Come, tell me, What will you do? Divorce me? Defy your precious Church, sin and burn forever in hellfire...damnation, forever..."

Her head was thrown back, her lovely throat, fine shoulders, the delicate curves of her breasts only a touch away and her laughter, rippling through his body and his dream and…

Suddenly she was gone, taking all light and colour with her, and he was plunging down, down into a well of blackness, falling, falling, hearing only the hollow sound of her laughter, echoing as he fell and her words, 'Divorce', 'Sin', 'Hell', the unthinkable darkness of the soul, endless damnation...

He awoke with a shudder, sweat-soaked and afraid, out of the blackness of his dream, into a dread-drenched darkness, trembling, cold, not knowing where he was or what had woken him. The fire had long died out. The wicks in the lamps had burned away. Silence, dead and heavy closed in on him. He was horribly aware of his loneliness, his isolation. With an effort he rose, groped his way towards the door and pulled it open. There was no sign of life. Virgo had gone to wherever he went, when he was not needed.

The dark beyond the door was thick, impenetrable, without end. Seized by an appalling and irrational horror he pushed it shut and leaned against it. Beset by premonitions he fumbled in his pocket for a light. The match flared. The flickering flame summoned shadows from the sombre recesses of the room, to move like phantoms against the old, stone walls.

Slowly, a faint dimness shaped a window's outline on the far wall. Thankfully, he moved towards it and from the stronghold of the castle looked down upon the valley. Above the mountains, the thin, silver slipper of a crescent moon hung in a blue black sky, its reflection gleaming like steel on the curving arc of the Guadalquiver, as scimitar-like, the river cleaved its course across the lowlands below, the lands from which his forefathers had driven the non-believers centuries ago.

Their crescent emblem flag no longer flew, but now another enemy, the Communists, with flag also bearing the emblem of a sickle blade, menaced and it was he who must hold fast...and again, the chill of fear touched him.

CHAPTER ELEVEN

Lancashire May 1919

*A*s before it was Anna who brought word to Claire that she was wanted at the Hall. They were sitting in the corner cafe, across from the lending library in Manchester's Albert Square.

"Well," said Anna. "I was told to give you the message and I have."

Claire was silent, stirring her tea.

Anna waited for her reply. But Claire could not answer. She did not want her aunt to offer advice or ask her how she felt, for she did not know. It had all come so unexpectedly. Her mind was reeling.

Sitting opposite, Anna watched her, trying to fathom what was in the young woman's mind before speaking again.

"Well, as I said, there's a job there, an' Lady Margaret wants to see you. It'll be helping with young Lady Leonora."

"In what way?" asked Claire, aware of her aunt's eagle eye upon her and striving not to let her voice betray the gamut of emotions assailing her.

"Oh you'll be busy enough, seeing to her gowns an' gloves, making sure they're all clean an' ready t' hand when she wants them...and her mending, you'll be doing that too, seeing that the buttons an' trimmings are all in place. Then there's her room, keepin' her cupboards and drawers tidy...and helping with her hair, washing, an' brushing an' braiding it when she's going out...yes, you'll be busy enough."

Watching her niece Anna waited, unable to make out what was upsetting her. She had never understood why she had rushed off the way she had, right after Christmas. If it was something to do with young James she wanted to know...yes, yes, Lord James as he was now, but he had been in and out of her little parlour often enough as a child for her still to think of him as she used to.

She had questioned Cook, but she knew no more than she did herself.

"So, what's it to be?" she ventured, after a long pause.

Claire straightened her back, took a deep breath and then hunched forward, leaning her elbow on the table, cupping her chin in one hand, looking down, fiddling with her fork at the leftover cake on her plate and Anna could not see her face.

'Oh do stop that,' she wanted to say but bit her tongue, for although Claire appeared composed, she could sense the tension gripping her.

Giving her time, she spoke again, "...and she's back at Ardleagh every weekend now, Lady Leonora that is...an' not boarding full time as she was, so that's something else you'll be wanted to do, be a sort of companion to her...you know, play croquet, or a board game, or go with her for a walk if that's what she'd like."

Anna glanced up at the town hall clock. She could not stay much longer. The bus she had to catch was almost due. No point in her asking her niece again, she knew by now she was not going to get an answer. She picked up her coat and started pulling on her gloves.

"And remember, it's not the housekeeper who'll be interviewing you this time. It's Lady Margaret herself, so try not to delay. Think about it will you, and get in touch."

After her aunt had left, Claire waited a while before leaving the cafe. She was shaken, in turmoil with no idea what to do and could not have answered. She wished she had had the courage to refuse, but the plight she was in was too awful to turn down anything that offered escape and she could not have told Anna, for it was much worse than anything she could have envisaged.

As Jimmy the carter had warned, a lot of women had lost their jobs to the demilitarised men. There were many still out of work and they were all on the same mission. The bigger, better establishments and department stores were fully staffed and had long waiting lists and the smaller, meaner ones demanded appallingly long hours for pitifully little pay.

After leaving the Hall, despite her constant searching, Claire had been unemployed for weeks. Her lodgings had cost far too much and had taken almost all her savings. Close to despair, she had finally got a job in a shoe factory in an industrial, rundown part of Salford adjacent to the city, an area only her desperation had compelled her to consider. The building housing it was cramped and airless, squeezed in between taller, grime-blackened workplaces on one side and a railway track on the other.

Her surprise on first seeing the notice for a vacancy faded as soon as she saw the conditions. She promised herself it would only be for a few weeks, just enough to tide her over, but her endless hunting around had gained her nothing.

Though better than some, the factory pay was small. The hours were long and her shifts varied, which meant she could not take a course at the library as she had wanted. Her time at work however, was proving the better part of her life. The foreman was kind and cheerful and the place was reasonably well run.

The offer of a room to let had been displayed on a handwritten card in the window of a small, nearby shop. It had been put there by Mrs Sugden herself, a prematurely aged, exhausted looking woman in her late forties, who had recently had another baby. The infant was sickly and the mother had not properly recovered from the birth.

Having got the job and desperate to find somewhere to live that she could afford, Claire had gone to see the place. The door was answered by a young girl, a neighbour's child, who said she was "keepin' an eye on't baby an' toddler while the Mrs is out," but made no mention of the other children in the family.

Claire saw the portioned off part of the room that was to be hers and also the small front room. It was dampish, but on that first visit had not smelled so, thanks to the dismal little fire just managing to hold its own in the grate, which kept sending forth sporadic puffs of smoke to prove it was doing its best. It had not been called upon to put in a repeat performance during the rest of her stay because the family purse did not stretch to two fires and the room remained cold and unused.

In Mrs Sugden's absence, Claire had thought it not her business to ask to see the rest of the house. As she later realised, the little she had seen had been especially tidied for her visit, another effort that was not repeated. When she moved in she found conditions to be nothing like what she had been told and the girl was never to be seen again, leaving Claire unable to assert what had been said. But the price was low, her savings were gone and finding nowhere else, it was at least a roof over her head.

With her aunt in charge of the laundry at the Hall, crisp, clean linen was a thing Claire had always taken for granted. Never had she considered the difficulties of washing for a whole family, with only one sink and the sole drying place, a tiny backyard. On wet days, of which there were many, the rain brought dirt with it, soiling the clothes before they were dry. On such days the washing was hung onto the backs of chairs and draped on clothes-maidens, rickety folding frames which were then arranged around the fire, hiding it from view and causing steam to make the one and only living room more miserable than ever.

On the draining board a seemingly unending supply of washed nappies, squashed into long, flat slices by the heavy, wooden rollers of the mangle, waited their turn to take the place of those partly dried. In addition to serving as a laundry, the crowded living room was also where the cooking and the eating took place. But worse than all of this, were the smells.

The house was one of several hunched closely in unbroken rows on a narrow stretch of land beside the river Irwell. On the opposite bank the ground rose steeply and the river changed course creating a sluggish backwater into which sank the putrid wastes from several factories upstream. As they settled they formed a dark grey sludge, commonly known as sink-slutch from which, when the waters failed to cover it, there arose large bubbles of sulphurous gas that burst on its surface and gave off an evil stench.

Inside the house there were other odours too, of damp flag floors, stale cooking smells and that which came from the bucket of soiled nappies waiting to be washed that was a permanent feature beneath the sink. They combined into that unmistakable, distinctive odour that speaks of poverty more descriptively than any words can tell, that reeks of neediness and deprivation and clings to clothes and persons alike.

Against all of this, Mr Sugden, a heavily built, taciturn man, had equipped himself with his own private defence, a fumigation device consisting of one permanently lit pipe. It stuck out from between his yellowed teeth and at regular intervals, billowed clouds of obnoxious tobacco smoke that effectively screened him from the worst of this malodorous world.

It was obvious that for Mrs Sugden, giving birth was a yearly occurrence and Claire strongly suspected she was suffering from morning sickness again. No woman, Claire reasoned, would ever have wittingly walked into this. It had somehow evolved around her, little by little, day after day, stone upon stone, one thing the inevitable result of another, each ineluctably taking its toll until, dragged down by the pitiless law of cause and effect, she had sunk to where she was now, too enmeshed, too trapped, too robbed of herself to fight free.

Seeing all too clearly how this had come about, Claire felt afraid not only on behalf of Mrs Sugden, but at how easily the trap had closed.

Then Anna came with news from the Hall.

Ardleagh Hall, just to think of it was a release, its cleanliness, fresh air and peace, rhododendron-flanked paths, moss covered stones, the light-filled spaces of its gracious lawns dappled by the shadow patterns of tall, protecting trees...and James.

Over and over in her mind, she turned the implications of the offer her aunt had brought. Given the present state she was in, the decision should have been easily made for on the scales of choice the determining factors seemed all weighted on one side, except for those concerning James. Ardleagh was his home, one day to be his and he belonged and she, as she was only too aware, did not.

But then...being at Cambridge, his life would now be on a different course. During the holidays she could hide away, be busy with Leonora. It was unlikely he would notice. But no, she could not go back, for nothing would be different to how it was before. This she had accepted, yet even so, every glimpse she had caught of him last Christmas, had hurt.

Throughout the night she could not rest. Her mind swirled in the confusion of her thoughts stirred by a truth cloaked from her by her pride, that acceptance of the offer was also an acceptance of defeat, an admission of her failure.

It was the finding of Elvira's letter, shortly after James had made his suggestion of a maid for Leonora that had finally decided Lady Margaret to send the message to Claire. Fortuitously, the letter had slipped from a pile of correspondence placed on the table outside Frederick's study. In falling it had come to rest against the white skirting and there it had remained, until Margaret noticed it later in the day.

Surprised to see it was addressed to her she opened it, to be even more surprised that Elvira, Alva's mother, was anxious at not having received a reply to her earlier letter. Margaret was thoughtful for a moment, then slipped the letter into her handbag and went to her room.

She did not waste time wondering how the earlier letter may have gone astray. During the weeks that she had spent in that awful Clinic, Frederick had allowed himself the liberty of opening and attending to her post. Compared to what she was undergoing at the time it had been a mere trifle, certainly not one to risk making a fuss about and she had raised no objection. Probably he was still continuing the practice and had intended to answer the earlier letter but preoccupied with his worries, it must have slipped his mind.

Closing the door of her room firmly behind her Margaret took the closely written pages from her bag and settled down to give them her full attention. The old lady was seeking Margaret's assurance that the arrangements being made for Leonora were not causing too much disruption or inconvenience for her and, in her womanly way she was interested and wished to know what the arrangements were.

She wrote of Spain and of the uncontrolled violence that was destroying the well-established routine of life there, even in the capital, Madrid. But her greatest emphasis was reserved, not for the political outcome, but for the affect it was having on the domestic lives of those around her.

The way in which Elvira outlined her cares and concerns regarding the importance and immediacy of family matters, the attention she paid to detail and her recognition of the true value that lies in the sometimes seemingly small aspects of daily life, left Margaret in no doubt that had Elvira been in charge at Ardleagh Hall, Leonora's future and wellbeing would have been accorded at least as much, and probably more, importance than that of the future of England's entire coal industry.

This made Margaret conscious of what little thought she herself had given to Leonora's arrival and how neglectful she had been of certain spheres of her own life in which she could undoubtedly have made more of a mark. Unable to contend with Frederick's overbearing ways and submerged by her loss she had been easy prey to the notions of inadequacy that assailed her. Not having fought back she had allowed these feelings to overwhelm her, to diminish her sense of self-worth and had come to regard her daily round as petty and trivial, of no consequence, and she herself in the middle of it as being of no real standing.

In fact the letter, or more truly the personality of its writer emanating from its pages, did a great deal for Margaret. It was to prove a turning point, for under Elvira's unwitting guidance she saw she still had a role to play and viewed the influence and advantage that came with it from a totally different standpoint, affording her a perspective quite the opposite of her previous one.

Down the years, she had not questioned Frederick's mandates regarding what really mattered and what did not. Topping the list of his priorities were profit margins and the maintenance of control, for these were the things that kept their ship afloat. They were the lynchpins around which all else of importance revolved, their financial security, social standing, upkeep of their properties and the advantages that followed. When, from time to time these values had appeared to her to be not quite right she had deemed herself to be mistaken, for how much did she understand of market forces, politics and economics. Not relying on her own judgement, she had ceased to hold to her own point of view.

But at base, she mused, might it not be that in all the striving the truest of all values had been discarded, namely, that of being at peace in oneself and with others and the contentment that comes from knowing, enough is enough.

Margaret made up her mind. She resolved to reclaim her independence, to win back some of that which she had lost. It would take patience and she must tread carefully, one step at a time. True to her intentions she had delayed no longer and sent for Anna. Yes, Anna had assured her, she would take word to her niece the following day.

After Anna had left Margaret had remained for a long time, thinking. Dusk fell. The lamps were lit and the heavy, velvet curtains drawn, shutting out the world beyond, enclosing her in her own domain. In the stillness she remembered how eleven years ago, she had readily given Anna permission to bring her orphaned niece to live with her, but had she ever enquired of Anna, how she would cope? No. Anna was Anna, competent, efficient and untiring, of course she would cope. But just now, chatting to her face to face she had noticed the lines of exhaustion around her eyes, the anxious clasping of her hands from time to time and guessed it was endurance more than capability that kept Anna going.

On bringing her breakfast tray the following morning, Lady Margaret's maid found her already at her writing desk sealing a letter which she then handed to her.

"Please take this and see that it is posted without delay."

The letter was to Elvira. For the first time in longer than she remembered, Margaret had a sense of purpose. This next part would not be easy but it had to be faced. In automatic gesture her chin lifted and she set off down the corridor to the old nursery.

How long since she had turned this handle? Time had passed, but all was as it had always been, the way she had wanted it left. Its windows were shuttered but all else was the same. In the dark, just inside the door she stood, resolutely tightening her eyes against the tears as powerful memory had its way with her. Then, swallowing the hard lump that had risen in her throat she walked quickly past the cupboards, the rocking horse and with fumbling hands threw back the shutters, pushed the French windows open and stepped through onto the securely balustraded balcony.

The memories were precious and she would treasure them always. Forever a part of her she did not need a room to keep them in. She would, of course, keep the toys. They would, one day, add fresh memories unto the old when her grandchildren would play with them.

The sun streamed through the open windows letting in the light on two sides, making it the brightest room in the house. Yes, for the next couple of years or so, which was the length of time Elvira had mentioned, this would be Leonora's room and the adjoining chamber that used to be the nanny's, could become her maid's.

It was some time later. Margaret was seated on the sofa, on the large central landing overlooking the front gardens. A few hours ago, Frederick had sent word he would like her to take tea with him in the drawing room at four o'clock. While waiting the appointed hour, she was looking through a book of fabric samples for the new curtains she had decided to have made.

She was also wondering as she usually did when Frederick made these appointments, what it was about and what sort of mood he would be in. His patience was awfully thin these days, but then he was terribly on edge. He seemed to have so many things bothering him, especially the hold he claimed this new Labour Party was getting on the Government, and the National Industrial Conference that had been held at Westminster, as well as his anxieties over Nationalisation.

That day in February, when the Labour man, Arthur Henderson, had made his speech and the Union Leaders all began clamouring about organised Labour being determined to get a bigger piece of the national post-war pie, he really had not been fit to be spoken to. He had gone around grim-faced and silent except for his grumbles, invariably ending with the phrase,

"It needs to have a stop put to it."

How often she had heard that said of late. Whether it was about the workers demanding better conditions, the spread of Communism, the increasing strength of the Trade Unions, James wanting his own way, the growth of the feminist movement, the waning influence of the Clergy, the threatened decline of the Empire, each and every one, according to Frederick needed to have a stop put to it, not modified, nor redirected, but stopped, so that they could all get back to their once civilised way of life.

Amelia's last visit had not done him any good. He was forever worrying she was up to something without his even knowing what it was. Margaret on the other hand, had been glad of Amelia's company and had learned much from her.

While at the Hall, Amelia had given no indication of having noticed any difficulties Margaret may be having. Amelia would not pass comments on such matters. She had on occasion however, whilst making no reference to any particular problems, aired various ideas which Margaret intended to act upon. The main prop of her good counselling was that Margaret should without delay change her doctor to one of her own choosing. Amelia had even gone so far as offering to recommend one and the subtle, slightly offside emphasis she had laid on the choice of one, "'not necessarily, a friend of Frederick's", had given Margaret the clue that her new doctor should, necessarily not be a friend of Frederick's.

Margaret smiled to herself. Amelia was shrewd, artful even, but why be surprised? Growing up with Frederick as an older brother, knowing him as well as he knew her, sharing the same background, she had seen all the gambits in operation. Now that Leonora would be staying at the Hall during her school holidays Margaret was hoping to see more of Amelia. She strongly suspected however that Frederick, finding his sister an irritation, did not.

Without warning, the peace of the place was shattered. Bursts of thunderous sound, as of an erupting volcano on wheels, were coming alarmingly closer and closer. Swiftly laying aside the book of curtain samples, Margaret crossed to the window and looked out. In a shroud of exhaust and with several grinding shrieks, what she still thought of as a horseless carriage, had propelled itself up the drive and lurched itself to a spanking stop in the centre of the Hall's gravelled forecourt.

As the smoggy haze it had belched slowly wafted away, she took a good look. It was brand new and brash, all bright yellow and polished brass. Immediately behind it, two dark, scarred bare patches of ground, testified to the efficacy of its braking power and she was just in time to see a whistling Ralph disappearing under the colonnaded portico of the front entrance. Caught unawares, Margaret's dislike of him reared up. She groaned inwardly as the thought occurred that he may be taking tea with them.

It was too bad of Frederick, why had he not said? Probably because he suspected I would find an excuse, she supposed. It was not yet four and Margaret sat down again, mentally preparing herself to be nice to Ralph if he were to join them. She had after all, no intention of upsetting Frederick. There would be upset enough, when she told him she was not coming on the Tour.

She had given the matter a great deal of thought. This last twelve months had been a long, bleak tunnel down which she had stumbled her way, not knowing where it was leading, nor if it had an end. But she had kept going and if the light into which she had emerged, was illumining everything differently to before, so be it.

Her journey through had done much to corrode the thought habits she had once let bind her. She had no homage now for what she saw as pomposity and pretension. She was finding the threads of a new life and was not going to weave with them the same patterns of the old. She knew exactly why she was not going on this trip. She knew from experience what it would be like.

Nothing would be changed. Nothing ever was. Frederick did not like change. They would stay in the same hotels where his long patronage had rendered them the most revered and welcome of guests. They would even stay in the same rooms, his favourites, especially reserved for them and their entourage. The way he had it planned, their progress would be one big cavalcade and she knew full well that whatever his promises beforehand, once they had embarked they would all have to keep to the overall pace that was set.

They would be accompanied by the same friends, the same travelling companions they always invited. Their visits would be to the antiquities of Italy and Greece, the same she had seen countless times before. As his wife, she would be obliged to always say the polite thing, make the right moves, conform to what was required but if, or rather when, any one of the men behaved badly, slipped his leash, got drunk, gambled too much, or otherwise fell off his perch in one or other of several imaginable ways, gazes would be averted until he was safely back in his boots, after which all would be glazed over. No mention of it would be made. The women guests would be expected to behave exactly as they had before and the caravan would keep rolling.

All that exhausting adorning oneself for dinner, having one's hair dressed, unpacking and packing and moving on. Yes, there had been a time when she had accepted it all as part of their lives' necessary formula, but it simply was not what she now wanted. Frederick would not be happy with her changed attitude. He would, most likely, regard it as a symptom of what he still referred to as her illness.

Four o'clock, time to go. Margaret rose and reluctantly made her way to the drawing room. If discussion were to centre round the Tour, things could get tricky. She did not want to tell him just yet. She was not properly prepared for the argument that might follow. Nonetheless, she felt obliged to let him know. But why should she? After all she had never said she would go. She had never been consulted. He had simply made his plans, taking her compliance for granted the way he always did. She paused on the stairs for a moment, whispered to herself, "Steady, remember now, one step at a time," and continued her descent.

Ralph and Frederick were already in the drawing room when she entered. The young man seemed in good form, Frederick less so. Margaret's state was best described as one of readiness to breast the waves. She looked around, thinking to see James. Maybe he's just been delayed she hoped, but then noticed the tea tray was laid for only three.

James had phoned that morning to say he would not be down from Cambridge after all. "Blast it," Frederick had muttered as he put down the phone, for he had already invited Ralph and now it would be just the two of them and he hardly knew the boy. A one to one would not be easy, not at all what he had had in mind when he had issued his casual, drop-in-for-tea, invitation.

The whole point in courting the Rawlinsons was to prepare the ground, create an atmosphere of informal bonhomie. Rawlinson was a wary old fox, but inviting the son on the Tour would simply be seen, so Frederick hoped, as a magnanimous gesture, nothing more than a show of concern that a young man who had lost his friend should not lose out further. It was a perfect first feeler. The deal with the father would come about as they went along the way. Well, if James would not be here, Margaret would have to fill the bill. She would see off any silences with small talk. She was quiet, even dull these days, but still gracious and socially adept. She would take the edge off any awkward moments. She was good at oiling wheels.

Margaret greeted them both with a smile and crossing the room, seated herself in a large armchair in much the same manner of Amelia, whose flair for sailing serenely through difficult occasions she was endeavouring to cultivate. She crossed her legs, smoothed the folds of her skirt, leaned comfortably back in her chair and was quite surprised at the sense of calm this Amelia-like posture induced.

Sooner or later the moment may come when Frederick would have to know of her intention. If it did, she assured herself she would simply state her case and stick to her guns.

In the event, the episode passed agreeably. Ralph seemed to have matured since she last saw him. The tea was poured. The cakes were handed round. Pleasantries were exchanged and the moments passed. Frederick spoke about the Tour and gave Ralph details of the itinerary. Margaret, though showing no enthusiasm, made no waves nor threw cold water on any of the arrangements when the Tour was being discussed. Ralph was pleased and expressed his appreciation and Frederick saw him to the door.

The tea party over, Frederick returned to his study. He was now sitting at his desk, staring at the silver and ivory paper knife he was turning over in his hands. After a while his gaze moved to the jumble of papers in front of him, "and every one a worry," he protested, decisions he had to make, burdens he did not want to bear. He felt empty and exhausted, not capable of dealing with matters the way he once did, but the worst was that he felt nobody cared.

Laying aside the paper knife, he picked up a letter bearing the Cambridge crest. It was an outspoken statement from James' tutor extolling his son's giftedness and strongly advising that he study music. Frederick knew the tutor in question, a youngish man and he took exception to his tone. He regarded it as disrespectful, implying as it did, that he did not know what was best for his own son. It was not a question of talent. Music was not an appropriate career and that was final.

He put the letter to one side. That at least, was one with which he could deal. The thought afforded him some satisfaction, but not enough. He sighed, put his elbows on the desk and rested his head in his strongly boned, cupped hands. James, what the hell was it with that boy? Every advantage and he turns out like this. Socialism indeed, but give it time, he'll prove no different to the rest of us when he finds he has to pay out of his own pocket for the better things in life, rare wine, fine food, seats in the front row and the best hotels. Then, there was his wife. Now that she no longer shut herself up in her room, all she seemed to do was wander, Ophelia like, around the garden. As for the Tour, initially she had been reluctant but there had been no sign of that this afternoon. Come to think of it there had been no signs at all. She could have shown some interest, not just sit there listening to Ralph.

They would be meeting people on their travels. She was meant to entertain their guests, show some enthusiasm, circulate, be amusing and…if not exactly scintillating, at least lend a sparkle to the proceedings. This was a time for everyone to pull together, well, everyone that counted, and not sit back as if success in business were automatic as James seemed to think and did he seriously believe he could make a lucrative career, playing a piano?

"Still," muttered Frederick, "…he'll change his tune quickly enough when some little lady starts playing on his heart strings. Come to think of it, that's not a bad idea," and he decided there and then to renew old acquaintances and widen their social circle. It was after all, the life blood of their class. He would pick out families with suitable daughters, debutantes, 'Fillies ready for the Race,' as they were somewhat crudely termed and get back to the way things used to be.

Used to be…those halcyon days of that last, lovely summer before the war, the boating parties, the picnics, the afternoons spent at the races or riding in the London parks, the ladies on show in their carriages, seeing and being seen, the nights of music, the balls, the carefree gaiety of it all, how self-possessed and focussed they had been in their ordered domain.

In those last, unrecognised days of peace, that summer of 1914, when Russia's Czar Nicholas was sending desperate pleas to his German cousin Kaiser Wilhelm11 for his help in trying to stop the war about to be declared by Austria's Emperor Franz Joseph, they had not deemed it a cause for their concern, but then they had not thought it was their world that was under threat. But it had been and when the war came, it had destroyed the very things it had been intended to uphold and those three great Royal dynasties, the Romanovs of Russia, the Hohenzollerns of Germany and the Hapsburgs of Austria, had met their end and still the fighting had not stopped.

The open pages of the newspapers littering his table by the window were full of it. The troubles in Russia were far from over. In Germany, Bavaria had declared herself a Soviet Republic and there were running battles in the streets to overturn it and then, there was Spain. "Bloody Spain…" he groaned at the prospect of more visits from Amelia and to cap it all, even the government at Westminster was appeasing the rowdies. Frederick went to the window, scraped up the papers from the table and shoved them in the bin.

He stayed, looking out into the garden. It was springtime. The birds still sang. The flowers still bloomed. The time-weathered little summerhouse was still there and there arose in him an intensity of longing for those bygone days, for his world as it had been, now forever severed from the present, irredeemable, unreachable, far away.

For like a swathe cut by the sweep of some cruel scythe, those four years of war lay as a no-man's land, strewn with mown-down men, crushed hopes and dreams, forever separating the survivors from all that had once been and to which they could never now return.

How cheerfully they had marched to war, never thinking it would come to this. They had simply been going to teach the opposition a lesson, show them where to draw the line, fly the flag and be home again by Christmas.

How horribly wrong they had been.

CHAPTER TWELVE

Cordoba, Spain. May 1919.

Bringing with him all the vigour and freshness of the bright new morning Raimundo arrived at the castle. Unannounced but expected, he entered Alva's rooms, briefly greeting Virgo before nodding questioningly in the direction of the door on the far side.

"In there, General," Virgo's reply was quiet and unruffled and he continued undisturbed with what he was doing. Raimundo's footsteps sounded his approach and Alva's voice could be heard to call, "Come in."

Alva was seated. He seemed a little moody and was less than effusive in his welcome. Unperturbed, Raimundo exuded his cheerful bonhomie and moved across in greeting, giving him a warm, friendly grasp before taking the chair opposite.

Unabashed by the somewhat cool reception he had received, he promptly declared.

"Alva, my friend, you look dreadful, too many late nights, too much worrying? Amelia not back yet?"

"Those and other things," Alva replied. He nodded towards the newspaper on the table. "I've been trying to get in touch with you."

"Hmm, 'El Corrio de Andalucia', yes, I saw it. Don't let it excite you. That's what they want," he smiled sympathetically. "Although I'd feel the same if I was an estate owner."

Alva did not find his good cheer infectious. His expression remained unsmiling.

Raimundo plucked a grape from the platter on the table. Popping it into his mouth, his lips twisted into a knowing smile as he chewed and his eyes met those of his friend.

"Well, go on," prompted Alva. "It's obvious you know something."

Raimundo rose, taking a turn around the room as though even his large frame could hardly contain his jubilation.

"Monedero, there's confirmation of his appointment," he replied.

"Director General of Agriculture...?" Alva questioned.

"Yes. Antonio Monedero Martin. The placement was made last week."

"Good," responded Alva. "But I'd like to have got to know him better before it was made."

Raimundo burst out laughing. "Ah, the old story, easier to make a friend who acquires power, than to acquire a powerful friend. But don't worry. It would make no difference. Monedero's too strong to be influenced by any but his own ideas. You're right to be pleased though, I gather his thinking concurs with our own. Yes, all's working out nicely." He returned to his seat and sat down facing Alva.

"And Herrera, have you any news of him? I tried to contact him, but he was out of reach, like you." Alva's comment had the tone of a complaint.

Raimundo scrutinised the bunch of grapes before choosing another.

"He's been abroad again. He keeps his comings and goings to himself, but he gets around, has an ear to the ground. You know of his liaison with the Vatican? He doesn't broadcast his politico-ecclesiastical dealings, but the news from Rome is interesting."

"Tell me," said Alva, taking a cigar from the open case Raimundo was holding out to him.

"Well, it's rather strange really, concerns a young man who goes by the name of Benito Mussolini of whom little is known as yet, but who's beginning to cause quite a stir in certain circles. You know the loathing the Church has of the Communists and that Italy's also suffering from the unrest troubling Europe. Well, with so many monarchies having fallen, the Italian King, Victor Emmanuel, is naturally nervous about his own throne. He's still managing to keep his balance on it, but it's a precarious one and it would appear that this young fellow Mussolini is beginning to win favour with certain elements in the Establishment and, so it seems, with certain members of the Hierarchy as well."

"And..." said Alva, not wanting to appear ill-informed, but not yet seeing the connection.

"And..." continued the General, "this Mussolini's of low birth, son of a blacksmith, just one of the masses, a one-time journalist who used to describe himself as a revolutionary, although there are those who say, an armchair revolutionary, but he certainly belonged to the Left before the war, was a member of the Italian Socialist party. The curious aspect in all of this is that whilst having no connections with the Establishment to begin with, he's just formed his own party, El Fasci Italiani di Combattimento, small to begin with but which appears to be anything but Left Wing."

Alva's brow puckered momentarily, as he searched his memory.

"Yes, of course, the name, it comes from Fasces, the bundle of rods and an axe, symbolically displayed by the magistrates of ancient Rome, designating authority."

"Well, that's just what this Mussolini says he is offering, the restoration of order and authority and a laying down of the law and it goes without saying, that anyone who can deliver that would certainly be of interest to the Establishment and to the Vatican as well."

"It's a tall order in these troubled times. What sort of a following has this man? Has he much of one?" asked Alva.

"That's what's interesting," replied Raimundo. "It seems that despite this new Fascist Party being committed to fighting Liberalism and Communism and hence gaining the ear of the Right Wing, it is at the same time, attracting a large following from the masses. The main unifying factor seems to be a fierce nationalism and he's drawing a great deal of support from the war veterans, many of whom are angry at their raw deal since the war ended, and also from the have-nots and malcontents, promising them better things to come. Seems he has an uncanny ability to inspire confidence and that's what's lacking at the moment, leadership and confidence."

"He certainly seems to have inspired you," said Alva, a faint, but unmistakable note of scepticism in his tone.

Raimundo refused to be ruffled. "True," he answered. "A man like Benito Mussolini who comes from nowhere, with no background, no influence to speak of, no heritage nor possessions to protect, not one of the elite, but notwithstanding, finds favour at the highest levels, gets the ear of the Establishment, vows to put down Communism, yet simultaneously rallies the masses to his cause and all this at a time of such uncertainty. Yes, I am impressed."

Alva disagreed. "All things to all men, I wouldn't trust him. Having come from the masses himself, he's in a good position to persuade the workers he'll improve their lot when he's in power but I doubt he will, not once he's got what he wants which is, as always, the spoils that go with being at the top."

"That's not the point," the General countered emphatically. "The point is that by that time, he'll have done the work of the Right Wing for them and if it can be done in Italy it can be done elsewhere. Take Germany, Berlin and Munich and their trouble with the revolutionary Spartacists and Communists. Now if a similar leader could rise up from the masses there, a diamond to cut diamond, someone who understands the common man but is also a leader with ambitions of his own, then he can take advantage of the very factors that are causing the unrest, namely, the aggression and resentments of the people and use them to serve his cause instead. Don't you see?"

'So many unsolved problems in Spain,' thought Alva impatiently, '…and all Raimundo is talking about is Italy and Germany. I want to hear more about what Herrera's been up to at the Vatican not the rest, but I can't just ignore him.'

"And you really think events in Italy and Germany are of concern to us?" he asked, somewhat disparagingly.

"Of course," Raimundo replied. "Obviously our situation's different. Our Army has a strong political influence and a say in government and isn't weakened by war, but yes, what happens in Germany and Italy can affect us. We can't afford for them to fall to Communism, leaving us isolated as a solitary Right Wing regime."

"Which brings me back to my question, what's your Army doing to ensure that we do remain a Right Wing regime?" asked Alva. "For weeks, we, the landowners have been holding meetings, readying our caciques and their armed men, but you and the others weren't even at the last meeting."

"It was decided better that we weren't. When the Army strikes we don't want our action to be seen as calculated and pre-planned, but as a necessarily swift response to…how shall I say…some particularly unpleasant incident, which is how it will be seen if properly reported as arranged. That way it will lose sympathy for the Anarchists and, given what's coming, we won't have long to wait."

Raimundo leaned forward confidentially, an affectation of manner, for who was there around to hear? Virgo was going about his business, his presence given as little attention as the furniture itself. Both men deemed Virgo to be uninterested in such matters.

"Monedero plays by the book, but he's tough," said the General. "He's already closed the working class socialist clubs, los casas del pueblo, banned their meetings and more besides. There's bound to be a reaction, there always is, then there'll be more arrests of strike organisers and ringleaders and their imprisonment and deportations will provoke more outrage. There will be explosive reactions up and down the province, leading to more uprisings…"

"The backlash the Liberals are forever warning about, you mean?" agreed Alva, pleased with what he had just heard.

"Exactly, and once that happens there'll be no shortage of villainy, any number of incidents from which we can choose. That's where you and yours come in. The activities of your caciques and their non-uniformed gangs can be of help there, creating incidents for which the Anarchists will be blamed, thus justifying a thorough clampdown by the Military and the Civil Guards, vindicating our actions, giving us cover against the accusations of the Liberals and the protests of the mealy mouthed. But heed my advice. When the trouble really starts, take no chances."

Alva looked across at Raimundo, "When?" he asked.

"…in about a month or so. Cavalry units will reinforce the Civil Guard. General Emilio Barrera will be the one in command. This time the Anarchists must be thoroughly crushed, taught a lesson they won't forget. We want no come-back."

It did not strike Alva as at all unjust that the clampdown by the Army was to be in response to incidents commissioned and perpetrated by the Right Wing, in order to flame the fuse. Nor did he question where the moral responsibility lay, for he judged that given the need to restore order, such actions were necessary.

"Civil war…is that what this may come to?" he asked.

"No, for if it comes to that, the people will be up against the Army and they don't have the resources to last out the fight," answered Raimundo.

As he spoke all hint of his previous bonhomie had disappeared. His face was that of the other man in him, the one that bore the steel-hard nature of the ruthless militarist. It was not that the mask of joviality had slipped. It was that this other personality, the one that grappled and clawed for him when the need demanded, had come to the fore.

The change did not go unnoticed by Virgo who had been waiting near the door he had left open. Seeing it, and noticing also that the sun no longer cast its rays into the room, he entered silently as always, ostensibly to raise the window's upper shutter, but more intentionally, to listen.

Unlike Virgo, Amelia had never actually seen this change in the General, but she knew this other man existed in her husband's military friend. She loathed Bastanta but at least Bastanta made no pretence about what he was. Raimundo fooled many, but not Amelia. Deeply intuitive and astute, she had long since seen beyond the stage-props of his plump and patting hands, the kindly twinkling of the eyes that guised this other very different self.

Alva also knew of Raimundo's other side, but his knowing came from having seen it first hand and he did not find the General's ruthlessness disturbing, for both men adhered to the precept, 'One does what must be done to achieve one's goals.' There was however a crucial difference between the two men.

To Alva, morality mattered. It was the guiding beacon of his life, the dictate defining his decisions. He believed that the morality of an act is defined by the worthiness of the cause it serves and Alva believed totally in the justness of his chosen causes. In the main they consisted of the defence of the Faith and the retention by the upper classes of the ruling hand, both of which he believed essential for the survival of civilisation itself. If the rabble were to get its way, a Hobbesian state of lawlessness would prevail. Just how this mayhem would come about Alva had not thought through, for such things were too awful for him to contemplate.

But in the absence of a conscious appraisal of his fears, Alva remained the victim of his dread. He was not a bad or selfish man, simply an indoctrinated one who behaved in the only way he knew how, which meant, according to the way he had been conditioned. Nevertheless, he still truly believed himself to be free, a freedom he was determined to preserve.

Raimundo was about to take his leave. He paused in the archway of the entrance before crossing the courtyard to his carriage.

"And you say Leonora's in England now. You feel that's wise?" he asked, his tone disapproving.

Alva looked sharply across at him. He had not invited Raimundo to hear his views on the upbringing of his daughter and he was still put out by his friend's earlier remark regarding his wife.

"By the time she's finished her education the troubles here will be over if the Army does as it should, and she will return to Spain," he replied, changing the subject and pressing a point.

But that apart, Alva was doubly anxious for the Army to get on with their task. The peasants' revolt in the province had worsened. Even Bastanta conceded it was getting out of control and the strikes and insurgency in Cordoba city were continuing, giving Amelia every excuse not to come back and…Damn it, he wanted her back.

For some time after his friend's departure Alva brooded on his situation. He would not admit it, but the isolation had begun to affect him badly. He had not recovered his spirits since that awful night of the meeting a couple of weeks ago when he had been beset by eerie, unnatural premonitions and forebodings that he was still unable to shake off. His nerves had never troubled him like this before. He felt dreadful and it had not been helpful to be told by Raimundo that he looked dreadful as well. He tried to reassure himself that it was only to be expected. The hostility in and around the countryside was palpable and he had not been sleeping properly. It had, once or twice, occurred to him to leave, but he could not be seen to be backing down, not after the stance he had taken. How would he explain himself?

He could move to Madrid where, as Amelia kept saying, security was more easily organised than here and help more readily to hand. If questioned by acquaintances and friends, he could claim it was due to an interest in civic affairs, in politics. He did, after all, still have governmental connections there from his father's day. But he would not mention politics to Amelia, not yet. Knowing she preferred Madrid to Cordoba, he would let her think of the move as a peace offering, with politics as a consideration that came later.

He would say nothing to his military friend either. 'As my father used to tell me,' mused Alva, 'when you tell someone something, you give them the right to ask questions,' and Raimundo was far too good at putting two and two together.

"In about a month or so," his Army friend had said. Once the Army made its move the bloodshed would quickly worsen. It would not reflect at all well on him if he moved then. He would talk to Amelia as soon as she returned. Meanwhile he would put on a good show of sticking it out. It would not do for her to get the impression she had been right all along.

THREE YEARS LATER

CHAPTER THIRTEEN

Ardleagh Hall. Summer 1922.

*A*lthough Lord Frederick's worries had not materialised, his outlook could not be said to have improved. The threat of Nationalisation had receded, but there had been no celebratory moment of relief nor assurance that the worst was not to be, and the lurking possibility that what was his by right could still be taken from him, resulting in developments beyond his control, riled him and raised spectres from the past.

He and Lady Margaret saw relatively little of each other these days except at dinner and at other such set times, during which she found it preferable to be placatory. It kept the peace and created a more pleasant atmosphere.

This was the summer of James final exams. Happily he had, to a certain extent, managed to get his own way. His tutor had been sympathetic and enabled him to continue his music studies. He had found an excellent instructor for him who, on hearing of the situation and having heard James play, had readily entered into the covert arrangement put to him.

The time and money James might have spent on other pursuits, he had given to his music which had received more attention than his other studies, but by dint of intensive last minute cramming he had managed to pass his exams and so Lord Frederick had never known. Neither did his father know that in the spring of this year, he had won first place in a prestigious competition for young musicians. Part of the prize was a three month course at a Berlin music academy, of which he intended to avail during the summer.

He still had not decided quite how or when to tell his father, but tell him he would have to and before very long. The consequences would be anybody's guess but of one thing James was clear. His father had to accept that he no longer owned him, estate, inheritance, or not.

All unwittingly his mother had been instrumental in firming his resolve. Her journey back from the depths to which her grief had pushed her had been slow, but the little steps that had inched her forward, minuscule as they may be, were successes nonetheless and little by little, her confidence and peace of mind had returned.

No big, onward strides had marked her progress save that one in the summer of 1919, when she had refused to go on Frederick's planned Grand Tour. There had been no adamant putting down of her foot to make her point, no justificatory rambling on, nor long winded excuses in defence, simply because she could find nothing adequate to say. She had dredged her mind repeatedly hoping to come up with something sufficiently weighty to counter Frederick's logic, but in vain. The trouble with logic, as she had found to her cost, was that its arguments can still be valid even when they are not true and so her only answer when finally challenged, had been one carefully enunciated sentence. "No dear, I will not be coming."

She had uttered it that memorable afternoon when the three of them were in the study and Frederick, suddenly aware that in all their discussions about the Tour she had played no part, asked no questions, nor shown an interest as one would expect, had commented on her silence.

It was the moment against which Margaret had been steeling herself. On hearing her decision, Frederick had put on quite an act. She had watched for some moments, waiting for him to calm down, but on seeing he was gearing up instead, she had risen and with no more than a quietly spoken plea of, "Frederick…please," had left the room.

Perhaps because of its simplicity, James had been impressed. He mentioned this to her later and she told him how she had been dreading a row and bracing herself against it for some time. Knowing from experience her hopelessness in arguing with him she had decided to copy Amelia's example and simply listen and, for the first time, had actually heard how much of what he was saying was untrue. The realisation robbed his words of what would otherwise have been their power and it had seemed as pointless to continue listening as it would have been to argue. "Of course," she had added, "if I had thought for a moment that he would listen to me, I would have tried to explain."

It had been a totally passive victory but Margaret's silent rejoicing was not over her husband. It was over herself and thereafter she had found herself able to withstand the pressures he applied, most notably that of guilt, blaming her, saying she was ruining the Tour for James and Ralph and, although she could not see how, for their other friends as well. Sorely vexed by his wife's refusal but not wanting her recalcitrance known, especially to the Rawlinsons, Frederick had put out excuses that she was not well and that the itinerary had been shortened to a few weeks in Greece, due to the turmoil the Communists were causing on the Continent.

The repercussions of his upset had echoed for some time. His wife's stance worried him. She had never behaved like this before. Of course, he knew where the blame lay. She had been seeing too much of that sister of his, Amelia and her flaming bad example. It had been a bad idea to have her come in the first place. She had far too much of an effect on Margaret. He was desperately hoping that the clampdown the Spanish Army had embarked upon two or three years ago would eventually prove effective and Amelia would go home and stay put where she belonged.

"To hell with the Spanish insurgents and the Communists and the Trade Unions and our own blasted Government for giving in to them."

But Frederick's hopes continued to be dashed. The predicted backlash to the Army's clampdown in Spain had been far fiercer than expected. The cavalry under La Barrera, backed by the Civil Guard, had closed in but despite their ruthless efficiency the insurrectionists had not been wiped out. Their numbers were growing and the rebellions in Andalucia and Catalonia had spread to other regions. As arbitrary action and sentences against selected ringleaders were carried out the retaliation worsened. The enmity between classes intensified and the viciousness of internecine warfare was keeping pace.

Now, in 1922, it was still on-going and another General strike, with more killing and blood-letting, was creating havoc as the so-called Forces of Law and Order continued their deadly struggle to get the upper hand. In the areas of Andalucia's vast estates, attacks tended to be motivated by personal vengeance and individual gain and hence specifically targeted against land owners and others of obvious power and wealth. Despite their brutality, the caciques and their strong armed men were no longer able to assert themselves as once they had and though still leaving the running of the estate to Bastanta, Alva had engaged extra forces.

Raimundo however remained confident the Army would succeed, for how could it be otherwise? The military had far more forces at its disposal than the rebels.

This was the year Alva had hoped to see Leonora married, instead of which

Amelia was making arrangements for her Court debut in London. Georgio was now serving with the Army in Catalonia and Raimundo had been assured by the General in command that the increasing unrest in the province would provide his nephew with excellent opportunities for promotion. Giving priority to Georgio's career, Raimundo was not pressing for his return.

Alva was becoming impatient. He had taken care not to let Amelia know of his arrangement with Raimundo regarding their daughter's marriage otherwise she would almost certainly try to prevent it. If the wedding were delayed too long however, Leonora may begin to get ideas of her own. All in all, Alva was not happy.

With no resources and nowhere to go, acceptance of the position at the Hall had been Claire's only realistic option. She was still unaware that the offer of the post was thanks to James and since returning three years ago, had resolutely stuck to her decision to avoid him. If she could put an end to what James stirred in her, how much easier all would be, but her feelings for him remained as strong as always. Mindful of the barriers, the impassable divides that separated them, she knew she should come to her senses, but knowing did not help. Her only ally was her pride.

At first, James had repeatedly tried to meet her, to speak with her, but it soon became evident she was eluding him. It hurt and he was at a loss to understand. After his many attempts had failed, he had stopped trying. Given the boundaries she had set up, there was nothing he could do and their relationship had remained at an impasse.

Claire had spoken to no-one about her time with the Sugdens. The sights she had seen in her daily encounters in the Salford slums had shattered her previously held assumptions about life in general. She had seen first-hand the effects of dire poverty. Severely chastened she could not talk about it, not even to Anna. The memory of Mrs Sugden's ill-health, her deprivation of opportunity and lack of choice, resulting in the appalling circumstances in which she had become ensnared, had induced a dread in Claire she could not overcome. Never, never again she vowed, would she leap into waters, not knowing their depth.

All that apart, her present situation had many advantages and Claire had tried, as Anna would have put it, to be 'worthy of her keep'. She was able to be reasonably dressed and well groomed. The work was not heavy and she had time to read. It was not what she wished for permanently, but that would not happen because in the not too distant future, Leonora would leave.

She was to have attended a Swiss finishing school during this summer, to be groomed in the social graces, but concerned at the amount of freedom the young women there were allowed, her father had decided on an Academy for Young Ladies in London instead. On leaving she would make her debut and, aware of the extensive wardrobe no debutante could afford to be without, Claire envisaged a busy time ahead. There would be trips to the fashion houses, fittings for her gowns and matching accessories to be chosen, wraps and hats, bags and belts and shoes.

Leonora was now eighteen, a tall, slim, alluring young woman with pale olive skin, dark amber coloured eyes, lissom limbs and silken, auburn hair. When the time came she would surely be in the forefront for the title Debutante of the Year. She had certainly attracted the attention of Ralph Rawlinson, a development that in turn had attracted the attention of Claire.

During the last strike, his father had put him in charge of the village mill. Initially it had been something of a trial run and Ralph had risen to the challenge brilliantly. His first move had been to call a meeting and in the echoing silence of the idly standing looms, the persuasive powers of his strong voice and resolute stance had partly bullied, partly cajoled, the workers to return. The crescendo of their clogs, clattering in the yard and the rumble of the dray carts as they lumbered to the warehouse doors, sounded sweet as music to old Albert's ears.

In the time since, the young man had proved himself a strong support to his ageing father and had certainly earned his wages. Albert had never stinted his son and though he rarely visited London himself, he had recently made him the gift of a small townhouse in Mayfair. It was a generous gesture, but property was a sound investment and he believed the money was well spent. Ever the proud father, he loved to see his son in the role of man about town. It also pleased him that Ralph was still on the Hall's guest list despite, or perhaps because of, his not having parted with the land he knew Lord Frederick wanted. It confirmed old Rawlinson's crass belief, hold onto the bone and the dog will follow.

As his businesses flourished, Rawlinson senior had taken an interest in racing and now had two horses in training. He had also taken a box in the Grand Stand at the racecourse where the Eglinton family had, for years, had theirs. Ralph's favourite flutter was not on the horses, but at the card and gaming tables. It was however, at a race meeting that Ralph had first noticed the lovely Leonora since when, his interest in racing had become quite keen and he sought even more excuses to visit the Hall.

Having lived in the village whilst at the Pendles, Claire had heard the whispers regarding Ralph in connection with more than one mill girl, but owing to the anxiety of the girl's family to hush the slur on her honour, they had remained little more than rumour. There had however, been no gossip regarding him for some time now and Lady Margaret seemed to have warmed to the young man. He appeared to have settled down, matured, become responsible and after keeping an eye on him, Claire had concluded there really was no cause for concern.

The reality was that Ralph, now an affluent young man of means, had lost his taste for mill girls. He preferred the fan and feathered females of the girlie shows and cabarets he frequented when in London and enjoyed the excitement of the city's dimly lit, sybaritic haunts, its casinos and gambling dens.

Having gained his degree, James had left Cambridge University and was on a celebratory holiday somewhere in the Mediterranean with friends from his year. He was expected back shortly but as was usual these days, no-one seemed to know quite when. Together with the way Claire organised her days, it was not uncommon for months to pass without her seeing him.

Tomorrow was her day off and she was planning to spend it in Manchester, mainly at the central library where she could spend time undisturbed in its quiet, spacious rooms. As usual she would set off early and take the train from the village.

On arriving in Manchester the following day, Claire left the station and walked through the city's crowded streets to Albert Square. On one side was the Town Hall, ornate and imposing, but black from years in the grime-laden atmosphere. On the opposite side stood the library, its large round, central dome, a landmark in the city.

It was a haven in the busy metropolis, a world apart from the bustle in the streets outside and she anticipated the subtle scent of paper and polished wood, the pervading, peace-inducing silence of the reference rooms where books lined the walls from ceiling to floor. Here she could find out everything she wished to know.

The sun was shining as she ran up the wide steps at its front entrance and into the large, circular reception hall. Waiting at the desk to show her ticket, she heard a familiar voice. Instantaneously her skin tingled and she froze.

"Claire," his hand touched her elbow and she turned to find herself face to face with James, close beside her. Reaching out, he offered to take her books. She felt the tweed of his jacket as his hand touched hers, could faintly discern the indefinable, attractive aroma that always surrounded him and, as the strong sensation of that first moment drained away, it left behind a residue of weakness and disquiet and the colour faded from her face.

"I'm sorry. I startled you," he said, studying her.

'He's noticed, oh Heaven it's obvious,' she thought as she stumbled out some comment about not having expected him to be here.

"No, well…it was very late last night when I got back. This morning Leonora said you'd left for Manchester. She thought you'd be at the library. I drove here, raced the train. Claire I have to talk to you."

It was something James had decided upon before leaving Cambridge that, come hell or high water he was going to see her even if he did upset her, or Anna, or his mother or anybody else. He had had enough of being upset himself, by her attitude and by not knowing why. Whatever the reason was, he needed to be told. He also wanted to tell her about Germany and that he was planning to leave for a while…though that was something still to be finalised.

It was quite busy where they were standing and he suggested they move to one side. He started to tell her about the competition he had won then broke off saying,

"It's difficult to talk here. I want to go to the Lakes, to Lake Coniston where Austen and I spent our holidays as children and again on his last leave and I want you to come with me, now, today." He stood, waiting for her answer.

Overcome by the long-denied emotions his nearness had released, Claire was silent.

"I can't explain standing here," he added.

No, they could not talk here. The reception area was busy and all the rooms had 'Silence Please' notices pinned onto their doors.

She was feeling calmer now after listening to his voice, its intonation creating a sense of ease the way it always did.

Turning back to face him, she was caught in the intensity of his eyes, so familiar, so loved. As the seconds passed they held each other's gaze. She did not answer. There was no need. He took her arm and they moved towards the door.

She recognised his car, parked some way down the street, an immaculate looking dark blue, twenty-first birthday present from his parents. Opening the door he handed her in and whilst he was starting the engine, she leaned back into the thickly upholstered seat. It had all happened so quickly, heightening her senses, how rich the leather of the interior, the smooth graining of the dashboard's burnished wood, the softness of the carpeting underfoot. Closing her eyes she was conscious also of the swifter beating of her heart.

The engine of the automobile throbbed to life. Through the windscreen, she watched him, strapping down the starter handle. A day, a whole day with him and in the potency of that moment, her resolutions faltered and she prayed. "Please God…let time stand still."

They left the city behind. The scenery became prettier, more picturesque. Claire had never before been to the Lakes. Gradually, the countryside became more wooded, the hawthorn hedgerows, thick with small, white blossoms, were higher and the lanes were narrower, steeper. The sound of the engine altered as the gears changed and the car climbed the hills. They had been driving for some time and the views from both sides of the twisting and turning lane were breathtakingly beautiful and far across the valley, they saw the gleam of the first lake.

Deep in his thoughts, James had spoken very little during the drive. They drew up at a small inn and over lunch he reminded Claire of the Wordsworth book of poetry and the letter he had sent to her more than three years ago, in which he had written of visiting the Lakes with her one day.

"You never wrote back to me."

"I was afraid that if I did, my letter might be found."

"Would that have been so awful, yet wasn't your fear, your silence, more awful still," but James smiled gently as he spoke and she knew it was a comment, the offering of a ventured thought...not a question.

They drove on and he told her he could no longer accept the dictates of his father. Music was his choice but he had become uncertain about taking up the prize. He was troubled. Austen had been killed while fighting Germany. Was he disloyal to take advantage of what was now on offer there?

"The war's over," she answered. "Taking up the offer isn't the issue, not of itself. I think what disturbs you, what you really want to know is how Austen would feel about it," and she suggested they go to the places that were Austen's favourites when he and James were there together, the places where the memories were strong and his spirit would be close and James would know intuitively what Austen would have him do.

And for the next several hours that was what they did.

It was late in the afternoon. They were on the far side of the lake across from his family's retreat. Its backcloth of wooded rise and foreground of gardens sweeping to the water's edge made an idyllic and romantic view. A light breeze, warm and laden with the scents of summer was drifting over the soft earth, rustling the trees. They were half lying on a grassy bank by the lakeside. From its pure, clear depths, fish could be seen rising until with tiny, pinpoint touch they pricked the under-surface to make ever widening, gently spreading, rippling rings. The lap of water played upon the quiet, listening stillness surrounding them and, as Claire had begged, time itself had ceased to be.

She had been listening to James, quoting a passage from Wordsworth's poetry, one he had once marked for her, his last words barely audible on the air. He turned, raising his shoulders and moved to lean across her. She felt his breath soft upon her skin and she also, lured by her longing far deeper than she could deny drew close to him. Their lips touched and in abandon to each other, they were in each other's arms.

Locked deep in those moments was an awareness such as she had never known. Her fingers touched his hair, his throat. With every perception magnified she longed as lovers down the years have longed that all could cease to be, save what was theirs to know and feel in this the very core of feeling and of life. Tears stung her eyes. The pent up yearnings of the many un-dared dreams that she had caged, now freed themselves, miming their intentions, swirling and stepping in wild joy through her being, weaving her desires and beckoning her to join them in the rhythm of their dance.

Closely entwined they wanted their togetherness to never end, but though it sometimes may pretend, Time never does stand still and when at last the sun began to sink into the far off hills, slowly, gently, softly clinging yet letting go, they came from depths that reason could not reach and James spoke of their always being together, of what could be if she would come with him to Berlin and marry him and of breaking free from his father, if that was how it had to be.

But the words he spoke reminded Claire of that other world, that lay beyond this one of sky and water, rocks and trees, of fierce love and gentleness and the beauty of the oneness of an earth where Nature knew, that the essence of survival is the harmony and balance of all things.

It was in that other world that they would have to live, that world on which Domination had stencilled its fixed limits, that world defined by barriers and distinctions and divides, that world in which Convention, when decoded, spells 'Thou shall not cross' and the chill she felt was not the cool of evening, it was the prescience of loss.

What they had had in these short hours by the lake, they had taken by stealth and, furtively, they must return. There was no other way. If his parents found out about today, they would believe only what would appear to them as obvious, and not what really was. If they knew what existed between her and their son, they would never allow it to just be. Something would have to be done about it. She would have to leave. The repercussions and the list of slurs against her would be long. She would be branded scheming. James would be considered to have taken advantage. She would be given notice and word would be passed around and Anna also would be affected.

A row with his father was inevitable given his career plans. Once it started who knew what may be said. Claire hoped he would not be reckless, would not throw caution to the winds. She stole a sideways glance at him, noting his firm profile, strong jaw line, the expression lines around his eyes. He could be as determined as his father, but his father had weapons that James did not. He had the influence and power to affect his son's future and the ability to be ruthless without a qualm, if necessary to retain control.

They had spoken little on the journey back and as they reached the road that bordered the Hall grounds, she wondered what he would tell his parents if they asked how he had spent the day. It was his first day home. They would have been expecting to see him. She could not ask him to lie, but for both their sakes it was important he did not say.

James swung the car into the back drive and approached the garages from the rear. As the car came to a halt Eric, the chauffeur, appeared. He had been standing for quite some time by the wall close to where the car pulled up, awaiting James' return.

"The Earl asked me to find you Sir. He wanted me to let you know your mother has visitors. Lady Arrabella Barrington Curzon and her father are in the drawing room."

Eric addressed James respectfully but his manner towards Claire was pointedly less so and there was no mistaking the way he looked at her.

Quickly she murmured some form of thanks to James and not letting him stop her, walked away. He called out and began to follow. Although she heard him, she did not look round. She knew Eric was still standing, and watching.

Oh why did that have to happen? But it will…always. If we are together it will always be this way, manipulated by his parents, gossiped over by the servants, disregarded by his friends. She wanted to run but stopped herself and took the path leading to a side door that gave onto the corridor close by the servants' lavatories. Thankful to find nobody there, she quickly entered the nearest cubicle. 'Stupid, stupid to imagine it could ever be other than this,' she told herself. Despairingly the thought remained, that no amount of longing and wanting could make things different to the way they were in this, the other world, the one they could not change and to which, wishing it were different, would make no difference at all.

This afternoon when James had spoken of breaking from his father and being free, she had listened, longing for it to be possible. In his words it had sounded simple. In reality it was far from being so, but when she had tried to warn him he had simply said, "So be it."

Later that night, alone in her room, Claire faced with realism the pitfalls James could not envisage. James had never seen how poverty could grind a person down, the despairing hopelessness of clinging day to day without a proper hold, without the safety-net of family connections, influential friends and the granted guarantee of who-he-was.

James was gifted. Music was as integral to his being as is the rhythm of the universe to the galaxies and spheres. It was intrinsic to his life, a fundamental part of him but it would take years of training and practice, time and money for him to realise his potential and achieve his dream. For all of this he needed his family's support and to be free, not burdened with someone from her walk of life who had nothing to bring to the relationship.

From the many wealthy, willing and well-bred young lovelies in James social circuit he could take his pick, but as long as he was with her he would be cut off from his family and inheritance. As he struggled in the years ahead he would come to see how she had held him back and the old saying could prove true once more,

"When Poverty knocks at the door, Love flies out of the window."

And Claire knew that what she longed for could not be.

Amelia and Leonora arrived, laden with purchases for Leonora's forthcoming debut. Each and every outfit had to be sorted and put away. It seemed every last belt and button had to be checked, together with the accessories to match, and in the days that followed Lady Margaret kept Claire under pressure with so much additional work she had no free time. When at last she and James managed to talk, Claire failed completely in her persuasions to have him understand. He was hurt and tense and that evening, threw his father's plans awry by telling him he was leaving for Berlin.

The row that followed was, as all rows are, an event unto itself, for of their nature rows have no rules, no formulae to guide their course. James' refusal to have his future shaped for him was regarded by his father as shattering the mould being handed to him and as such, was unacceptable. But no matter how jagged, nor how many the pieces to befall, James' mind was made up.

With their deadlock unresolved, his father said he would speak to him in the morning, but the following morning, the household awoke to find that James had gone. The note he left gave no cause for concern. Low-keyed and courteous, it simply let them know he had decided to avail of the prize he had won and wished them well.

CHAPTER FOURTEEN

Lancashire. England Autumn 1922

In the centre of the city of Manchester, the town-hall clock struck one. It rang out across the Albert Memorial, which gave its name to the main square in which it stood. For the last several days, many a wall, lamppost and hoarding had displayed black and white printed posters telling of the Trade Union meeting and demonstration to be held here this afternoon. Already the crowds were gathering, wandering around or taking up positions close to the newly erected, wooden platforms from which the speeches would be made. It was a golden, autumnal day and a massive turnout of workers, strikers and the unemployed, was expected. At strategic points, clusters of helmeted police were checking that the barriers were securely in place.

The clock's sonorous chime was also faintly heard in the fashionable area of boutiques and cafes, a few streets away. Here, in a quiet restaurant, catering for a wealthy few, sat Lady Margaret, Leonora and Claire. The luncheon room's wide but discreetly netted windows looked out onto St Anne's Square, a pretty, pedestrian area, its paving dotted with flowerboxes and shrubs and in the windows of the nearby shops, luxury goods, furs, jewellery and valuable antiques were on display. Inside the restaurant the atmosphere was leisured, the food tasteful and deferentially served.

The date of Leonora's presentation at Court was drawing near and a final fitting for her gown and the purchase of yet more necessities had once again brought her and her aunt to Manchester. The whole procedure was being complicated by Leonora's frequent changes of mind, whims which the various establishments graciously accommodated thanks to Lady Margaret's much valued patronage. Although their parcels could readily have been delivered, Leonora liked to take them home with her and Claire had been brought along to carry them.

The decorative, ribbon-tied boxes were at this moment discreetly stacked close by the restaurant's entrance. They had finished their meal earlier than expected and were now waiting for Eric, their chauffeur, who was not due to collect them for a while. As they sipped their coffee, Leonora and her aunt were discussing the choice of outfit, handbag and footwear most suitable for each of the various occasions in her calendar. As before, there was much differing of opinion. Claire was only half listening, knowing full well that no matter what was finally decided all would be changed and changed again before the time came.

The morning had passed agreeably. They were in the most expensive part of the city and during the long intervals while Leonora was making up her mind, Claire had taken the time to look around, luxuriating in the ambiance of the select boutiques, the cushioning of thick carpets, the faint trace of expensive perfume lingering in the air and the ostentatious display of wealth on show in the display cases.

After a morning of being at her employer's beck and call and following behind, she was thankful to sit back and relax. The boxes had not been heavy but were cumbersome and she was looking forward to the unfamiliar pleasure of being chauffeured home. How could Claire know these passing moments were as grains of sand slipping through the hourglass of her life, bringing her closer and closer to the first of a series of events that would alter everything?

In the small kiosk by the wall a telephone was ringing, signalling the first in the sequence, but the triviality of the incident gave no warning of its being so. It was answered by a young man who then came to tell Lady Margaret her husband wished to speak to her. On picking up the receiver she was told there was to be a change of plan. Contrary to earlier intentions, Frederick's horse, Past Master, would be racing that afternoon at a course some miles outside the city. Heavy, overnight rain had rendered the going favourable for him and his trainer had decided to race him after all. In view of the congestion in the city Lord Frederick told his wife not to wait for Eric, but to take a taxi and go straight to the course.

Margaret, who had no interest whatever in racing, was put out at the prospect of the boring afternoon in store. At the same time as summoning a waiter for their bill and asking for a taxi to be called, she made a vague comment about having to arrange some way to get Claire home. Leonora's reaction to the news was to choose a suitable hat from the selection she had just bought. Claire went to attend to the boxes and returned just in time to hear the end of something Lady Margaret was saying to her niece.

"...and of all things, just imagine, James is returning from Berlin, well so your uncle said." But just then, the taxi arrived and whilst aunt and niece were climbing in, Claire was obliged to go with the driver to make sure the boxes would not be crushed in the boot.

She so wanted to know if she had heard correctly but it was not her place to ask and certainly not when she had eavesdropped.

The traffic was dreadfully heavy. Owing to the demonstration, police barricades were preventing entry to many of the streets around Albert Square. Soon their car was at a standstill, locked into a jam of automobiles, horse drawn vehicles and throngs of people heading to the Trade Union Rally.

For Leonora, the sense of being trapped, with workers pressing round the taxi trying to get past, revived memories of the carriage incident in Cordoba and she was restless and on edge. Lady Margaret, also harassed by the noise and confusion, began fussing the taxi driver, telling him what best to do and insisting he find a route to get them out of wherever it was they were. They were already behind time and this would surely cause them to miss the race and Frederick would be in a hubbub wanting to know why they were late, as though it were her fault.

The taxi driver stayed stony-faced and did not answer. The car continued, in little fits and starts, to edge and jerk forward without seeming to get anywhere. Eventually they got out of the city and picked up speed.

James' return that morning from Germany was totally unexpected. His three months tuition had not ended, but he had been offered the chance to join one of the good orchestras in Berlin. With little time to decide he had taken the plunge and accepted. It would mean staying in Germany indefinitely. In her letters his mother had said his father was hoping his time in Berlin would get music out of his system and that on his return he would see things differently, for which read, 'he's hoping I'll come to my senses, come back and manage the mines', ruminated James.

He was not looking forward to breaking the news to them, but they had to know and it would be so much better if they could understand. The matter had been bothering him and wanting to get it over with he made a sudden decision to tell them in person. He also decided to say nothing about his coming until shortly before he was due, for if his father knew too long in advance he would start asking questions and maybe get worked up before he arrived.

Finding no-one in when he got there, James went to the stables where Martin was already saddling his mare. The hunting season was due to start in a few weeks and he was aiming to get her fit. During their ride, their talk turned to the mines. Martin updated James on recent developments within the Trade Unions and mentioned he was going to the Rally that afternoon.

"If you really want to know how things stand, why not come along?" he suggested.

Although James had no intention of ever taking over the mines he was interested in the politics of the situation and agreed to join Martin later. At worst it would be a waste of time. At best, by being there he would get a better feel for what was going on than by reading second hand reports and newspaper editorials. He was not planning to tell his father of his decision until tomorrow and meanwhile the more he knew, the better he could answer him if his news caused an argument.

On hearing his trainer's opinion after inspecting the course, Frederick had phoned a few friends inviting them to watch the horse run and having learned that James was on his way home, he had included the Barrington Curzons. Their daughter, Arrabella, was a lovely girl. If only he could get James to take an interest. His horse was in fine fettle. The going suited him and the trainer was confident they could count on a win. Yes, it was going to be a good day, high time for something nice to happen for a change.

Shortly after returning from his trainer's yard, a problem arose. Eric had misunderstood the message not to collect Lady Margaret and had already left. The driver who normally stood in for him could not be found and Frederick, who did not drive, was flustered. He had to get to the racetrack. He was still trying to organise something when James walked in.

"Oh, good," were Frederick's first words as James came through the door.

Driving to the races was the last thing James wanted to do. It was miles away and having arranged to meet Martin he could not leave him hanging around at the Rally, the place would be packed. However, anxious to keep things on an even keel, he would oblige, but he was not going to stay.

"Your mother should be here by now. She'll be delighted to see you," said Frederick as they arrived at the course.

They made their way to the paddock. On the bright green turf in the centre of the enclosure, individual groups of owners with their wives, friends and trainers were standing around the horses. As James approached however, it was not his mother who came to greet him but Arrabella, followed by her agreeably smiling father. James smiled too, but it was not how he felt. She was very sweet, but he knew her being here was his father's idea with which he would be expected to conform. 'Ah, well,' he thought, 'nothing for it but to stand around making pleasantries until mother arrives. It's not Arrabella's fault.'

While they were waiting, Frederick saw that one of the groups on the turf was made up of Albert Rawlinson with his wife, Ralph and the rest of his entourage. Albert also had a horse running, Mr Sandman, and together with the trainer they were attracting a fair share of attention. This was something Frederick had not expected. Not having intended to run his horse today and in the rush following the change of plan, he had not checked the other entries. Albert's horse, a chestnut, looked damned good, too damned good and the odds on it were short.

Strong as the temptation was, there was no way Frederick could not acknowledge them. Better not to upset Rawlinson, he still had not parted with that land, but much as Frederick tried not to let him, the man was getting under his skin. He turned his back and tried to put him from his mind but his pleasure in the afternoon had diminished and his mood was not the same.

When Lady Margaret's taxi finally arrived, an attendant was on hand to meet her. He escorted her and the two young ladies along the finely gritted paths between the lawns towards the white railed, paddock enclosure. It was surrounded by stylishly dressed throngs. Though not exactly dressed for the races, Leonora and her aunt were elegantly garbed, gloved and millinered as always, though it must be admitted, Lady Margaret looked tired and a little faded in contrast to Leonora who, in her stylish, new hat, looked very much the part. Claire, on the other hand, hatless and in her dark more serviceable coat, was fervently wishing herself somewhere else, anywhere else but here.

The three of them reached the paddock as the horses entered for the race were about to be paraded. At Lady Margaret's approach, the paddock gate was opened to receive her. As she passed through, Leonora was about to follow, but Claire hung back, not knowing what to do or where to go. Leonora hesitated, then turned and touched Claire's arm.

"Just...wait here a moment..." she murmured uncertainly before walking on.

Margaret quickened her pace and hastened across the turf to where her husband was waiting. A magnificent looking Past Master was being calmed by his handler and standing beside him was James. In her surprise and excitement, Claire slipped from Margaret's mind.

Hordes of spectators were jostling outside the rails. A crowd had bunched around the gate with people passing to and fro. Behind the barrier, others were pushing to get to the front, trying to get a good view of the horses, their owners and trainers and Claire was lost in the crush.

James' attention was taken in greeting his mother. Arrabella, looking exquisite, was standing close by him. Dressed in fashionable eau-de-nil chiffon of palest green, she looked fragile and delicate. Beneath a matching hat adorned with satiny, cream roses, her shining, blonde hair was drawn into a chignon at the nape of her neck. Pearls, the elegance of kid gloves and shoes and a little parasol completed the picture and, a picture, she truly was.

Soon it was time for the parade to end and for the horses to be brought back on the turf. The jockeys in their brilliantly patterned racing colours were being given last minute instructions by their trainers. The enthusiasm was infectious. The bell rang and the jockeys were hoisted aboard. The Rawlinson's entry for the race was getting considerable attention. Albert Rawlinson, his face flushed with pleasure and anticipation looked ready for the fun to begin as also did Ralph, who had just caught sight of Leonora.

Fuss and fanfare surrounded those at the centre of the scene, their banter and rivalry entertaining the onlookers. Now, the horses and riders were leaving the paddock and cantering down to the start. Still waiting by the rails, Claire was thronged on all sides by eager race-goers wanting to see what was happening. Laughing and exuberant and with many a true word spoken in jest, owners continued to chaff and call across to each other on their way to the Stand. All was excitement, but James' mind was on other things. It never entered his head Claire might be around. His mother's late appearance had made him late for the Rally and he wanted to get away as soon as he could.

Now was his moment. He whispered a few words to Leonora, asking her to make his excuses to his parents for him. As his father's group moved to the exit gate on the opposite side, James turned to leave. Arrabella noticed and came back, giving a little tug at his sleeve. As he looked towards her, she pulled him closer, standing on tiptoe, whispering something in his ear. From the midst of the throng outside the enclosure rails Claire watched her putting her lips close to his face and saw him turn towards her, smiling at whatever she had said and then the crowd closed around them and they were hidden from view.

Was it jealousy, grudging? In that moment Claire did not know what she felt, only how much it hurt. Spectators and punters went to watch the race, leaving the paddock deserted and Claire was left standing alone. Feeling conspicuous, she also wanted to leave but Leonora had said to wait here. She fervently wished they would hurry.

Meanwhile, in the Stand, everyone was settling into their places. Ralph, on the pretext of lending her a pair of binoculars had joined Leonora in the Eglinton seats. Knowing the race was about to begin he remained chatting while calculating exactly how long to overstay. His timing was perfect. He was just about to leave, when,

'Under Starter's Orders' boomed the megaphone. Feigning surprise, a well practised art, Ralph made a helpless little gesture, signifying his inability to return to his seat in time and readily accepted Leonora's gracious response that there were sufficient seats for him to watch the race from where he was. Peering through field glasses, all eyes were now riveted on the restive horses in the starting stalls. Suddenly,

"THEY'RE OFF". The words cracked across the racecourse like canon shot and, like canon balls, the horses shot out of their stalls and thundered up the track. For weeks Leonora had been on the receiving end of an interplay of looks and glances from Ralph, another of his skills. Now, he deemed, was the time for him to chance his arm, literally and metaphorically. Seated close by her side and in what could be excused as the exuberance of the moment, he put his arm around her shoulders. The general excitement served as cover for Leonora's uncertainty. She had not been oblivious of Ralph's attentions, but now that he had made a move, she was utterly unsure how to react and was glad that the ever growing, almost ear-numbing noise of fevered shouting and cheering, afforded her a few moments in which to collect herself.

As the crowd's urgings of the leading horses swelled to an outright roar, the spectators in the box rose to their feet. Dropping his arm from her shoulder, he moved it to around her waist. Caught off guard, her lashes fluttered as she glanced at him a genuine, wide-eyed look of shy regard.

The expression of obvious enjoyment on his laughing face was disarming. His audaciously good-natured sense of fun amused her too. The reverberations in the Stand rose to a crescendo as the battling horses hammered the ground and shortened the distance between themselves and the winning post. The attention of everyone was glued on them. Nobody was watching Ralph and Leonora. The winner shot past the post. The tumult began to die down and as it subsided, the announcer's voice could be heard declaring,

"And the winner is...Mr Sandman."

It was the perfect moment for congratulatory hugs and kisses and Ralph took full advantage of the opportunity. There were great goings on and much jubilation from the Rawlinsons and Ralph invited Leonora to join in the rejoicing. Albert delightedly welcomed her as an honoured guest and as they readied themselves to descend the stairs and take up their envied positions in the winner's enclosure, he insisted she come too.

The much vaunted Past Master was neither placed nor mentioned. Perhaps it had not rained quite hard enough after all, last night. Valiantly Frederick brushed aside his guests' commiserations with a sporting, 'all in the game' joviality that no-one could have guessed was faked. It was bad enough his wretched horse not winning but to watch it put up a second rate showing, and now, the sight of the Rawlinsons being congratulated on their way down to the winner's enclosure, was salt in the wound. 'Hell and Damnation,' fumed Frederick to himself. 'Why did it have to go his way? The man knows nothing about racing yet he'll come back up here gloating and asking how Past Master got on, knowing damn well he never got a mention and Leonora, going off with them, damned discourteous of her to leave her aunt like that.'

Frederick made an excuse and left the box for a few minutes. He needed to be on his own. He was frustrated, on several counts. Where the hell was James, disappearing again when Barrington Curzon and his girl were here? Her father was not going to let her be messed about much more, couldn't afford to. And Margaret, she was not even trying to put on a front and what was it with that b——- trainer? 'Doesn't the man know what he's doing?' Frederick asked himself. 'The devil he should…he charges enough.'

Returning to his box, he decided he was not going to have it said he was piqued or put out, or have the Rawlinsons steal the thunder with noisy celebrations in their box and the usual well wishers joining in the junketing. No, he would turn this round to some advantage.

He would be magnanimous. As the Rawlinsons returned from the winner's enclosure, he would have the champagne on ice, waiting. He would look pleased for them, tell them the celebrations were on him and have the corks popping in his territory, not listening to them popping in theirs. Any horse could lose a race and if Albert asked any putdown questions he would say the vet had been to see his horse, had pronounced him lame and was taking some tests. Signalling a hovering steward, Frederick placed his order.

As before, the crowds gathered round the paddock ready for the next race and as before, when the horses left the parade-ring the crowds left also and Claire, still waiting, was left behind. She glanced up at the pavilion clock and seeing the time, a kernel of anger began to sprout. Was she expected to stand here all afternoon she wondered? Not knowing James had left the racecourse, she imagined him with the lovely Arrabella in the Grandstand, all of them laughing and joking and making merry. She looked again at the clock but its fingers had not moved. Fifteen minutes more she decided and that would be it.

It was not until Margaret saw Leonora returning from the winner's enclosure with Ralph that she suddenly remembered Claire. Oh Lord how dreadful, she had quite forgotten her. She had meant to organise something, but James' unexpected arrival, together with her harassment at being late and afterwards in all the excitement, it had completely slipped her mind.

When the attendant arrived he told Claire the luggage van was waiting at the delivery entrance to take her to the nearby station. He would show her where. The boxes, now labelled, had already been put in and the instructions were for her to take them on the train and leave them with the stationmaster when the train arrived at Ardleagh village.

Claire climbed into the back of the waiting vehicle. It had no passenger seats and its load of freight and boxes left little space. She made room for herself on the corner of a large crate and sat down. The driver slammed the back doors shut and the vehicle jolted off. She tried to tell herself the afternoon was just one of those things, but that was not how it seemed. She felt belittled and bruised and it was not from the bumping and rattling on the rutted road.

Again she imagined James in the Grandstand and Arrabella making little overtures to him, as of course she would. It was two or three seasons since she had made her debut, so she had overheard Lady Margaret say, and like most young women of her age and class she was, to put it bluntly, husband hunting and time was not to be wasted.

But if James had seen her, what could he have done? He could not have invited her to join him and his parents and guests. No, but he could have organised something. Well, maybe he had. Maybe it was he who had organised the van and Claire stared glumly out of its little back window at the road stretching out between her and the receding Stand.

If she stayed at the Hall the same sort of thing as of today, would happen over and over again, in different circumstances, on different occasions, for different reasons, but always inflicting the same hurt. Miserably close to tears, Claire battled with her injured pride.

Within minutes of having been beckoned, the steward had performed a conjuring act, producing a small white clothed leaf-table, champagne in ice buckets, sparkling glasses and salvers of appetising canapés, exactly as Frederick had ordered. The Rawlinsons returned. Bottles popped their corks. The champagne frothed. The bubbles burst. No glass stayed empty and all went well.

But as the afternoon wore on, the champagne's first energising flush began to be overtaken by the heaviness of its full effect and Frederick was not feeling well. Champagne was not his favourite drink, but it had seemed right for the occasion. It certainly had not been right for him. It had soured his stomach and he had a headache coming on.

Not so for Ralph, its effect on him had been to make him heady in quite a different way and he was well into his stride. The camaraderie and close rapport between him and his father had been evident all afternoon. It pierced Frederick with a thorn of envy and as the friendly banter between them continued Albert laughingly recounted how during a recent bout of trouble at the mill, Ralph had managed to get his mill-hands to end their Go Slow. Frederick listened, remembering how during last year's long drawn-out strike when production in the collieries ceased, his own son had rowed with him about the miners' plight. Ralph's affection for his father, his support and loyalty, caught Frederick on the raw and festered.

James had only just got back from abroad. He should have stayed with the family.

It was at this point that Albert spilled the beans that his day's success was thanks to Martin, Lord Frederick's engineer, whom he had happened to see whilst on a visit to the Doncaster sales a couple of years ago. Knowing him to be a judge of horseflesh, Albert had taken a place next to him as the entries were being walked round the ring. It was no more than a passing comment by the engineer as one young colt was being shown, but Albert had taken note and bought the yearling and, in the hope that he may become the stuff of dreams, had named him Mr Sandman.

Frederick shifted uncomfortably in his seat and passed no comment. What ailed him now was more than the sour stomach that had troubled him earlier. He was not at all his normal self. His headache had worsened considerably. True, he had drunk a little more than usual but not enough to cause this. Nor was he happy about having invited the Rawlinsons. It had been a mistake. Far from being appreciative, they had, as the afternoon wore on, started to overstep the mark, taking too much for granted, a classic case of, familiarity breeds contempt. 'I've done myself no favours there,' thought Frederick. 'He'll be even more difficult to deal with now.'

They had moved onto the terrace. The sun was beating strongly through the striped, red and green canvas awning, casting psychedelic colour on all beneath. Frederick experienced a strange surrealism descending on the scene, amplifying noise and laughter. He loosened his collar and breathed deeply, waiting for the moment to pass, promising himself to have a thorough check up with his doctor first thing in the morning.

A few miles away, the goods van grated to a halt at a wayside station. Its back doors clanked open and along with the freight that was being unloaded, Claire got out, thanked the driver and with as much dignity as she could muster, waited again like the boxes on the platform. She had been standing there some time, when the railway porter approached.

"Sorry miss. Trains are all held up. It's to do wi' them Trade Unions an' their Rally up the line. There's bin trouble already an' wi there bein' so many folk, police is a' feared o' crowds not bein' able t' get home an' are keepin' trains in't sidings to 'ave 'em ready fo' when it's all o'er. Sorry miss."

Claire thanked him.

'So, what now?' she asked herself. Noticing a dingy door bearing the sign, Rest Room, she went in. But the rank smell of the place, long unused and uncared for, the lack of light, the closet with a hand-basin and tap that turned but gave no water, sent her quickly outside. Back on the platform, she assessed the situation and went to find the station master. He confirmed her fears. All was as the porter had said.

"Lord alone knows when the trains'll come, could be real late and when they do they'll be packed... an' if there's been trouble and some o' the men have been drinkin'..." He did not finish his sentence.

After further questioning he told her there was an inn close by, The Pack Horse. It had once been a hostelry and was very comfortable. Leaving the parcels with him, Claire set off, hoping the inn would live up to his promise. She would ring the Hall from there and surely Jimmy the carter, or someone, would come to collect her.

The Inn surpassed her expectations. It was surrounded by well kept gardens where customers were seated, taking their ease. Walking up the sunlit path, taking in the pleasant atmosphere, hearing the birds and hum of quiet conversation, Claire relaxed. The miserable afternoon was over. She glanced around and what she saw reminded her that there was more to life than acting as a lackey for others.

She entered the inn and went straight to the Ladies Powder Room. It was a far cry from the station's Rest Room. This was luxury indeed. Together with what was in her handbag she had everything she needed to restore her amour-propre and sitting on a small stool before an ornate mirror, she set to work. After the discomfiture of the past few hours, it pleased her to make the best of herself, applying her make-up and putting up her hair.

It had never occurred to Claire to assess her looks. Hers was a beauty, gifted not only by flawlessness of feature, but one born of character, by her manner, an unaffected air of calm composure of which she herself was unaware.

She finished her grooming and, though not vain, was pleased with the reflection she saw. Taking a clothes brush from its peg, she subjected her coat to several vigorous strokes. It was cut on simple classic lines with high collar, long narrow sleeves and slim waist, one Leonora had brought from Spain and handed on to her. Its folds fell smoothly over her hips and flared towards the hem. Claire fastened all of its long line of buttons to the high collar at her throat and twirled around in front of the full length mirror. Away from the fragile fabrics, frills and floral hats in evidence at the races, the coat came into its own. She no longer saw herself as the 'nobody' the afternoon's events had conspired to make her feel.

On a wave of confidence and with her head held high, she went to the reception desk and asked to send a message to the Hall. The man behind the counter entered a small cubicle and Claire could hear the cranking as the phone's handle rotated. After several unsuccessful attempts he returned. He was, he told her, unable to get through to the village switchboard. If she would like to wait he would try again later. What else was there to do? Claire went back outside and after what seemed a long time, returned. Again he tried, to no avail.

She sat in the garden awhile, taking in the peace, trying to quell the unfamiliar emotion the James and Arrabella image had aroused and to accept how inappropriate her feelings were, for James was destined to marry, if not Arrabella, then another, cast in similar mould and all her hurting could not change that one jot. The time she had spent with him in the Lakes, would she have been wiser not to have gone? But she had been through that many times already. She should be glad of the insights the afternoon had brought.

Maybe she should go back to the station and wait in hope. She was on the verge of leaving, when a shadow fell across her. A tall man, of good physique, well dressed, possibly in his early thirties, was standing before her.

When he spoke, his English was perfect, but bore traces of a foreign accent. He told her he had overheard at the reception that she was having difficulties. It would please him, if in some way, he could be of help. Striving to match his self possession, Claire assured him that, whilst appreciating his kindness, it really was not necessary.

"You mentioned Ardleagh Hall. I know of the place. It is en-route to my destination. Perhaps, if the telephone still fails, you would accept I drive you there," he offered.

Claire softened her refusal with a smile. She had no wish to encourage him, but his considerate manner was balm indeed to the bruises of the day. She raised her eyes to his. They were dark, very dark. He roused her interest, intrigued her. When he suggested that if she intended to continue waiting, maybe she would consent to pass the time by taking a glass of wine with him, it seemed unnecessarily churlish to refuse. His persuasive charm was such she had no wish to appear ungracious.

The wine was served, white and chilled, in long stemmed glasses, but it was of this man's courtesy that Claire deeply drank. He offered what she needed at that moment and it was a potent brew. He was in the right place, at the right time and Claire was vulnerable to the aura he exuded, appreciative of his old world manners. Excusing herself she rose, returned to the desk and waited a little nervously as the phone proved its unreliability yet again. Having followed her, the stranger again proposed he drive her home. What should she do? She did not know this man.

But it was soon obvious that the receptionist, not only knew him, but held him in high regard and sensing Claire's uncertainty, intimated how fortuitous the offer was, because as he pointed out, even when the trains were running, not all would stop at Ardleagh. The luxuriously large, black automobile belonging to her new found friend was parked outside. Of the two options available it seemed the safer to accept. Thinking of the boxes Claire decided that they, like her, would have to take their chance.

Soon, the unknown man had steered the car onto the road and they were heading for the Hall. During the journey, Claire learned he was Rumanian and endowed with an unpronounceable name. He suggested she simply address him as Bude. According to his story, his family had lost a great deal owing to the two Balkan and 1914-18 wars. He was, so Claire supposed, one of the many European exiles one often read about in the newspapers, flotsam on the waves of revolution still flooding the continent. Bude did not drive quickly nor, so it seemed to Claire, did he take the shortest route, but she was pleasantly disposed towards him and after the wine and in the cushioned comfort of the car, she was content to take the longer, prettier road.

After some time, the lanes began to look familiar. As they approached the Hall Claire decided, having given the matter some thought, that she was not going to direct this handsome man in his splendid car to the servants' entrance. For once, she was going to be swept in through the tall, grand gates of the front entrance, up the imposing drive in style, right up to the portico and stately front door. The afternoon had hardened her and if complaint were made, she would stand her ground. She had complaints of her own she would put forward.

It felt quite wonderful. The car drew to a standstill and he handed her out. With characteristic gallantry, he took her finger tips kissing the air a little above them and courteously took his leave.

Stepping back into the shadows she watched his car roll smoothly down the drive. Other than the grounds-man there was nobody around. Claire made her way to the rear of the house. The servants, save for the one on duty at the back entrance, were busy elsewhere. The family had not yet returned from the races and taking advantage of the moment, Claire passed by the back stairway and ventured down the hall into the family's private domain.

As it was now, with no other presence to disturb the flow of feeling, no other element to weaken the bond of enchantment it cast, she could feel the true atmosphere of the house itself. In the doorway of the gracious drawing room Claire remained quite still, absorbing the loveliness, savouring this opportunity to have it to herself and for this little while, to imagine she had a right to be there.

The evening sun was streaming through the old, mullioned windows, shedding their diamond patterns on the floor's ancient wood and Claire wondered, how many long bygone summers had passed, since the sun had nurtured the oak from which it came, and she thought also of the summers yet to come in which James' children would play upon these very boards, patterned again by the sun's rays gleaming through these panes.

'Whatever darkens his relationship with his father,' reflected Claire, 'his father's attitude is not integral to James' nature. He cannot let his father dictate to him, nor must he turn his back and walk away, but face him and stand firm for this is where he was born, is the place where he belongs.'

Our true heritage is more than parents and possessions. It is what we are. It is the bonds woven into our being, the talents, aptitudes and abilities gifted to us at our birth, realities that do not change. We may not like what life hands on, but we do not change it by throwing it aside. We change it by accepting it and making it the best that it, and we, can be.

Yet, in the Lakes James had spoken as if it could be tossed away, neither knowing nor considering the consequences, perhaps realising only when, irredeemably, it was too late and he was living his regrets…regrets for which she could not allow herself to be the cause.

Today's happenings were no different to what had gone before and, if she stayed, would be so again.

She should be glad James was with Arrabella. It showed he had accepted what she had said, as she must accept. It was the price to pay. She must go. This was James' world and soon he would be arriving home.

CHAPTER FIFTEEN

Later the same day

For all of them the day was to prove one of portent and change. For weeks past Ralph had been trying to create a rapport between Leonora and himself and although he had been doing well it had not been the plain sailing to which he was accustomed. The combination of her rigidly structured life at boarding school, the emotional sterility of her father's control laced through with his religion's dogma and dictate, together with the ingrained correctness of her Spanish upbringing had not exactly tutored her in the art of flirtation. But Ralph had advantage on his side, for neither had it provided her with the know-how of keeping her balance when dealing with the ploys of a male, skilled in sweeping comely maidens off their feet.

At twenty-four, Ralph Rawlinson was as attractive as they come. The combination of his manly physique, intensely blue eyes, ready wit and almost feline nonchalance of manner was magnetic. He had doubled his efforts this afternoon. Calculatedly, but with sensitivity and subtle charm, he had succeeded in awakening in Leonora her first awareness of desire. His whispered asides hinted of both romance and intrigue but, by being six years older and knowing his way around, he conveyed the impression she was safe with him.

By the time the party was breaking up, a certain understanding had been established between them. His father, not unaware of his son's success, was amused and in a further flush of generosity, indulged in the expansive gesture of making Ralph a gift of Mr Sandman. Ralph was delighted. The horse would be running again soon and Leonora happily accepted an invitation to the race.

The long afternoon was drawing to a close, but the forces that had set it in motion were not yet spent. In Manchester, the demonstration and speeches were over. Martin had arranged to meet with his Union friends and had invited James to come along.

"If it's what you wish, you're very welcome," he said. Then, sensing James' hesitation, added, part in truth, part jokingly, "…and don't worry, as a friend of mine, you won't have to say who you are. No-one will question your credentials."

James was pleased. It was a good opportunity to see things from a different perspective and he was in no rush to go home. He had planned to break his news to his parents tomorrow. Tonight would not be a good time to discuss it.

The meeting was being held in a large, upstairs room in one of the city's better known public houses. By the time James and Martin arrived, the air was already thick with honest talk and tobacco smoke. The topics being discussed ranged across a wide political spectrum and opinions concerning them were vastly different, but right or wrong and however varied, their common ground was their unity of purpose in the betterment of the common man. Martin was greeted on all sides as he shouldered his way through the crush to the raised table where representatives of the Trade Unions and a committee of sorts, were loosely gathered. Unobtrusively James found a seat near the front and settled down to listen. It was going to be a long night.

Back at Ardleagh, Frederick was alone in his study. He was waiting for James to come home, not something he would normally do but tonight was different. In his unsettled state Frederick was convinced that his son's unannounced appearance and unexplained absence were definitely linked and he needed to know what he was doing.

It was late. Margaret had gone to bed long ago, but she was not sleeping. She also was sitting up, waiting. She had tried to read, but the silence was strangely ominous and she was uneasy, unable to keep her mind off the storm that was brewing between her husband and son. She knew it was coming. Frederick had got into a dreadful mood this afternoon and it had worsened when he started to be unwell. Of course, with Rawlinson there he had tried not show it, but she knew.

He was often indisposed these days, easily hassled, but his complaints of late were mostly because things were not as he wanted, or as he put it, not 'right and proper', by which needless to say, he meant, not the way they used to be. "Well of course they're not. They never can be, but that's what he won't accept. He thinks the clock can be turned back," she grumbled…adding, not without a touch of sarcasm, "…if we all keep pushing hard enough, for what's 'right and proper'."

She had seen it at the races this afternoon, how he could not enjoy himself if things did not turn out as planned and it had not pleased him to hear Rawlinson's luck was thanks to his own engineer. He had tried to laugh it off, but it had needled him. So, he had lost the race, well actually it was the horse that lost it, but it was only a horse for goodness' sake. It was not as though he and Rawlinson were competing athletes and Rawlinson had run faster. Why let the man, irk him so? It must be something to do with that land deal, whatever that was and why on earth had he invited him and his party to join them? He knew Rawlinson was a man to crow about his triumphs, so why not let him crow in his own box. She herself had been stuck with Rawlinson's over-talkative wife and Arrabella had been no help. She was not talking at all, poor girl. She was far too upset at James spurning her like that and Leonora neglecting her as well, going off with Ralph who, in total contrast, was all attention to her. Really, it had been this, that and the other all afternoon.

Downstairs, Frederick was still in his study, brooding, his imagination taunting him. He would have liked to go to bed, but not until he knew what James was up to. When inviting the Barrington Curzons he never thought James would behave as he had, and why had he come back so suddenly from Berlin? He had volunteered nothing during their drive to the races, though heaven knows he had prompted him enough and where the hell was he now?

Frederick still had his headache. He had had it a lot of late. He was not coping as well as he used to, was worrying more, but in times past his worries had been only what he could expect, given his position and lifestyle and there had always been ready answers. It had been easier to delegate. Staff stayed at their posts for years and knew what they were doing.

Not so now, too much was uncertain. Fears that the Labour Party with their threats of Nationalisation may seize power in the coming election, the Trade Unions encouraging strikes and who knew what may come out of their Rally in Manchester this afternoon. Could that be where James was? If he were, what the hell was he doing mixing with a conglomeration of rowdy Lefties? It was not something young Rawlinson would do. Ralph may have his faults but, as had been obvious this afternoon, disloyalty was not one. Thoughts of Rawlinson triggered the worry that he still had not parted with the land he needed. Damn it, whenever it crossed his mind without warning it unnerved him. He sat back in his chair and closed his eyes. His head was throbbing. He ought not to have drunk the champagne. A top-up of brandy usually settled his stomach, but it had not worked tonight.

He leaned forward, reaching for the brandy on the table and, stretching a little further, half rose. His arm, still extended, felt strangely stiff and heavy. As he lifted the heavy decanter, it was afflicted by an incapacitating numbness and his fingers lost their grip. The crystal container fell, bouncing off the fender onto the tiled hearth and the splintering smash that followed, pierced his head. With shards of pain searing inside his skull, he reached out blindly to save himself.

Already insensate, he did not hear the second, heavier crash as it resounded through the Hall, but Margaret, still awake heard it and came running. Struggling to help himself, Frederick had lost consciousness and slumped across the nearby occasional table, sending it and the weighty marble lamp upon it hurtling to the floor. He was, when she found him, sprawled out awkwardly among the debris, his limbs at strange angles.

James had found the meeting interesting and the attitude of the Union members seemed constructive. Lloyd George, a liberal, was currently Prime Minister but was expected to fall from office soon and preparations for a general election were being made. The Labour Party was gaining support and judging from what was said, its leaders were set on proving themselves worthy if they came to power, respecting tradition and observing established practice.

The talk had gone on for ages and it was very late when he left. His parents would have retired hours ago. He would be careful to make no noise. He wanted no bother in the morning when talking to his father, but if there were, he consoled himself the unpleasantness would be of short duration because he would soon be leaving for Berlin. He must see Claire before he went. She was still very much in his thoughts and on hearing of his place in the orchestra, maybe she would change her mind.

Arriving at Ardleagh, he swung his car in through the front gates. He realised immediately something was amiss. Two large cars he did not recognise were at the front entrance and the windows along the upper landing of the great house were in darkness. He sped up the drive and, forgetting his resolve, braked sharply scattering the gravel. His father did not hear the sound he had so long awaited. He was lying unconscious in one of the downstairs rooms. The specialist, waiting in the Hall, informed James his father had suffered a severe stroke.

James thanked him and hurried to be with his mother. She was sitting by her husband's bed, her clasped hands resting in her lap. On first seeing her he was relieved to find her so composed, until he realised she was still in shock, clinging to a firm belief that the specialist's diagnosis was wrong and that Frederick's loss of consciousness was due to a severe blow to his head, inflicted by the heavy marble lamp when falling from the table as it overturned.

"You'll see," she assured him. " When he regains consciousness he may be suffering from concussion, but he will be fine."

James knew differently, but aware of the comfort her erroneous belief was affording her, he hesitated to reply. 'Given what she must have suffered on finding him, it would be unkind to distress her further tonight,' he concluded. 'The hard truth will make itself known soon enough.'

The long drawn-out waiting which the physician had said was all that one could do, was just beginning and James stayed with his mother throughout the night. The helpless man on the bed bore no resemblance to the father he had always known, dominant and in control. He could only pray that any incapacity the stroke may cause, would be minimal and of short duration.

The hours passed, until slowly, the dawn began to lighten the dark sky. James crossed to the window. The coming day would change his life completely.

How could he tell his mother now, that he was leaving for Berlin?

Claire woke early, knowing nothing of the calamity that had occurred. The room she was now in was cramped and dingy, in the attic on the far side of the house, with only one tiny window and no view. The one that had been hers was now fitted with extra hanging rails, cupboards for accessories, shelves and shoe racks for Leonora's expanded wardrobe.

It was one of her rare, free days and she planned to visit the public park on the outskirts of the city, walk in its extensive grounds, listen to the concert in the bandstand and perhaps take a rowboat on the lake. It would help to take her thoughts off yesterday and restore her peace of mind. She decided against going down for breakfast. Had she done so, she would have learned of the Earl's stroke, for Elliott was there, telling the staff of the happenings of the night. His demeanour dismally befitted the pervading gloom, for in trying to help Lady Margaret when first finding the Earl unconscious, he had badly strained his back and was still suffering the pain.

The park was very beautiful at this time of the year. Autumn, it was her favourite season. It was, as one poet had written, "When Nature unburdens herself of her harvest and takes rest." Coming to a bench, she sat down and, conscious of the peace surrounding her, closed her eyes, listening intently to every sound both near and far. The beauty and constancy of the natural world blunted the sharp edges of her cares, lessening their power to hurt and she became content. During the journey back, her calm remained and she felt more confident than she had for some time.

All was very different at the Hall. As she entered the cobbled yard, Anna came to meet her and give her the news. But it was not the whole story. The staff had been told little and much of what Claire was hearing was what the servants had surmised.

Lady Margaret had been up all night and had been advised to get some rest. James was in his father's room keeping vigil over the sick man. Frederick had recovered consciousness early that morning and tried to speak, but the specialist who was with him had been unable to tell what he was saying and, becoming agitated, he had blacked out again. Stressing the importance of his father not being upset and, knowing James would understand him much better, he had strongly advised James not to leave his bedside and James had agreed.

Amelia was due to arrive. Amelia who in the past had at times been dubbed too carefree, was now the one towards whose coming all were looking forward. Her very presence would help lift the gloom and breathe sound sense into the air of despair that was threatening to take hold.

" 'Er 'll 'elp get rid o' the misery alright. 'Er won't be able to mek it right nor 'im any better but 'er 'll be like a breath o' spring an' er'll mek it all feel better, an' us wi' it," said one of the older housemaids who had known Amelia for years. On arrival, Amelia displayed an ability to organise of which Margaret would not have deemed her capable. She promptly arranged the appointment of a live-in nurse and had followed this by engaging a second, highly recommended specialist to thoroughly appraise her brother's condition and give advice on the best available treatment. As soon as Frederick could be moved, he was to occupy a room on the sunnier south side of the house, overlooking the garden.

At first, when hearing of his brother-in-law's illness, Alva had hoped the changes at the Hall would speed his daughter's return to Spain. It took him no more than a couple of days to realise that far from being the proverbial ill wind, there was nothing at all fortuitous about it. Frederick had been Alva's ally in his battle with Amelia, for he, like Alva, also wished her permanently back in Spain. In fact, hoping that his niece's debut would prove a finale to the arrangement that had necessitated his sister's visits, Frederick, had been very cooperative and had offered the Park Lane House as a venue for her Coming-Out Ball and other entertaining. He was also to have presented his niece at Court when she made her debut. These arrangements were now to be cancelled along with those of his and his wife's calendar for the London Season. It was agreed however that there was nothing to be gained by postponing Leonora's debut and, in lieu of the Park Lane House Amelia decided to take a house in Belgravia.

This was not at all what Alva wanted, but given the changed circumstances how could he refuse? Apart from the loss of Frederick's support, Alva was further chafed that Fate, once again, had played into his wife's hands. For years she had wanted to have a place abroad and scheming she may be, but he had to admit, Frederick's stroke had nothing to do with her, except, so he imagined, trying to put the dark thought from his mind, she had more than likely raised her brother's stress levels. The whole performance of this debutante business was something Alva could well do without and he was far from happy with the Englishness of it all. He wanted Leonora married without delay, but he could hardly use that as argument for her return to Spain, not when Amelia still knew nothing of his plans.

After two more days of lying comatose, Frederick again regained consciousness. James was at his bedside. Distressing moments followed in which his father tried to talk. His speech was slurred, almost incoherent, but James understood only too well what was being asked of him. Margaret had watched her son battling within himself before hearing him tell his father he must not worry, that yes, he would stay at Ardleagh and do all he could to help in the running of the mines, adding, in a caveat born of desperate hope, "until you recover". Margaret was relieved. It meant James would be at home and settled and the rift between him and his father would be healed.

Initially it had been Claire's intention to take a governess course when her position as Leonora's maid ended and for the last three years she had been putting her savings into a Post Office account. Surprised however at the pleasure she found in caring for Leonora's beautiful gowns, their exquisite colours and fabrics, the soft velvets and silken satins, she had begun to take an interest in fashion. Designer dresses were expensive and many society women were cutting costs by having dress-makers copy the latest models. It appeared an attractive alternative to being a governess. It was also more lucrative and although money could not buy happiness, it was certainly the key to education, health, freedom and independence. It offered choices and could buy time and other life-enhancing advantages. She had decided therefore to take a course in dress design and tailoring instead, but owing to her having been asked to remain as maid to Leonora during her debut Season, Claire had believed the time for her departure was still some months away.

This was no longer so. Amelia's plans for her daughter's debut were different now and, concerned at what the changes would mean for Claire, she spoke to Margaret who said other work would be found for her. Totally distracted however by what had happened to her husband, some days elapsed before Margaret informed the housekeeper. With no suitable vacancy available, there was a further delay and the housekeeper eventually passed the problem over to Cook.

James' hopes of persuading Claire to go back with him to Berlin were cruelly dashed. He now had no contract and nothing to go back to. Everything was in the air and he himself was tied down at Ardleagh. He was beginning to question the wisdom of his promise to his father, for surely there were others who could have taken over, but he could not back out. The present domestic upheaval, his mother's dependency on him, the need to sort out precisely what was now required of him and his angst at the disruption to his career, fully absorbed James' time and attention.

Meanwhile Claire had received a letter from Bude. There was he wrote, something he wished to discuss. Remembering the receptionist at the inn, she was reasonably confident regarding his respectability and agreed. In her present circumstances, with previous plans cancelled and no replacement offered, what was there to lose?

Bude was a man for whom nothing was mundane, an artist who had made photography his medium. He looked on all objects and encounters as worthy of assessment, perusing them for whatever possibility they may hold. His skill was more than mere portrayal, more than camera, light and shade alone could achieve. His technique lay in bringing forth underlying aspects he observed in the subjects he worked on, hidden facets that he, and possibly only he had noticed. Then, as he focussed upon them, he changed them, transforming them into becoming what he alone had seen. This was his way of possessing, of moulding what he saw to his own imagery, shaping its potential into the form that he intended it to be.

That instance in the garden of the inn, when he had first caught sight of Claire, lost in private thought, still and motionless, he had pledged himself to satisfy the urge she aroused in him to capture and create.

During their meeting Bude spoke of his agency in fashion photography and advertising and that he had been approached by a well-known clothing store in Manchester. Without further preamble, he told Claire he wished to employ her and take her portrait. He knew the result would be special. She hesitated but on parting agreed to consider it. Within days he contacted her again. The contract with the clothing store had been signed. If Claire refused, he must use another model. The firm was waiting. How quickly could she let him know?

Shakespeare's words, "There is a tide in the affairs of man, that taken at the flood leads on to fortune," flashed across Claire's mind, along with the truism, "More men miss their chance, than are missed by chance." Having turned down Cook's offer of helping in the kitchen, was this the chance she must not miss? Fashion was certainly in keeping with her own interests and intentions.

She still believed James was with Arrabella. Why otherwise had he returned to Ardleagh prior to his father's stroke before his three month's tuition had ended and was now staying, running the mines. Surely he knew she was no longer employed at the Hall.

But James did not know. He simply assumed Amelia and Leonora were in London on another shopping spree. He was totally unaware their departure was final and believed Claire was still in her post as Leonora's maid-companion.

Bude's contract offered a year's guarantee and a salary beyond Claire's expectations and with no other options, it seemed her only viable alternative and she accepted.

Hearing Claire was no longer at the Hall James was both shocked and confused. He knew nothing of the events that had occurred on the day of the race, nor of her misconceptions regarding him and Arrabella. Learning later, of her loss of employment and how she had been treated, his anger rose. Now she had gone, his musical career was thwarted and he was back at Ardleagh, committed to doing the very things he had vowed he never would.

When John Barrington Curzon called to enquire about Frederick's health, Margaret pressed him to visit again with Arrabella, but he had not done so. It was disheartening particularly so since the young woman had discreetly indicated she was favourably disposed. The specialists could not tell Margaret when, or even if, Frederick would recover. Her own life was in limbo. Amelia and Leonora were away in London. James was behaving strangely. He had practically hammered the piano this afternoon and Arrabella, dear girl, was upset and let down.

'Oh, the obduracy of it all,' she sighed, so many lives at crossroads with no signposts telling where they may lead.

How strange it is. We follow our hopes, draw up our plans, plot our lives on the drawing board of our dreams, all unaware, never seeing nor suspecting how each private dream becomes a public property when once one starts to build, never knowing how much it may be altered or impaired by others in their efforts to build theirs.

...and therein lies the rub, for all too often, the others are part of the dream.

CHAPTER SIXTEEN

Madrid, Spain. Summer, 1923.

Alva was seated in the window of his drawing room overlooking the well-tended rear gardens of his extensive Madrid home.

It was well into the afternoon and the city was stirring again after the siesta. Rising from his chair, he crossed to the long windows and went out onto the balcony, leaned against its decorative, iron-lace surround and looked down into the flower-filled patio below. All appeared to be well, tranquil and calm. An unknowing observer could be absolved from believing that here was a most contented man. The reality was different.

Alva was concerned. There had been disturbances and during the night gunfire had been heard, two, single, assured shots, those of a marksman who knows his bullets will strike home. Raimundo had warned of a crisis in the offing but was being tight-lipped, refusing to say more on the excuse that certain issues had yet to be resolved. Alva found the uncertainty unsettling. He dearly wanted to know, but meanwhile was following his friend's advice and not pressing for his family's return.

He had planned, when Leonora's season came to an end, to take his wife and daughter on a continental holiday during which he intended to inform Amelia of Georgio's, as yet unmentioned, 'offer' for their daughter's hand, to persuade her of the young man's suitability as a husband, of the fortuity of his proposal and of the several advantages attaching to it. He had been hoping both she and Leonora would be pleased, excited even for Georgio had matured into a most eligible suitor. His battle experience at Annual had etched hardness on his once boyish looks and endowed him with self-assurance, best seen in uniform with his newly acquired decorations on display.

To all of this Raimundo's cooperation was vital, yet here he was, insisting on a delay. Clearly, whatever the impending crisis, the Army was involved and without a doubt, Raimundo was putting his career before all else. Alva had therefore cancelled the continental holiday for he had no intention of unveiling any of his plans to Amelia until they could be implemented without delay He knew to his cost the folly of giving her time to think. Even so, he was chafing over this further hindrance for time was of the essence, especially since Amelia's wish for Leonora to remain in England was now being aided and abetted by Leonora herself who, for no reason known to him, was behaving quite petulantly whenever spoken to about returning to Spain.

During his daughter's coming out Season he had complied with all requests made of him and had visited London several times. But he had not enjoyed it and was glad when it was over. Having done his duty he had insisted they vacate the large and expensive house in Belgravia that Amelia had rented to serve in place of the one in Park Lane. It was gratifying that she had agreed without protest. At least it was until he learned that on relinquishing the large house, she had bought another, with his money. 'A teeny, pied-a-terre, tres petit', was how she described it when breaking the news.

Given that the transaction had already taken place, there was little he could do. He could of course, legally refuse to pay debts incurred by his wife without his knowledge but his action would be reported in the gossip columns portraying him as mean and petty, something she had known he would not consider. Again he was in a situation not of his choosing, for it facilitated her staying in London with Leonora, shopping for essentials, which basically meant for clothes, or to attend the opera, or the ballet, concerts and art galleries, museums and 'must see' exhibitions, all of which were made to sound intrinsic to Leonora's education but which were anything but. It was giving his daughter all the wrong ideas, teaching her to be extravagant, and would make it far more difficult to settle her down afterwards.

Compared with the decorum of lifestyle in Spain, London society was far too liberal, licentious even and he viewed the modern trends in fashion with extreme distaste. He particularly abhorred the changes in female dress, the bobbed hair, uncorseted torsos, short skirts, exposed legs, dropped waists and flat chests adorned by long, swinging ropes of pearls as worn by the un-chaperoned, young women now flaunting themselves. 'Flappers', he had heard them called.

He was no happier when dining in the evenings. Dressed for dinner, skirts were back to full length but this modicum of modesty was more than offset by the low décolletage displayed by some women, the nearly backless cut of their evening gowns and the figure-clinging flimsiness of the chiffon from which they were made, all evidence of the decadence the new modernity had spawned. London was not the place it once was and it was quite unsuitable for his wife and daughter to be there unescorted.

It was while he had been pondering his options that Raimundo had advised him to leave his wife and daughter where they were for the time being and although frustrated, Alva was biding his time. Confrontations with Amelia availed him little and Amelia had ammunition of her own. As she had more than once reminded him, his promises that calm would be restored to Spain, made yet again, so convincingly to her four years ago, had still not materialised.

The backlash that had been provoked and the military's brutal repression had taken place according to plan, but the scale and ferocity of the insurgents' retaliation had exceeded all expectation and was not being contained. As reprisal followed reprisal, atrocities intensified and on both sides, revenge begot revenge. Men died, but the hatred lived on and in and around estates in Cordoba, unrest was rife and the violence was increasing.

Hoping to weaken the peasants, the Andalucian landowners had withdrawn concessions. The watering of animals, the gathering of windfall crops, collection of firewood and even the rebusca, the gleaning of the fallen olives left on the ground after the harvest, all had been denied them. The measures had afforded no gain to the landowners for though they did debilitate the peasants, they greatly strengthened their resentment and the parched, dry air of Andalucia was taut with fears of worse to come.

There had been a worrying incident a few weeks ago. Bastanta had been missing for two days before turning up in a state of utter exhaustion, sullen, bruised and determinedly uncommunicative.

"...could get nothing from him." Virgo had reported. "...nothing. It bodes badly for those gone against him."

'Yes,' thought Alva, concerned by the implication of Bastanta's silence, 'it bodes badly.' Whatever it was his cacique had been given a taste of in the two days before escaping, which he certainly must have done for his captors would not have just let him go unharmed, it had dented Bastanta's confidence if not his courage, for in the past when satisfying his lust for revenge, Bastanta had always been bold, boastful and unafraid to claim credit for his deeds, a warning to others to stay away from the Arradova preserves.

This time was different. Bastanta's tight-lipped concealment of the identity of those responsible, would render him less likely to be seen as the all too obvious perpetrator of the vengeance he would undoubtedly later inflict and the significance of Bastanta's change of behaviour filled Alva with foreboding.

'Even he has come to realise we're now up against something bigger than in the past,' Alva reasoned, 'an enemy no longer easily cowed, an enemy stronger and more organised and capable of striking back and this way, keeping the identity of his attackers to himself, he's less likely to be targeted for his reprisals after making his aggressors his victims. Yes, Bastanta also has become wary. He too has sensed a change taking place.'

Finally, news came from Raimundo. It seemed insignificant, but was far from being so. It concerned the conclusions of the Enquiry into the Army's crushingly disastrous defeat and appalling loss of life at Annual in Morocco, two years ago. Hopelessly overpowered by the Riffian tribesmen, the Spanish Army had totally lost control. As one fort after another had fallen into the hands of the tribal hordes, there had been panic. Fifteen thousand Spanish soldiers and civilians had been massacred, with Melilla itself in danger of being taken. The General in charge, Fernandez Silvestre, had committed suicide. The findings of the Enquiry were now being made known.

The King was said to have contributed to the calamity. Once again, Alphonse X111's irresponsible interference in military matters had resulted in dire consequences and much of the responsibility for the catastrophe was now laid upon him. He was blamed for the rash telegram he had sent on the eve of battle, to General Silvestre, a close personal friend of his. It was reputed to have read, 'Ole, boys, I'm waiting for the 25th,' and was believed to have induced a madcap recklessness in Silvestre's decisions. The King's informal friendship with General Silvestre had already caused concern and the imprudence of his ill-considered incitement to the incautious Silvestre was believed to have spurred that General to impulsive and foolhardy action.

"The King's not going to be forgiven," declared Raimundo. "It's not the first time his familiarity with Army officers, favouring them at the expense of the politicians, has had serious repercussions. His attitude stems from his resentment at having had his wishes thwarted during his minority. Twenty years on, and his attitude is still the same. When the Enquiry's verdict's made public there'll be an angry response. It could affect the survival of the monarchy itself."

"I doubt it..." responded Alva. "Any fuss will be the usual much ado about nothing." He was irritated at Raimundo's attempt to endow this boring report with a sense of drama. After waiting to learn about the crisis, was this it? He had been hoping to hear some real news, something that would cut ice with Amelia.

"So, is that all?" he asked, sounding bored.

"Oh, there's more to come. There needs to be if confidence in the Monarchy and the Military is to be restored."

"So now what?" queried Alva, not expecting much of an answer.

"A Military Dictatorship," came the reply

"What?" Alva's attitude changed abruptly.

"You heard," Raimundo said calmly. "We had a good idea of the report's findings and had a meeting a few weeks ago, but had to wait for its release."

"We? Who's we...and when?" Alva asked, startled at the decision.

"The leading Generals, we're all agreed and the King has acquiesced. He knows he can't survive without the Military. General Miguel Primo de Rivera is the chosen man. He was Captain General of Catalonia, very capable, and the Dictatorship will support the King much in the way this Mussolini fellow in Italy and his black shirted Fascist Party are helping King Victor Emmanuel keep his throne. We're not expecting any opposition. The people have had enough of this government and its politicians. They'll accept a popular General, especially when it's known the King's agreed and that Largo Cabellero has vouched for the Socialists. He says they'll cooperate, make no trouble."

"Cabellero," Alva's tone was one of outrage, "you mean to say you've had Cabellero in on your talks...that Socialist."

"Alright. Admit it. You've a bee in your bonnet about the man, but it's only now, now that we know the Enquiry's findings and will definitely be carrying out our plans, that we've been talking to him. We do need to gauge what, if anything, we might run up against."

Trying to cloak his bad feeling Alva shifted in his seat but did not reply. There was no denying what his friend said. His dislike of Cabellero was intense. The man was the mainstay of the 'Union General de Trabajadores, the Socialist Workers' Trade Union, known in short as the U.G.T. He was nonviolent, strictly observing all legalities, and had become too well regarded, too important a figure. He was far too respected for a Socialist, plus having gathered too much of a following, more by his example than his words, for the man was no orator. 'But that was only to be expected,' reflected Alva, 'given that he had been nothing more than a common plasterer before becoming a Union official.'

Raimundo did not press his point. He knew he had touched a nerve and rose to take his leave.

"I'm staying in Madrid, in readiness for the Proclamation. We'll meet again soon." He looked cheerful, in robust health, "...and don't worry, my friend," he added, exuding his usual confidence. "There'll be no trouble, but I'd leave your wife and daughter where they are for a while."

After his military friend had departed, Alva was uneasy. "No trouble," the General had said. 'But maybe he's right,' reasoned Alva, resigning himself. 'Anything's bound to be better than what we have now.'

It was in 1868 that, due to her immoral ways, the then reigning Queen Isabella11 had been banished from the Spanish throne by the aptly named General Prim. She had been handed in marriage to her cousin, a sore misfortune for according to Court gossip he was impotent. Her courtiers had more to gossip about when it was rumoured she was indulging in sexual affairs with different men, behaviour for which her unhappy situation was not considered sufficient excuse.

The tittle-tattle had continued. The prattle spread beyond Court circles into the public domain and she was labelled a nymphomaniac. Talk that her children had been sired by different men called into question the paternity of the heir to the throne, causing not only serious scandal but playing straight into the Carlists' hands. The empty throne spurred them on afresh and there was turmoil in the land.

Different solutions were sought and tried, but to no avail. Spain's First Republic was formed, but did not last. As the Army battled to maintain order its generals decided to restore the Monarchy and Queen Isabella's son, a cadet at Sandhurst in England at the time, became King Alphonse X11. Sadly however, in 1885 the new King died while his son, the present King Alphonse X111, was still in the womb.

Once again, the Army became the protector of the Throne, thus increasing its power and influence and entrenching itself even more in the domestic affairs of government.

'So who else but the Army, to restore order?' Alva asked himself. 'Even so...a Military Dictatorship, is it legal, in accord with the Constitution?'

But there was much already that was neither legal nor in accord with the Constitution. The political system was riddled with corruption. Threats were commonplace. Elections were rigged. Peasants were attacked if not voting as ordered and glass urns were often used as ballet boxes, making secrecy impossible. The law courts provided no redress. Witnesses were intimidated and it seemed that those in charge cared only about feathering their own nests. In the last five years a succession of Conservative governments had failed and only two years ago the Prime Minister, Eduardo Dato, had been murdered. Small wonder many saw violence as their only way to help themselves.

One could only hope the Military Dictatorship would succeed.

It was in September that the Proclamation was made and the Cortes suspended. It was not legal, but it was what happened. The Directorate was set up and General Primo de Rivera became Military Dictator of Spain. In Madrid the Commander in Chief declared his troops to be at the disposal of the King and with the backing of the King and the cooperation of the Socialists, all promised to go as intended.

In the evening Raimundo and Alva went out to dine. The new Dictator had spoken at length and much of what was said could not be denied. The parliamentary regime had been corrupt. Tampering with the voting system had enabled it to retain its hold on power. The Army, he stated, had no need to justify its action, "...for the people and their common sense demand it." Primo de Rivera was right on many counts but most of all he was right about the people and their common sense, for when he told them, "...the garrisons would not agree to anything other than a Military Dictatorship and the Army was resolved to be moderate, but would not shrink from bloodshed if opposed," his listeners' common sense came greatly to the fore.

The Anarchists were still at daggers drawn with the Military, but it seemed their reserves were depleted. The Socialists' Union, the U.G.T., had gained the respect of the bourgeoisie due to its discipline and reasonable way of conducting itself. It had no wish to lose its good name and provided Largo Cabellero led them, the Socialists would collaborate with the Dictatorship.

For the Army it was a day of triumph, for Alva and Raimundo, a night of celebration. They talked and, along with other topics, spoke of their arrangement. With the Army in power and Raimundo's prestigious elevation to The Directorate, the opportunity for Georgio to gain further promotion was enhanced.

Having finished their meal, the port was poured. Exchanging knowing glances, they raised their glasses.

'Leonora', thought Alva, '...will make a lovely bride.'

CHAPTER SEVENTEEN

Ardleagh Hall. Autumn. 1923

Lady Margaret followed the manservant as he pushed her husband's wheelchair along the path. Between the freshly cut lawns they trundled, her two newly acquired pet Pekinese trotting at her heels. Each to his own gait the small procession pressed on until it reached the favoured spot, whereupon it stopped and the customary, complicated performance of comfortably settling Lord Frederick began.

The choice of place varied, according to the weather. Today was dry and sunny and the wheeled canvas chair was turned and brought to rest in the dappling shade of the old chestnut tree. The procedure took some time but finally everything was properly arranged and Lady Margaret took out her book and having ensured that her husband was at ease, began to read aloud.

Considering how desperately ill Frederick had been at the time of his stroke twelve months ago, he had made better progress than expected, at least so his doctor insisted. His left side however was still very much affected, most particularly his leg. Margaret credited much of the improvement to James' consideration. He had been as good as his word in taking care of things and given his dislike of the mines, Margaret was surprised how knowledgeable he was. She supposed it due to the studies Frederick had insisted he undertake. Of course, he consulted with the managers and overseers but liaised mainly with the young engineer Martin Donnington from whom he obtained information about what was happening at grass-root level.

There had been fewer disputes of late but she put this down to the consequences of that major strike that began in October 1920. The government was so alarmed, a national emergency had been declared. The strike ended, but began again and was not settled until the following year when the government agreed to subsidise the coal industry.

Not long after Frederick's stroke, the Tories withdrew their support for the coalition and the Liberal Prime Minister, Lloyd George, fell from office. It had been a considerable relief when, in the election that followed, the Conservatives gained a large majority. They were sure to nail the coffin lid on the threats of Nationalisation that so worried her husband. It was unfortunate though that in May this year, the Tory Prime Minister had to resign because of ill-health and a House of Commons man, Stanley Baldwin, had taken over. It seemed he may unsettle things. 'Oh well, time will tell,' she thought.

As she often did, Margaret had paused in her reading. It gave the invalid the chance to fall asleep. She glanced across at him. Thankfully, he had. She closed the book and picked up a piece of fine lace she was working on. It was one of life's rare and tranquil moments. The mellow autumn sun shone golden. A hint of harvest was in the air. Apples were being brought in from the orchard and the chrysanthemum buds were showing peeps of their strong and glorious colours to come. The breath of a breeze rustled the leaves and as always in the fall, the heat and hurry of summer was giving way to September's gentleness.

How closely the seasons had followed one upon the other. It seemed so short a time since Leonora's debut, yet already it was over and she had been launched. In fact, Margaret was somewhat surprised at how smoothly all was running despite Frederick not being in charge. Leonora's presentation had been a great success. From all accounts, she had looked very lovely, her rich auburn colouring and delicate olive skin, strikingly offset against the white of her dress.

Margaret had been sadly disappointed not to have been there. The whole procedure was so traditional it would have changed little if at all, from when she herself had been presented. Like most debutantes, she also had been plunged, straight from the schoolroom into the grownup world, caterpillar to butterfly with barely a chrysalis stage in between.

How well she remembered it, the long queue of carriages in the Mall, moving slowly and orderly only a few yards at a time towards Buckingham Palace where crowds were waiting to catch glimpses of the debutantes, many with names already famous, some with names to become so.

Once inside the Palace, the radiance and spaciousness surrounding her had quite distracted Margaret from her nervousness. Dressed in their gowns of white, adorned with headdresses or tiaras and other accessories, many of which included ostrich feathers, the debutantes were noticeable against the lavish display of silks and taffetas of every hue worn by mothers and sisters. Some of the fathers and brothers had been in uniform, a few others in the black velvet of Court dress, complete with steel swords.

Yeomen of the Guard, as upright as their halberds, remained as ornamentally unbending as the statuary in the background. She could still recall the grandeur of it all, the upward sweep of the magnificent staircase, the profusion of white roses, the Picture Gallery, the three great drawing rooms and the shine of parquet flooring reflecting the radiant chandeliers that hung above the dense throng of guests.

A long continuing rumble of drums coming from Margaret knew not where, had announced the Royal procession's approach. Ladies sank low in curtseys. Chamberlains bowed over their white wands of office and the King and Queen mounted the dais. La crème-de-la-creme of society was present, members of Royalty and the nobility, the Corps Diplomatique and those prominent in politics, all were there in their specified positions, predetermined by protocol. A gleaming display of ceremonial paraphernalia, uniforms and gowns, medals and stars, set the scene and the debutantes had filed forth to pay their homage and to be acknowledged by their King and Queen.

Had it all been worth it, all that and The Season that followed, where had it led? It had not led anywhere really. One just rode round and round on the gay carousel of parties and outings and boating on the river, riding in the park, attending the regattas and the races and dancing through the night, all of which was what The Season was about. One met the same people, in different settings and kept circulating until, sooner or later, like the little balls in roulette wheels, many of the maidens dropped into prize slots, winning eligible future husbands for themselves or, if not so lucky or not so pretty, into merely suitable ones or, after The Season ended and months and even years began to pass, into whatever niche they could find.

She had been lucky. The Earl of Eglinton had asked for her hand. He was the most estimable of men, a very good catch indeed. Yes, she had been lucky, so she had always supposed.

The striking of the old clock in the tower sounded the hour of four and to the minute, the manservant reappeared coming back across the garden. The Pekinese stood in readiness wagging their tails and the procession reformed and wound its slow way back to the house.

When the planned continental holiday had been postponed, Amelia and Leonora had remained in London, waiting. Alva had hinted at possible political changes in the form of government in Spain. Amelia sensed the Army was in some way involved, as it always was, but whether Alva was remaining in Madrid to assist or to help prevent, what he hoped for or feared, Amelia had no idea nor did she wish to know since as far as she had seen, nothing in that country ended as intended. Promises did not come to pass. Calamities struck without warning and there was little one could do but wait and see.

In contrast, the summer in London had passed pleasantly. Her daughter's debut had been one of life's welcome distractions. Alva's absences had not created the awkwardness that, once or twice, she had feared they may and there was enough excitement left over from the fun, for invitations to be still arriving and neither she nor Leonora had been bored. Taking the smaller London house, not too far away from the one Alva had insisted they vacate had been fortuitous, despite his not having been too happy when she told him.

A young man, a Ralph Rawlinson, whom Leonora already knew and whose company she obviously enjoyed, owned a delightful little townhouse in Mayfair which he visited frequently and on the rare occasions when plans had gone askew, had proved a presentable and reliable escort. Although not exactly from the top drawer, he was well educated and wealthy, compliant to a fault and, given his courtesy and impeccable manners, she was sufficiently broadminded to let that be of no account. Certainly her brother regarded him as responsible otherwise he would not have invited him to join the Grand Tour.

Amelia had just returned from a day out to find several letters awaiting her. An ominous looking one bearing a Spanish postmark lay on the top of the pile. Its tone was dramatic and struck her as quite pompous until she realised it was not actually Alva himself speaking, but that he was quoting from some document or long winded speech. It informed her that, "on this day, the 13th September 1923, the Spanish Army, as its privilege and its tradition permit, has taken upon itself the task of restoring the honour and glory of our beloved Spain and of taking up....."

'Ah,' she thought as she read on, 'so the Army's taken over. Why not just say so?' She skipped through the next several passages, missing out all the bits about The Eternal Values and Spain being the Guardian appointed by God. The letter was lengthy, but Amelia had become adept at picking out whatever was relevant to her and flipped quickly through the remaining pages.

Pouting a little, she kicked off her shoes and poured herself a drink. So that's what all the waiting's been about. Crossing to the sofa she cupped her chin in her hand and curled herself up for a long think, after which she picked up the letter again.

'The situation in Spain will now radically change. Without question, order will now be restored,' so Alva had written. He wanted her to call to mind how patient he had been and how he was prepared to continue being so while the necessary adjustments to the new regime were taking place, but, thereafter, he was adamant, both she and Leonora must return.

Amelia gasped. "He's been patient. He's been patient, oh the effrontery!" she exclaimed. She looked again at the letter. 'The situation in Spain will now radically change,' she read. 'Oh you can bet it will.' she told herself. 'Nothing's more certain. The situation in Spain's been radically changing for the last several years, why would it stop now?'

Clearly her husband felt Right was on his side, never a good auspice. She needed a plan and allies and time. She had to work out a strategy. Her sister-in-law had repeatedly said she would welcome their company, especially now with her husband laid low. A retreat north was called for. She would start to pack and so must Leonora, for she knew Leonora did not wish to go back to Spain. Her academic results had not been good and Amelia was concerned for her future. Alva however, appeared to have no thoughts other than getting her back to Spain, why...for what? She was certain he was keeping something from her.

When word arrived from Amelia that she would like to visit Ardleagh, Margaret was delighted. She was finding the daily round trying and Amelia could cope with her brother so much better. At first, Frederick's every improvement had been an occasion for thankfulness, but as the rate of his recovery slowed, he became more impatient with what he still could not do and the atmosphere in the house was often strained.

Aware of the dangers in the mines, James was constantly concerned about conditions underground and Frederick's interference of late, giving instructions to the foremen, cancelling those James had issued without telling him, was causing friction. James' reply to his father's standard complaint that improving conditions did not come cheap was to ask, at which point did the cost become greater than men's lives, or had he not yet worked that one out? It was an impossible situation, distressing for everyone. But Frederick was in no state to take over and knowing how incapacitating his stroke had been James was afraid of a recurrence if he seriously pressed the point. With the state of affairs as it was now, there were far too many problems pending.

It was some weeks before Christmas that Amelia brought news of Claire to James. She had been sitting in the salon of an exclusive haute couture fashion house in

London and while waiting for one of their mannequins to parade a couple of dresses for her, had been leafing through some fashion plates lying on the coffee table.

"James, I felt you must see this. So I commandeered it...very naughty I know, but there are times when...'needs must'." She opened the folder she was holding, slid out a fashion advertisement and handed it to him.

The image was of Claire, one of the most exquisitely beautiful portraits he had ever seen. There was a stillness, a timelessness about her, a quiet perfection, no smile, those long lashed expressive eyes casting their reflective gaze slightly away from the camera, the silken braids of her dark tresses drawn high, before falling to the nape of her neck, her shoulders visible above the soft folds of a cream evening dress and at her throat, a small cameo.

Amelia did not speak and nor did he. The very portrait itself seemed to have created an atmosphere in the room. Like any flawless work of art, it said all that there was to say about its subject...Claire. They both stood, silent, James continuing to look at it, first in wonder, then, wondering.

"Who took this and, where?"

Amelia shook her head.

"May I keep it?" he asked.

"Of course you may, that's why I brought it. James, I know how you feel about her...I've always known. There's something about the two of you, the way each one of you looks at the other, even when you're not actually together." Amelia glanced towards him. "It's a chemistry that goes right across a room."

For a few moments, James looked away. He walked to the window, desperately beating down his emotions. Amelia had said that on first seeing it she could hardly believe it was not just a likeness. But James knew it was Claire. There, in the photo, on the little finger of her left hand was the ring he had given her long ago, only days after she had come to the Hall when her father had been killed and he had found her crying and had wanted to give her something and had taken the ring from his finger. It was a small, gold signet ring engraved with his initials and he hugged to himself the knowledge that she was still wearing it.

Turning from the window, he picked up the photo again.

"Amelia, there has to be some way to reach her. I must find out which photographer took this."

Amelia hesitated. "It seems the advert was one of a series of four. The fashion house had commissioned the photographer but when published they were so successful he withdrew from the arrangement. They seemed annoyed, said he was supposed to do more work for them, something about their having a contract with him, but that's only their story. Either way the upshot is, they've disappeared."

"They've disappeared," echoed James. "You mean they've disappeared... together?"

"Well," said Amelia, seeing the expression in James' eyes, "...if they're working together, I guess that would be so."

James was silent, trying to adjust to what he had heard, but was too drained to grapple with it. Amelia sat beside him.

"Life, it's a devil," she murmured sympathetically.

"I must find her," he repeated.

Amelia looked at him. Something in the absolutely straight and honest depth of her gaze seemed to hold a warning he should prepare himself for whatever Life may throw.

"I'd say she isn't finding life any easier either," she said. "Think gently. Hold onto that."

December, and shop windows gaily dressed for Christmas, were adding to the traditionally festive air. Leonora had enjoyed the last several months in London. She liked England. There was freedom here, a freedom she had never before experienced, not just the freedom of being able to wear what one wanted, read what one chose, visit friends' houses and attend exhibitions and concerts, but freedom from the rigidity of her father's unrelenting strictness. His emphasis on adherence to the dictates of their religion was such that she had become over-scrupulous as a child. She had heard about the Inquisition and the state of her young mind had not been helped by seeing the pictures in one of the city's churches, of Dante's inferno and another of the day of Judgement and the casting down of sinners into hell. The truly awful dread implanted by the notion of everlasting hellfire was one she had never quite outgrown and conditioned as she had been by her upbringing, Leonora had never scented the relief that lay beyond her fears.

Ralph raised the issue as they were dancing one night.

"So tell me," he had asked. "...what exactly was it you were warned about if you committed a...what did you say it was called? Oh yes, a Mortal sin, well, whatever, it certainly inspired a mortal fear in you. Alright, alright...don't tell me. In Spain, they still tie people to the stake, burn them alive and all that. No, no, don't answer," he laughed. "Honestly, I know they don't, but you're still scared of something in all you were taught as a child - and don't tell me you're not. I see it.

The other night when I...alright, alright, we won't talk about that either," and Ralph laughed again, the curve of his sensuous lips revealing stunningly white teeth.

Suddenly serious, he had stopped speaking and, moving to the music of the dance, now slow, throbbing and romantic, had pulled her firmly, closely to him. Then, as they passed a marble pillar, he leaned her against it, pressing his body into hers and with strong yet gentle hands, had teasingly taken her wrists as if to tie them behind the column and Leonora felt her body throb and her heartbeat quicken. "Tie you...to the stake..." he whispered, his lips brushing her forehead. "No, I promise I won't light the fire, not yet, just...kindle a few flames?" and looking down at her, his face very close, he whispered tenderly, "Leonora," and brought his lips down on hers to kiss her, hard and passionately.

The dance floor was crowded. The lights were dim and nobody was paying attention to them. It was the first time she had been kissed...that way, the first time she had felt her body respond.

Later, they were sitting at a tiny table, an empty bottle of champagne between them. Ralph signalled a waiter. He came with another bottle and fresh glasses. Noisily the cork popped and after the cold, frothing contents had been poured and the waiter had gone, he returned to the topic of sin.

"So what is it with these hierarchs in the Vatican, with their rules and insistence on you confessing and telling all, your venial sins and all your Mortal sins and about you being guilty of sacrilege if you skip bits out and hellfire forever if you fib, or leave chunks out?" He shook his head incredulously.

"No-one should ever tell that to a child," he said glancing across at her, his face now quite solemn. "Certainly no adult should believe it but I can see you do...or you did. Did or do? Which? As a child you used to believe it...some of it...all of it? How much? ...a little bit...the lot?"

They began to talk and despite his incredulity, he listened seriously and did not scorn her fear, but was sympathetic and Leonora, instead of pushing all the indoctrination she had been fed even further to the back of her mind, admitted, yes, the concept of everlasting hellfire had absolutely terrified her as a child, so much so she had never been able to talk about it, and its legacy...did still linger, at times.

They carried on talking and he did not mock or laugh but something in the way he spoke and in the things he said, enabled her to laugh at herself and at the dread that had so beset her, and his impersonations and descriptions of those he imagined had caused them were so very funny, their domination was no more.

Never before had Leonora heard the institutionalised Church so taken to task and her father would have gone berserk to see Ralph breaking the bonds that had held his daughter and to hear her laughter as he did.

Was it the champagne, the atmosphere, the laughter, Ralph, the lateness of the hour, the sophistication of the grown-up world around her, which of these, or was it all of them that brought the sense of sudden release, of shackles falling from her, of her becoming autonomous, truly herself, a person in her own right, able to call her mind her own? The taste of freedom, mingled with the taste of kisses. She felt like the eagle she had watched that last evening on the escarpment, soaring freely high above the mountains in the sunset's golden sky.

She too could carve her arc, could let her spirit pattern her own future against the sky of her own life. Feeling freed from her father's dictates and overpowering authority that until now she had been unable to dismiss or rise above, Leonora was falling in love. Only occasionally afterwards, just once or twice, did her fears return, the way some people, lonely in the dark, are fearful of the ghosts in which they do not believe. But this never happened when she was with Ralph. Ralph's world, the world she entered when she was with him, was safe and sane and free from fear, rational and colourful and fun. He had a way of convincing her that many of the things of which she had been afraid were no more able to hurt her than the scary-looking cardboard cut-outs of witches and evil-looking goblins hung up at Halloween which could just as easily be taken down and thrown away, provided, as he said, nobody was getting hurt, and nobody was.

The Military Dictatorship in Spain appeared to be succeeding and Alva was adamant. His wife and daughter must return home. He was convinced that with the military in power the rule of law would prevail and Amelia was afraid, for if order really were restored she would lose her only excuse not to return. She was hoping he would agree to spend Christmas with her and Leonora in London, during which time she would try to turn the success of the Dictatorship to her advantage, arguing that, with order restored, Bastanta would be well able to look after the estate and with their interests no longer under threat there was no reason why they could not spend time abroad.

Expecting difficulty in getting him to London, his ready acquiescence left her uneasy. She was similarly disconcerted by her daughter, reluctant to spend Christmas in London one day and agreeable the next. It would be nice to think Alva was now seeing things her way and that her daughter's whims were due to adolescence but she suspected this was not so.

And she was right. The apparent inconsistencies were nothing of the kind.

Although implying he was coming to London to please his wife, Alva saw the festive season, while away from the pressures of Spain, as an opportunity to persuade Amelia how advantageous to their daughter's future was Georgio's proposal and of the happiness the forthcoming marriage would bring.

For her part, Leonora wanted to be with Ralph and Ralph was not saying where he would be spending Christmas. He could see the turn Leonora's feelings had taken and it was time to touch the brake. Fun was one thing. Getting serious was another. Resultantly, Leonora was hedging her bets. With her aunt low in spirit she offered to spend Christmas between London and Ardleagh and persuaded Margaret to ask her father to consent.

The cloaked agendas of the three of them were fated to collide.

The impact occurred when Amelia, weary of waiting for the opportune moment that never arrived, finally put forward her proposals. Alva totally rejected them. She dug in her heels. His attempt to play the heavy husband met with no success. Despite appearing to be standing her ground, Amelia was nervous for Alva had kept the agreement regarding Leonora's debut and she had now run out of time. Nonetheless, she did not intend to let Leonora be hauled off to Spain when she clearly did not want to go. Stalling, she pointed out how kindly Frederick and Margaret had cared for their daughter for the last few years. Surely Alva would not now refuse Margaret's request.

Sensing the battle to come, Alva considered it wiser not to reveal his arrangement with Raimundo. After much wrangling, Amelia, conscious of the chink in her armour, conceded to go back to Spain provided their daughter could stay on at Ardleagh until Margaret was feeling better and on this they agreed.

Christmas at Ardleagh was not a cheerful affair. The atmosphere was far from merry. Even the decorations just dangled, neglected, with nobody really noticing them. Leonora was out of sorts, seemingly because Ralph had not called and when James wanted to take them all out for dinner, she did not want to leave the house in case he came when she was not there. Frederick also baulked at the idea, saying he did not want to go out in his wheelchair. More to the truth, it was because he was in no mood to celebrate, given the political situation.

When the Conservative Prime Minister's health had failed during the summer, Lord Curzon of the House of Lords had not become his successor as expected, but a man from the Commons, Stanley Baldwin. The hope was that being 'a man of the people', he would prove more acceptable to the populace. All had not gone as planned. Declaring he needed a new mandate to carry out his reforms, Baldwin had called for a snap election in November. When, in early December, the results came in, the Conservatives had lost ninety seats, forty to the Liberals and fifty to Labour. Unable to survive the combination of Labour and Liberals, the Conservatives were certain to lose office. Needless to say, the news had done Frederick no good and Christmas had not been a jolly time.

Despite having a live-in nurse, he insisted on having Margaret care for him, something she would have been glad to do if only he would try harder to be happy and thankful for the improvements he had made. Given their wealth there were so many pleasures to be enjoyed but no, the highlight of each day was their routine perambulation round the garden, weather permitting. Times were, when she was ready to believe it was a perverse way of punishing them all himself included, ridiculous though that may seem, for the misfortune that had befallen him, but at least he was alive, not like Austen.

Shortly after Austen had joined the Army, she and Frederick had called at Asprey's in Bond Street, one of London's 'finest purveyors of fine things' and found what they were looking for, a powerful periscope, the very best available. Frederick had heard a little about trench warfare and had thought it would prove useful. It came lying in its perfectly fitted, red velvet lined leather case, complete with a quite lovely clasp. Only much later when the war was over and Margaret saw those awful newsreels of shell splattered, dazed and wounded men staggering in mud-filled trenches, or lost deep in mud bogs or holed up like animals in earth burrows, in one long, misery-sodden nightmare of no awakening in a war of no end, had she come to understand the twisted half-smile that had come over Austen's face when, during his all too short last leave, she had asked why he had left the periscope in his room.

Thinking again of the incongruity of the gift in its velvet case and the living conditions in the filth-flooded, rat-infested trenches, she felt ashamed at not having understood why he had not taken it and at having been puzzled when he had not answered her. Knowing what she knew now, she could bear neither to look at it, nor give it away and it was still in his room with his other belongings, just as they had been when he was alive.

That war, those months and months of killing, maiming and suffering, their dreams of when it would be over…but it would never be 'over', for there was no way of bringing back those whom they had lost.

How unaware, how mindless they had been of the realities of war.

CHAPTER EIGHTEEN

Ardleagh, January 1924.

*I*t was January when the full force of realisation struck Leonora that something was horribly, horribly wrong. She came out of her bathroom, cold and sick. The unthinkable suspicion that had been haunting her now overwhelmed her with nauseous panic. Her period had been late before but not like this, for there had been no other accompanying signs. At first she had not paid much heed, just assumed it would start the way it always did, but that had not happened and she was now numb with horror. Slowly she crossed the room to her bed. Rigidly she sat, staring at the floor, twisting her lace handkerchief in her fingers until it tore.

She could not be. But she knew she was.

Her guilt felt very real. Black garbed patriarchal condemnation, its talons vicelike as a strong clawed bird of prey, had her in its grip. Pregnant, she could never tell her father, but sooner or later he would have to know. She put her hands to her head. Her very scalp was prickling and her mouth was dry. She remained where she was, scarcely able to think. Like an overpowering wave, fear again washed over her. She waited for the strength of feeling to pass, then pulling out her bedside-table drawer she slipped her fingers to the back, pulled out her diary, turned the pages and counted. She was even later than she feared.

She stayed quite still, not daring to consider the days ahead in which she would become more and more late, more afraid and swollen. No. No, maybe it was something else. Maybe it would start tomorrow and the awful sickening hope against hope began, alternating with equally sickening despair.

She spent the morning in her room. The only idea to come to her was to get in touch with Ralph but when she phoned, his mother answered telling her that he was out and no, she did not know when he would be back. Whenever she phoned after that, he still was not in. After a nightmare week of terrible loneliness his father answered and said his son was in London.

Nobody, as yet, knew anything was wrong. In her better moments Leonora had tried to hope that by some extreme chance her period would start and she would not be pregnant, but she knew by now that was not going to be. It was intended she join her parents at the end of January. She had only a week or so left. Distraught and in desperation, she decided to go to London.

Having made her plans, she took some of her mother's letters from her writing desk and for a long time practised copying her hand. Very, very carefully she forged a letter from her mother to herself, one she would show to her aunt. She was taking a ghastly chance and could only gamble her luck would hold.

The letter to herself over which Leonora had so painstakingly laboured, told her that she had been invited by the parents of one of her debutante friends, to spend a few days with them in London and that provided it upset no arrangements at Ardleagh, her mother was happy for her to go. Leonora waited anxiously until shortly after the post arrived and then, feigning pleasure at the news, took the letter to her aunt. Margaret was an unsuspecting soul and her niece trusted she would simply go along with what the letter said. Her aunt was agreeable and provided her mother made no contact whilst she was away, her ruse could work and hopefully, she would not be found out.

The journey to London was long, but at last, late in the evening, she arrived at Ralph's door. Nobody answered when she rang the bell. She tried again, still no answer. It was an eventuality she had considered and fervently hoped the spare key was hidden in the same place.

Wearily she let herself in, pushed open the sitting room door, curled into the corner of a deep settee and while waiting, fell into exhausted sleep. It was later, much later, long after midnight when Ralph returned but Leonora did not hear. She did not hear the voices, the giggling and fooling around as he climbed the stairs, but then some noise disturbed her and a little while later, hearing sounds overhead, she half awoke. For several seconds after opening her eyes she stayed quite still. Slowly she began to recollect where she was. Of course, she was in Ralph's house. Oh, thank goodness, he had come back.

Not bothering to fumble for her shoes, she climbed the thickly carpeted stairs. The landing light was on and seeing his door ajar, she crossed towards his room. It was dark inside, but she saw him in the narrow shaft of light slanting through the slightly open door, slanting across his naked back, slanting also across the girl, almost hidden by him as the two of them moved, tangled together, barely covered by the crumpled, silken sheets, the same sheets, the same bed, all just the same.

Motionless, she stood, then, shaking and with limbs trembling, silently pulled back into the shadow of the wall. For how long, for only an instance or...numbed, she knew not. Then, with the fear of an intruder who must not be caught, hurrying unsteadily, she went down the stairs to the front door. Her case, she must take her case. The realisation overcame her that she had no right to be here, spying on him, at night, in his own home. He must not know.

Her shoes, where were her shoes? She tried to be calm. 'Think, move slowly,' she told herself. Groping in the darkness near the settee, not daring to put on the light, she found them, but did not wait to put them on, not until she stood on the cold flags of the pavement in the street outside. With the night air cool upon her face, she leaned against the wall, flooded with relief that she had got away unseen, unheard.

Shattered by what she had just witnessed, struggling in her heightened state of nerves to survive the happenings upon her, she was feeling no sympathy for herself. Anxiety had rendered her incapable of forming those insights that would have enabled her to take up a position, a stance from which she might fight back. Overcome by stress and worry she had lost touch with her inner self. Fear of her father's anger on learning of her pregnancy, fear of Ralph's anger if discovering he had been seen, had obliterated all awareness of her own right and entitlement to react against unfairness to herself, to retaliate at this violation of her own emotions and still in a dazed state, she started walking with no idea where to go.

Instinctively she went to where the lights were and the signs of life and after wandering for a while came upon an all-night cafe and went in. It was now almost four in the morning.

That night, when Ralph had come unexpectedly to London and called to their house and she had left a note for her mother and he had taken her to dance and dine, that night when she had drunk too much champagne and his words had fuelled her with defiance and desire and had freed her mind of fetters and bathed her world in different light, it was so short a time and yet, how long ago it all now seemed.

Now Ralph had gone and with him had also gone the illusion of a world of freedom in which nobody got hurt. Was the loss of it, part of the reason why she so needed him? Cut off from him as she was now, it were as if his going had struck the midnight hour and the glass slippers, the white horses and carriage were no more than the shabby shoes, the mice and pumpkin they had always been.

In her exhausted state, the silly thought of Cinders sitting on her pumpkin prompted an urge to hysterically laugh and cry and as the waiter set down her cup, her lips were quivering and her "Thank you," made no sound.

She stayed staring at the newspaper she had spread before her, killing time, not knowing what to do. Her plight was such, she must do something. She could not remain sitting here. Past five in the morning now, but where to go? She could not face returning to Ardleagh and if she told her mother, to what good, for sooner or later her father would have to know. This was not the sort of secret one could continue keeping to oneself. Prodding in the scrimmage of her jumbled thoughts, grabbing at ideas all contradictory and pointing different ways and then discarding them, she tried to form some plan.

What if she said nothing, waited until they noticed? No, no, for what then? The very thought was ludicrous, so what if she went somewhere by herself? No, the thought was just as senseless for she had no money to speak of, and could not manage on her own. Staying at Ardleagh was not an option. Return to Spain? No, for then events would take their course. She knew too well the consequence of that and, in her mind she clearly saw, 'El Torno', 'The Wheel', set in the convent's high wall that nobody approached except the families of women such as herself, unmarried mothers. Veiled and at night they came in secret, bearing the small bundles they would not keep. By the wheel was the handle of the bell. Deep within the confines of the convent its toll would sound the summons, unheard outside the walls. A little waiting and the wheel would slowly turn and the bundle of the baby that it bore would pass from view, unnamed, unwanted and unknown.

Leonora's thoughts circled. At last she made up her mind. She would take a taxi to the nearest main railway station, have breakfast there, then make her way back to her old Belgravia haunts and book in at a small hotel she knew. It was ironic, their Belgravia house was standing empty, but it was locked and shuttered and she had no key and in any case, she dare not stay there. Her deception could all too easily be found out.

It was a raw January day. The hotel receptionist told her the room would not be ready until after twelve and rather than hang around in the lobby and risk meeting someone she knew, Leonora went outside. Having wandered aimlessly the familiar streets, she sat on a park bench. The park itself was just a railed-in square of lawn with a few bare trees, empty earth beds in which nothing was growing, wet paths, a couple of iron lamp-posts and a litterbin, all very tidy and cold and across on the other side of the road, a row of grand-looking townhouses.

It was a common scene in this part of London and it was a while before it dawned on Leonora that there was something vaguely recognisable about it. Of course, that was it she had been here before, a day in the summer, months ago. A party held been held in one of the houses, a lunch party, before they all went boating on the river later in the afternoon. The little park had looked quite different then, rather pretty, and while the outing was being organised, they had spilled out of the house to promenade its paths and circulate and flirt informally.

How long ago it seemed. The debutante whose party it had been, Leonora remembered her well, a young woman one would not quickly forget and remembering, a faint smile twisted Leonora's lips. 'She would never have been stupid like this,' Leonora reflected, now seeing herself as a fool who had allowed herself to be duped, as well as degraded and sinful and all the other tormenting perceptions she now had of herself. To have come to this, after all those endless warnings and constant chaperoning that at the time, had merely seemed nothing more than the done-thing.

With nowhere to go, Leonora stayed where she was, looking at the row of houses opposite and remembering. She picked out the one where the party had been held and sat staring at its dark blue door as though it might suddenly open and the friends of last summer come out and she could go back and waken up in the past, where what was happening to her now could be put away like some horrible foreboding or bad dream.

Suddenly, the girl's name came back to her, Marianna Conningham. Was she still there, Leonora wondered, behind that door, all brash bright and self-confident and as seemingly invulnerable as ever? 'Marianna...if ever she did something so mindless,' mused Leonora, 'I know she would find an answer.' The thought stuck in Leonora's mind...'I know she would find an answer,' and again it echoed...'she would find an answer,' and as if compelled Leonora stood up and automatically began to walk towards the dark blue door with its shiny bell-pull and brass knocker at the top of the swept and well-scrubbed steps. She was not even thinking as she climbed the steps and pulled on the bell-pull and she had no idea what she might say to whoever answered.

The door opened and a maid in a black and white uniform was standing there. Expressionlessly, she looked at and listened to the young woman on the step and then opened the door a little wider and disappeared. Marianna promptly appeared in her stead.

"Leonora, Oh how divine to see you, do come in. You are the answer to my prayers. I was becoming so utterly, utterly bored." She hugged and kissed her visitor on both cheeks and turned and led the way towards a parlour, calling backwards over her shoulder and trailing a barely discernible, strangely scented fine strand of smoke in the air behind her as she went. It came from the tip of the long cigarette, jutting from the end of the even longer cigarette holder, held in the hand with which she beckoned Leonora on.

"Mumsy and Popsy are out, for which Saints be praised, and I have the house to myself," she informed her visitor. "Well almost…" she added, shooting a dark look at the maid, now standing at the foot of the staircase watching their progress with what Leonora could not but notice was an unmistakably dubious, almost mean, expression. Marianna closed the parlour door firmly and with satisfaction upon her, putting an end to her scrutiny.

The parlour they were in was warm and cosy and expensively furnished. A cheery fire burned in the ornate grate.

"She's such a dragon and she misses nothing, not a thing darling, not one thing and my parents always leave her on guard whenever they're not around, which will be for the rest of the day, until late tonight. They're visiting friends in the country, a very long drive away. Oh it's so splendid you've called. Now tell me, what's been happening in your world, tell all, but, first things first," and Marianna went across to a side table.

"What's it to be darling? Which cocktail do you favour? You don't, oh come, you must," she pressed as her guest shook her head. "I have here some of the newest, fruity recipes over from America, all the rage. You will? a teeny one, oh good. Of course Popsy disapproves, thinks cocktails are vulgar. He judges everything American, vulgar, including this craze for dancing in the mornings at friends' houses, especially when it's the Black Bottom and the Turkey Trot and the Cake Walk, also from across the Atlantic. I keep wishing to have a morning dance here," she added, waving her cigarette holder in the direction of a large, windup gramophone complete with its huge trumpet accoutrement and several records. "But Popsy's so stuffy. He hates jazz," and Marianna pulled a po-face and stood stiffly, screwing up one eye in imitation of her father, before coming to sit down opposite Leonora and handing her an intriguing looking drink.

Leonora had been watching her as she moved around. She was the very epitome of the new breed of woman known in current jargon as a Flapper, but taking the word in its other sense, Marianna Conningham looked like the last person to flap. There was a gritty worldliness about her and she gave the impression of being well able to find her way around.

She was dressed in a manner that would have made Alva blanch. The long legs she crossed were elegant, every inch of them, from the hem of her short, fine pleated skirt, until they disappeared into her strappy, very fashionable shoes. Her hair was bobbed, but framed her outstandingly pretty face to perfection. Her nails were long, very long. There was an affectation about her which Leonora sensed could not have been easily acquired, but it was attractive and amusing and conveyed Marianna's undoubted sense of wellbeing to those around her. She was chic and confident and just by being with her, Leonora felt a little better.

"It's been ages. You should have kept in touch darling, but never mind you're here now. Tell me, all your news. I want to hear everything."

Leonora raised her cocktail to her lips and took more of a gulp than a sip.

"I..." she began, but suddenly with no warning whatever, everything piled up inside her and was just too much. Her voice faltered and large tears began rolling down her face.

"What is it? Oh you must tell." Marianna was instantly kind and firmly insistent and Leonora had no resolve left to resist.

"I'm pregnant and...I'm not married," she blurted out.

With lightening-speed, Marianna rushed to the door and snatched it open. "Phew," she said, mock fanning herself in relief as she returned. "It's alright darling, she wasn't there. The dragon, she wasn't eavesdropping, but I'm sure she does at times."

She raised her finger to her lips. "Sh, don't say things like that, not out loud, not if others don't yet know. The father, does he know? Will he, I mean, can he, marry you?"

Leonora bit her lip, shaking her head. Her despair welled up again but the previous night was something she could not discuss.

"Are you sure, really sure? It would be best."

Leonora was frantic.

"No, no, I can't. Something happened and now...I can't. I can never tell him, not now."

Marianna watched her, her penetrating bright blue eyes shrewdly summing up the girl before her.

"Alright, but who does know. Does anybody?"

Leonora shook her head. "No, only you and nobody else, I've been too afraid."

"Then it's alright darling. It's alright." She said soothingly and crossing from the other side of the fireplace, she sat down beside her friend and put her arm around her.

"Sh. Hush," she said soothingly as Leonora shook with sobs. "It's alright, but not a word to anyone darling, not one word, not to anyone. Keep it absolutely hush-hush, otherwise, it's too dangerous if things…but don't worry. It can soon be all over, all over and forgotten."

Leonora looked up in disbelief.

"There is one thing though, one itsy-bitsy problem, money. He charges, quite a lot. Well it is against the law and it's a fearful risk for him if he's found out and so…but this isn't a backstreet job. He works from his own home in…but there's no need for you to know. We'll go by taxi. I'll take you to his surgery myself."

Gradually, some understanding of what she was saying penetrated through to Leonora. But it was all too strange. It sounded like something she had once read a bit about, but which she had found confusing and had not really understood. She listened, pale and afraid and the more she listened the more afraid she became. This made it a little tricky for Marianna and she tried again.

"You may feel a bit unwell afterwards, not likely but possibly, and yes, it is illegal and if it were known, there could be dreadful trouble and for the doctor as well."

But as her friend pointed out she was in dreadful trouble already and anyway it was all sure to go well and she would not be pregnant anymore and, ever practical, Marianna outlined what her position would be if she did not…do something. Her reputation would be ruined. She would lose respect, be shunned in society with scarcely any chance of making a good marriage afterwards and almost certainly be made to give her baby away, to be adopted.

Leonora knew only too well the truth of what she saying and thought again of her father's anger. She twisted the old, valuable ring on her finger, twisted it until it came off and held it out to Marianna. "Do you think this would raise enough to pay for it? It's all I have with me."

The doctor was able to see her immediately and arrangements were made. Marianna came with her, but the procedure was not straightforward and for two days everyone involved was very anxious and Leonora remained secluded at the doctor's home. But on the third day, she was back on her feet and Marianna came to collect her, then having made sure she would be met at her destination, saw her safely onto the Manchester train. The story they had concocted, was that Leonora had been thrown from her horse whilst riding out with her friend and had seriously wrenched her back, but had been seen by a doctor and there were no bones broken.

Back at Ardleagh Hall, Leonora took to her bed, making the excuse that her back was hurting and she thought she was sickening for flu. Although in pain, she tried to convince herself she was getting better. The complications she had suffered had been unforeseeable, the consequences possibly long term but fearing her symptoms would betray her secret and the loss of her virginity become known,

Leonora adopted a fatalistically uncaring attitude of either getting better on her own, or not, and sought no help.

The happy go lucky, freedom-seeking rationale, by which Ralph lived his life, how shallow and trite it now seemed. "As long as nobody gets hurt," he had said. But when people claim their freedom to do just as they like, almost always, somebody does get hurt and Leonora remembered the old Spanish saying. 'Take what you want - and pay for it,' and yes, there was always a price. Her father's values stood for permanence and continuity and he was loyal to what he believed in. Ralph was faithless and false and despite her fears and feelings towards the Church, she knew full well that if she had heeded what it taught, she would not be suffering in this mess now.

Freedom, as she now realised, was double-edged and she had come to understand the significant difference between, "Freedom from…" and "Freedom to…"

Leonora was sad for other reasons also and when Ralph came to the Hall, full of charm and good cheer, the images she had seen in the shaft of light slanting through his bedroom door, came vividly to mind and she refused to see him. Miserably she watched as he drove away and, for several minutes after his car disappeared down the wet and windswept drive, she stood, looking into emptiness. The things she once enjoyed no longer gave her pleasure and without Ralph, she no longer wanted to be here.

Perversely, she remembered the good things about Spain, its music and colour, its sunshine and vibrancy and she opened her father's unread last letter. He was insisting she return as agreed. With the Military Dictator in power and the Army in control it was safe to walk the streets. He reminded her, her education was complete, her 'season of partying' was over. Keeping the family name in mind, there were decisions to be made. She must accept her responsibilities, look to the future. These were matters not to be left to chance.

'Yes', Leonora reflected, 'I know about responsibilities and decisions. I've had to make the hardest one I ever will,' and she knew she could delay no longer. She must return to Spain.

CHAPTER NINETEEN

Berlin, Germany. February 1924

Wanting to renew the friendships he had made in Berlin, James was on holiday there. The Academy he had attended previously was situated in the suburbs. It was also self-contained and, engrossed in his music he had learned little of politics or life in the city. Now, with time to stroll and look around, the poverty and misery he saw were a far cry from his expectations.

Much had happened in Germany since the Armistice and the political scene was chaotic and confused. The so-called peace treaty of 1919, the Treaty of Versailles, was punitive. It required Germany to take full responsibility for the war, acknowledge her guilt, make reparation payments until the 1980's, surrender several territories and colonies and hand over her submarines and battle fleet to the Allies. It forbade tanks and offensive weapons, demanded that her Army be reduced to one hundred thousand men and that the Kaiser, Wilhelm the second, be handed over for trial on charges of violating the laws of war.

The Kaiser however had already abdicated on November the ninth, two days prior to the Armistice, and fled into exile in Holland, thus bringing the autocratic Hohenzollern dynasty to an end. The collapse of the monarchy had intensified the already existent revolutionary fever in the country and with the leaders of a large insurrectionary movement, the Spartacists, plotting to establish a Soviet Republic the threat of a Communist takeover was real. A Republic in the form of a Social Democracy was proclaimed and the authority of the Chancellor was surrendered to its interim president, Friedrich Ebert.

The crippling terms of the Versailles Treaty and the realisation that the reparation payments would bring ruin upon Germany had roused anger, despair and a lusting for revenge. The people had expected victory, not ignominy and penalties such as these. Nor had the land to which the soldiers returned, met with their expectations. The country that awaited them was not the one for which they thought they had been fighting. Mutiny had broken out in the German Navy and the insurrection had spread to the workers, setting elements within the country against each other. The Monarchy had fallen, political opponents were being killed and there were running battles in the streets.

But although the war had toppled the throne, it had not destroyed the social structures and traditions of the Establishment, the ruling elite that had held power prior to its fall. During the old monarchic, autocratic rule of the Kaiser, the Military top brass had long been involved in affairs of government and state. The Army's high ranking officers tended to be aristocratic, of Prussian stock, and the amalgam of ambitious, power-seeking personalities that made up the Army's Supreme Command existed as vigorously as ever. Proud, elitist and well educated, they were conscious of their social superiority and long tradition.

The Democratic members of the newly formed Weimar Republic had no such advantages. They were mostly working class, conditioned to respect authority and undermined by their inexperience. Their leader, Friederich Ebert, had previously been a saddle-maker and the Germany that now had to be dealt with was not ready for Democracy.

Even as the war ended, the German Army's high command was determined to retain its authority and consolidate its position and, seeing the young Republic threatened by revolutionary forces, had struck out to do a deal with it. The new Republic, believing itself to have little choice, had complied. In the subsequent agreement, the Army promised to protect the young Republic on condition that the Army retained all of its traditions and could take whatever measures it saw fit in dealing with insurrections.

In such an arrangement the new Republic scarcely stood a chance, for the Army was in league with the country's other Nationalistic Right Wing forces, namely, the industrial barons of the Rhur who supplied its armaments, the Junkers the feudal landowners of extensive estates, the Prussian aristocracy, the magnates of the great cartels, the Imperial Civil Service and even the Judiciary.

These groups despised the untrained, unqualified Republic now trying to govern in their stead. Additionally, most of the capital wealth of the country was in the hands of these Conservatives with their autocratic Right-Wing loyalties. They had vested interests in banking, commerce and industry and were prepared to contribute considerable amounts of their resources to support the Right-Wing and the press that put forward their views.

The Army's Supreme Command denied responsibility for Germany's overthrow, claiming that while they were still fighting on foreign soil, they had been let down and betrayed, by the revolutionaries at home. Thus, the myth of Der Dolchstoss, the Stab in the Back, was born. The Democratic members of the new Weimar Republic who had signed the Versailles Treaty were now blamed for the consequences of the Armistice and were branded 'The November Criminals'. These slurs were a gross distortion of the truth, for the signatories had had no choice. But the calumnies levelled against them served the vested interests of those aiming to get rid of the Weimar Republic, giving them a stick with which to beat it and justification for their attacks

So it was that as the war beyond Germany's borders ended, the war within them began and having started, was to continue for years to come.

Now, as James arrived in Berlin the newspapers were full of the on-going troubles. Every day or other, the headlines were captured by some fresh development on the political scene. The morass of confusion was worsened by the infighting between the many political parties that had sprung up since the war, reports of which were riddled with so many distortions and contradictions that few accounts read the same.

A great deal of news space was filled with accounts of the public trial of one named Adolf Hitler. James had heard of the man but knew little about him other than that he had already been imprisoned for a few weeks, back in 1922, because of his dubious activities. He was now the leader of a Workers Party, formed shortly after the war.

The general unrest had been increased by Germany having suffered the worst runaway inflation ever experienced by any country. Prior to the war the exchange rate had been around four marks to the dollar. By the autumn of last year it had spiralled unbelievably to the rate of hundreds of thousands of marks to the dollar and was still rising. As 1923 ended the German economy was in steep decline.

This rate of exchange benefitted foreign visitors, but brought misery to the German populace as a whole. As money bought less and less, the Government printed more and more. A large proportion of the middleclass lost their savings. Many of the once wealthy were destitute and there was massive unemployment and appalling poverty. There were others however, those in financial circles and possessing sufficient wherewithal to ride out the storm, who took advantage of the economic situation and had increased their fortunes.

James wanted to know how the orchestra he was to have joined had fared. One of the other ensembles in which he had played once or twice during his previous brief stay had been reduced in size and taken over by a private benefactor, Gustav Manstein, a wealthy antique dealer, art connoisseur and music lover. He was married to Ingmar, a much younger, very pretty socialite whose vanity to appear as patron of the arts, he was pleased to indulge. On hearing James was back in Berlin, Gustav invited him to a gathering at his home later in the week and said he would be happy to have him join his new ensemble. James explained he would be leaving soon but would be pleased to accept the evening invitation. At least on this occasion, he would know what to expect.

He was not mistaken. When the street-door of his host's home closed behind him, it was as if poverty, toil and turbulence had ceased to exist. In the opulent hall, as the liveried servant divested James of coat, scarf and gloves, the very atmosphere informed that here was a place in which civilised life was safe from strife, that war and hunger were as unrealities and would remain so. All was perfection. The soft light shedding from the chandeliers, the magnificence of heavy, antique furniture, the silver bowl of hot house roses, the portraits and carved panelling, expensive rugs and polished old oak floors, created, yet did not fully total, the air of secured, good order that unmistakably prevailed.

The sophistication that in those first few moments James sought to discern, was bestowed by a quality less material, less overt, by something in the faint strains of Schumann, the softness of tones of voice, the gallant gesture, the courtesy of manner, these were the living details that contributed to the all-pervading sense of graciousness of which he was so aware.

Having seen, during the past few days, so much of the city's harsh meanness of life while exploring on foot the city's dilapidated back streets, James suffered a strange unease. It did not stem however, from the luxury of such a lifestyle against a background of poverty, disturbing though that may be. It came from something other, and once again it was the less tangible, the less obvious, that was prodding his consciousness. An unexpected cynicism had arisen in him, not only in relation to the surrounding ambiance, but also to himself, prompted by the questions some voice was asking of his soul.

'How really enduring is this graciousness, or how skin deep only? Would this sophistication of manner, this gallantry, these qualities I now see, continue to exist if separated from this lifestyle. Stripped of this affluence, would they survive? How self-sustaining could they be?'

He longed to believe they would live on even if order and security were swept from them, but would they? Would they prevail if subjected to the sort of cruel happenings that were taking place outside these walls? He very much doubted it and his doubts were also about himself and his unease lay in the unwelcome presentiment that one day they may be put to the test.

Shrugging, he pushed away the morbid thought. Approaching the archway that led from the hall, he was greeted by his host before entering the extensive drawing room and mingling with the other guests. He knew only one or two of those present and having been introduced to several whom he had not met before, he opted to listen and learn, rather than talk. In any case he was still far from fluent in the language.

After the recital and whilst refreshments were being served, the talk was of Adolf Hitler and his attempted coup in Munich last November when he had intrigued to involve Right Wing elements in Bavaria, against the Weimar Republic. The man had misjudged the amount of support he had hoped to receive and his attempt had failed. Sixteen of his supporters had been killed and he was now in the dock along with Erich Ludendorff, the legendary war hero who, amongst others, had also taken part in the abortive coup.

The name of Ludendorff was revered in Germany. He had been second in command to Hindenburg and dictator of Germany in all but name during the closing years of the war. Hitler, despite having twice been awarded the Iron Cross, had risen no higher than corporal and his affiliation with the famous General was giving him a measure of acceptability his low status did not deserve.

Shortly after joining the Workers' Party at the end of the war, Hitler's overweening self-confidence and ambition had enabled him to become its leader. He had changed its name to the National Socialist German Workers' Party, now commonly known as the Nazi Party.

Not knowing much about the man James had deemed him little more than a rabble-rouser, but from what he was now hearing it seemed the man was regarded more seriously by the Mansteins and several of their guests. Much of the discussion was coming from a group surrounding Ingmar, Gustav's vivacious, blonde wife. Slim, attractive and expensively dressed, Ingmar loved to be at the centre, preferably at the forefront, of what was going on. Her soirees, held on the last Thursday of each month, were well known and she endeavoured always to have as centrepiece some guest of honour, a personage of note currently in the public eye.

The novelty of wealth and social position had worn thin for Ingmar. Life as the wife of Gustav Mannstein was not nearly as satisfying as she had anticipated it would be prior to her full immersion in the role. She had learned to her cost, that her husband was sensitive about his image, needing at all times to have it well reflected back upon him. He was an elderly man, tending to be difficult in ways she had not noticed before their wedding. True, he indulged her when he was not upset, but the avoidance of his becoming so was a constraint that did nothing to embellish her own personality and she had come to resent being rated as little more than the pretty, young wife of a much older man.

Recognition of her own identity, so she felt, was fading fast and her soirees were one of the ways she had devised of deflecting a much hungered need for attention onto herself. So far however, her field of conquest had been limited to the cultural, but once again, this was her husband's domain. When the opportunity presented itself of introducing a political flavour into her gatherings, she had been delighted.

It had come about through the diplomatic connections of a friend of hers, who was on close terms with a military attaché at one of the Embassies. It was at one of the Embassy gatherings that Ingmar first saw the National Socialist leader in person and had been impressed by the way his presence imposed itself. The ladies were certainly taking note. He was different, even a little coarse. Strangely that was part of his appeal, conveying an elemental, primal, masculine strength. There was a forceful magnetism in his brooding silences but when in unexpected response to some chance remark, he began to speak, his passionate conviction delivered in rather raucous tones killed conversation and captured the interest of others in the room.

It was not the done-thing at a private party. It rebuffed the usual conventions but Herr Hitler seemed to be set apart from such. It was obvious he was an unusual man, but as he himself had said, these were unusual times. After he left, the room had been abuzz with talk of him and his way-out ideas about what should be done, ideas many privately agreed with, but would have hesitated to voice publicly themselves. For such as these, his outburst had provided a banner under which they could now gather in consensus.

The man's presence and passion had excited Ingmar and thereafter, she attended his meetings. She was aroused by the way he could bring the focus of so many others onto himself and therein lay the thrill, for when she met the gaze of those deep-set, extraordinarily penetrating eyes, it were as if all that attention was being channelled upon her, filling her with an awareness of her own individuality and worth.

At the end of the last meeting, hoping to hand him an invitation to one of her evenings, she had waited to see him but too many others were also there and she had to leave it with an attendant. She later realised she should have first asked

Gustav and not knowing her husband's opinion of the man, nor how he may react, had been concerned. It would be very awkward if he proved difficult, but Adolf may not come so she decided to wait and see.

She was therefore very pleased this evening, to hear the opinion expressed, that the humble corporal turned fiery orator, had given a very good account of himself in Court and was becoming, a man to watch. Although Adolf had yet to make his mark, Ingmar had seen how he could control people, bring them to his way of thinking, play their mood, pause, then lead them on, stirring their frustration with invective until emotions became strung to the pitch at which the audience would arise en masse climaxing in orgiastic crescendos that continued on and on.

Afterwards, there was the sensation of being drained, emptied, but then the exhilaration would return and the 'high' could last for hours and in her aroused state, those nights with Gustav after she got home, were like no others. Adolf almost always spoke late for he believed that people became more receptive late at night. She wanted to promise funds to the Party for it seemed no more than the done-thing. It meant however, that she would have to tell Gustav, but she was sure she would find the right things to say and the right moment to say them.

In addition to Hitler broadcasting his boasts and declarations himself, they were published in the Party newspaper, The Beobachter Volkischer. The guests here this evening, approved of his adamant stance against the Communists and there were those, dare it be said, who even agreed with his attitude regarding the Jews.

His fanatical determination to crush Communism and his uncanny spellbinding ability to sway people and thus lure them away from it was endearing Hitler to the Nationalistic Right-Wing. The man may be a brawler, but his energy and determination were all the more impressive for that and his impassioned incantations incited a psychic energy which, once generated, seemed to feed off itself.

Of course Ingmar realised this was only half the picture for deprivation and despair had already conditioned the masses to listen to him and Hitler, a master of demagoguery and endowed with intuition, was able to bloat his listeners with the emotive power of his words. It was an uplifting experience for those contaminated with fear and hopelessness, to have their debilitation and weariness exchanged for a renewed belief in their country, their future and themselves. This was precisely what Hitler bestowed on the thousands who flocked to hear him and they came away buoyed with the belief that jobs, money in their pockets and food on their tables would again be theirs.

But if Hitler pleased the aggrieved masses and the Right-Wing, there were many who were far from happy with him, namely the Socialists and Democrats, the much maligned Weimar Republic and needless to say, the Communists. With Hitler now on trial for treason, Ingmar was concerned and was very much hoping the fuss would die down and the trial would not amount to much.

In truth, she was not as confident as she appeared and, wondering what that good looking, young Englishman may have to say, she took a seat next to him on the sofa.

"Of course," she explained, "…all this really started last September when the Republic resumed those awful reparation payments. Everyone was up in arms and the Republic became afraid of another attack on itself like the Kapp putsch back in 1920, when that powerful Freikorp faction, the Ehrhardt Brigade, staged a putsch and practically took over in Berlin, so you can see why the Government's put the leaders of this putsch on trial."

"Just what, or who, are the Freikorps?" asked James. "I keep hearing them mentioned."

"Oh! the Freikorps? Well, they're the armed groups, mostly from the units that have had to be disbanded from the Army in keeping with the dictates of that ghastly Versailles Treaty. And you can see how, with so many soldiers out of a job and roaming free, the Army thought it only sensible to use them. They're ready-made for the purpose, trained to kill, still have their old uniforms and weapons - the Army equips them anyway - and they're easy to organise because they're loyal to their old commanders and to the units they were in. So when the Army wanted help, there were plenty of volunteers.

"…and quite apart from the Freikorp, Adolf now has a squad of his own supporters. They're under the orders of one of the Party's early members, an ex-Army man, Ernst Rohm, who loathes the Weimar Republic. He calls them his Storm Troopers, Sturm Abteilung, the S.A. for short, his 'Brown Shirts'. They're to act as Adolf's bodyguards and protect The Party as well as breaking up their opponents' meetings and the like." Ingmar laughed and stubbed out her cigarette.

"…many of them…?" asked James.

"In Adolf's group…? Oh, I'd say thousands of them by now. Gustav says Mussolini's march on Rome with his black shirted Fascists, back in twenty-two, was what inspired Adolf to launch his putsch against the Weimar Republic, especially when Ludendorff agreed to join him. That in itself is a feather in Adolf's cap. Anyway he followed Mussolini's example and…"

"…got himself arrested. Not a very auspicious start to his career," said James, hoping to deflate her obvious adulation of the man and promptly feeling mean.

Undismayed, Ingmar again laughed her throaty laugh. "The Republic's tried many times to disband the Freikorps, but they just regroup and join one or other of the Right Wing parties that are looking for strong-arm protection and there's not much the Government can do, especially now that old General Ludendorff is encouraging counter-revolution by the Right-Wing…and of course, the trouble's been aggravated by that awful inflation…really awful." Ingmar sighed. "It's not right. This wretched Republic simply doesn't know how to govern. It's to Munich we'll have to look if we want to get rid of it. There are several Right-Wing groups based there now and Adolf was in league with them, well…he thought he was, but it turned out they had their own agenda and they let him down. But Gustav says he'll be treated leniently because he's against the Republic and the Communists. Gustav says it's a case of, 'The enemy of my enemy is my friend'."

Without wishing to appear rude, James looked around for a line of escape. Arnold was a possibility. He was the lead violin in the ensemble and James had come to know him during his previous stay in Berlin. He was standing by the far wall and had already cast a couple of sympathetically enquiring glances in James' direction. Choosing a safe moment James shot him an affirmative response.

A discreet lapse and Arnold came across with a tall, thoughtful looking man. Ingmar introduced him then captured the newcomer's attention, wanting his views on Adolf whom she was happy to say she knew personally, and also on the likely outcome of his failed putsch. The two were soon engrossed in deep discussion and claiming to need Arnold's advice on a musical score, James excused himself and moved with his friend to the adjoining room.

"Many thanks," smiled James.

Arnold grinned. "Could see you being tucked up there for the rest of the night, so what's this score you're having trouble with?"

"My trouble's in knowing the score on the political scene here, so many different factions and divided loyalties. Each time I think I've got a handle on it, I hear something to make me think I have it all back to front."

James glanced around. The gathering was thinning and in the hall, fur coats, cloaks and wraps, gloves, hats and canes were being brought. He glanced at his watch.

"What say you to coming back to my hotel for a nightcap, have you time?"

"Love to," Arnold agreed.

Out in the street, the snow was falling. It was bitterly cold but the night was fresh and clear and they set off at a brisk walk. The hotel was only a few blocks away.

"So what did you learn from Ingmar, apart from how wonderful Adolf is?"

"She thinks he's become the one to watch and that he'll get off lightly," answered James.

Arnold gave a hollow laugh. "She's right about him being one to watch, though I doubt she meant it in quite the same way. She's also right about him getting off lightly. The Army and its cohorts in the judiciary believe he'll be useful to them, but they're wrong. They are more seasoned in Establishment circles than Hitler is, but the sheer exclusivity of those circles in which things are done this way and not that, is the truss that binds them. Their conformity to certain codes of conduct, good form, call it what you will, makes them predictable. It's Hitler's crystal ball for knowing how they'll behave.

"In moral terms the Establishment is also dubious, but in a different way because they can't be seen to be so, at least not if they want to retain their status and claim to superiority. They're manacled in a way Hitler will never be. It's their Achilles heel. Hitler's strength lies in his having no regard for codes of conduct and conformity, except as guide ropes for knowing how to bind others. Hitler isn't hamstrung by any pretention to Honour. He's come up from the bottom. His behaviour is that of the gutters, dirty dealing, double crossing, doing down his opponents and getting rid of them any which way he can. He's more than just streetwise. Hitler knows his way through the sewers. He'll run rings round them and they don't yet see it."

"You've obviously been watching him," commented James, surprised at his friend's conviction.

"Yes, not because I like him, but because I don't."

Arnold had been living in Berlin for some years and was interested in politics. They reached the hotel and settled themselves comfortably in the lounge. The place was restful, a legacy of the pre-war era, betraying none of the scars of the interim years.

"So you think Hitler could make trouble?" questioned James, anxious to know more.

"Hitler doesn't so much make trouble as latch on to it and use it to stir resentment and fear in others. In all his ranting there's not a single new idea. It's a hash of bits and pieces from this and that other theory and philosophy, taken out of context and distorted to convince others of what he wants them to believe so as to serve his purpose. When this latest trouble flared in the autumn over the government paying the reparations, he kept barking on about the 'November criminals' and the Versailles treaty. There was uproar and Ebert, the President, knew he couldn't trust the Army for support, not after what happened with the Kapp Putsch."

"Yes Ingmar also mentioned that. What's its significance...?"James asked.

"The Kapp Putsch...it happened back in 1920, because the Republic was cutting down the Army to a hundred thousand, in line with the Versailles Treaty. The Commander of the Army in the Berlin district hates the Republic and wanted the Helmut Erhardt's Brigade that had been disbanded, to be reinstated. When Friedrich Ebert refused, the Commander gave orders for Erhardt's Brigade, which had already joined the Freikorps, to march on Berlin, overthrow the Republic and set up a Military Dictatorship with a Right Winger, Wolfgang Kapp, as Chancellor. When Ebert appealed to the Army for support, the Army simply said it couldn't fire on its own soldiers and just stood by, waiting to see what would happen."

"...and what did?" asked James.

"Erhardt's Brigade almost took over. The Government fled to Dresden, then on to Stuttgard and appealed to the workers to strike. They did and the country practically came to a standstill. The Putsch failed and the Government returned. But the Army's attitude had been revealed - quick to let the Freikorps loose against the Communists, the Left Wing and such, but refusing to defend the Republic when it's under threat from those whose views the Army shares," explained Arnold.

"It seems to me, that with not actually being in the Army, the Freikorps have a free hand." ventured James.

"You mean rights without rules," replied Arnold. "The Freikorps is the Army's brain child and serves the Army's purpose. And remember, Freikorp leaders are not demobbed conscripts, glad to get home. They're the men who've made the Army their career, their profession. The Army was their life and in Germany, Army officers rank way above civilians. They bitterly resent being disbanded and make very willing volunteers when the Army puts out an appeal. Initially the Army was using the Freikorps to reinforce Germany's borders where territory had been lost because of the Versailles Treaty, but they then began using them against Communists and rebels at home and now the country's a battleground between extremists. Three leading politicians were murdered by the Freikorps, but nobody was called to account because the judiciary's also in on the act.

"The Republic's now in a double bind because when trouble began again last September, Ebert, doubting he could trust the Army, called on the President. But in the subsequent State of Emergency that was declared, power was handed over to the Army.

And Hitler's now got his own gang of street fighters, his Storm Troopers, the S.A.

Amongst them are several demobbed conscripts who can't settle to civilian life and footloose ruffians, handy for attacking opponents and breaking up their meetings." Arnold paused looking thoughtful, "but this violence augurs ill. It's conditioning a 'Might is Right' mentality, an attitude of 'Anything Goes,' sanctioned by a uniform."

"Why did Ingmar say Munich, Bavaria, is the one to bring down the Republic?" asked James.

"Bavaria resents the Republic because when Bismark unified Germany during the Hohenzollern dynasty, Bavaria remained a kingdom in its own right with its own royalty, the Wittelsbach dynasty, and a semi-autonomous parliament. At the war's end it lost its monarchy and its status as a kingdom and became just another province under the Weimar Republic, something it still finds very hard to accept.

"Around the time of the Armistice, an Independent Socialist, Eisner, attempted to set up a Socialist Republic in Munich. He was assassinated and the Communists took over. A month later, the Army moved in with the Freikorps, the same Erhardt Brigade. When the fighting began several hundred were slaughtered and the Right Wing gained control. See how useful the Freikorps can be," said Arnold, raising an eyebrow.

"Bavaria's been a Right-Wing stronghold ever since and its capital, Munich, is becoming a rallying point for those wanting to get rid of the Republic. The country's now unstable, impossible to predict. We'll have to see. But it's late, time I was on my way. You're returning to England soon, any plans to come back?"

"My life's changing too, impossible to predict. We'll have to see..." said James, smiling as he echoed Arnold's words.

"Well, either way, keep in touch," said Arnold as they made their farewells.

James ordered coffee and sat mulling over what had been said. Despite the beggars, the soup kitchens and other tell-tale signs of poverty, Berlin was still a vibrant city. The Weimar Republic had made for the beginnings of freedom. Its new Constitution was the most democratic in the world and the city had become a mecca of the arts. Its nightlife throbbed with vitality, but the current tensions and violence were impossible to ignore.

Nor was James looking forward to returning to Ardleagh. His father's attitude and his own aversion to the mines, the strikes and threats of them, made for too much disquiet. Martin was convinced there was a crisis in the offing.

England, Germany and Spain, three different countries, three different governments, yet suffering conflicts rooted in the same causes of exploitation injustice and greed.

'Must it be ever thus?' James questioned...'when will we ever learn?

CHAPTER TWENTY

Spring 1924. Cordoba. SPAIN

*I*nside the great Cathedral, all was sombre and still. The heavy, entrance door Leonora had just pushed open and passed through clunked softly and closed behind her. From where she stood she could see the confessional boxes on the side wall, with penitents kneeling in rows, waiting their turn. Every so often, a confessional door would open, someone would leave, another would enter and there was shuffling in the pew, as each moved up in line.

With every confidence that under the Military Dictatorship order would be maintained, the Arradova family had returned to Cordoba. Their presence in the city was another emblem of normality, so Alva maintained, and accordingly in two weeks time on Easter Sunday, the Arradovas would attend High Mass here in this Cathedral, conspicuously occupying the family pew. This was why Leonora was in the Cathedral now.

Leonora had come to the Cathedral to make her 'Easter Duties', the common name for one of the Church Commandments which ruled that every Catholic must, 'Go to Confession and Communion at least once a year, at Easter or thereabouts'. The Church taught that obedience was compulsory, that its Commandments were binding and obligatory because the Pope was the direct successor of St Peter on whom this power had been conferred by Christ when he said, "To thee I will give the keys of the Kingdom of Heaven. Whatsoever thou shall bind upon earth shall be bound also in Heaven and whatsoever thou shall loose upon earth shall be loosed also in Heaven."

This was the power, so she had been taught, by which she would be released from her sins. It was all laid down, more fixedly than in stone, in the thick and awesome volumes, which spelt out Church laws and decrees.

She had also been taught, "The Pope is infallible in matters of faith and morals to be held by the whole Church." But James had told her it was only in July 1870, when, thanks to Garibaldi and others, Italy had finally been united and the Papacy had suffered the loss of its temporal power that The Ecumenical Council had voted to declare the Pope infallible.

Even so, the dread she had so lightly cast aside when Ralph was with her to make nonsense of her fears, now clutched her anew, seemingly drawing its strength from the very desperation with which she fought it.

The Cathedral in which she stood was a building of great pomp and grandeur but it arose out of the interior of another much older one namely, the Mezquita, the Mosque of Cordoba, an ancient edifice of imposing splendour that embodied the very essence of Spanish Moorish art. The Mesquita had stood for more than a thousand years. It had been built by the Moors who had conquered and held much of southern Spain for several centuries and its classical lines were very much in contrast to the Baroque embellishments of the Cathedral. Within the Mesquita's massive walls, the symmetry of its columns and arches stretched out on all sides receding as though without end. Over the centuries, the enduring artistic quality of distinctive patterns and arabesque designs had come to bestow upon the ancient building, an atmosphere of timelessness and quiet calm.

When the Christians re-conquered Cordoba, a large section of the interior of the Mezquita had been ripped out and the Cathedral had been built in its centre, a kind of symbolic rape of this emblematic edifice of the Moors. But Leonora liked to think of both the religious buildings as One, a symbolism of peace between the two religions each offering in its own way, devotion to what is surely the One and Only, all loving God. Why could they not exist in harmony, each to his own, 'doing as they would be done by', instead of in an enmity-fuelled struggle for dominance and power?

She had entered with Letitia through the Mesquita's main portal, the Gate of Pardon, of Absolution, but wanting to be alone had asked her old nurse, whose role now was that of chaperone and companion, to wait for her there. Inside the Mosque, in a corner on the right, was the small postern, Postigo de la Leche, The Milk Gate, so named because, it was the gate to which orphans, or otherwise lost or abandoned children, were brought to be cared for. It reminded Leonora that in her troubles she was not alone and for a short while, she had lingered in the quiet stillness.

Now, from the back of the Cathedral, she watched the line of penitents grow shorter. The red light above the confessional door still burned, signifying the confessor's presence. Miserably, she fingered the pretty, black lace of her mantilla, moving its folds to veil her face more closely, before summoning her resolve and walking down the aisle.

Kneeling, she waited. She had become thinner in the last few months. Physical pain, together with anxiety over what she had done and the misery of her rejection by Ralph still tired and tensed her. Her hands resting on the rail were tightly clasped. But she was not praying for it seemed the obstacle of confession lay between her and whoever might listen. Trying to distract herself she looked around.

As was usual during the Lenten season, the tall interior walls of the Cathedral were stripped bare of ornament. No flowers, no polished candlesticks, nothing that may lift the spirit or gladden the eye had been left on view. All was shrouded in black or purple cloth and would remain so until Easter Sunday. On that day the Church would be crowded. During the High Mass the congregation would move in solemn file to kneel at the altar rails and receive communion. Those in the family pews at the front were expected to lead the way. But, she could not receive Communion unless she had confessed, neither could she remain behind alone in the family pew, for it would be noticed and her father would demand to know why and insist on an explanation.

The number of penitents before her, lessened. Only two before her now, minutes passed, now only one. Still weak and exhausted by her illness she was unable to overcome the superstitions her phobia was inflicting upon her. Her mouth was dry and her fingers, clammy on the varnished hand rest, left little imprints as she rose, for it was now her turn.

The door shut behind her. Heavy with the smell of dry wood and beeswax, lit only by the tiny shaft of light from the side of a small, curtained grille, the claustrophobic confines of the confessional closed in on her. Her scrupulously guarded secret she had paid such price to conceal, she must now reveal. Confession was confidential, but perversely, only if she kept it to herself could she feel certain she was safe. A Mortal sin must be revealed in full. How could she tell all she had done that night and what she had done later? How would he react? It was illegal and what if…she must reveal the doctor's name? The 'what if's now haunting her joined forces with her fears and crumpled her resolve. Backing towards the door she stumbled in her haste to leave and with tears wet upon her face hurried down the aisle looking neither right nor left. Struggling to regain her composure she found a quiet cloister where she could be alone and remained there for some time for she could not meet Letitia in this state.

Preoccupied during the journey home she claimed a headache as excuse and on arrival went straight to her room. She wanted to think, but the thinking made the worry worse and gave no answer and there was no-one in whom she could confide. She was utterly unable to contend with her father while living under his roof. Furthermore, if he knew, he would hold her mother responsible, blaming her for taking her daughter to England and she could not bear to have her mother know she had broken her trust.

It was later in the week that Georgio came again to the Arradova household. Raimundo had tactfully secured a posting for him in the province and he was now stationed not far away. As on previous occasions, Alva welcomed him warmly. Amelia, still unaware of her husband's arrangement and hoping the young man's company may help to raise her daughter's spirits, was also quite pleased to see him. Leonora had attached no significance to his visits, not until his last one when he presented himself, carrying a bouquet of deep red roses.

It was her first inkling that his calling might be more than casual. Even so, she had been disinclined to give much thought to him, but looking back, could see the signs were there and on giving consideration to the matter realised there had been other token indications also. Ailing and preoccupied she had not been reading them as might have been expected. Several times of late, her father had openly questioned her regarding her wishes for her future, advising her that, "the years before a young woman's twenty-fifth birthday are consequential to her subsequent happiness and you must pay attention to such matters." ...and now, Georgio had called again.

It was a warm spring evening and she was seated in the small bower of the patio garden in view of the drawing room's large, French windows. Her father brought the uniformed, young officer to greet her and after a few moments of pleasantries, returned to his study leaving the two of them together.

So, thought Leonora as she took a few moments to fold and lay aside her embroidery, if this is how things are, the situation must be as I imagine, in which case it can only be that Georgio has made his intentions known to my father and has been favourably received. Leonora knew well enough the procedure in such matters.

She could refuse of course, but how without unpleasantness? She needed time to sort her thoughts, to find a way not to allow the opportunity to arise. Smiling sweetly at Georgio, she rose from the bench and asked if he would care to take a turn around the garden. After a few circuits and having kept the conversation steered to general topics, she now steered their steps towards the drawing room's open windows, knowing her mother was inside. Once seated, the conversation was somewhat slow. Leonora did not help and in due course her mother rang the bell for refreshments to be served. After a polite interval the young man took his leave and shortly afterwards Leonora declared she was tired and withdrew to her room.

Amelia watched with concern as the door closed behind her daughter. It was now her turn to get an inkling of what may be about to happen and she was worried. Not for this had she gone to such lengths for the last three years to ensure her daughter did not become incarcerated in this land of little freedom, where life was too regulated and stultified by protocol on the inside, and too volatile and lawless on the outside, both of which meant one could neither do what one wanted, nor go where one chose. It was obvious Leonora was not happy but Amelia had no way of finding out why.

But if her mother was in a state of uncertainty, Leonora was seeing things clearly and was now quite certain Georgio was about to propose. She had no doubts that having hinted pointedly regarding her future, it would be only a matter of time before her father spoke frankly. She knew him well enough to know, that if she were not compliant with what he deemed to be in her best interests, one clever chess move would follow another, until she was left with virtually no alternative.

Even then there would be the question of her dowry and in that also, she was dependent on her father and there was no provision for her from a family trust, such as her mother had enjoyed. He would, if she married in accordance with his wishes, be very generous. But what if she chose not to? She had no professional training nor would her father fund such, given his belief it would demean the family to have a daughter in employment.

So what else, here in Spain, where everything was so different from England? And she could not go back to England, for what was there to go back to? As her father had implied, the choice of acceptable suitors would diminish with the passing of the years and if not marriage, what else, other than to remain under her father's roof and being under his roof, also under his rule, with little more autonomy than a child.

Once she was married, the loss of her virginity would be of neither relevance, nor concern, provided Georgio did not suspect and that was another worry, although judging him objectively, he did not appear to be a knowing man. From what she could gather, his career in the Army had been his one absorbing interest until now. She was not in love but realistically Leonora asked herself, 'How many women of good family are in love when marrying into a good family?' More important was that as a married woman she would be mistress in her own home, no longer under her father's dominance. Viewed fairly, marriage offered advantages, a new life, a fresh start, a measure of independence and autonomy that she certainly did not enjoy at present and so, if Georgio proposed as she expected, Leonora, calmly and clinically resolved to accept.

Amelia was upset. She had so wanted a different, freer life than this for her daughter. Tactfully, as much as she could, she questioned Leonora, "Why?" and doubted not only the truth of her answers, but the wisdom of her decision. Alva however, along with Raimundo and not least Georgio, was delighted. Hiding her anxiety Amelia wished her daughter much happiness. She would have preferred a longer engagement but Alva had already embarked on the arrangements and her protest, "Why this rush to the altar?" fell on deaf ears.

From now until her wedding day, Leonora would be chaperoned. 'How little they know,' she reflected, 'the damage has already been done.'

On the night of her engagement she wanted to be glad, to feel the way she thought she should, but was too tired, too drained and the words of the old Spanish proverb she had heard Letitia quote, came to her mind.

"Hoy casado. Manana cansado." "Married today. Tired tomorrow." Well, "Hoy cansado." She was tired today, but surely everything would now be better.

It was a summer wedding, a glittering affair. The sun was shining brightly. The Cathedral was full and the crowds outside were waiting as the bride arrived in the splendid, family crested landau drawn by four white Arab horses. Apart from the brass and paintwork of the coach, the whole ensemble was a study in virginal white.

The first chords of music announced the bride's approach. The heavy crescendo of the organ began The Wedding March and to Leonora it seemed in that moment, as if her marriage contract was already sealed. There was no going back now and as the chords of the organ merged into one sonorous, drawn-out weight of sound, Alva took his daughter's arm and slowly, with steady pace, began the long walk down the aisle.

In those endless moments as Alva's unhurried and deliberate tread brought them ever closer to the altar rails, there flashed before Leonora's eyes the sequence of events from the moment she had realised she was pregnant up to this instance and it seemed she had been on a predetermined course. She could think of no one point at which she could have changed the direction or forward movement of her decisions any more than she could stop time itself, or let go of her father's arm, cease walking down the aisle and tell him she had changed her mind.

What choices had she had? To run away with no means of supporting herself, to where? to what? Or to have barged in through the bedroom door on Ralph and...whoever she was, and told him she was pregnant, or have turned down Marianna's offer and simply let things be until her growing waistline made her grand announcement for her and then be shut away until the birth and have her child taken from her. But in none of those moments had she had the courage, or the confidence, or the wisdom, to do other than she had.

She had not yet taken her vows. The contract had not yet been signed. She was still unmarried and, as she moved steadily forward by her father's side, her forearm resting on his, she reminded herself that, in actuality, she still could change her mind. But the thought was nonsense for of course she knew that she could not, not now, and by the same token, it seemed to her she could no more have acted differently in any one of those moments that had just been flashing through her memory, for then as now, she had been hemmed in by circumstances she could not change and the road ahead had led only in the one direction she had taken.

But no, that was not so. What had happened had not been predetermined. None of these events amounted to the triumph of Determinism over Freewill, for free choice had been hers...in the beginning. In those moments of that evening with Ralph, she had had free choice then. She had been on no treadmill then. She could have acted other than she had. She could have turned aside. She could have chosen differently...back then...back at the beginning.

Alva slowed his pace. The High Altar loomed. From the front pew her mother smiled at her and, in the rush of love Leonora felt, was deep gladness that she had not lost her trust. It was the kernel of precious joy to which she must hold.

Her long, silk train tended by her bridesmaids, swept the floor as they drew near to where Georgio stood waiting and Alva, releasing his hold, led her to him. Turning to hand over her bouquet, Leonora momentarily glanced at the congregation of family members and friends, the cream of Cordoba's high society, guests from Madrid, representatives from the Army and judiciary and many politicians. Splashes of bright colours and pastel shades worn by the women interspersed the square cut, sombre suits and uniforms of the men and across on the far wall Leonora caught sight of the confessional door and quickly looked away.

All appeared unreal as if events were unfolding in disregard of her. The altar rails opened. The bishop stepped forward. The dissonance of the organ died away and the long, solemn ceremony began. London, her debut season, the life that she had lived there, Ralph, Ardleagh, all had existed in another realm, belonging to a world very different to the one in which she must now act out her life.

Having missed Leonora's debut and her presentation at Court, Margaret had been doubly anxious to attend her niece's wedding. Getting away had not been easy. Unable to make the journey himself, Frederick had been fractious and her departure with James had been delayed. Eventually however, all details had been finalised and they had arrived in Cordoba with just one day to spare. Margaret was now enjoying it all immensely, but James was concerned. Leonora was not at all the girl she had once been. She had lost weight and looked strained. He watched her now as the marriage service came to an end and she descended the altar steps. Her every movement was too measured too guarded and he knew her well enough to know something was amiss.

A while later, as James was waiting in the throng of well wishers surrounding her, he caught her eye and for an instant the mask of her facade failed. The expression in those soft, deep dark, amber eyes was an appeal. Swiftly, reacting to instinct, James brusquely pushed his way through the crowd but when he reached her, the smile had been put back in place.

For the last several weeks, teams of workmen had been employed, restoring and renovating the ancient castle's main hall and several of its rooms. Alva had decided that after the reception and the departure of the bride and groom, the rest of the celebratory days would, for tradition's sake, be held there.

So it was that after the wedding, the carriages and cars of chosen guests made the journey to the castle on the estate. No expense had been spared. Political friends had been invited, along with Raimundo and several from the Army. It seemed to James the festivities were as much in celebration of the success of the new Dictatorship with its promise of power and control, as they were of Leonora's marriage and still troubled by the change in her, he could not get into the party spirit.

Raimundo however was in excellent form. He had spent the last several minutes regaling the guests with an entertaining account of a dialogue between King Alphonse and the Italian ambassador, in which the King had continually referred to Primo as 'My Mussolini'.

"One must admit," another guest volunteered "…there are parallels to be drawn, politically of course, not socially, although for a man of low birth Mussolini has done well to win the approval of the Monarchy, the Establishment and by all accounts, the Vatican also. I gather the Hierarchy is pleased with him. His new Fascist Party is now indisputably in control. It scored a resounding victory in Italy's general election in April, gaining nearly four hundred seats of the five hundred and thirty-five available. It may serve us well to cultivate a cordial relationship."

The brandy and the port flowed, tongues loosened and discussions, though still political, turned to matters closer to home. Arguments became more frank, more to the point, and it became evident that the issues of greatest interest were rooted more in the events affecting each man's individual prospects, the retention of his inheritance and security, than in the state of the country as a whole.

'Amelia was right,' reflected James. 'They're forever afraid of losing what they have, when others have nothing and then, when there's strife, they think they're the ones with all the worries. They forget the old Spanish proverb,

'The bigger your roof, the more snow will fall on it'.

"You're very quiet James." said one of Alva's political friends, "You were in Berlin at the time of Hitler's trial. Shouldn't you be telling us about it?"

"Yes, but..." James paused, thankful to see the musicians moving to their places, "...the music is about to start and before it does I'd like to propose a toast, 'To Leonora, to her happiness and that of Georgio.'"

There was a scraping of chairs and a raising of glasses. James' words were echoed and the toast was drunk.

'And where does Leonora come in all of this,' he pondered. His good wishes went out to her but, of themselves were not enough, for 'If wishes were horses then beggars would ride.'

CHAPTER TWENTY-ONE

Lancashire. August 1924

*I*t was not long after Leonora's wedding that Amelia's letter to James arrived at Ardleagh Hall. She confessed she was writing somewhat hesitantly and hoped she was not doing the wrong thing, but she had chanced upon a couple of photographs of Claire in a haute-couture fashion magazine and was wondering if James wished to see them or was he endeavouring to put her from his mind. If this were so, he must ignore her letter. James rang Amelia at once. She told him the fashion house had been of no help whatever.

"Either they don't know the photographer's whereabouts or they're not saying. When I pressed them they became quite distant indicating the phone number was private. A couple of days later I contacted them again in a roundabout way and learned that 'the model in the fashion-plate', Claire, to you and me James, had not modelled any of the gowns on the catwalk at the show, nor appeared in person. Her only part to play had been to be photographed in one or two of the most costly garments in the collection and it seemed the shoots had taken place behind the scenes. I was told the photographer is very selective about what he will and will not do and sets a strict limit on the number. The adverts in which his shots of Claire are used are without exception extremely successful, so the fashion houses reserve their quota to display their most exclusive and expensive creations, with the result that many a rich, society woman feels almost a need to be seen wearing one.

"From what I could gather, she doesn't work for anyone other than him. I suppose that must be a condition of her contract for it seems he behaves quite proprietarily towards her. He's Rumanian by the way. The result is that she remains the exquisite beauty whom nobody knows. Of course James, we both know Claire is lovely but the shots this Rumanian takes of her portray her as utterly stunning. Her features and qualities are there already, but he has a way of accentuating them and the mystery he's surrounding her with, does add to the allure."

It was a relief to know Claire was well and successful in her new life, especially so given the high unemployment and political uncertainties elsewhere, but James could not help wondering whether she and the Rumanian were together in ways other than their work. The thought was tormenting, but no good came from brooding. He would do what he always did when trying to get his mind off things, saddle his horse and go cross-country, or turn to his music.

Today, it was towards the stable yard he headed. He would put his new horse, a strong well-boned bay to the gallop, take everything that lay in his path in his stride, open no gates and avoid no ditches. It would make him concentrate.

He headed in the direction of Martin's cottage, a small, detached, stone house on the edge of a farm a few miles outside the village where he was renting a couple of fields to graze the brood mares he had bought.

By the time James arrived at his place he had managed to get a handle on his mood with strictures to himself to stop acting like an adolescent chasing foolish notions about Claire. She had managed to make the fresh start she wanted. It was up to him to do the same. It had been her decision to leave and the last thing she needed was for him to drag up the past when, as was evident, she was putting it behind her.

Martin came out to meet him. He cast an expert eye on the gelding.

"Yes," he pronounced, "...looks the part. Turn him loose in the back paddock for a breather and we'll go inside."

He led the way into a clean, well-kept parlour. On the table was a wireless set with some parts beside it. It was only recently that the B.B.C. had begun broadcasting and Martin had been trying to tune into their wavelength.

"Reception's erratic at times," he said, pulling out a chair and inviting James to sit down, "... hard to know if the fault's with this set or due to transmission. When it's working, I'll take it down to the Labour Club where the Union meetings are held. It's another source of information. Even if there's bias, at least the men will get to hear what's being said and maybe get a different slant on the news they read in the papers."

James looked at the bits and pieces. "I'm afraid I can't be of any help," he said, smiling ruefully.

"No? Well I have to admit if you sat me down at your piano it's not much I'd able to do with that either," conceded the engineer.

He tidied the table moving the wireless and parts to one side and sat down opposite James. He seemed discouraged and as he ran his hand through his tousled hair, the look in his black-brown eyes was troubled. It was unlike him to be sombre.

"...trouble in the mines?" asked James.

"No. Well...yes and no, I suppose. It's the men. Nothing specific, not at the moment, but there's an undercurrent, hard to pinpoint, something in the atmosphere."

"Well, you would know," said James and waited, wanting to hear what was on his mind. Since working closely with Martin, he had come to respect the engineer's intuitive powers.

Martin remained thoughtful. After a minute or two, shrugging as if to shake off his mood, he replied.

"Oh, it's just that after all those promises from Lloyd George when the war ended, about a land fit for heroes, getting rid of the slums, every man a decent wage and the like and then the let-down that followed when nothing improved..." Martin sighed as he spoke.

"The National Debt was enormous at the end of the war," volunteered James. "It drained resources, left little for bettering conditions and...it was a Coalition at the time. The Liberals had to keep in with the Conservatives and social reform's never been a Tory priority."

"All the same, given the promises, the workers expected something."

"The Conservatives have their own agenda," said James. "Coalitions have never been to their liking. A couple of years ago, late in twenty-two they knew exactly what they were doing when they voted to end it. Lloyd George fell from office and the Conservatives got into power with an overall majority."

"Yes, smart move," agreed Martin, "but it wasn't such a smart move late last year when Stanley Baldwin, decided he needed a mandate to put through his reforms, called another election, lost their overall majority and fell from office, leaving the way open for Labour to come to power, with Ramsey Macdonald as Prime Minister."

"Yes, I remember," said James. "My father was furious, no longer just 'out-of-office agitators' as he once labelled the Labour Party, but actually in power and threatening not only to nationalise the mines, but to impose a levy on individual fortunes as well."

"The first Labour government ever and the Unions had struggled for it for so long. But Labour's been in charge for seven months, since January, and the men reckon Macdonald has done damn all for them," commented Martin.

"True, but as MacDonald himself said, he may be in office but he's not in power, not real power. Labour's way short of the majority needed for that. It's Labour's turn now to keep the Liberals sweet and MacDonald's admitted he's had to lower his socialist sights."

"Try telling that to the men at the coal face. They say they've been badly treated. They expected better than this. It's not only that things haven't improved," replied Martin, who had been studying the figures, "...they've got steadily worse with no sign of the tide turning. It's being said MacDonald's more concerned with foreign policy than with what's happening at home. Late in nineteen-nineteen, unemployment stood at three hundred thousand. Two years later in twenty-one, it was past two million and still rising with wages falling. That was the year there was coal rationing and a State of Emergency and the miners' National strike ended only when the Government agreed to subsidise the coal industry, but the men have still not felt the benefit.

"The improvements you introduced," he continued, "taking electricity below ground, better safety regulations and the like, have kept our men from striking but there've been strikes in other pits this year. There's a bad feeling that they've been short-changed and given the solidarity that exists among miners due to the dangers they face, they pull together and it doesn't take long for resentment to spread."

"Labour took over at a bad time," ventured James. "There isn't the money for a public works programme to reduce unemployment and being the first Labour Government to come to power, they're trying to show they're responsible, balancing the Budget, keeping the Liberals onside, all the while knowing they'll be out of office if they don't."

"...seems to me that day's not far off," responded Martin. "As you said, first time in office, the odds are stacked against them. The cabinet includes those from less privileged backgrounds and schooling and to score in party politics one needs experience in the manoeuvring that takes place. MacDonald's worst moves come from not knowing what goes on behind the scenes and while the Conservatives are jockeying and juggling and pulling strings, he's doing everything straight up and by the book, afraid of losing votes next time round."

"...and the Conservatives are doing their damnedest to make sure they do, constantly playing the Communist card against them," added James.

"True," agreed Martin. "Although," he added after some moments, a wry smile twisting his lips, "...it would help Labour's image if they'd stop singing 'The Red Flag' at the end of their meetings. But I guess old habits die hard."

He raised himself out of his chair, settled the kettle into the embers in the grate and, having offered James tea, took cups and saucers and a big tin of biscuits from the cupboard.

Riding home, James was thoughtful. He would hate events to prove Martin right, but looking at what was happening, could well see they might. His comment about the singing of 'The Red Flag' was very apt. Given the bullish mood of the opposition, the anthem might as well be called 'The Red Rag'. It was certainly doing nothing to dissuade his father and friends from arguing that Socialism was little other than Communism in a less virulent form.

Since becoming involved in the mines James had taken advantage of every opportunity to improve conditions. Martin had proved invaluable and James had promoted him. The two of them worked well together and it had begun to look as though, given time, things would change for the better, but these last months had thrown cold water on such hopes. His father's overall health had improved and he was stronger in himself, but his physical disabilities had remained the same and his resentment at his handicaps, possibly permanent, made him irascible and subject to abrupt mood changes.

The specialist had warned Margaret that a stroke often affects a patient's personality and advised her not to take it personally, nor let it upset her. She had done her best to be understanding but it had to be admitted that over the past months, she and Frederick had had their moments. She continued to hope that as time passed he would adjust to his changed circumstances, but hoped in vain. His increase in energy went measure for measure with his mounting frustration at being disabled. When Margaret mentioned this to the new specialist Frederick had appointed, he advised her this was a symptom over which, due to changes in the brain, her husband would have little control and he firmly cautioned her not to exacerbate the situation by disagreeing or arguing with him, since this would provoke further irritability and could seriously set him back.

Unable to ascertain the form a serious setback may take and left to contend with him as best she could, she dared not defy the instructions in case something ghastly befell. Knowing the dreadful remorse she would suffer if that happened, she considered it better to pander to him, to keep her patience and the peace, except that the peace was exactly what his moods overturned.

James considered the advice misguided. Whilst agreeing that keeping one's patience and making allowances were essential, he did not believe that never remonstrating with him was the answer. Far from helping matters it seemed to be developing into a situation of 'an inch given, a yard taken'. Frederick was continuing to make his presence felt and Margaret's reserves were wearing thin.

Prospects on the economic front were also bleak. Labour's coming to power had not helped. Imports of foreign coal undercut the price and profits were tight. Many mine owners were reducing wages and extending hours, thus aggravating the situation further. Dock workers, tram drivers and railwaymen were also striking and the Cabinet was ready to introduce the Emergency Powers Act, causing Labour's own supporters to accuse them of behaving like Capitalists. There was no telling how the situation would develop.

Although there had been virtually no trouble in his own mines Frederick was convinced that given the state of affairs, it was only a matter of time before there would be and he had been checking the profit margins. Improving working conditions was costly and, looked at on a weekly basis, returns were reduced. The fact that this was off-set in the long run by the unbroken continuity of production, and that improved attitudes and an increase in safety resulted in greater efficiency, cut no ice with Frederick because he maintained there would be less inefficiency and fewer stoppages anyway if the workers were kept in their place, as they would be if proper action were taken.

The long held differences between father and son were souring their relationship once more. Attempts to talk things through led to arguments and in really difficult moments James found himself almost wishing Labour would carry out its election manifesto, introduce Nationalisation and so relieve him of his task. But then the spectre of the Brackworth mine would rise again and he tempered the disloyalty of such thoughts with the realisation that Labour was unlikely to survive.

The fall was not long in coming.

It was provoked by Labour having signed an Anglo-Soviet Treaty recognising the U.S.S.R. and was further aggravated by the Campbell case and the Zinoviev letter.

When J.R. Campbell, editor of the Communist Workers Weekly, wrote to the Armed Forces requesting them not to allow themselves to be involved in strike-breaking, he was accused of sedition. He had been decorated for gallantry while in the armed forces and Ramsey MacDonald intervened on his behalf. The Attorney General dropped the charge, whereupon Labour was accused of having interfered with the course of justice on behalf of the Communists. Not wishing to be associated, the Liberals threw in their lot with the Conservatives and in early October the Labour government fell.

In the forthcoming election, the Conservatives trump card was a letter purporting to have been written by Zinoviev, President of the Communist Third International, and sent from Moscow to the Communist Party in England urging them to revolt. It was published by the foreign Office five days before polling and proof of its forgery was not made public until after the voting had taken place.

Causing panic, it had swung the vote against Labour and the Tories were returned to power in a sweeping victory. The Labour Party's howls of protest about a dirty tricks campaign were as water off a duck's back to the Conservatives. They were in power again with a strong, working majority and secure tenure of office and would be able to take the steps they had considered needed since the end of the war.

During the celebration at Ardleagh Hall much was said about change, but not the kind of change James wanted. There was a great deal of talk from his father and the other mine-owners about settling disputes, but hearing them speak, it was obvious their chosen method of achieving this would be to stand firm until the other side was forced to give way.

Clearly the battle lines were being drawn. Both sides were bracing themselves for the struggle. The crisis that was brewing had been too long in the making for it not to happen. The only uncertainty remaining…was when?

CHAPTER TWENTY-TWO.

Lancashire. Ardleagh. Late April 1926

*T*he smooth, polished steel of the oven's heavy latch, slid softly forwards onto its keeper, rose evenly and clicked home. It was a gentle, familiar sound. Martin awoke and stirred, recollecting where he was and lay listening to the reassuring sounds as his uncle moved about the room, quietly making ready for the day. He had stayed the night in his uncle's small, terraced house in the village and slept on a makeshift bed of two armchairs pushed together in front of the grate of the big, black-leaded, iron and steel range.

The range, it was the mainstay and comfort of the house, its heart and focal point, and was common and identical to each house in the row. As a child, Martin had looked upon it as a thing of wonder. The admiration he had bestowed upon it then still lingered so that even now through half closed eyes, he still appreciated the ingenuity of its design.

A multipurpose contraption, it comprised a large oven and a smaller one for baking bread, several recesses with cavities for anything needing to be kept warm and a wide mantle-piece that overhung the rails for drying clothes. On either side of its open fire, were grids and racks on which stood kettles and cooking pans. Heavier containers for heating water, hung from hooks at the ends of hinged, iron arms that could be raised or lowered to swing over or away from the flames.

Rarely was its fire allowed to die. At night, its glowing embers were banked down with ashes to still give of their heat to the oven wherein a billycan of tea leaves and hot water was always placed to brew throughout the night in readiness for the morning, for although the house had gas for lighting, it did not serve for cooking or heating purposes.

The light of dawn was showing through the curtain's chink. The day upon them was the day Martin had hoped would never come. He roused himself, rose and doused his head under the tap above the only sink. To the side of it, a long, tin bath hung on the wall, for none of these houses boasted a bathroom. The table was already set with mugs and plates, a crusty, home baked loaf, a pot of jam, milk and the billycan of tea. It had a tangy flavour, fruit of stewing all night in the oven, but it was hot and strong and welcome.

Martin had stayed in the village overnight. He wanted to be close to the station to catch the first train of the morning to Manchester. Six o'clock and the clatter of clogs that had been making a racket on the pavement outside the window had almost ceased. The morning shifts of mine and mill would now begin. At Pendle's bakery where Claire had worked, women would have left their homemade hotpots to cook slowly in the shop's large, communal ovens while they were at work. They would collect them on their way home in readiness for the family supper.

It was hard life, but it was ordered. There was no other way these people could survive. The long hours of their grinding, dangerous and exhausting work rendered scant comfort and left them little time. Their living was eked out and measured to the penny, to the hour. Always on the edge of poverty with no reserves, no margin for false moves, they could not afford to make mistakes.

The crisis that all those in the mining industry had long known to be brewing had finally come to a head. The government subsidy to the coal industry had been meant to end last summer. The price of coal had been falling and the mine owners had pressed hard to reduce wages and extend working hours. The miners had fiercely opposed them. Their slogan was, "Not a penny off the pay, not an hour on the day," or, as their President Herbert Smith had more succinctly phrased his response, "Now't doing."

The government had averted a lockout by offering to continue the subsidy for another nine months and by setting up a Coal Commission under the chairmanship of Sir Herbert Sankey, to look into things. The miners had cooperated and agreed to wait.

Five weeks ago, in March this year, the findings of the Commission had been made known. The Commission's report favoured the colliery owners. It supported the owners' demands. The report's three hundred pages stated that although the mines were making sufficient profits, some sections of the industry were less remunerative and a cut in wages and a 'temporary' increase of the working day were recommended. The subsidy was to be discontinued. An improvement in conditions was advised.

The Conservative government accepted the proposals. Disregarding the amount of profit being made by the owners, the Prime Minister agreed to a cut in the miners' wages of around thirteen per cent. The miners were angry, anxious and helpless. Their average wage was three pounds a week. They did not want the fight but had no choice. If the owners got their way, longer hours and a cut in pay would drive even deeper the knife already cutting to the bone.

The owners wanted both concessions, a cut in wages and longer hours. The Miners' Federation rejected both proposals and the wrangling began. There was a great deal of sympathy for the miners from the other main Unions, those of the transport and heavy industry, construction, the railways, gas and electricity and the printing trade. The General Council of the Trade Union Congress gave approval for a General Strike. It was to be nationwide, a combined, massive show of strength supported by eighty per cent of the Trade Union movement. The country would grind to a halt. On hearing this, the Government immediately began to prepare as if for war, mobilising all resources, including the Armed Forces. The Conservatives claimed the threatened strike was 'An Organised Attempt to Starve the Nation' and was 'Nothing less than an Attempt to overthrow the Government of the Day.' At strategic points in London, armoured cars were assembled complete with machine guns protruding from their turrets. An Organisation for the 'Maintenance of Supplies' was set up and plans were made for Hyde Park to be closed to the public and used as a milk and supplies depot. The workers were referred to as the enemy and calls were put out to the middle and upper classes asking them to volunteer to fight.

The Government, having got its defences and emergency measures in place now welcomed the confrontation. It was the showdown the ruling classes had been waiting for since the war, their chance to demonstrate their strength. They viewed the T.U.C.'s threat of a General strike as a challenge. Having accepted it and readied themselves for the struggle, those in power had no intention of backing down. They had locked horns with the workforce and were not going to show weakness by compromise. The Government was confident of its power. Well it might be. It had troops, Army and Naval forces and thousands of special constables on alert and standing by.

Fears of what might happen were growing and some of the Union leaders were making last minute appeals for moderation and compromise. The Labour Party itself, whilst deeply concerned about the miners' plight, was also anxious to avoid the situation being used to portray the Unions as spearheading what the Conservatives were now saying was not a strike, but a revolution. Many in the miners' ranks were hoping that a solution could still be found but the crisis point had been reached and this weekend, the last in April, would prove decisive.

The mood of the meeting at the Labour Club last night had been bitter and depressed. After the meeting, Martin met James and they had talked long into the night. James knew the adamant stance of the owners. They were not going to back down. The majority the Conservatives had gained at the last election meant they were faced with little real opposition. As James said, "Too much power makes for bad government." The mine owners had the wealth and resources to see the strike through. Whatever the strike may cost, they did not intend to let the workers get the upper hand. The miners' situation was very different and Union leaders from around the country had agreed to meet in London for further discussion. Their final decision would fatefully dictate the matter. The outcome would be irrevocable. Before going to the London however, they wanted to talk with the various representatives of the local branches, hence Martin's early departure for Manchester.

The government subsidy was due to end on Friday, the thirtieth of April. If the Unions' final decision was to declare for the strike, then the stoppage of the subsidy would determine the time for the miners to cease work. Martin glanced at the wall clock, ticking away the seconds. Time to the deadline was running out. If work stopped, a lockout by the owners would follow. He felt a chill, for the anxious, sinking sensation gripping him was not fear in its normal form with which one could grapple. This was the inexorable approach of something that could neither be turned back nor overcome.

He finished his tea, put down his mug and looked across at his uncle's face. The stamp of honesty was clearly marked upon it. It was strong and resolute, lined and set, pitted with small abrasions that had healed over, sealing in the coal grit where it had embedded beneath the skin.

"Well lad, you'd best be on your way," he said, glancing across at his nephew. There was kindness and a knowing empathy in the eyes of the older man. He rose, giving a gentle touch to Martin's shoulder as he passed behind his chair and moved towards the door to take his coat down from the peg in readiness for him.

"They'll have their talks, but the bosses already have their minds made up," he added.

Martin nodded in agreement. In his heart he knew it too.

Outside the wind was blowing chill, spewing a steady drizzle down the valley against the smoke-grimed cottages. Hunching his shoulders he turned up his coat collar and walked steadily past the long lines of identical, terraced houses. He knew the families in most of them, many with sons as well as fathers working down the pits. With the breadwinners no longer earning, the strike would hit hard.

Mid-afternoon and the Union leaders were already on their way to London. Travelling home by train, Martin, conscious of his weariness, tried to relax to the wheels' rhythmic rumble as the carriage belted out its speed along the track, but he was too much in the grip of things. The atmosphere at the meeting had been tense. The general consensus among the miners had been that the Government must put forward something more, but Martin was anxious, for as James had said, neither the Government nor the owners would make concessions. This strike, the first General strike in British history, would be unlike any that had gone before.

The General Strike of 1926, 'Yes, this one will be different,' gauged Martin. 'Its outcome will set a precedent for the future and therefore, once begun, it must be fought to the finish.' He leaned against the plank-hard upholstery of the carriage seat and closed his eyes, trying to shut out the worry facing him that not only was there no other option, there was no real hope, for the opposition they were up against had far more means than they had to weather out the storm.

As expected, the talks availed nothing. The subsidy was discontinued and across the country, work stopped on Monday, the third of May. The Conservatives branded the strike a revolution and blackened the strikers for holding the country to ransom. The Government produced its own news-sheet, The British Gazette, and printed its own propaganda. Troops and armoured vehicles paraded on the streets. Soldiers were marched ostentatiously through the main thoroughfares. It created an air of urgency and danger and was quite unnecessary, but it gave the Government the opportunity to show its strength and intimidate the strikers, which was of course, the object of the exercise.

The T. U. C. had said it would distribute essential foodstuffs. Almost all the Unions had come out in support of the miners. Had it not been for the Government's emergency measures and its appeal to the middle and upper classes to come forward as volunteers, the stoppage would have been virtually complete.

A few days after the strike began Martin saw Ralph. He was actually acting as stoker on one of the trains whistling its nonstop way through the village level crossing. His bon-viveur energy and exuberance were bursting from him as he leaned out from the footplate, seemingly very proud of himself, calling and waving to Martin. He was obviously having great fun in his new role as one of those who had responded to the Government's appeal for help to break the strike. Martin ignored him. What else did he expect?

There were many such volunteers from Government supporters, so many in fact that tasks could not be found for all of them, but they sorted themselves out, lending their services to the various organising bodies that had sprung up, all bent on playing a part in defeating the strikers who were still being accused of 'Holding a Pistol to the Nation's Head'.

Several offering to help in this way were wealthy with no real jobs, social dilettantes and debutantes. There was a great spirit amongst them and they joined enthusiastically in what many of them saw as a splendid opportunity to have a jolly time. Never before had they had the chance to keep the buses running or issue tickets on a tram. It was all quite a lark. There was however, a distinct shortage of volunteers to go down the mines.

Almost a week into the strike, the former Home Secretary, Sir John Simon, had the bright idea of declaring the strike illegal. He claimed that it was not covered by the 1906 Act and therefore the Trade Unions' funds were not immune from payment for damages caused by the strike. The accuracy of this was arguable, but arguable by whom? The judges, almost to a man, were from the ruling classes. But on hearing about it many Union leaders took fright and a rift opened up between the Miners' Union and others in the T.U.C. In any case, the strike was beginning to be seen as not working and support for the miners from the rest of the Unions, was beginning to collapse.

On May 13th, the Daily Mail, a newspaper that spoke for the Government, announced, 'The Surrender of the Revolutionaries'. Other headlines were, 'Victory for The People' and, 'T.U.C. Strike called off unconditionally'. The other Unions had ended their strike.

The miners now stood alone. James was utterly opposed to his father's attitude and that of certain other owners with whom he had spoken. Their stance was dictated solely by concern for their lifestyles and he was galled at the callousness of some of their remarks. Like Martin he knew the situation was destroying the livelihood of the mining community, that the meagre fabric of their lives was being ripped apart. But the owners remained adamant and although the strike was certainly not solely his father's fault, his attitude was totally in keeping with those whose collective fault it was. James realised how genuinely unable were many of those on the Government's side, to look at matters from angles other their own and how well this incapacity worked to their advantage, for not only did it save them from wasting time and energy pondering the merits of the case, it also blessed them with immunity from moral guilt since, seeing only their own viewpoint, they were oblivious to the damage they inflicted.

The strike dragged on. The miners scraped to survive, snaring rabbits, scouring the countryside, leaving their families to look for work further afield and sending their wages home. The first sign that money was running out was the disappearance, one by one, of the ribbons of smoke that in better times, trailed upwards from the cottage chimneys. In some homes, the big, black grates were now cold, chilling to the touch. There was no heat in the house, no hot water and no means of cooking.

Women and children climbed the slag heaps on the outskirts of the village, those great, grey, mountainous heaps of 'slack', the name given to the broken slate-shale that was the waste and debris of the mines. Swarming up and over it, they rooted and sifted it through for whatever bits of coal may still be found, anything they could use to light a fire. Then there were the other signs, the listlessness of children, the skin sores, the down-at-heel appearance, lank hair and other betrayals that poverty and hunger were biting hard. Of course, people pretended otherwise and put on a brave face, a face in which the lines were deepening in the sallow skin.

Soon they would be forced to admit defeat, for the determination of the Government and mine-owners, was as grim and unyielding as it had been in the beginning. Signs of neglect and deprivation were everywhere. The slag heaps had been thoroughly sifted and picked clean. No-one climbed them now. With no fuel, grates were empty and for many there was little food. Now and then a house was seen with blinds drawn in mourning, as deaths occurred from malnutrition, disease and ailments that at other times would have been resisted.

The miners were finished, locked out and desperate, and on the streets small groups of gaunt, ill-clad men leaned against the walls of half-empty corner shops or stood around as if waiting, but for what? Seeing the telltale signs James checked on the statistics.

Not wanting to hear his father's comments he began avoiding him, but there was no avoiding the facts. Deaths had increased. Not knowing what to do, he called on the village doctor. Dr Sarson was a kindly man living in frugal fashion with his wife and only daughter. His dispensary was a small, neat kitchen type room behind the surgery, where his wife helped with the work of mixing potions and ointments, sterilising bottles and other tasks. It was she who opened the door to James and led him through to the back of the house.

James did not know the doctor well and had not seen him for several weeks. He was past middle age and as he got up from his chair, James was shaken at the change in his appearance. He did not just look strained, he looked haggard. Greetings over, James took the chair he offered hardly knowing what to say, but there was no need. It was one of those moments when understanding takes the place of words. The issue in question was there in the room with them, invisible, but tangible as a third presence waiting to be addressed.

Without preliminary, the younger man broke the silence.

"It's a bad business. Is there anything I can do?"

Dr Sarson shifted in his chair and for a few moments did not reply. James waited, taking in the shabby cleanliness of his surroundings. Mrs Sarson came in carrying a tray of tea. She too looked worn, but cheerful in a resolute way, as though fixedly determined not to let slip the attitude of positive purpose she had managed to adopt. Excusing herself on account of being busy, she withdrew.

"Well, at the end of the day, what it comes down to is, as always, money. It's as basic as that," said Dr.Sarson, in reply to James' query. "It's not a question of my not attending them if they can't pay. I do that more than often. But conditions are so bad now there's very real hunger, toting up to what amounts to slow starvation or 'nutritional deficiency', to use the more acceptable term. The Cooperative Society has been supplying free milk to the children but ailments are multiplying and folk are coming down with things they'd normally withstand.

"But they won't admit that they're defeated, that they've reached the end and by then it's often too late. It's not so much their pride," the doctor continued, "it's that the alternative, defeat, will force them into appalling, long term conditions with wages cut still further. I had been thinking that maybe, just maybe, seeing the suffering, the government would do something but..." Dr. Sarson broke off. What more was there to say?

James shook his head. "Neither the government nor the mine-owners will do anything."

"I'm pushed to the limit with the work load," explained Dr Sarson. "There's only one of me and it's not merely the matter of diagnosis. It's the medicines they need. We mix our own here, but how do I buy supplies and how am I and my family to live if I'm not paid something?" The older man sighed. When he continued, he was clearly disturbed.

"But it's far worse when they don't call me...when the first I hear is a request to sign a death certificate and that is happening now. Some of them, when they've no hope of paying and all that is left to them, is their dignity...they just die."

James had known the screw was tightening, but not to the extent it had. He had been relying on Martin for information until he realised that even Martin had become tight-lipped.

"Yes, it's as one of the engineers was saying. They keep it to themselves and you can't get behind closed doors," said James. "When things are only moderately bad and there's still hope, they'll talk. But when things get to extremes they do the opposite, clam up completely, refusing to admit to the awfulness they can do nothing about."

A few days after talking to Dr. Sarson James drove down to London. He was lucky. The dealer in the Mayfair showrooms gave him a good price for his car. 'So he should, that Lagonda was a beauty', thought James. He had a few other ideas also on how to help what he called the Dr. Sarson fund. He would not tell his father. He would only be accused of subsidising the opposition, of being a traitor to one's class. James did however hope to be there if his father found out. After the happenings of these last months he would be almost glad to see him vexed.

October and the dark evenings were closing in. When night fell, families still with money for the meter could put a match to the gas mantle, but the guttering, greenish-tinged light was dreary in a cold room with an empty hearth. Those without fuel depended on neighbours to boil water for them or cook whatever food they could obtain. Some houses were almost bare of furniture. Whatever they had once owned had long been sold. For those with no other skills and no resources to fall back on, the choice was stark. Return to work or starve. The strike finished officially on the twelfth of November. The miners must now work longer hours for less pay, with no prospect of improvement in conditions.

Frederick was relieved. With spirits raised he was in an almost expansive mood. Wine was brought from the cellar. Toasts were drunk. Despite the wooden immobility of his left leg he had managed to get himself upright and with the help of two specially designed supports was able to stand and move around a little, albeit shakily.

James was noticeably absent. Later in the evening, his father found him in the library.

"Oh, come James...at least show a little family unity in front of our guests. Join the rest of us in the drawing room and raise a glass, claret, I had the '99' opened, damned good, excellent, better than I expected."

Raising his head from the book he was reading James looked across at him.

"Thank you. I prefer not," he replied, trying to keep the coldness from his tone. He had his own reasons for being glad to see his father well again, but he could never overlook what the miners had been put through.

"Oh, I know how you're thinking. You still don't see it as to the miner's good. If we'd agreed to what they were striking for, they would have priced themselves out of their jobs."

"They weren't striking 'For' anything. They were striking 'Against'." He responded more aggressively than he had intended, "...against a cut in their wages and longer hours when they were pushed to the limit already." He put down his book. His voice had hardened. "One way and another, this strike lost the industry millions of pounds. Over fifteen million tons of coal has been imported. If such costs and losses could be sustained, the miners could have been treated with fairness and decency."

Having made his point, James chose to leave it at that and rose to go to his room, but his father, having had suspicions for some time that James had aided the miners, now asked out-right. His son's free admission led to their final showdown. Their attitudes were totally disparate. Once begun, the argument intensified and as emotions took hold, his father made it very evident that, with the help of his foremen and managers he considered himself able to take over.

It was all his son had been waiting for.

Back in his room, James knew he could no longer live under father's roof. For reasons of self-respect, he wished he had kept his silence. The owners' stance had been about maintaining the upper hand. Aware of how the mines would now be managed James wanted no benefit. Better to write his father a letter and leave it at that.

The house was in darkness. All was quiet. The tall clock in the hall below had struck midnight long ago. James pulled a couple of suitcases and two or three boxes from a high cupboard and in the pool of soft light from one small lamp, began to pack. Thinking he heard a sound he paused and listened but all was still. A gentle peace lay over the old house. He would miss this place. Yes, there it was again, a quiet tap on his door. It was his mother.

"I knew you would be awake. I heard the row between you," she said as she entered. She took in the scene at a glance. It was as she expected. For a few moments she stood in the shadows of the room, an elegant, graceful figure, the lamplight falling across her, on her hair and the folds of her long robe. She looked down at something she held in her hand.

"I believe the time has come for you to have this." she said softly as she came towards him holding out a letter. The stiff envelope bore James' name in a copperplate handwriting he recognised, but had not seen for a very long time. The mark of the seal was familiar also. It was that of his beloved grandfather, his mother's father, who had died years ago when James was in his teens. Mystified, he looked at her for explanation.

But Margaret raised her hands a little as if to say she had none to give.

"I can tell you, but little," she said gently. "Only that my father gave it to me, just before he died. His only words were that I was to wait, for a time would come...and when it did I, as his daughter, would know and must then give this to you."

"He said nothing else?" asked James.

"Nothing and I know nothing of its contents and he gave no other indication as to why or when I was to give it to you, only that I was to wait, and his promise to me as a father, that when the time came…I would know," she paused…

"It may sound strange…but a while ago in my room, in the stillness I knew he was with me…and that the time had come when I must give this to you." Silently she pressed the letter into his hand.

James thanked her. Margaret put her arms around him and held him close, then turned to leave.

Left alone he waited a while before slowly breaking the seal.

As James began to read, the shadows seemingly extended beyond the sphere of the lamp's light, past all boundaries of time and from across the years, his grandfather was speaking to him once more. His message was that James was now reading the letter because, of his own volition, he had made a certain choice, a choice regarding an impasse that he, his grandfather, had long believed would one day have to be resolved. You will have come to a crossroads and I believe I have long known the road that you will take.

Given that this matter concerns you and your father, then any decision concerning it had to be yours and yours alone, determined solely by your own inner promptings and certainly not influenced by any act or word of mine.

Often, when at the Hall, I would stroll in the garden outside the music room windows to hear you play and sometimes I would see a young, dark haired girl, half hidden by the shrubbery listening also and sometimes we listened together.

Having chosen your freedom, you are free to accept this help. Your life lies ahead of you. The values you espouse will be its determining influence and force. Some men have a love of power, but stronger and above all else, is the Power of Love. Music also, is of itself a living influence and keeping in mind the legacy that both endow, I ask you to accept the bequest I offer, for I believe that as you stand at this parting of the ways, it is the path of music you will chose.

Please accept my blessings along with the enclosed for the years of training that lie ahead, a gift to help you nurture your potential which will in turn, be your gift to the world."

"My love will be with you always,
Your grandfather,
Thomas."

The enclosed was the pass book to an account in James' name that his grandfather had opened for him many years ago.

His mother's timing had been perfect and James could only wonder at the depth of intuition existing still between a father and his daughter.

He must thank her again, early in the morning and explain to her. Then if he had her blessing also, he would leave as soon as possible, for Vienna.

CHAPTER TWENTY-THREE

Lancashire. December 1926

*T*he heavy locomotive dragged itself into Manchester's busy Piccadilly station and with the usual clanking and grinding of brakes, grated its wheels to a stop. The carriages jerked and then were still.

As the train had journeyed on through the north of England, Claire had seen for herself the sad effects of the long drawn out strike. The dingy side streets and overcrowded backyards visible through the soot-speckled carriage window conveyed impressions of families miserably lacking the barest of needs. It was depressing and all the more so by bringing into sharp focus, the contrast with extreme wealth she had seen elsewhere. In all honesty Claire asked herself, could she envisage returning to this?

Picking up her portmanteau she stepped down onto the platform. Inside the station nothing much had changed. Everything was just so much shabbier than when she was last here, or was it that in those days she was conditioned not to notice? It was noisy and cold. Carriage doors slammed. Whistles pierced the ears and swirls of grit eddied in the draughts. She crossed to the ticket office to enquire the time of the next train to the village, but she did not intend to go so far. She would get off at one of the outlying stations and take a taxi from there.

About a mile from Ardleagh, Claire asked the taxi driver to wait for her and took the lane from where a short distance on, the Hall would come into view. How often she had walked this way. Since then how much her life had changed, but when the Hall became visible on the rise of land, its timeless loveliness was as if the intervening years had never been.

At first sight she stopped, her breath catching in her throat. Tears stung her eyes. How could it move her so, yet at the same time bring such peace? For several moments she stood quite still, absorbing the reality of which she so often dreamed.

Back in the taxi she directed the driver to take the narrow road bordering the garden's high wall. On seeing the little gate, she paid the driver and let him go. The latch had rusted but it was, as Anna had promised, unlocked. She had agreed to keep her visit secret for Claire had no wish to be questioned by others. She had too many unanswered questions of her own, a state of affairs that had prompted her return.

Four years ago when she had accepted Bude's offer, she had simply wanted work. When the promotion for the clothing firm had ended, Bude had closed his agency in Manchester and she had accepted his offer to continue working for him in the one he was opening in Paris. She had never supposed the work he offered would take her so far from her roots. Their success had been unexpected and there had been little time to look back or even, so it seemed, to look forward. Now she was wondering if she had gone too far.

At all times their relationship had been purely one of work. In the beginning it had been simple but as the various contracts and commissions had come their way, they entailed the making of decisions over which he had assumed control. She had not much minded at first, but now Bude rarely told her what was happening unless, or until, it was necessary for her to know and slowly drip by drip, her independence was seeping from her.

As time passed she was finding the possessive attitude he had adopted towards her, disturbing. Initially she had welcomed his protective warmth but now sensed it was keeping others at bay. She had also, of late, become concerned about her reputation. Her face was well known, but not her name. Bude had surrounded her identity with mystery. No-one really knew her. The life she had embarked upon was changing her. She used to know who and what she was, but did she know now? She had wanted, as the saying goes, to make something of herself. Was that something to be nothing more than a beautiful image, his artistic creation?

There was also another drawback. Only recently had she come to realise their liaison had given rise to speculation or, put more bluntly, gossip. She could see she had been naive, stupid even, not to be aware of this before. Although her arrangement with Bude was solely a business one, was she now being labelled like certain other women, as 'Une dame de demi-monde', one of those women of the twilight world, that questionable realm that fringes high society, dimly lit by its reflection? It is the half-world to which some women are drawn and into which others, whose reputations are regarded as somewhat shady, simply fall.

She had seen such women, always beautiful and bejewelled. They were discreetly brought by their protectors into the salons to be dressed, women who because of what they were, could never share the real lives of those whose property they had virtually become, women who looked at you with empty eyes.

It was not at all like that between her and Bude, but in truth was this how she was now regarded. Claire was no longer at ease. She had tried to explain and he had been courteous and listened, but had made no response and made no changes either. She was restless. Soon she would be twenty-seven. Was this the way her life was to continue until her looks began to fade and she was no longer needed, or things just fell apart the way they sometimes do? What then? What did she want from life? The answer was simple…but James she knew, she could never have and for that reason must not let him into her thoughts.

Anna had left the door to her rooms off the latch and Claire slipped in quickly and unnoticed. Her aunt was somewhere in the house and would be back soon. For the next few days Claire would stay here, shut away, listening to her advice and taking time to think. James was not here. He had left home and was in Vienna. That much she already knew. Had the situation been otherwise she would not have come.

The December light was fading into dusk. The fire, burning quietly in the grate, cast its glow. A kettle sizzled on the bars. Slipping off her shoes, Claire sank into the comfortably worn armchair, thankful for this place where nothing changed and for the sense of continuity it offered. Here, everything was real, the way it had always been.

While waiting, she reflected again on Bude, wondering how he had reacted when he read her message. She had tried to make herself understood, but believed she had failed. How did one describe a lack? It was like trying to paint a picture of something that was not there? Whatever she wrote seemed ungrateful. She had tried to explain her concern for her future security, pointing out that the agency was his, not theirs. But then she had destroyed that note for it seemed to say she wanted something to which she was not entitled, for of course the business was his.

He had built it up. The ideas, the expertise were his. He was the one with the connections, the one who negotiated the contracts. It was he who had made her what she was, or phrased more exactly, it was his discerning, aesthetic eye and skill that made her appear as she did in the photographs. She had no wish to argue with any of that. On the other hand, without her as a subject for his camera, their success would not have been as it was. She had been, she still was, uniquely essential to that section of his work.

In the end, she simply said how she would prefer the situation not to be, rather than how she wished it would be. She had told him she needed time alone and that she may find work here instead and had given him the forwarding address of a hotel in Manchester.

At the end of her stay with Anna, Claire returned to her hotel. While in Lancashire she wanted to see how much if anything had changed and went by bus to visit the neighbouring towns and outlying districts. She called in at the corner shops, chatted to the women as they bought their necessities for the family meal and could not but notice how old before their time so many of them were. The results of the miners' strike were obvious. Money was scarce, meat a rarity. Potatoes, root vegetables cooked in bone stock, bread, margarine, perhaps some offal and dripping that the butcher sold off cheaply, were the staple commodities of many a family's meal. She saw the effects the toll of industrial diseases had taken on the aged and that of rickets and impetigo on the young and all the other scourges of neediness that blight the destitute and the resolve arose. 'No, not for any child of mine, no child of mine will be born to live in circumstances such as these.'

Claire spent the next two weeks searching for whatever prospects Lancashire had to offer, but nothing available was of interest to her. Her inability to regard as acceptable anything she came across was due in no small measure, so she supposed, to its comparison with the scenario of wealth and luxury of which she had been so much a part in Paris. No, she corrected herself. She had not been part of it. No place in it, had she thought of as her own. The false stylized images had their place, but not her, and she had known not what her life may have in store. The time had come when she wanted to plan her future, to be settled and secure. She must make up her mind. Her savings would not last forever.

Collecting her room-key after yet another day of fruitless searching, the receptionist handed Claire a telegram. Once inside her room, she thumbed it open. The message on the small square of paper was brief and to the point.

It was from Bude and read, 'Marry me.'

She had given no thought to an eventuality such as this. A proposal was not what she had expected. She had not supposed him to be the marrying kind. For a long time Claire sat on the edge of the bed, occasionally rereading his message as though its meaning may change, but it stared back at her, stark, commanding and the same, 'Marry me'. She remained where she was, telegram in hand. Later, much later, she simply turned off the light, lay back against the pillows and, fully clothed and exhausted, fell into a deep sleep in which her worried and uncertain thoughts took her back to the time when she was staying with the Sugdens. Vividly she dreamed she was in their house and was again living in the wretched conditions that beset them. It was night, she was alone and in the blackness of the dream, could find no door and could not leave. Submerged in the strange horror that nightmares possess, she was once more encased in the awfulness of the slums, the smell of the sickly baby filling her nostrils...then she awoke.

Rising quickly she stood in the dark hotel room, willing herself to be calm, recalling where she was, and lifted her wrist to her face. Reassuringly, the fragrance of her perfume was still there. Comforted, she breathed deeply and slowly the other smells, of sickness and decay and unwashed bodies faded, but her memories of that time, of failure with its attendant guilt and helplessness, lingered on to plague and intensify her loneliness.

Groping in the darkness for the switch, she turned on the light. With reality around her once more a sense of normality returned and she attempted again to rationalise her fear. Why did that house and her memories of it fill her with such horror? She had no answer only that it was somehow entangled in the dread of ever being encased in a situation of the same crushing hopelessness as that of Mrs Sugden, ailing and impoverished with needy children she could not support, in circumstances she had never envisaged nor opted for. Her entrapment had somehow just come about, the result of one false step inexorably leading to another, each one diminishing still further, her life's choices and chances of escape.

Again, the question came to her mind. What to do with the rest of her own life, almost twenty-seven, still alone, her love for James unchanged. Hurriedly she pushed such thoughts aside for all was very different for him now. The breach with his father was healed. It must be so or James would not have worked for him these last four years and his attendance at the Viennese Conservatoire was, no doubt, his father's thanks to him for his support after his stroke. It was all so much better for James this way, for music was his joy, his raison d'etre and none of this would come about if he had left home and married her. It validated her decision not to come between him and his family and, with no way of knowing differently, this was what Claire believed.

She had no wish to be alone all her life but alone or not, she must work, apply herself to something. Resolutely Claire turned her mind to all and other possibilities, including her interest in Fashion when caring for Leonora's beautiful gowns. Her work for Bude however had been solely in modelling, advertising and marketing and although successful, it was not what she wanted. Making clothes, not marketing them, had been in her mind when refusing work in the kitchen at Ardleigh. Choosing fabrics, handling silks and velvets, colour coordinating, designing, was what appealed to her, and so, '…why not now?' Claire asked herself. Why not create her own place and space in the sphere in which Bude worked?

A few more disturbing dreams and sleepless nights until one morning she awoke, her mind made up. There was to be no changing it. Resolutely she came downstairs, took her seat in the dining room and ordered coffee, but no breakfast. Breakfast would have been more than she could manage. When she had finished, she put down her cup, crumpled her napkin and with deliberate step walked to the reception desk.

She wished to send a telegram. Her message was simple and to the point. It was to Bude and read, 'Why not? Claire'.

He responded and it was agreed that they would marry in Paris, later in January when he returned from Rumania where he was going to visit his family and give them the news. He would contact her on his return. Three weeks later, his message arrived.

As her train pulled into the Paris station, she caught a glimpse of him on the platform, suave, self-possessed and as immaculately dressed as ever.

Later over dinner in one of the city's expensive restaurants, he explained his delay. There had been unexpected complications with his father who had kept insisting that his only son must marry in his native land. Claire listened, not happy with what she was hearing.

"Why is that so all important?" she asked.

"Well, it was important to me not to fall out with him and also, there was truth in part of what he said."

"Which was?" she enquired, toying with the fish on her plate.

"Well…he spoke bitterly of the forced redistribution of land in the aftermath of war, of government corruption, of our still having claim to title and continually reminded me we were an old and established family, but how would it be if his only son married a foreigner abroad, 'an alien' was how he put it, a woman he had never met, of whose family he knew nothing. Who was she? Where did she come from?" Bude paused, shaking his head as if to convey his own bewilderment at his father's obstinacy.

Claire waited. "And…?" she queried after some moments, putting down her fork.

"Oh, he simply continued to say that I could not do this, that I must marry in Rumania and so on and so on…you can see why it took three weeks."

Again, Claire waited and then asked. "And what did you say to this?"

In the soft candlelight Bude smiled at her and reached for her hand.

"I told my father that I was marrying the most beautiful woman in the world," he murmured, his dark eyes, gentle and sincere.

"But Bude," Claire protested taking back her hand, "...listen to me and please understand. I am not interested in the family title to the lands or the gain that goes with them. If your father is upset yes, I care about that and yes, I admit to being afraid of becoming dependent with children that I...that we, may be unable to support but we are earning more than enough to avoid that. We can save and invest. We need nothing from your family." As Claire spoke there was strength in her voice.

"Claire, you must not be concerned," he reassured her. "There was a problem with my father. He is an old man, he becomes confused, but he accepted." Bude paused. "We came to an agreement and we marry in Paris at the end of the month. Nothing changes that." Bude's voice was decisive. "The arrangements are made," he continued, "...all is well and now no more of this. We talk now only of the good things ahead," and speaking soothingly, he went on to tell her about the plans he had made.

Claire had to admit that what he had organised was exactly as she would have wished. The wedding was to be simple with just two witnesses provided by the Church. This suited Claire. There was no need for more. After all, whom would they ask? Her only family, Anna, was in England and his family was miles away in Rumania, which was as well if his father was being difficult.

After the ceremony, they were to lunch at Maxim's before flying to the sun and spending their honeymoon on the lovely, flower-filled island of Madeira. Then, Bude really surprised her by telling her they were to begin their married life in New York. They had been commissioned to do an extensive photographic spread for a prestigious fashion magazine in circulation there. Meticulously he had finalised every detail and they were to arrive in style, having sailed on the ocean liner, the Mauretania.

Claire was enthusiastic at the thought of working in New York. She began to relax, telling herself that she really must stop looking at life as if it were one big problem. As Bude had said, "All was well."

And, on the wedding day, all was well, except that the registrar was late. At least, Claire thought he was late, but then learned after the wedding, that his presence was not required. The vicar seemed surprised that Claire had expected otherwise.

"A Church ceremony here and a legal marriage in Rumania, that was what I was told," he said by way of explanation.

Claire moved aside out of the vicar's hearing and spoke to Bude.

"Bude, you arranged this and you did not tell me," she protested.

"But Claire, I did tell you," he said, in a manner which suggested that she had forgotten. "I remember very well explaining to you. I told you of the difficulty I was having with my father and of his concerns and his insistence that I marry in Rumania, but that we came to an agreement. I thought you understood all of this."

"You spoke of the lands, of title to lands or some such thing. But you did not tell me that we were not to..." She hesitated, disturbed, uncertain how to phrase what she wanted to say. She tried again. "When you spoke of your father's concerns, of the lands, of the family interests, I told you that I wasn't interested in...." but as she was speaking Bude interrupted her.

"Exactly," he said "and when you said you were not interested I did not pursue the matter. But you did say you were concerned my father was upset and I appreciated that, for he is an old man and I also have been concerned. That is why this was arranged."

He looked at her almost plaintively as if searching her face for a sign of understanding or remembrance and agreement of their discussion. Claire was perturbed, not knowing what to think, or feel. She turned again towards the vicar.

"But am I married. I mean, really married?" she asked.

"Certainly you are really married. It is now down in the parish records," he assured her.

"But then...surely, the registrar should at least have been present. So why not?" she persisted.

"Because, as your husband informed me, your wedding is to be legalised in his native land. That is where the civil ceremony will take place and for that there will be a registrar." His manner had an air of detached finality. It was clear that having done what had been requested he was not going to be drawn further and wishing them a long and happily married life, he ushered them towards the vestry door and bade them farewell.

Bude and Claire were alone and Bude was looking at his watch. "We mustn't waste time Claire," he urged her. "If we are late for lunch it will throw out our plans."

The misunderstanding was bothering her but nothing was to be helped by standing in the cold of the stone-floored vestry. 'How would it be,' she silently asked herself, 'if she said she did not want to go?' It would raise all manner of difficulties. Furthermore, Bude would think she did not trust him, hardly an auspicious start to their marriage. But this was totally unexpected. Desperately she wished she had been told in time for her to think about it, not now when there was little she could do.

Bude took her hand in his. "Claire, you are freezing," he exclaimed. "We must hurry, the taxi is waiting."

The next moment they were outside on the pavement, with the chauffeur holding open the car door and Bude handing her in. As they seated themselves he pulled the screens across to shield them from the driver's view and took her firmly in his arms.

"To a new life…" he whispered.

"To a new beginning." she answered softly.

She must look forward now. There was no going back.

CHAPTER TWENTY-FOUR

February 1927. Ardleagh village

*I*t was around six in the evening and the late winter sky that had doused the village all day, pulled darker shrouds across itself and gave way unto the night. In the mill's warehouse Ralph switched on the lights and cast his eye around. A satisfied smile spread itself across his face. The building was fully packed with bales, stacked and ready to be loaded in the morning. He moved down a narrow aisle between them, patting the odd one as he went before calling out to the overseer to say he was leaving.

As he strode across the yard to his car, he began to whistle. 'It's certainly an ill wind that blows nobody any good,' he thought. 'That miners' strike was a stroke of luck.'

It had certainly made his work force more amenable. The village was a community that hung together. Those with money coming in helped those without and with so many of the breadwinners unable to put anything on the table, nobody who had a job was going to chance losing it. After the other Unions had given in, the continued work stoppage in the mines had made for a trouble free time in the cotton mills. It had served Ralph well. He would never otherwise have got away with the changes he had made.

Unlike mining, the cotton industry was an innovative one. Anyone who could find a suitable building and had enough money for machines was able to set up in the business provided he knew what he was doing and almost anyone could learn. The mills were a different enterprise to the mines. The financial returns from cotton came in more quickly and correspondingly it was easier to raise capital. It meant however, more Johnnies-come-lately were attracted to the trade and the competition between operators was keen to the point of being cut-throat.

It was not the same with the mines. The colliery owners were often from the old landed gentry and they stuck together. A mill-owner aimed to be a jump ahead. Ralph, young and keen, was determined to get to the front of the field.

He had wanted to make changes for some time and he just had. He had sold off almost all the old machines his father had installed years ago. They were cumbersome and outdated but he had managed to get rid of them to someone just starting up. The replacements he had bought were the latest to come on the market. They had more shuttles, were faster and equally important, they were compact.

Being able to fit more in, the floors were even more crowded. Being faster, the operators were going to have to concentrate harder, be even quicker off the mark. There was also more noise with the new machines. With more of them squeezed into the same space, the din was deafening. Ralph had to admit, but only to himself, that he wondered how the workers stuck it. Even with the old machines, the mill-hands had always had to lip read or use sign language. The racket had always been far too great to hear others speak even face to face and there were many complaints about permanent hearing loss. In normal times the workers would have been showing the usual signs, looking for an increase in wages but not these last several months. Many of the mill workers had miners in the family and although the strike was over, their wages had been cut. With little in the family coffers, they would be struggling to pay off their debts for many months to come, by which time the impetus to strike would have passed.

However, the changes made the mill more lucrative and profits had soared. Ralph had extended the loading bays to cope with the increased output and arranged with the hauliers to collect more often. It was a very satisfactory state of affairs altogether, which was why he was whistling so cheerfully. He was delighted with himself and confirmed in the opinion he had long held, that he was a fine fellow. His mood gave rise to that other thought that had kept occurring to him of late. Maybe he should get married. He was in his late twenties and had sown a fair amount of wild oats, but provided he chose with care, his freedom need not be curtailed. Given his advantages, he would have a wide selection of women from which to take his pick.

That time some years ago, when Leonora had behaved in such a fickle way, he had been more than a little miffed. Women did not just give him the brush off and walk out on him like that. Her behaviour had rankled but he had put it behind him. There were plenty of compensations. Life is a succession of phases. One must move on and enjoy each to the full. The idea of a wife and a fine house in the country with all the accoutrements and pleasures that go with them, entertaining at home, dinner parties, being regarded as a man of substance, yes, it appealed to him.

Her family would of course, have to be well-heeled, a good, sound, respectable Lancashire family and the girl herself would have to be sensible, for Ralph intended his future family life to be an extension of his present modus vivendi, something to be enjoyed as well as his present diversions, not instead of them. Her father also would have to be sensible, a man who did not cease to see things from a man's point of view just because his daughter had got married.

Since he intended to keep his London life separate from his wedded one, he decided that his bride must be a Lancashire lass with family, friends and pass-times to keep her orientated in the North. This, together with his other specifications would narrow down the field. The sooner he started looking, the better.

It was a choice demanding much care and forethought. His search was systematic. He quickly ran through the short lists of possibilities, his own and those helpfully provided by friends. Not having found the lucky lady, he extended his search and began to work his way steadily through the more respectable nightclubs and hot-spots currently in vogue with the up and coming young generation.

His presumptions were quite right. There were indeed many attractive, well groomed, fashionably dressed, robustly healthy young women whose attitudes signalled they were on the husband hunting trail. Regarding his objective however, Ralph stayed strictly on track. He neither dallied, nor allowed himself to be waylaid and, in fairness to the young women concerned, it must be said, nor did they.

Like him, they knew exactly what they were looking for and were not prepared to squander their favours on unpromising prospects. To their credit, they were not over demanding. The prerequisites on their wish lists were limited, but those that were on it were absolute and essential. They asked that a man be reasonably attractive, socially presentable, comfortably off, with a good, solid background behind him and good solid prospects in front of him.

In the main, they were nice, young women who knew what their chances and choices were. They were quite happy to conform to the middleclass, Lancashire society into which they had been born and to fit into the stereotyped, bourgeois lifestyles of their parents and peers. For this, a husband was necessary and like Ralph, they were not wasting time. They had their futures to consider.

It did not take him long to find what he was seeking. Nor was Barbara long in making up her mind. Like any young woman in her position, she was pleased and hopeful that her prospects may soon cease to be uncertain. She took Ralph home to meet her parents. Her father owned a shirt-making factory and a string of outlet shops. Within a few months, the deal was struck and Ralph took his fiancée to the best-known jewellers in the city and placed an expensive, ruby and diamond engagement ring on her finger.

Ralph had chosen well, His bride to be was a warm-hearted girl. Good natured and easygoing she was popular in the set to which she belonged. She was a member of both the County tennis club and the local hunt, was the product of a reasonably good, finishing school and was attractive in many ways, being endowed with a superb figure, shining, blonde hair and deep violet eyes and, as Ralph had decided she must be, she appeared to be down to earth and sensible.

She was indeed, for she also was getting what she wanted. Henceforth, she would be well provided for. She was confident that as a husband, Ralph would give her a good life. He would look after her, protect her and within his ample means see to it that she and their children were cared for. All that being so and not unaware of the ways of the world, she was prepared to abide by what were often, the unspoken rules. She was going into this marriage with both eyes wide open. She would, once securely wedded and provided he also adhered to the aforementioned unspoken rules, close one.

The wedding was a showy affair, a little overdone, but that was the price to pay.

It was essential to make a noticeable splash in the provincial pool, if one were not well known but wishing to become so. Subsequently, both families were duly gratified to see themselves and their guests on the full two page spread of Lancashire Life, the monthly magazine that informed folk in the county, what the county folk were doing.

After the honeymoon, for which Barbara's father had generously insisted he pay, the happy couple settled in a large modern house in the countryside to the south of the city. The furnishings were exactly to Barbara's liking, which was not surprising because she had chosen them and Ralph had been happy that she do so, which was equally not surprising because once again her father had offered to foot the bill. Ralph had, of course been very helpful and forthcoming with his suggestions.

Margaret came in from her morning walk. She had covered quite a distance today and felt better for the exercise. She was trying to find more things to fill her life since James had left. She missed him dreadfully. Always understanding of her difficulties, he was the one to whom she had always turned for good advice.

On entering the morning room, she rang the bell for coffee and picked up the magazine she found lying on the table. 'Now where has this come from?' she wondered, '...it wasn't there when I went out.' Flicking through the periodical's glossy pages, she wandered over to the sofa by the drawing room window and comfortably settled herself down.

Oh yes of course, Ralph must have brought it.

She remembered him mentioning something about his wedding photos being in Lancashire Life. He was in the study now with Frederick. He still called on her. It was sweet of him to find the time especially now that he was married.

The photographs displayed on the glossy pages did Barbara justice. She looked quite superb but a perusal of the others in the pictures, of Albert Rawlinson, his wife and guests, occasioned Margaret to appreciate anew the wisdom of having tactfully claimed a prior engagement and declined the invitation extended to her and Frederick.

Looking at some of the shots taken later at the reception where the dancing had continued into the early hours, she could not imagine they would have experienced any comfort or enjoyment in the atmosphere that all too obviously had prevailed. Several of the revellers were wearing paper hats with bits of torn streamers adhering to their shoulders and the glassy-eyed look of some, close up and staring into the camera was clear indication they had had too much to drink. She put the magazine aside. 'Oh well,' she mused, 'young Ralph has made his bed and now must lie on it'.

She need not have been concerned. The truth was that despite having seen quite a lot of Ralph, Margaret did not really know him. He had gone up in her estimation by behaving well when Leonora had acted in a somewhat erratic manner shortly before leaving for Spain and she appreciated the way he still continued to call, to enquire about Frederick's health. It was kind of him.

The reality was not quite so.

On those occasions when Ralph had escorted Leonora during her Season, she had opened a door for him onto a world of wealth and sophistication surpassing anything he had previously encountered. It was a world of which he wanted to learn more but was astute enough to know, given his background, his chances of achieving this on his own were slim. It was therefore a serious letdown when for no apparent reason Leonora rebuffed him as she had. He had promptly decided not to allow this setback to sever his connections to the Hall for, artful as ever, he had worked out that if he were to maintain his entry to the higher social sphere to which he had been introduced, he needs must cultivate a relationship with her aunt. It was to this end that, at appropriately spaced intervals, he had continued to visit expressing his concern for Lord Frederick.

Ralph had an animal instinct regarding those of value to him. Over the last few years it had become patently obvious that Lord Frederick could be a demanding patient and that, in certain moods, try as she may, there was little Lady Margaret could do to please him, yet could not bring herself to walk away. On such occasions, by glance or subtle gesture Ralph conveyed sympathy and understanding and of late, a discreet readiness to assist.

Now that James' departure looked like being final, Margaret appreciated Ralph's consideration even more. With James abroad, she no longer had a pretext to present the house as a venue for the young, a meeting place where the eligible could mix and mingle. No longer were there tennis and croquet parties, music drifting from the ballroom in the evenings and handholding young couples slipping into the flower-fringed conservatory, to be hidden by the potted palms when stealing their first kiss.

Where now, the young women who in anticipation of meeting James, had been delighted to visit? Not that he had ever shown much interest, but there had always been the hope. They were so sweet and solicitous, Arrabella particularly so, but she never saw her now and when James wrote, he never asked about the young women he had known. Nor did he mention having met anyone new, but that was as well, for he was unlikely to meet nice, young English women in Vienna and Margaret certainly did not want him marrying a foreigner. It seldom worked. Look at what had happened to Amelia.

Yes, poor Amelia, that was a dreadful business some weeks ago when her letter to Frederick arrived, saying she had received word from her bank, informing her, in effect, her account was no longer operative save for a paltry overdraft they had patronisingly stated they were prepared to waive. Enclosed were documents Amelia had signed a few years previously at a time when the income on her capital was not as it had been, and she had agreed to invest in a fund yielding a higher return.

Now, the worst had befallen and Amelia was pleading her case that it was ridiculous, that this simply could not happen, that she had always been able to rely on her assets. How could it possibly be that she would waken one morning to be told her money was no longer there, when she had not spent it?

Margaret had tried to persuade her husband to send funds to his sister, so she could visit them and the matter be settled. She totally agreed with Amelia that surely there were safeguards against this sort of thing. There she was, stuck in the middle of Spain and helpless, for how could she consult an advisor to sort out the matter for her, when she had no money with which to pay him...and it seemed

Alva was doing nothing to help her, so Frederick simply must speak to his lawyer on his sister's behalf. She was still an Eglinton, despite her marriage.

Frederick had remained intractable. Amelia was her husband's responsibility. He was merely her brother and she had cost him enough already, for in upholding the family name, he had told the Bank he would pay the 'paltry overdraft', only to discover when the Bank dipped into his account, that it was anything but.

Winning the battle with the miners, had restored some of Frederick's old determination and on the evening of their celebratory party Margaret had been thankful to see that with the aid of his specially designed supports he had actually managed to get himself upright and move from one room to the next. Sadly however, he had woken up during the small hours with a very bad back pain and despite all her persuasions, flatly refused to try to walk again. It was such a pity. If only she could find someone who could talk him into trying once more. Margaret stared down at the carpet thinking hard, a small frown puckering her brow. Slowly her expression lightened and a slightly smug look stole across her face.

"Now, there's an idea," she said softly. "Ralph, he's still in the study with Frederick. It's worth a try. Frederick gets on well with him, better than with his own son. He was full of praise for the young man when he acted as a stoker during the strike, said it was more than James would ever do."

Yes, she would invite Ralph to stay for lunch. She was sure he would. He seemed to quite like being at the Hall and later, while Frederick was having his early afternoon nap, she would have a straightforward talk with him, see what he had to say.

After all, he had on more than one occasion, offered his help.

CHAPTER TWENTY-FIVE

Vienna. 1928

*J*ames looked down from the parapet of the bridge into the murky, brown waters of the Danube and wondered, 'Was it ever really blue?' "Probably, it was blue once," he murmured, "...long ago, before men got at it, too long ago for anyone to remember." But memory was an odd thing. It could play tricks, rewrite history to suit one's purpose or remain quite untouched, a precious treasure to be locked away for consolation in times of need. Absentmindedly he gazed for a few moments, watching the waters swirl as they flowed between the embankments and passed on.

He turned away and took from his pocket the letter that had been waiting for him that morning, pinned on the notice board in the Conservatoire's main hall. It informed him that his tutor, who had been one of the mainstays of the school for many years and had proved himself invaluable to James, was leaving. James accepted most of what he read, but not the reasons given. It was a blow but not entirely unexpected for as he had learned, the Conservatoire was not the Elysian Fields that on his arrival, he had naively expected it to be.

Even in such a place there were undercurrents, power struggles and professional jealousies, which were anything but professional especially when applied to music. During his time at the Conservatoire James had been forced to the conclusion that manipulation, the ability to climb over others to get what one wanted and the artful practice of undermining and discrediting those who stood in one's way, were talents in themselves.

He folded the letter and crossing the street made his way towards one of the coffee houses for which the city was famous. Determined to validate his grandfather's faith in him he had, since coming to Vienna two years ago, focussed solely on his studies. Recently however his path had crossed with that of a young woman violinist. Quite unexpectedly, James found that whenever she was around he could not help noticing her. Not too surprising, he told himself for she was after all, noticeably attractive. Tall with an alluring figure, golden-brown, waist length hair, green eyes, she certainly turned heads but he knew that was not the reason. His attention was taken by a quality that was other than 'pretty-woman' looks. Rather it was her manner, her calm attention to whatever she was doing, at peace in the given moment...a characteristic that reminded him very much of Claire.

Her name, which he troubled to find out, was Johanna von Cours. He would have liked to know her better, but when she disappeared from the scene, he thought no more about her.

Much had changed in Vienna since the last war. Even before it began in 1914, the old Imperial Austro-Hungarian Empire of the Hapsburgs that had reigned there for many generations had been finding it harder to hold together all the different elements and nationalities coexisting under its rule. When the Great War ended in 1918, its Empire had collapsed. Enhanced by the music of Johann Strauss however, romantic images of Vienna lingered on, as a city in which elegant carriages were drawn by prancing horses, where lovers lived fairy-tale lives strolling hand in hand along the banks of the Danube or in Vienna's woods, and waltzed the night away gliding over polished floors beneath glittering chandeliers. None of this matched up to what James had seen while he had been there but the impressions were still potent and though they better befitted what had become a bygone age, they still came to mind when one thought of Vienna. James smiled. It said much for the power of music.

Arriving at the coffee house, he went inside. These at least were places that had not changed and this one was much the same as many others, a cosy room, a meeting place that functioned almost as a club where people, predominantly male, spent hours reading newspapers, drinking coffee, which it had to be admitted was the best to be found anywhere, and discussing what else, but politics. It seemed as if no other conversational topic existed.

James sat and listened. He was fluent in the language by now, but his understanding of what was actually going on benefitted little from what he heard. The city was suffering the Austrian version of what was happening in many other European capitals. Speculation fed the rumours, exaggerated by the gossip that passed them on. But however many tales did the rounds, there was never a shortage of material for more.

There was the same bitter infighting between rival political parties, some old and established, others new and up and coming, the same clash of extremes between Communists determined to seize power and the old Establishment equally adamantly trying to get rid of them and the usual 'muddle in the middle' of splinter groups, monarchists, conservatives, liberals and what all.

There had been rioting again in the summer when the Courts released three men belonging to an anti-Socialist group, the Kaempfers, who had been charged with murdering two Communists. Their acquittal had outraged the Communists and editorials had appeared in certain papers inciting the killing of judges and jurors. The insurrections that followed were fierce. Fires were started, shops looted and thousands of marchers had converged on the Ministry of Justice and set it alight. The debris still lay around.

The police at the scene had proved unable to control them. By the time the armed reinforcements arrived however the violence appeared to be abating and instructions were sent to them to await further orders, but too late. Having been told that some of their comrades had been beaten to death, they fired, killing eighty workers. The wound cut deep and in the bitterness, refused to heal.

James finished his coffee and left. The more he heard of the happenings in the various countries across Europe the more they sounded the same. Names and places differed, but the tales told varied little, save for the complications of the intrigues hatched by politically motivated men serving their own self-interests.

James did not consider himself a political animal, but he strongly believed that, "Peace without Justice is no peace at all."

At the time of the 1926 General Strike in England, there had been nothing comparable to what was taking place on the Continent, but then, the structure of Government in England, of King and Commons, had remained virtually untouched by the war. The horrors of its battles had not taken place on British soil. The English applecart had not been overturned and the apples were not rolling around to be grabbed in the confusion by others, as in other parts of Europe. In England, the Establishment had remained intact. The forces of authority and order had remained in place and those beneath them had been kept in theirs.

He picked his way through the rubble lying on the pavement. There had been more skirmishes in the city overnight and in certain areas the streets were littered. Keeping his head down, he continued walking. He was making his way to the home of his tutor who, judging by the letter was unlikely to return to the Conservatoire.

Later in the morning as he and James sat in his study, he told James he intended to retire and that he thought the time had come for James to move on also.

"It might be a wise move, if you were to go to Berlin," he advised him. "Artistically, it's a little decadent at present, but that's the swing of the pendulum, the release of energies that follow the removal of restraints. You're a young man at life's crossroads with a great deal of potential still to realise. Lost opportunities and wrong choices now could spell regret for you in years to come. Look around. Take your time. There's more on offer to you in Berlin than here."

"Vienna's a beautiful city..." volunteered James hoping to probe more into his thoughts.

"Yes, but a spent one, a reflection of its past," responded the ageing man swiftly. "It was the hub of its Empire, the seat of its Emperor. Now, they've gone and without that support and direction, the heart's gone out of the city as well. It lacks a focal point...it's little more than a shell."

"And," James asked quizzically, "...you mean?"

"I mean...well, look at the opulence of the magnificent homes and buildings on the Ringstrasse. Yes, they still stand there unchanged and there are still those with wealth, the lucky ones, the cream of society, promenading in the squares and boulevards, seeing and being seen. But look behind the grand facades and closed doors of many of the others, desperate to keep up appearances.

"Look at the rooms sealed off, the windows kept closed to conserve the heat, the unlit corridors, the understaffed kitchens with stale cooking smells, and then, look further down the ladder to where the gut has been kicked from society and to those even further beneath, at the bottom of the pile..." he broke off.

"What we now call Austria," he added, "is but the rump of what she was. Her identity was determined by the Empire she has lost and she has not yet redefined herself, knows not quite what she is, nor where she's going...and she's vulnerable, being on the door step of a Germany now increasing in strength. In truth James, I do not believe Austria will survive as she is. My advice to you is to leave and go to Berlin."

"But isn't it only a couple of weeks since you said you didn't believe Weimar would last?" protested James.

"And I don't," his tutor responded swiftly. "But before you ask," he added, smiling as he watched the question forming on James' lips. "My reason lies not in the essence of the Republic itself, although it has made many mistakes, not least by not having hobbled the Military and the upper crust on first coming to power when it had the chance, instead of compromising itself by entering into that disastrous agreement with the Army...but because of the country and the people themselves."

The cultured, elderly man spoke with conviction as he looked up at James.

"Democracy, as I'm sure you know, is not something that can be imposed upon a people from above. There has to be willingness in the grass roots stemming upwards from its base. In order for Democracy to be accepted and to function, a nation must be ready for it. Coming so abruptly after a monarchic, militaristic regime Germany is simply not prepared. The country is unified, yes, but it's still not 'One'. I don't see that yet in Germany. She hasn't had the time to evolve into a homogeneous whole, to attain the cohesion necessary for her to become a democratic state.

"There are too many prejudices to be overcome, too many diverse classes amongst its people and too many inequalities dividing them. The industrialists, they don't want Democracy and a Republic, nor do the Nationalists, nor any of the hard, Right Wing factions. And at the other end of the scale, but for quite different reasons, nor do the peasants. Well I should not call them that. One does not speak of the peasantry any more, so I say, the farmers, and in Germany there are many of them. They're still steeped in their ancient ways, bound by the old fashioned customs and rituals rooting them almost religiously to their land, to the soil, a kind of mysticism virtually holding them in the feudal tradition of looking to an overlord. These attitudes run deep in their blood. They look for a leader. They aren't ready to govern themselves, nor do they want to. And the upper classes, they certainly don't want to be ruled by the people."

He looked across at James, leaning forward a little, as if to give emphasis to the commonplace truth of his words. "Always remember...military regimes can break all the pledges they've ever made once they are in power, for they assert authority from the top down. But Democracies, their power can only come from the people and without it they fall. No James, the way things stand at present, I do not believe the Weimar Republic can last. But for the time being it's still in place and in certain spheres is throbbing with new ideas. You know the city. You have spent time and have friends there. There's little more I can teach you but I know someone who can and I say you should go."

So it was that some weeks later, James arrived in Berlin. He had already contacted his mother telling her of his move. He was surprised however, during his first few days there, to receive a visiting card from an acquaintance of his father, Sir Charles Rotherman, who was in Berlin for several days as a member of a visiting British delegation. They met and Sir Charles invited James to a social gathering the following week. It was being hosted by a German friend of one of the delegation, at his home in Dahlem, one of Berlin's most exclusive areas.

The house was situated in a prestigious and very desirable location and more than lived up to James' expectations. From the moment he arrived he could clearly see that his host was not a man who did things by halves yet at the same time nor was there sign of ostentation.

It is, as they say, a small world at the top and James had been hoping he may have already met some of the guests there, but as the welcoming preliminaries proceeded and he was taken into the spacious drawing room, he saw only a couple of vaguely familiar faces. On being introduced, he discovered that most of the people present belonged to tightly-knit banking or industrial coteries, liaison with which was what the visiting British delegation was about.

The room James had just entered was airy and elegant. Along its far side the extensive French windows, one or two of which were open, afforded a view of the well-tended garden. A faint breeze wafted the long, muslin curtains and on the patio beyond, in the last slanting rays of the sun, several guests with drinks in hand, were laughing and chatting, enjoying the conviviality.

As the day drew to a close, the evening air grew chill and the guests coming in from the terrace were mingling and circulating. It was then that James saw Johanna. She saw him too and for both of them there was the pleasure of instant recognition. In the sudden spontaneity, neither felt the need for formal introduction.

Immediately they crossed the room, greeting each other with the usual questions and remarks, appropriate to the situation.

"I wasn't expecting to see you here?"

"I thought you were in Vienna."

She told him later she had been somewhat bored by the occasion, owing to those present belonging almost exclusively to her father's generation. For James also it was a relief to meet someone he recognised who shared a common interest. It turned out that Johanna was younger than her looks made her appear. She was, as she told him when explaining the reason for leaving the Conservatoire, only eighteen and still very much under the auspices of her father.

Her father was a banker, a powerful but discreet man, who listened rather than spoke and who, although very well known in his professional circles, preferred to keep a low profile. He was scarcely ever without an expensive cigar, which he rarely smoked, but found a useful thing to have in hand. It could claim his attention, requiring its ash to be meticulously tapped into a nearby ashtray whenever he sensed during one of his many business deals, that an awkward, drawn-out moment was in danger of becoming overstretched.

It was convenient in other ways also and he would raise it slowly to his lips, to ease but not betray the silence if, in negotiating a business deal, he intuitively sensed the other party was about to concede, or if his astute and quickly working brain required a little extra time. When Johanna pointed out her father to him, he was not all as James had expected. From the near reverence with which his daughter had spoken of him James had formed an image of a tall, distinguished looking man, but this was not the case. Nonetheless Hans von Cours was a man pleasing to behold.

He was handsome and although of slightly less than average height and inclined to corpulence, his physique was considerably enhanced by an obviously excellent tailor. He was immaculately garbed and from the brilliance of his highly polished, black shoes, to the gleam of his bald pate, he exuded an aura of well-groomed affluence and comfort. Even so, the impression he created was due much more to his attitude and way of conducting himself, than to his physical appearance. He bore the air of a man who commanded respect and an element of warning was soon to be detected in his manner, if this were not forthcoming.

"I'd introduce you to him but it looks to me as though this would not be a good moment." Johanna paused before adding by way of explanation, "…one gets to know when one may and when not." She glanced around and added, "Mama's not here, she's…" she hesitated, as if unsure of quite what to say, then pressing her lips together, she gave them a slight twist and raised her shoulders a little in a resigned gesture, "she's…indisposed. Do you have a cigarette, please?"

James had been watching her attentively. "No, it's not good for you and besides you don't really want one," he said, in a frank but gentle tone.

His reply was unexpected, but instead of offence Johanna felt a sudden closeness to him. It was reassuring that, having recognised her unease, he had acknowledged rather than ignored it and from the way he had spoken she knew instinctively that he was someone to be trusted if she ever needed to confide."

James grinned and relented. "I don't smoke so I haven't one on me, but give me a moment. I'll get one for you."

Quickly she reached out, taking his arm, restraining him as he turned to go.

"No. You're right and anyway, with you, I think I don't need one," she said, smiling up at him.

The party was almost over. The guests were taking their leave and Sir Charles approached the young couple. He would be returning to England shortly and wished to say goodbye. As James prepared to introduce Johanna, Sir Charles smiled.

"No necessity for introductions here," he said easily, inclining courteously towards her.

"Johanna and I know each other well. Her father and I are old friends and it's always my pleasure to visit the family whenever I'm in Berlin."

The trio stood chatting for a few moments. It was clear from his conversation that Sir Charles was unaware of the rift that had taken place between father and son and James was relieved because what had happened with his father still grieved him and he preferred not to think about it. He had been back to visit his parents since leaving for Vienna but on each occasion, realising that his son was resolute about living his own life and pursuing music as a career, his father had been quite distant towards him.

On the other side of the room, Hans von Cours parted company from the man with whom he had been speaking and came across to join his daughter. Introductions were followed by a little polite conversation and then Hans took his daughter aside. He was anxious to conclude certain negotiations with the man he had just left and had arranged to dine with him later in the evening. His chauffeur therefore, would drop him off at his club and then continue on to take Johanna home. A few moments later, farewells having been made, the banker, lightly but firmly, took his daughter's arm, steered her in the direction of their host and then out of the door.

As they disappeared James caught Sir Charles' eye. The older man's expression was one of amused understanding.

"Watches her like a hawk poor girl, but he does it so nicely. Hans is one of those of whom one says, he has eyes in the back of his head. But he's just the same in business. He's always ahead of what's happening even when he seems to be paying no attention."

"He seemed engrossed in the discussion he was having this evening," commented James.

"And I'm sure he was," Sir Charles replied. "But if you were to ask him six months from now who, of any importance, was here tonight, whom they spoke to and for how long, he very probably would be able to tell you. Although he would be much more likely to ask you why you wanted to know."

Sharing a taxi home, James learned more about Johanna. She was, so he was told, practically engaged to Fritz, the son of an industrialist, a close friend of her father and a business associate of the man with whom he would be dining that night.

"Well, when I say practically engaged, perhaps I should qualify that," explained Sir Charles. "What it means is that both sets of parents are set on their marrying. The two families spend considerable time together, not only in Berlin but also on vacation and there are business interests to be considered. You can imagine how it is in these uncertain times...keep it in the family. With Johanna and Fritz being the only children of their parents, they have been constantly in each other's company, except for the time Johanna was in Vienna. I sense that's the reason she's been brought back here."

"But was that what she wanted?" asked James, sounding disconcerted.

"Who would know? I'd very much doubt she was asked," his companion replied, somewhat ruefully.

"But she still came anyway, just like that, without saying whether or not it was what she wished?"

"Maybe, she didn't really mind one way or the other. I've watched Johanna grow up. In the main she goes along with what's arranged, until it comes to something she really does or doesn't want and then she's capable of being very shrewd, very canny indeed, chooses her tactics and battleground with care. I must say, it's amused me to watch her down the years mainly because when she does get her own way, her parents never seem to realise it was what she had wanted all along. But such occurrences are rare. She goes to lengths not to put them on their guard and I've never seen her behave contentiously. But I believe they're making a wrong move this time."

"Why so?" asked James.

"Because the signs as I read them, tell me she has lost interest in Fritz, possibly due to there being someone else. But again, her parents seem not to have noticed."

"And Fritz..." asked James, "What's he like?"

"Pleasant, but not awfully bright, there was difficulty getting him into university, but he's enrolled now, in Munich and I hear Johanna will also be going there in the autumn, to read philosophy,

"But Munich of all places," said James sounding concerned, "...isn't that where they're having trouble with the S.A., those brown shirted thugs of Rohm and Hitler, who go around beating people up on the streets?" asked James.

Sir Charles looked questioningly at James, not quite knowing what to say.

In answer to your question," he ventured after a pause, "it depends on whom you mean by 'they' when you ask if they're having trouble. The S.A would not be getting away with their behaviour if the Munich police were not in connivance with them, which they are."

"You mean...?" questioned James

"I mean," the older man added in an almost expressionless tone that carried the ring of objective truth, "that those currently in control in Bavaria are very Right

Wing and would love to see the demise of the Weimar Republic and that being the case, the forces of law and order there, if one can call them that, are not unhappy to have the S.A., Hitler's brown shirted thugs as you rightly called them, doing their work for them, including beating up the Communists and keeping them off the streets, work they prefer not to be openly seen to be doing themselves."

"But doesn't that make the city unsafe?" asked James.

"Not for the likes of you and me, or Johanna and Fritz. Provided one is not a Communist, nor an active socialist, nor any other kind of liberal agitator, which is how the Bavarian regime regards all those who do not agree with it, then Munich is a safe place to be at present. Provided one is Right Wing and does nothing to ruffle or rub up the Nazis the wrong way, like advocating freedom of speech, or defending Left Wing radicals, or Jews, or being a supporter of those who do, then the answer to your question is, No, Munich is not that place where they are having trouble with the S.A. The regime there is glad to have their help and welcomes what they are doing, which is why the authorities there lifted the ban last year that had been imposed on Hitler speaking in public."

Sir Charles sounded cynical and James felt he knew him well enough to say as much.

"I prefer the word realist," he replied. "But yes, you're right. Maybe I should not have expressed my feelings quite so frankly, although on the other hand, if you're about to make your home here, I believe it's better for you to know. You're safe enough as a foreign national, but be careful not to get involved James."

"It sounds a dangerous game, like keeping a nasty dog, all very well as long as it doesn't turn on you one day. What do your German friends think about what's happening in Berlin?"

"Being English it's difficult to know what they think," Sir Charles replied. "I get the impression they're keeping their cards close to their chest, waiting to see what, in the end, will be in their own best interests. One has to keep in mind that the Versailles Treaty was deeply humiliating. They saw it as an attack on themselves and the blockade the Allies imposed as the war ended created dreadful destitution...and Hitler made good use of their bitterness and fear. Now however, the economy is recovering and there isn't the same anger and resentment around for Hitler to exploit and as you would know, Weimar's attracted a lot of writers, artists and musicians.

James smiled. "Yes Berlin seems to be making its mark as quite a Mecca of the Arts. It's certainly much less staid than back home. Nightlife here is thriving, new theatres and cabarets have opened and concerts halls are well attended. The sudden changes made space for new opportunities and ideas and it seems a pity Johanna's going to be sent to Munich."

"You're right. Her parents have set her course for her for too long, she should be allowed to get around on her own for a while. It would be good for her to spread her wings before she settles down." Pondering on what he had just said, Sir Charles frowned and when he spoke again, James could hear the cautious resignation of increasing age in his voice.

"But it's hard to judge, difficult to know what the future holds and young women can behave very unexpectedly at times. At least with Fritz her future would be secure. She'd be safe."

""Yes," agreed James, thinking of Claire. "Young women do unexpected things," and for the rest of their journey, each deep in his own thoughts, they spoke little.

CHAPTER TWENTY-SIX

Cordoba. May 1929

*D*arkness had long fallen. The strumming of the guitar, soft and languid as the warm night air, began again, the way it had the night before. Curiosity stirred her and leaving her bed, Leonora pulled on a robe and on bare feet quietly crossed the wooden floor to the window. It was open, but the latticed ironwork outside the casement, thwarted her from seeing who played. Somewhere out there, by some other iron-latticed open window, a young woman would be sitting listening to her would-be lover's serenade. It was allowed. The lateness of the hour was no matter for, as any watchful father knew, the laced-iron grille through which his daughter's inviting glances and her suitor's whispered words would be exchanged, was chaperone more guardant than any sleepy or indulgent nurse.

Beyond the quiet of her room were other sounds. In the city's streets and crowded squares, the revelry was continuing into the night for this was a time of celebration, the first fortnight of May, when the gay and colourful Festival of the Patios of Cordoba took place. Boulevards and cafes, open to the fragrant air, were overflowing with families and couples enjoying themselves. The town was full of flowers for soon the judging would take place and terraces, courtyards, walls and windows adorned with carefully tended, perfect blooms, would vie for first prize.

Leonora listened. Beyond the plaintive sound of the guitar, she could faintly hear the music of the dancing. She longed to be a part of that vitality, to be held in the arms of a man, to feel her body pulse to the flamenco's throb as the quickening vibrant rhythm of the dancers' hammering heels drummed faster ever faster into a rapid continuity of sound, until, struck to sudden stillness, by arrogant staccato stamp.

In that instant, the partners, proud and poised stayed statuesque, dark eyes exchanging potent glances, only the deep, blood red lace of skirt still moved, to swish its layered frills against the black and tightly fitted costume of the male.

In her imagination she could see the scene, music and happiness, laughter and love and as she sat by the casement of her window, not merely alone but lonely, she tried to put such thoughts from her mind. The house was quiet. The servants would have slipped out to join the merrymakers, but by morning they would be back in their places and if need be, feigning innocence as they covered for each other with excuses.

It was always the same, these first two weeks in May. Routine went by the board but there was little one could do. The Festival followed so quickly after Easter it seemed to be the recognition of necessary release after the sacrifice and self-denial of penitential Lent.

Leonora still recoiled from thoughts of Easter for it brought home to her anew, her self-inflicted severance from her Church. She had not been to Confession and when following her husband to the altar rails, her act of defiance flying in the face of all she been taught, became harder to perform. What other could she have done, or do? The questions she had so often asked herself came back, even as she tried to close her memory against that awful time. Years had passed, but her anxiety at being outside her Church, the sense of emptiness that came with the thought of her severance from grace, persisted.

Nor was this Leonora's only sense of loss, of something lacking in her life. She had been married for five years now and her deepest impulses were telling her, this cannot be all there is. There had to be more, much more to marriage and, of course there was, for it was going on right now in lives around her, but not in hers and she went slowly back to bed.

As Georgio's wife, she knew no other way and being one of the Arradova family was not helpful, always recognisable, yet set apart, corralled by an invisible barrier of separation, contained within an unchanging circle of select companions, and all the while, out there in the world, others were living their lives to the full.

Adding to this sense of aloneness was Georgio, or more accurately, the lack of Georgio, since almost always, he was away. He had returned two weeks ago, but his leave was only for a few days and he had been tired. He had wanted to rest and they had gone out very little. The Army belonged to a seemingly sealed world and most of their acquaintances were his military associates and their families. Sons followed fathers, or uncles into the service and Army families tended to remain so, due to the military equivalent of endogamous marriage. There was little scope for Leonora to meet others outside their realm and none in whom she felt she could confide.

On the other hand, when Georgio left he returned to the life he loved. Dedicated to his career, he had risen in the ranks and found the promotion and prestige gratifying. His latest posting to Morocco was an enviable one, a place well known for the sybaritic, pleasure-filled life it offered to the military stationed there. Georgio enjoyed the freedom it afforded him when not on duty, the company of his comrades, the drinking and gaming with them at the card tables. As an Army officer, it was the best of both worlds.

Lying in the dark, Leonora wondered if this time she would have become pregnant. Sometimes, in her worst moments, she believed this was the only reason he bothered to return. Her continuing failure to conceive did not please him. Maybe it was the reason for his increasing coolness towards her. She knew the sort of macho comment made during the rib-digging, horseplay that took place in the officers' mess.

She was equally worried regarding the reason for her apparent infertility. Already there was talk, whispered behind raised hands. Other brides who had married around the same time as herself had at least one child by now, if not more. When socialising, their nannies and children came also and in the main, the conversation was of them. At such times, Leonora concentrated on being a good listener, there being little she could add. Her mother had delicately raised the topic and her father had dropped heavy hints, but she was afraid to go for tests. What may be found? Georgio had never doubted her virginity.

After life in London, the lack of freedom was stifling and, without children, empty. She had no career. Her sense of purpose lay in her marriage and she appeared to have failed.

The void over which she swung in her empty cage was soul deadening and the thought of continuing like this frightened her. It had not been this way for her mother who had been part of a far more emancipated environment prior to her marriage and had come to Spain in totally different circumstances. A wealthy woman in her own right, Amelia had been able to keep in touch with the social circle of her youth. Her financial independence had enabled her to maintain her individual outlook and attitude, to take trips abroad and make forays to Biarritz.

Now, even her mother's situation was drastically changed. The bad news from her bank came shortly after she had invited Leonora to Biarritz and Leonora had been looking forward to going, but the trip had necessarily been cancelled. When the blow fell, Alva had solicitously expressed his sympathy to his wife concerning her unfortunate news, but his commiseration went no further. After years of putting up with her wayward ways, he was secretly relieved and had no intention of making up for any shortfalls in her income. Her brother, far from offering consolation, had informed her he had worries of his own and could not help. After surreptitiously listening when Amelia had phoned Frederick, Alva had taken pains to conceal his delight. He had been somewhat anxious about the possibility of a rescue package from Frederick and was glad to know it would not be forthcoming. No longer need he feign nonchalance in reply to Raimundo's questions regarding his wife's whereabouts. From now on Amelia would be where she should be, at home.

After speaking to her brother, Amelia had not let the matter rest there, but to no avail. To add to her misfortune she was now humiliatingly dependent on her husband and the effect of his dominance, now that she could no longer escape, impinged upon her even more.

The guitar's evocative strains had ceased. The long vibrations of its strumming, the throbbing as the fingers plucked and played, had quivered Leonora's heartstrings. The music had been for another but had filled her with longings such as she never felt with Georgio. With Georgio there was no shoreless sea of emotion, no surging of love's waves, tempestuous, until…drenched in the delight of passion-spent they lay gently cradling, caressingly entwined.

How different love could be…and long into the night Leonora lay awake, remembering Ralph, thinking of what might have been.

Lancashire, November 1929

The funeral was overlong and standing on the damp grass in the chill graveyard, Barbara Rawlinson felt both cold and sick. The last few days had been trying, probably due to her nerves. She had been scarcely able to eat at breakfast and felt quite ghastly.

A mean, bone-piercing wind was cutting through her new, black coat. She had chosen it in a hurry not realising it was not nearly warm enough, but worse than any of these discomforts was that which at first she had refused even to contemplate, but which had actually come to pass. Albert Rawlinson's death, or more accurately, the consequences of it, had been too baulking for her even to consider. The old man's illness had dragged on through the summer. The finale was inevitable but desperately hoping that the gods-that-be would follow her example, Barbara had persistently and resolutely, willed otherwise. Come November and the gods had gone ahead without her.

Barbara's persona, the outer image she presented to the world, was that of a woman blessed with an even temperament, capable of taking things as they came. She could, but it was not an innate ability. It was one at which she had to work hard and she kept her act together by dint of always being one jump ahead, with an eye on the next fence. That way, more often than not, she was able to sidestep most pitfalls, circumvent the insurmountable and take the rest in her stride, relying heavily on her down to earth Lancastrian realism to let her know which was which.

On this occasion however, not having been ready for it, the last few days had been a fearful rush for although Barbara had made no plans, the old man had and throughout his last, long drawn out summer, he had given considerable thought to his impending demise. He had been widely known. He therefore intended his passing to be much noticed, if not much mourned. The announcement of his funeral in the local press, including details of its arrangements, had certainly been noticed.

Standing under her dripping, black brolly listening to the vicar's unending lauding of Albert's virtues, Barbara cast her eye upon the multitude. Masses of mourners, rank upon rank, crowded the wintry Pennine slope and her heart sank lower still. They were expecting to be fed for as they now knew, all attending the funeral were invited back to the house and a free meal was not something to be missed. To her jaundiced eye it was surreal, a Lancashire re-enactment of the feeding of the five thousand and a miracle too much to hope for.

Worse still, the house they would be coming back to was not her house, that lovely, modern, sun filled, architecturally designed dream home with all mod-cons, situated on Manchester's south side close to the Cheshire plain, where she and Ralph had lived since their marriage. No, they would be flocking back to The House, Prospect House the Rawlinson old home, that big, dark, Victorian mausoleum of a house that jutted out in ungainly fashion from the ravine's northern, cliff-like face and overlooked the village mill.

It had been constructed with no eye for beauty, in the middle of the last century, by the man also responsible for the building of the mill and the back-to-back terraces that housed the workers. The view of those ugly little houses and the even uglier big mill was the only one visible from its protruding front bay windows, but at the time no doubt, the outlook had rewarded its proud owner with a sense of power and achievement as he looked down on the new community and workplace his enterprise had brought into being. Perhaps in those days, she mused, when the river was clean and the valley still green, it all looked better than it did now, some eighty years on.

The vicar was still intoning eulogies and the proceedings were still dragging on. She had not been overly fond of her father-in-law and at this moment, the only fervour in her breast, was for the vicar to hurry up, but hopefully it would end soon and they would all file past the grave and throw their handfuls of earth upon the coffin. So many of them, she wondered whether the gaping hole might be completely filled and the gravediggers spared a job.

She was so cold she could have cried and was sure she looked as miserable as she felt, but at least it spared her the effort of having to put on an appropriate act.

Albert had caught 'flu last winter. It had turned into a nasty bout of pneumonia from which he had never fully recovered. It was sad, but the deep seated cause of his daughter-in-law's desolation was still, that House, for with his death the house was now to pass to Ralph with provision for the widow to live there for the rest of her natural life and Ralph, she knew, was determined to move in. There had been neither discussion nor argument regarding the move, for in Ralph's mind taking up residence at Prospect House was as predestined and ordained as that of a newly anointed King occupying his Throne.

In situations such as this, battling with him was useless. No matter what was said, he would still go ahead in the end with what he wanted. Disagreement would be pointless and its souring of their relationship would preclude the compensations she would undoubtedly be able to wheedle from him later, if she behaved in an apparently selfless mode, insisting that 'if that is what you really want darling, then of course you must', for Ralph was not ungenerous, when pleased.

During Albert's stay in hospital his wife Florence had taken the opportunity to get rid of the domestic help owing to her longstanding objection to charwomen, as she christened all servants regardless of their function, poking their noses around in her house. Lacking the stimulus of her husband's directions and energy she had, as the saying goes, 'let herself go' and needless to say the house was also showing serious signs of neglect.

Albert however had specified it as the venue for his funeral feast. In the short time available Barbara had done her best to open up the place, but it had not been cared for, was badly in need of redecorating and there was little to show for her efforts. It was a hard-work house that did not respond to cleaning and would break the heart of any cleaning lady conscientious enough to care, the sort of house that would have been manageable before the war when servants were plentiful, trained by their predecessors and prepared to work long hours for little pay. Given changed attitudes and the present shortage of good staff however, Barbara feared the task of running it was beyond her and the prospect of living there appalled her.

The heating facilities were dreadfully antiquated and the kitchen was a huge, stone-floored room in the basement. True, there was a serving hatch to bring food up to the dining room level, but it was a cranky old contraption raised in a series of food-slopping jerks, by means of a pulley requiring an expertise of long practice that she, nor any other operator, was ever likely to possess.

Situated as it was, in the rising vapours from the river and, on occasion, fumes from the mill-chimney, the house had acquired considerable grime down the years. Its elevated dominance of the village and the status that went with it however, enabled its occupant to look upon himself as the industrial equivalent of the village squire and it was this, so Barbara suspected, that was the real reason for her husband's determination to move in.

She had come to know her husband well. He was a good husband and there had been no surprises. She had known when marrying him what to expect and Ralph had lived up to the expectation, in every way. He had his trips to London, but he was sufficiently sophisticated to abide by the unspoken rules. She, for her part, being exceedingly well looked after, made no fuss and, so far so good.

Barbara was realistic. She knew her limitations. They had been fully tested over the last few days. The house was unmanageable and not only was his mother no help she had been interfering, complaining and downright difficult. Given her grief it was understandable so Barbara told herself and she had made allowances, but the strain was taking a toll and how would it be over a much longer span of time? Alarm bells rang. The old lady was tough. She could live for years.

As was her wont, Barbara was already looking ahead and what lay there had her aghast. It had been in the small hours, a couple of sleepless nights ago, that desperation had set in. Thoughts of the changes threatening to wreck her life were just too stressful. She and Ralph had been happy and she was not going to let things get out of line, especially not now when they were hoping to start a family. Lying very still, thinking long and hard, slowly the steel in her came to the fore. If changes there had to be, changes there would be.

In the middle of last night, very quietly and without waking the lightly snoring Ralph, mouse-like, she had crept downstairs. By the time the alarm clock woke him, she had accomplished the tasks she had set herself. She had been busy, 'getting everything ready', so she told him when he came downstairs and asked what she had been doing. Getting everything ready, she had indeed, according to what she had in mind.

The vicar finally made it to the end. The remaining rituals had been performed and cars, carts and crowds on foot, were now headed in the direction of the House.

A while later and the rooms were as jam-packed with people as she had known they would be. Squashed up against each other they stood in their damp coats and sodden shoes, their smiles of expectation fading from their faces. Barbara was by the big tea urn dispensing stewed and lukewarm tea into the empty cups held out to her.

As the queue shortened, she glanced around and took stock. All was happening as she had intended. The boiler, in response to having been got-at overnight, was putting out no heat at all. The feeble spluttering in its pipes was doing no good whatever. To accommodate the crowds, all the doors downstairs were wide open to each other and according to location the rooms were either very chilly or downright cold. The food, such as it was, would be likewise when it finally arrived, but that would not be for some time yet because after the first couple of heave-ho's on the antiquated pulley, the so-called serving hatch that had never really worked had become irremovably stuck halfway up between the floors. There was a call out for more trays to bring up the edibles by the stairs, but they had not yet arrived.

Watching what was happening, Barbara's nerves were shot with guilt for all this was just as she had planned. If she had to live in Prospect House with his mother and all as it was now, she needed no crystal ball to see how things would be. When telling Ralph how difficult the house was to manage, he had not listened. Further attempts had been of no avail. The only way for him to be made to realise, was not simply for him to be told, was not even for him to see, but was for him to suffer it himself.

The food was now starting to arrive, piecemeal, one tray...then another. Those not yet served were becoming disgruntled, but no more so than those who had been and were now looking at what was on their plates. It was unlikely they would hang around for long. A most embarrassed Ralph was apologising profusely. Now, judged Barbara, was the time for a word in his ear about the kitchen. That done and still well within earshot of her husband, she related at length to anyone who would listen, the endless catalogue of time and effort she had spent in trying to avoid such a situation, but as she pointed out, "in houses like this, one is fighting a battle lost before it has begun." She then smiled wanly and looked around, awaiting sympathy for having had to be up since the small hours of the morning, 'getting everything ready'.

Yes, after today, Ralph would surely have grasped the fact that his own lifestyle and comfort were at stake. Chilled to the bone and persuaded by his wife that the boiler had been doing its utmost and could do no better, there was little doubt he would agree to its replacement. Once she had his say-so on the boiler and after work had begun, she had decided that one thing would lead to another as defect after defect came to light...the existing heating pipes would be found to have rusted and...oh well, whatever...she would think of something to prove to him that the fabric of the house in the basement had needed replacing.

Meanwhile, given that moving house takes time, she and Ralph would continue to live in their Cheshire home. Barbara intended to wait until his next trip to London and then let in the posse of workers she had lined up and when he returned, she would not mention what was happening at Prospect House. She did not envisage a problem with his mother who was in something of a parlous state at present, disorientated by her loss and looking for sympathy from any quarter it could be got. Barbara was giving her all she could want and was absolutely insisting, she simply would not take no for an answer, that as the doctor had advised she must not be left on her own at such a time and must come and live with them for a while.

In the event, Barbara had a splendid piece of luck. Ralph was strong but like many of his kind, was not a hardy creature when physical discomfort had to be endured. The day after of the funeral, he complained, not very surprisingly, of not being able to stop shivering. He thought he had caught a cold and by the time he returned from London, was sure he was suffering from 'flu. Reminding him of his father and what a bad dose of 'flu could lead to she had no problem persuading him to stay in bed. Before long it would be Christmas. No-one moved house before Christmas and with all the Yuletide preparations, partying and present buying, there were enough distractions to keep Ralph and his mother's attentions diverted from what was happening at Prospect House.

In the meantime she would make sure the builder and his men continued hard at work, very hard indeed, for when the old boiler came out, the rest of the basement kitchen would come out with it and a well-equipped laundry was to be installed in its stead.

That took care of the subterranean regions, now for the ground level. Adjacent to the dining room, there would be a modern kitchen. The front room and the room next to it, the ones with the North facing bay windows overlooking the mill, were to become a self-contained granny-flat with its own separate entrance. Situated at the very front of the house it was, as Barbara would stress, in the very best position. How could his mother complain?

The large, first floor master bedroom room at the back of the house, with windows facing south overlooking the garden, would become a spacious sitting room for her and Ralph. It was a good place to have it because the old lady did not like climbing stairs.

Time was of the essence for Barbara was operating on the principle of 'fait accompli' and once the work was half-done there could be no going back. Her main concern was Ralph's reaction when the bills began to arrive, but she would think about that when the time came.

She did not intend to lose her nerve worrying about it now. To be prepared she had already thought out some excuses, the first of which was that she had not told him because she wanted it to be a Big Surprise.

If the 'Big Surprise' story was not going down well she would say the wood in the basement had been found to have dry-rot and had to be ripped out and knowing how much he loved the old place she could not risk taking chances for who knew where the spores might have spread. If Ralph checked with the building firm, her story would hold good for Barbara had chosen her contractor with care and the man in question, delighted at the prospect of the extra work, had readily agreed. He was certainly not going to turn round now and tell Ralph the work had not been necessary and so be accused of having played on Barbara's fears. She would also remind him how sad she had been to move from where they were living, but how readily she had agreed to what he had wanted.

Ralph would of course, keep on groaning about the bills, but they could afford them and they were sure to get a good price for their present home.

She only hoped this Slump or Depression that he and her father kept going on about would not amount to much. The two of them sounded so nervous whenever they talked about it. Her father had been fretting about the market and raw materials and shirt sales, ever since that day late in October when that awful photo appeared on the front page of the newspaper, showing men in New York killing themselves, jumping out of windows and landing on the pavements.

The half-inch tall, black letters of the newspaper headline, had read
CATASTROPHIC FALL, WALL STREET CRASH.

It turned out however that the Fall and the Crash were about the collapsing prices on the New York Stock Exchange and not about the men landing on the side-walks as she had first thought, except that the fall in prices was the reason they had jumped out of the windows in the first place. But she was quite sure it would turn out to be alright. When it came to business Ralph and her father were always talking about what might happen, but everything kept going just the same and surely, so Barbara assured herself, New York was far too far away to have any effect on them.

But all was not alright and everything would not keep going just the same and New York was no longer too far away to have an effect on them. Across continents, dramatic changes were taking place. Communication between countries had increased at an unprecedented rate since the Great War. As never before, what affected one, affected another and the slump Barbara had heard about was not merely threatening. It was already happening.

Although it was to become known as the Great Depression of 1929, it was set to continue into the nineteen-thirties with calamitous results. It spread rapidly affecting many countries, not least England and Germany. Stocks and Shares were wiped out. Monetary policies failed and production slumped. Government measures were proving ineffective. Unemployment continued to rise. Politicians and economists put their heads together and produced various theories, but theories do not feed people and as economic statistics translated into harsh, physical conditions the Depression spelled hunger and destitution for many of the working class. By and large, the wealthy would restructure their affairs and insulate themselves against the worst, making few if any changes to their way of life. In fact, there were even those who would do quite well out of the disaster.

In situations such as these it was too much to expect calm to prevail and across Europe, once again, Communism threatened.

CHAPTER TWENTY-SEVEN

Paris. Early February 1930

Claire picked up the slim, leather bound folder, one of a limited edition containing portraits of her modelling garments from the latest collections. Spoken for in advance, demand for them had increased and they were coming to be regarded as Collector's Items.

Turning the pages, she looked in wonder at the images Bude had created. His artistry was more than mere skill. By what wizardry did he produce such icons of elegance? It was all an illusion, one she certainly did not share, fantasy images she did not measure up to in reality. Claire smiled, shaking her head. Small wonder he wanted her kept under wraps, her identity shrouded in secrecy. She could well understand his not wanting the legend blown out of the water, for thereby lay his commercial success, greater than they had expected.

Counting her blessings, Claire told herself she had been fortunate. As a husband, Bude had lived up to her expectations. She did not measure her present life against what had gone before, nor allow the shadows of what could not be to cloud her peace of mind. The past was a place she did not visit. She still saw Anna, but not wanting to awaken poignant memories, did not go to the Hall. Timing her visits to coincide with days when Anna was free, they met in a small hotel a few miles from the village. She kept her niece updated on the lives of Lady Margaret and Lord Frederick. "He never did recover, poor man." She also relayed news about Amelia and Leonora but, possibly having sensed something in Claire's attitude, did not mention James and Claire was grateful.

She laid the folder aside and sat for some moments, taking stock. Having come to know Bude well, she could not but admire his extraordinarily even temperament, his unfailing courtesy and consideration. She had grown accustomed to his reserve, to his somewhat aloof manner and occasional moodiness, supposing it to be due to the time of his youth in Rumania during the wars and felt compassion for him when he spoke of his sense of isolation from his native land. In other moments though, he excluded her, barring and retreating behind the shutters of his emotions. Claire knew there were tracts of his soul she could never traverse but she could understand this also, for she too had her unopened doors, memories, feelings and longings she could never share.

Their upbringing and cultures were very different but they had their similarities. They were both exiles from their past. Bude had never told her he loved her and she had never asked. From time to time she felt uneasy that her marriage had not yet been formalised and had continued to remind him, but when they first returned from America there had been so much to attend to and afterwards things had just seemed to drift. His father had not been well of late and his illness had begun to intrude upon their lives. His frequent letters, continually demanding that Bude visit him, were a strain.

There were signs that the economic Depression resulting from the 1929 Wall Street Stock Exchange collapse, was affecting the fashion business and certain sections of the trade were becoming concerned. Bude had been approached last month however, by an English fashion house that was taking a far more pragmatic approach than that of the high fashion haute couture so beloved by the Parisian establishments.

The promotion in question was to be of garments designed to appeal to a far wider market. 'The Truly Modern Woman' was its slogan and 'Versatility', its theme. The advertising angle was its claim that women of today with fewer servants and more dependent on household machines, needed clothes that would accommodate the many different demands and situations now facing them. Much of this would depend on Claire. The hope was that her appearance in contrasting roles would add a touch of realism to the boast of a woman's ability to adapt to the diverse tasks of modern life. The adverts would illustrate the various ways in which the multipurpose garments could be worn and their suitability for the wide range of activities now opening to the nineteen thirties woman.

On learning that the project was a launch into the prêt-a-porter market or, as Bude disparagingly referred to it, ready-to-wear, off-the-peg, mass-produced apparel, he had turned it down. He considered the offer was downgrading and would impair the image he had created. Claire however had pushed for it. Constantly living in the reflection of the exclusive effigies he constructed had become an unwelcome imposition. Not only was the continual and artificial presentation of her at odds with her own personality, it was stultifying her identity. She was beginning to question who she truly was. Unlike the haute couture gowns she had modelled previously, the clothes displayed in this promotion would be functional, illustrating real life situations. This commission would be the perfect opportunity for her to express her individuality. She would be able to act out her own character and she did not intend to let the chance slip by.

After much persuasion, Bude very reluctantly agreed, but as Claire was to find out later, he had pushed up their price unrealistically high, presumably in the hope that it would be refused. Notwithstanding, the fashion house had agreed the figure. Despite the different portrayals required, they had faith in Claire. The boost to her confidence was gratifying.

The promotion was to take place in a glamorous location in Spain. All had seemed settled, but at the end of January, the Military Dictator of Spain, Primo de Rivera, due to his own misjudgement, had fallen from the favour of the King, Alphonse X111, and also from power.

Once again, the situation in that explosive country was highly charged. The King's handling of the affair was severely criticised by the Army and the loyalty of certain sections of the military was in doubt. Few had faith in the King's acumen and there was wild speculation about what might happen next. Claire's thoughts were of Leonora, tied to a man whose life was bound to the Army in a country where marriage was set in concrete and also for Amelia dependent on a husband who, if the servants' bush telegraph at the Hall was to be believed, had total confidence that the military and their henchmen could maintain control, thereby ensuring the safety of his wife and daughter. But could they if the worst came to the worst?

Certainly, the fashion house was taking no risk and was making plans to switch the venue from Spain to one of the quiet Canary Islands. Claire very much hoped the work would take place on time. He had only agreed to this commission on sufferance, but was always at his best immediately after a successful modelling session. It would be an ideal time to ask him again about registering their marriage.

Three months later

Bude was due back home from Rumania tonight. He had been away for almost three weeks and should have returned a few days ago. She had been let down when he had not arrived. His father had been ailing again and had become demanding, pressing him to visit. Claire was finding his frequent absences unsettling and was somewhat disconcerted at his not yet having asked her to accompany him. She had still not met his family and was beginning to dislike his continually returning to his native land without her.

Their work for the fashion house promotion had gone well, despite Bude having been rather withdrawn. Claire put it down to the fact that he was still none too happy with this particular assignment. When the photos were submitted to the fashion house, they had been pleased. This time however the work on location had been of quite a different nature, with much more active input from Claire. The company they were dealing with now was appealing to a wider, tougher market and was far more commercialised and hard headed than the ones they had worked with previously. Safeguarding itself against any possible future claims, it stipulated that in addition to Claire signing the contract, each one of the portraits it selected for use must bear her signature of consent. It was said that this photographer could be difficult, even rumoured that he had once reneged on an assignment and the fashion house was taking no chances.

It was shortly after he had received another letter from his father and was about to leave that the last of the documents arrived for signing. Afraid his father may now be dying Bude had insisted he must not delay. Genuinely failing health or just old age and petulance, Claire was not sure, but Bude was anxious and before leaving had paid a hurried visit to his lawyer and signed all that was required of him.

Wanting no further delay, Claire was glad when the last of the photos the fashion house had finally decided upon had been delivered a couple of days ago. She had her signature witnessed as she put pen to them, then placed them in their special pouch together with the documents already signed by Bude, locked them in the safe and informed the fashion house they were ready for collection.

At last, all was in order. Leaning back in her chair she noticed again the untidiness on his desk. The clutter and unpaid bills she had come across when putting away his post, perturbed her. It was unlike him. He was usually so meticulous but in fairness his father's letter had harassed him and he had been rushed on leaving, searching for papers seemingly essential to take with him.

Tonight was the occasion she had been waiting for. They were to dine out and she knew exactly what she was going to wear. He would want her to look her best and she intended to ensure he would be proud to have her on his arm. With the contract now complete she would to speak to him about making arrangements for their civil wedding and was looking forward to meeting his family, visiting Rumania and seeing the scenes of his boyhood.

The cherry trees were already shedding their blossoms, their pink petals swirling in the air like confetti as they approached the entrance to the restaurant. Faint strains of music could be heard as they were ushered in and the attendant took their coats. The atmosphere would have pleased the most discerning bon viveur, warmth, soft lights, small intimate tables, here and there a delicate flower arrangement, superb food and in the air the fragrant hint of aromatic cuisine.

'Small wonder this is his favourite place to dine,' thought Claire as she followed the head waiter to their table, but her enjoyment was momentarily spoilt as unbidden there flashed across her mind, the memory of the restaurant's unpaid bills. Bude dealt with the contractual and financial matters. Payments went into his account and Claire did not object. As his wife she shared their high standard of living and left it at that. She had seen the high figures on some of their contracts and knew he could well afford to pay.

The waiter drew out her chair out and handed her a menu. His manner was as always charm itself, but conscious of their debt, Claire was discomfited. 'It's just an oversight, nothing more', she told herself. Even so, it should not happen. Trying to put such thoughts from her mind, she concentrated on the menu. The list of specialities was long. They would all be equally delicious, spoiling one for choice. Having decided, she was pondering whether to ask him before or after their meal about registering their marriage. She glanced towards him, but he was conferring with the wine waiter, discussing the various vintages and commenting on which wines to have with this, or that, dish.

He was extremely knowledgeable on the subject and turned to her once or twice, asking what she had chosen and appearing slightly dismayed on realising that the wine he had selected to suit his choice of meal, would not go well with hers. Perhaps he would choose something else, or she may not mind changing dishes, or perhaps he should go for a different wine altogether. The debate continued.

It was a procedure Claire did not enjoy. She would be glad when he had finally made up his mind and it was over. But even after he had chosen, she knew that there would still be some way to go before that happy moment arrived. He could be difficult again when the bottles were brought to the table and become pernickety after tasting, sending them back after they had been uncorked. As in other matters, Bude knew exactly what he wanted and would not accept what did not conform to his wishes. Not until the wine had been poured and he had pronounced it to his satisfaction, would they be able to settle down to enjoy the evening and she would be able to talk to him properly, without distraction.

While watching and waiting for the wine waiter to leave, it occurred to Claire how it was only at times and in places such as these, over well-ordered tables, in good restaurants or other similar venues where everything was pleasing and exactly to their taste, that she and Bude talked seriously to each other. It were as if they could only communicate properly in formalised set aside moments, as though neither dared risk baring their feelings to the other save at specially appointed times and in safe settings. It was not just him, it was her also, for once the modelling sessions were finished, she could have asked at any time about their wedding, but no, she had particularly chosen now. Was it only in such moments, when, knowing she would be free to concentrate, interpret each inflection, pick up on every nuance of tone, that she dared unlock the closets of her mind and if so...why?

At last, the wine waiter left and she and Bude were alone facing each other across the snow-white, starched cloth. He raised his glass to hers. Fondly she looked at him. The pale liquid caught the candlelight and sparkled. She smiled, but he did not smile back and it was then she noticed the unusual pallor of his skin. Silence hung between them, as though each had something to say, but was waiting for the other to begin.

Suddenly, both spoke at once and just as suddenly, stopped.

"You say"..."No, you".

Claire began by speaking of her pleasure at the thought of meeting his relatives and seeing his home country, before leading on to ask him about the arrangements for their wedding there.

Later, but too late, she knew she should have waited. Would things have turned out differently if she had? But no, for however long she may have waited the facts would still have been the same.

Slowly he put down his glass and remained quite still, looking away from her, not answering. It did not take Claire long to know something was wrong, very wrong, something in his manner, in the tension between them, in the very air itself.

"Bude, the arrangements..." she prompted him, the sound of her voice more forceful than she would have wished.

He looked across at her, expressionless, unflinching, betraying nothing of his feelings, but it was evident there was no cause for joy. Finally he spoke.

"Claire...I must tell you. There is," he paused, searching his mind, "...difficulty." He said at last.

"The arrangements...?" she queried, trying to speak more gently.

"Yes, the arrangements made with my father who..."

But he got no further as, overanxiously, Claire cut across him. "And you have not told me," she blurted out.

Impassively, Bude deliberated before replying.

"No," he said at last, his voice calculatedly calm. "I did not tell you. It was not necessary. It needed not concern you, at the time."

She glanced across at him, but his eyes were on his wineglass, his only movement, one finger slowly stroking its long, cool stem.

His words conveyed nothing to her. His tone, devoid of meaning, had the same quality of nondisclosure as in a guessing game. But this was not a game. This was real. She had always known he had a strong, authoritarian side to his nature, a rocklike quality on which she could depend, but it was now opposed to her, an intransigent bulwark he was using against her. She still did not understand and still he was silent.

When nothing further was forthcoming, "So, what is the...difficulty?" Claire queried endeavouring to sound unperturbed.

"Claire, I want very much for you to understand that the arrangements my father has made for, yes for the wedding, and about which you must now be told, will make no difference to our relationship. You and I will go on as before. It only means," he hesitated, then spoke again. "The only difference will be that I will be away...more often."

His expressions, the emanations of his manner were chilling. The atmosphere was fraught, his words an ominous weight on her. The suspicions now crossing her mind were cutting her loose from her psychic bearings, leaving her emotions veering this way and that as she tried to quell the panic rising in her and catch on to something to hold to. What was he telling her?

No, no, he was not telling her anything. He was forcing her to ask questions in the hope that she would hit on the right one and thus spare him the difficulty of having to tell her and that her search for the right question would in some way, prepare her for the shock of his reply.

Was this process, this pushing her to draw her own conclusions, intended to steady her in readiness for what was to come?

She cared nothing for the niceties of strategy or the refinements of the game. She had already guessed that her wish to have her marriage registered was not to be fulfilled, for if it were, he would have said. Clearly, something, or someone, his father, or some bureaucratic Rumanian red tape, or some other impediment about which she did not know, had already destroyed her chance of that.

Silently she had been studying the look on his face. In the dark she may be but one thing she now saw clearly. This difficulty of his was not one he intended to put on the table for the two of them to discuss and hopefully resolve. She could tell from his attitude that whatever difficulty there had been had already been resolved and his difficulty now, was in putting that resolution on the table.

Devastated, she needed to hear the truth outright and cutting to the chase, thrust her suspicion at him.

"You speak of the wedding, our wedding?" she asked.

He sighed, as though it were she who was being difficult, forcing him to spell out something she already knew, as if he had already told her.

But he hadn't told her. True, she had guessed but if she were right, the facts were so opposed to what she had believed, guessing was not enough. She had to hear it said.

"Your wedding...to me?" she asked, and when in response he simply breathed deeply and looked away as if in an effort to restrain himself, she asked outright, "...or to another?"

Seconds passed. "To another," he answered.

Her mind reeled. Huge chunks of what had been her world, fell away, cleaved from her by some gigantic axe of Fate, but although she was aware that she was trembling, she felt no emotion. The impact was too great for feeling. That would come later. Right now, his betrayal was too much to take. She wanted only to get away from him.

They were seated in a small alcove. Her fingers closed upon her evening bag and she moved to leave. He rose swiftly blocking her way, gripping her wrist.

"Sit down. Allow me to explain and try to understand." The tone was low pitched but there was force in the words, imperious, dominant and hard and they were spoken by a man she no longer knew. Not wishing to create a scene, there was little she could do. She stood motionless, feeling nothing, seized by a numbing stillness as though none of this was happening, and she herself, no longer part of it. It was too removed from actuality, from what was real and true, or was it simply that her mind, knowing that the truth had become too much, was...in its wisdom, tripping switches?

Her chair had become pushed back against the wall. Holding her shoulders, he pressed her to sit before returning to his place. He began to speak, telling her again that none of this changed their relationship.

The statement was so outlandish Claire did not reply. She was listening, and thinking.

He continued speaking, saying the meetings had been long and the talks drawn out, but a settlement had finally been reached. The key figure in the bargaining and on whom its ultimate success had depended was the neighbour of the adjoining lands. He also, was seeking restoration of title to his estate and had, by one means and another, inveigled himself into a position of influence with the powers-that-be. It was this man's daughter who was to be Bude's wife. She was still a spinster and her string-pulling father, having lost his sons in the wars, was anxious to see her married.

"Claire, you must understand," he continued, "...none of this affects us. Our relationship continues as it is. The woman is...she is still of childbearing age, but past her youth and I am not in love."

Claire bit her tongue, refraining from saying sarcastically, "Ah…yes I can see how that makes everything alright."

"Unfortunately," added Bude, "…there was a delay. In addition to other costs, the officially authorised approval required a reward, necessitating the payment of more monies than originally agreed and the bartering was difficult, with many aspects involved...each dependent on another."

'He means bribes, hence the bills', she thought.

He added that he would be marrying into a very old Rumanian family of considerable wealth. After the marriage was sealed, the addition of adjacent tracts of land would further co-join their two estates. In explanation of why he had not told Claire earlier, Bude said it was because the transactions had been difficult and all could have come to nought. Had that happened, he would have remained married to her.

"You still are married to me." said Claire.

Her comment brought Bude to the rest of his story. At the time of their wedding his father had promised, that if Bude agreed to have the marriage legalised in Rumania, he would obtain the dispensation necessary for a Catholic to marry outside his religion. There would be no problem for he knew the Bishop well. But the dispensation for a mixed marriage had not been granted and his father was not now prepared to recognise Claire as his son's wife, claiming that in the eyes of their Church, their marriage was no marriage at all.

"My father also demands that with the restoration of title to our lands and inheritance, my sons must be raised in Rumania, in their fatherland, in accordance with their culture."

Bude carried on speaking and Claire heard the words duty, family, honour, repeated many times, but such concepts had nothing to do with this. This was simply a scheme enabling his family to have title to their estate legally restored, together with the material advantage that undoubtedly went with it.

While waiting for him to finish, Claire's mind had not been idle. She had always known he could be unyielding at times, but nothing had prepared her for the ruthlessness she had come up against tonight. The brunt of his words had pushed her to the edge of her restraint and it was now she who fixed her eyes on the wineglass. When at last he fell silent, she made no comment. Then, on pretext of being upset, she rose. She must go to the Ladies' Powder Room, would he please let her pass. Accepting this, Bude moved aside. Claire left the alcove, collected her wrap and walked from the building.

Seated in a taxi, she waited until she was almost home before asking the driver to stop at a telephone kiosk. Her phone call was to the restaurant. The receptionist was to inform the gentleman she had been with, not to wait for her, that there had been a change of plan and she would call on him in the morning.

On arriving home Claire went straight upstairs to the bedroom. There was little time to waste. When Bude received her message he would most likely come back to the house. Quickly she changed from what she was wearing, thrust a torch, some clothes and other essentials into a suitcase and, leaving no trace of her visit, hurried downstairs to the garden summerhouse from where she could see when he came home.

While waiting, Claire assessed the situation. Had the evening been less catastrophic, she would have been more confused in her reactions, but the extent of the shock seemed to have cleared her mind. All Bude's scheming had been centred on himself. He had spoken of his planned wedding as making no difference to their relationship. Did he really believe she would become his mistress? In effect, he had abandoned her and given his betrayal and deceit, she wanted no further dealings with him.

Everything however, including money, was in his name. She had a small amount, nothing much. But the fashion houses had recognised her as indispensible and without her, their work would not have met with such success.

Within moments of hearing his car the light shone from their bedroom window. A while later and all was dark once more. She would wait a further hour or so. He should be asleep by then. A nearby clock sounded the passing hours. When at last it struck three, tense and nervous, she stood in the darkness outside their front door, then quietly turned her key and entered. Fervently she hoped he had been given her message and was not still awake and waiting for her. Making no sound, she crossed the hall into the office and lifted a corner of the window blind. A glimmer from the street gaslight dimly lit the room, enough to see by. Opening the safe, she worked quickly and quietly, checking all the items required by the contract and putting them into her shoulder satchel. More minutes passed as she repacked the pouch she had just emptied, placed it in the safe and with trembling fingers, closed and locked it again. When the courier called, the pouch would be waiting for him where it should be. Bude would not check it. He knew she was always careful and correct. He would simply hand it over, full of useless old proofs.

The satchel she had just packed, contained the original contracts, documents, photos, proofs of the printouts together with the other indispensables the fashion house required. Bude had already put his hand to all requiring his signature, prior to visiting his father. The stipulations in the contract requiring her signature rendered anything now left behind with Bude, quite worthless.

The hall's wardrobe door creaked when she opened it. She froze, holding her breath, but no sound came from upstairs where Bude lay asleep, or was he awake? She waited, listening, for what seemed an age then gently unhooked a daytime coat from its peg. In her suitcase and satchel, she had all she needed. She checked again and glanced around. She must leave nothing to betray she had been back to the house.

As noiselessly as she had come, she went.

It was still dark when she arrived at the main railway station. Seated in the carriage waiting for the early morning train to leave, she was anxious and on edge. At last, the carriages lurched, the engine shunted, chugging slowly before swiftly gathering speed on its journey through the sleeping city. Soon, it was passing through the open countryside on its way towards the coast. As streaks of dawn slit the charcoal sky and widened the slashes to let in the day, Claire relaxed. By nightfall she would be in London and she had her plans worked out.

The following morning, she called at the fashion house that had commissioned them. They had been pleased with what she had contributed on location and several of the ideas they had incorporated had been hers. The outlets were already waiting for the adverts. There was no time to lose. She had the only prints that could be used. Claire made her requirements clear. If they wanted to benefit from this promotion it was with her they had to deal. Mindful of their doubts regarding the photographer's reliability, wishing to have the business finalised and very conscious of the fact that all the necessary documentation, legally stamped and signed, was in her possession, they raised no objection. She would meet with them at their convenience wherever it was necessary for the exchange to take place. Duly they met. All went as planned. The ordeal was over. All previous payments had gone into Bude's bank account. This one would remain in her possession.

The riches and security so seemingly a part of the high life she had been living, how ephemeral they had proved to be and Bude, the man whom she had thought she knew, how very different from reality, her perception of him had been.

CHAPTER TWENTY-EIGHT

Summer 1930, Ardleagh Hall

*M*argaret checked the drawing room that gave onto the terrace one last time, making sure all was in order for the guests arriving later in the day. It was ages since she had entertained so large a number and she wanted everything to be perfect. 'But it's not a really large gathering, not like the ones we used to have,' she reflected.

The weather was hot and dry, promising to stay sunny until late. It was a shame not to have the celebration on the terrace. The flowerbeds of dark blue delphiniums and pale pink climbing roses looked quite lovely and showed to advantage against the old, stone walls, but no, it would involve too much moving around and she must have them all seated and settled before the broadcast began. Thinking of the broadcast, Margaret glanced at her watch. "The wireless technician, he should be here by now." She spoke aloud to herself as she did increasingly of late and left the room.

It was the occasion of James' first public broadcast live from the B.B.C. in London. Reception still tended to be not quite reliable, crackling and coming in waves, but she would ensure that the technician was on hand. How proud his grandfather would have been. She only wished Frederick would show more pleasure in his son's success, but taking pleasure was something he seemed to have lost the feel for these days. His zest for life had quite disappeared. 'Perhaps if he stops upsetting himself so much or so often, over things he can do nothing about, political decisions of the government and such-like, it may come back,' she mused.

It used to be that his grumbles were, more or less, confined to when he was reading the newspapers at breakfast. These days however, the wireless broadcasts fed his exasperation during the day as well and as the doctor kept saying, becoming irritated increased the flow of bile and contributed to his nasty liverish attacks.

When Labour got back in power again in June last year, he got himself frightfully upset, not only about Ramsey McDonald being Prime Minister again and there being a woman in the cabinet for the first time, but with Stanley Baldwin the Conservative leader, for being, as Frederick put it, dumb enough to let Labour in a second time. The reckoning showed that Labour had two hundred and eighty-eight seats and the Tories only two hundred and sixty, but the Tories had most votes. With neither party having a sufficient majority, the Liberals held the balance once more but rather than try to strike a deal with Lloyd George, their leader, the Conservative cabinet had resigned and so let Labour gain power.

Frederick's stroke was still affecting his reasoning and Labour's threats of Nationalisation left him very much on edge. He muddled and argued about things that happened yesterday, but his long-term memory was good and he could well recall events of twenty years ago, which needless to say, included his recollections about the Brackworth. Margaret kept telling him to forget it, that everyone else had, but she knew that was not so. There were those in the village who could recount in detail, everything related to the disaster, as clearly as on the day it struck.

They had quite cut themselves off from the village now. There was not the respect there, the way there once had been, and when the Trade Unionists opened their new Social Rooms and plastered the walls with their placards, Frederick gave his chauffeur instructions to detour round and use the back roads instead. Trade had slumped since the collapse of the New York Stock Exchange last October and the number out of work was now more than double the figure it had been when Labour took over. The mills were on short time. The demand for coal was falling and Frederick was not alone in fussing about lost profits. There were many like him, anxious about their holdings, saying that this was only the start and that worse was to come. Sadly events were proving them right. James said the effects of the downturn were even worse in Germany. America was calling in its loans. Companies were becoming bankrupt. People were committing suicide. The brawling between the Communists and the Nazis had flared up afresh and that Hitler fellow was making a name for himself again.

Margaret was sick of hearing of nothing but trouble. It was so unpleasant. People did not go on and on about politics in the old days, the way they did now. If only Frederick would turn the wireless off instead of up when the politicians came on air.

Well, at least today's broadcast would turn their minds to more pleasant topics. James' success was quite wonderful, but he maintained success was the joy one got from music, not the fame that sometimes followed. Nonetheless, she was glad he was becoming well known and his recordings were selling in the shops. Arrabella had married very well, but whenever Margaret mentioned marriage to James he would reply, "No woman wants to marry a man who's always on the move." But that was only an excuse. He had a beautiful apartment in Berlin, in Dahlem and did not spend too much time on tour.

Margaret checked the rooms again and, assured all was in order, relaxed. Amelia and Leonora were arriving later in the week. They were in London at present. Alva had agreed to their trip due to something about Leonora having tests done, but it was all a bit vague. Happily, their visit had coincided with James' concert, which they were attending this evening. Margaret had been hoping she and Frederick might also go and hold a reception for James at their Park Lane house after the concert, but Frederick had poured cold water on the idea. He abhorred the changes taking place in London, the new hotels and offices that had appeared in Park Lane, the screech and fumes of the traffic, all the rushing and busy bustle there was now. Consequently, they had not been to London for ages. In truth, they had not been anywhere for ages and she was looking forward to Amelia arriving and brightening things up.

Amelia also had been longing to get away. It had been awful in Spain this year. A fresh onslaught of violence was rocking the country brought on by the fall in January of the Military Dictator, Primo de Rivera. She was weary of living in strife-torn Madrid and yearned for the delights of London, strolling down Bond Street, calling in at Aspreys, having tea at the Dorchester, pleasing herself where she went without fear of riots and bloodshed.

Amelia was an English rose at heart and longed for the pleasures of a more temperate clime. The heat, the tumult, the baked landscape in summer and the sheer energies of the Spanish, drained her. Wilting, she thirsted for the cool dew of a morning that promised to become an English summer day, the freshly cut grass, the birdsong, the overall peace and calm that pervaded the gardens there. She had tried to persuade her husband that she ought to visit her brother, who was far from well.

When he remained deaf to her promptings, she had focussed her persuasions on a subject more welcome to his ear. Knowing it was an on-going cause of impatience to him that their daughter showed no sign of producing a grandson, the male heir he was still fretting for, and was refusing to seek medical advice,

Amelia hinted that the doctors in Spain were somewhat old fashioned and out of date and recommended the merits of a Harley Street specialist she knew.

As a mother, she was genuinely concerned about Leonora and was of the opinion that a trip abroad would be every bit as beneficial as the ministrations of some man in a white coat. Alva however continued to argue the merits of the Spanish gynaecologists and their marriage was suffering another of its strained periods, then, all unexpectedly, he went along with her idea. He had been generous with their allowance. They would be able visit the latest exhibitions, go to the theatres and choose from the new season's fashions and when she learned that her trip coincided with James' concert, it was the cherry on the cake.

In fact, it had suddenly suited Alva to have his wife take a trip abroad. He had become embroiled in politics and in certain machinations best kept quiet, involving a trip to Italy, to Rome with two of his associates. Of course, if Amelia had still been around he would have concocted some plausible excuse, but Amelia was no fool. She had a mind of her own and her intuitive abilities troubled him. It was as if she had the power to tune in on his private thoughts. She had ways of probing, of shooting in the dark and although such topics as 'arms-dealing' had not entered their conversations, he could tell she sensed there was something going on that he did not wish to talk about and the idea of her visiting London, was a relief.

The summer of 1930 was a dangerous time in Spain. There had been relatively little volatility during Primo's dictatorship, but his departure had resulted in great instability and fierce rioting had broken out the very same day. The bulletin on Primo de Rivera's resignation had said it was for health and personal reasons, but the real reason was that the King had got rid of him. The King's handling of the political situation was as inept as ever and support for him was waning drastically. Certain Army officers condemned the King for having acted dishonourably towards Primo de Rivera, his loyal and long-time defender. Even staunch monarchists were admitting that King Alphonse had been unwise. Pressure for a Republic was growing and there was intrigue afoot, but the King was not altogether to blame. Primo de Riviera had been at fault and, as is often the case, a scandal had triggered his fall.

After months of treading the straight and narrow, Primo de Rivera, an aging widower, had a tendency to suddenly break out and go on the razzle-dazzle. At such times while not quite himself, he was prone to making unfortunate and embarrassing statements it was necessary to retract. However, these interludes were regarded as separate from his professional life, until, La Caoba, a mahogany coloured beauty, crossed his path.

She was alluring and moved with discretion amongst the very best of people in the very best of circles, many of whom became extremely apprehensive, if not downright alarmed, when she became involved in a drug scandal and was facing prosecution with all its attendant publicity. She appealed to Primo, who took it upon himself to get her case dropped and obtain her discharge.

When the judge in question refused to cooperate, Primo ordered that La Caoba was to be released anyway. Again, the Judge refused and his decision received the full support of the President of the Supreme Court. Primo responded by dismissing the Supreme Court President from office and removing the judge. There was uproar. As was his wont, the Dictator tried to gag his opponents, many of whom were prominent figures. One of Rivera's victims was the well-known philosopher, Unamuno, who was in exile on one of the Canary Islands for voicing his disapproval. The whole affair epitomised Rivera's contempt for the law, which he tended to disregard or manipulate to suit himself. His conduct was diminishing respect for legality, bringing the regime into disrepute. Worse still, it was playing into the hands of the insurrectionists.

He had already upset many officers, by tampering with the Army's system of promotions and was no longer popular. With his health deteriorating and, uncertain about whether he should remain in office, Primo had instituted a referendum of the Captains General. Not one of them had answered 'Yes'. The King only learned of this when reading his morning newspaper. He was furious and accused Rivera of a violation of Royal Prerogative. He remained unforgiving of his onetime Little Mussolini and coldly banished him. According to the officer corps' code of honour, the King had acted disreputably and the Army was offended. A few weeks later, the old Dictator died alone in a Paris hotel bedroom and the King made the grievous mistake of refusing to attend his funeral.

Problems abounded, mismanagement from the top, insurrection from below, interference from the Church, political stalemate, corruption, the failure of the Military Dictatorship and now, dissatisfaction with the King himself. Even the massive construction schemes of Calvo Sotelo, Primo's darkly handsome, finance minister, which originally had been applauded for modernising and bringing Spain into the twentieth century, had ground to a halt in the slough of the Great Depression and were now seen as uselessly excessive and a wasted extravagance.

Nor had the conditions of the workers and peasants improved, half the country's land belonged to only twenty thousand men, some of whom owned almost whole provinces much of which they let go to waste. Two million peasants had no land at all and barely any means of livelihood. A third of the people continued to live in abject poverty and half the population of twenty-four million was unable to read or write.

Believing that an educated population was harder to govern than an illiterate mass, Primo de Rivera had discouraged education and had closed down places of learning even the notable Ateneo, thereby antagonising not only the Liberals, but many intellectuals in the Right Wing and demands for reform were coming from previously unexpected quarters.

The chaos continued throughout the hot summer. Strictly speaking, Primo's rule had been illegal. At the time of his takeover in 1923, the Cortes had been suspended and the setting up of the Dictatorship had not met the requirements of the Constitution. There was clamouring for a Clean Sweep, an end to the Monarchy and fighting flared between those in favour of a Republic and those against. Mobs were out in force on the streets and in many instances, what started as a demonstration ended in a full blown riot. Anarchists seized the moment and added to the ferment. Men, who only a decade ago, would not have considered Spain becoming a Republic, now believed that only the setting up of a Democracy could defuse the explosive atmosphere and channel it into a legalised form of government and that failing this, the outcome would be civil war.

They were not alone. Several high-ranking Army officers also, were concerned that unless reform came soon, they would be embroiled in the civil war they dreaded and were debating whether a Democratic Republic was the answer. Dissent was spreading in the ranks of the Army itself and Raimundo had heard rumours that an intrigue was afoot to bring down the Monarchy.

Spain a Republic, was it conceivable? Many whose loyalties had previously been clear-cut were now undecided, not knowing which option to favour. Alva and his ilk were not among them. The demand for reform, the oft-debated land question, could only be satisfied at their expense, by loss of their land. Their minds, never open to such a solution, became more tightly sealed. Raimundo and Georgio, the old and the young, were typical of those in the Army that would not accept a Republic either. The older officers, hard and entrenched, would never let go of their ways and traditions and the young ones, fresh from their military Academies, were burning with zeal, fired with idealistic notions of recreating the glorious Spain of old.

Word had reached Raimundo that those intriguing to set up a Republic, were meeting secretly at San Sebastian, a well-known Spanish spa, very popular during the summer months, situated on Spain's north-easterly coast, close to the border with France, near Biarritz.. With so many visitors coming and going, San Sebastian was the perfect rendezvous for the plotters to meet and liaise. Anxious to know just what was in the offing and who was involved, Raimundo suggested to Alva, that Amelia and Leonora should plan to visit Biarritz on their way back from England, breaking their journey at San Sebastian on route. Alva could join his wife and daughter there for a short holiday on his way back from Italy and he, Raimundo, could accompany his nephew Georgio, who could also spend time with his wife. It would provide the perfect cover for Raimundo to figure out what was happening. Amelia loved to mix and mingle it and it was always possible one way or another, to get to know what was going on if one were socially well connected.

Meanwhile in London, Amelia was having a splendid time, the best for ages. The concert had been a success and James had taken her and her daughter to dine and dance at the Savoy. Not for a long time had she tripped the light fantastic and James, rising to the occasion as he always did had acted as a charming escort for Leonora. She was still a little wan but as he swirled her around the floor, she too began to enjoy herself.

In the end, Leonora did not undergo an examination by a specialist. She baulked at each appointment made and Amelia, not knowing why, deemed it wise not to press the issue but she had no intention of letting Alva know. There was no point in making trouble. She would simply tell him they were waiting for the results and then say the results were inconclusive. Leonora had planned to slip away quietly by herself to visit a consultant unknown to her family, for her worries were still there in that closed off part of her mind, like a beehive she knew about but tried not to disturb. From time to time, anxieties escaped and, like bees, buzzed around. One by one, she could deal with them, but she dared not break open the place from whence they came. She had never told anyone. Was it advisable to tell this specialist? Again, like bees, the questions buzzed and again as always, fear spawned more fear. What if he put it in his records and what if… word got out? Dishonoured, a disgrace to the family, no, she was never going to admit to what she had done and knowing she could not force herself to tell the truth, she cancelled the consultation and despite her distress she still did not know what may be wrong.

Shortly after his concert, James travelled north with Amelia and Leonora to Ardleagh, but it was not the merriest of visits. Only for Leonora did a sharp prong of unsought excitement pierce the boredom. Would she, perchance see Ralph? Did she want to? Yes…No, not now that he was married. The thought of a chance encounter quickened her heart, but it was not a pleasant sensation. Ralph however, not wishing to meet James, did not put in an appearance and the matter resolved itself. Amelia had not expected to find life at the Hall enlivening, but never had she known it as lacklustre as it was now. Her own life was not a gay carousel, but this! How did Margaret get through the days?

When Alva rang, asking her and Leonora to meet him in Biarritz, she was pleased. She would have been more so if he had not said Raimundo was also coming. Hoping to alleviate the prospect of his company, she invited Margaret and James to join them. James agreed, but Margaret, having been advised by Frederick's specialist not to leave him, declined.

Nor was the stay in Biarritz the light-hearted interlude James had envisaged. The crisscross of relationships between Alva, Amelia and Raimundo was unsettling. Georgio was paying little attention to Leonora and Alva was doing nothing to ease the situation. He was irked by his suspicion that Amelia was withholding something from him. He considered her unsatisfactory account regarding the gynaecologist to be less than straightforward and was letting his annoyance at being no wiser regarding his chances of having a grandson, to express itself in unfortunate comments regarding the matter.

James would have dearly liked to ask Alva, if he had ever considered the non-fulfilment of his wishes could well be attributable to his son-in-law. Long postings in Morocco were not conducive to such hopes. It was a well-attested fact that that the lifestyle enjoyed by many officers stationed there could all too easily result in consequences injurious to their virility.

Georgio, Alva and Raimundo were forever putting their heads together, going off into huddles, speaking in rapid Spanish James did not understand. It was none of his business, but their anxiety was discernible. Sensing trouble, he was concerned for Amelia and Leonora They were not here on a family holiday any more than Alva's recent trip to Rome had been a holy pilgrimage. Alva had become involved in politics and the liaison between the Spanish authorities and the Vatican was strong. The name 'Herrera' needed no translation from the Spanish and James had overheard it mentioned several times.

With the atmosphere as it was, dinner tended to be an uneasy affair and Amelia, being Amelia, had also gauged there was more going on than met the eye, but had kept her opinions to herself and said nothing…until last night.

They were gathered at the table and Amelia, as before, had remained silent and straight-faced listening to Alva who, still brimming with recollections of his recent visit to the Rome, was treating them to a glowing account of the changes and improvements resulting from last year's Lateran Treaty between the Vatican and the Italian State.

"For which read, The Hierarchy and Mussolini," Amelia intercepted.

"…and how," continued Alva raising his voice a decibel and ignoring her interruption, "it has ended the tension that's existed between the State and the Vatican since the last century. The Church's spiritual power is being acknowledged and the Pope can venture outside the enclave of the Vatican for the first time since 1870."

Amelia strongly disliked and distrusted Mussolini and his black-shirted Fascists. The murder of his political opponents, particularly Matteotti, a respected and well-loved Italian politician, had given Mussolini a bad name. It angered Amelia that the Pope's official endorsement of Mussolini, declaring him to be, "A man sent by Providence", had made him and his regime internationally acceptable. Having listened to as much as she could take of Alva's commentary, she had created a flutter in the dovecote and livened up the evening, by denouncing Mussolini as a nasty bully and pointing out how well the Church had done out of its business deals with him.

"The Vatican's now a sovereign State; the Pope's been granted one thousand, seven hundred and fifty million lire for the loss of its former areas, a thousand million in interest-bearing Italian State bonds and clerical stipends are increased; Roman Catholicism's now the State religion; Catholic education's obligatory in schools; marriage bonds have been tightened; and inhabitants of the Vatican had been granted special immunities…to mention only some of the benefits." Listening to the heated arguments that followed, 'Good,' thought James, 'my aunt may have lost her money but she's lost none of her verve.'

But was not the world ever thus, with wrong whitewashed as right and morality and ethical values traded like commodities for material gain?

It was late in the afternoon, sunny as usual and James came onto the hotel terrace that overlooked the beach. Seated at a table at its other end were Georgio, Raimundo and Alva, engrossed in each other as usual. A man in civilian clothes joined them. Judging by his manner and the way they greeted him, James supposed him to be in the military also. Amelia and Leonora were at the hairdressers and James decided to take himself off for a swim.

The man who had just arrived had come with news of the San Sebastian conspirators. Raimundo had been right in his suspicions. Several Army officers were involved in the plot. They were, so he informed his listeners, supported by groups whose motivations differed, but were none the less effective for that. It figured, for although there had been little rebellion during Rivera's rule, there had been intrigues within military ranks and two unsuccessful military risings, pronunciamientos, against the Dictator.

The San Sebastian plotters were from various political factions; Socialists wanting reform; Intellectuals frustrated at having their work censored and their voices suppressed; Liberal politicians weary of Right Wing misrule and pressing for democratic change; Catalan separatists ready to support a Republic in return for their autonomy; anti-monarchists of long standing, always ready to topple the Throne and even the Anarchists, who had been biding their time, were now preparing to cooperate, for despite the different axes these miscellaneous elements had to grind, they were bonded together by the common aim of bringing down the existing regime.

The informer had much to tell and, although now far out from the beach, James could still see the four of them as he swam, small far away specks seated on the terrace, intently involved in their deliberations. Their unease gave no cause for surprise. The ruling classes were coming to realise they were no longer as insuperable as they had once supposed.

Was it really only thirteen years ago that his father, reading at the breakfast table, learned of an uprising in Russia, an uprising which, like others before it, would soon be put down, so it was thought. But it had not been put down and those one time rebels were now the recognised leaders of their country. With that in mind, Alva and Raimundo's disquiet was not hard to understand.

Facing the sun, floating in deep water, enjoying its gentle movements, James thoughts went back to his childhood. It was so short a time for such changes to have taken place. As always, recollections of his childhood brought haunting memories of Claire, her voice, her laughter, the way she moved, how it had felt to hold her in his arms, above all his longing for their wordless understanding, their oneness in a world that had been theirs, and theirs alone.

The images of her were gentle. The pain they brought was not. James drew a long, deliberate breath and dived deep, deeply down into the cool sea. When at last he surfaced, he struck out at a steady crawl. Already far from land, he swam on, putting distance between him and the shore, keeping only enough reserve of strength to return. His clean and powerful strokes cut swiftly though the waters playing across his shoulders, rippling on the bronzed muscles of his body.

When at last he left the sea, his energy was spent. Throwing down his towel, he stretched out on the beach. He must not think of her again. It hurt and was to no avail. He must get back to Berlin, back to his music. He lay enjoying the warmth of the breeze upon his skin, watching the changing light of the evening sun on the deep, unruffled sea and in those moments, there was peace.

But below the surface the undercurrents were pulling this way and that. The Pact of San Sebastian would soon be signed.

Spain, inexorably, was moving to the brink.

CHAPTER TWENTY-NINE

Berlin, Germany. Late summer 1930

*H*aving obtained a first class degree in economics, Kurt Krugenberg had embarked on a post graduation course at Berlin University. He had first met Johanna von Cours more than a couple of years ago and, unknown to her parents, they had continued to see each other since.

Kurt was four years older than Johanna. Though not outstandingly handsome, he was attractive, tall and of good physique, but it was his personality that carried the day. On first meeting him, the effect on Johanna of his strong, quiet self-assurance, the resonance and timbre of his voice, the depths of expression in his dark blue eyes, had been one of instant infatuation. Sir Jonathan's speculation had been accurate indeed. Johanna was in love.

One evening recently Kurt's father, an impoverished factory foreman, had offered his son a piece of advice, the drift of which was that if he continued to be seen with Johanna, her parents would expect him, in due course, to make a formal offer. To court her company and then choose elsewhere would leave her not only hurt, but compromised and would not be the act of a gentleman. Had Kurt considered this? he asked.

Kurt was bemused, but careful not to let it show. The very idea of choosing elsewhere had never entered his head. Not only was he highly intelligent he was also ambitious and had made up his mind to marry Johanna shortly after meeting her. He found other women attractive, but that was a different matter. Attraction, personal magnetism, as some called it, was certainly a bonus in marriage, but was far from essential and he was confident she would accept when he proposed.

She had persuaded her father to allow her to change courses and study in Berlin. It would be a further two or three years before she completed her degree.

The timing suited Kurt. He knew what he wanted in life and had a lot of ground to cover before settling down. He was not expecting a warm welcome from her parents, not from anything Johanna had said, but precisely from what she had not. He was astute enough to know why. It was easy to understand.

Put bluntly, he was not from the same social bracket as the von Cours. Not that Kurt considered this a shortcoming in himself, nor did he consider there to be anything at all wrong or lacking in him, but his family could certainly not be described in such terms as applied to her parents and their ilk. This being so, he lacked kudos and connections, the push and pull of power that money provides, in short, the necessary prerequisites for anyone wishing to circulate with ease in the realms of the von Cours.

It was a disparity of which he had long been aware, a yoke to be borne, one he had long been determined to discard. It was not a case of his having a chip on his shoulder, he simply viewed it as unfair, looked on it as a challenge and believed it could be done and with this in mind, he would avail himself of every advantage and opportunity that came his way.

In 1926, Germany's recovery was under way. The Dawes plan was working and a considerable amount of foreign money, especially American, had come into the country. Production had risen, inflation was under control, unemployment had fallen and with the coming of relative affluence, Communism together with the extremism and unrest that went with it, appeared to be in decline. To Kurt it was proof that rules could be brought to bear, economies could be regulated and provided one found the appropriate formula and applied it to the given problem, one got the right answer.

In June last year however, trouble had arisen due to the settlement made at a conference of international financiers, allowing a more flexible method of payment for the reparations demanded of Germany by the Versailles Treaty. It was named The Young Plan, after its chairman the American banker, Owen Young, but was mainly the work of Gustav Stresemann, the German foreign minister. It was to Germany's benefit. It eased Allied control over Germany's economy and included an agreement on the withdrawal in September, of Allied powers from the Rhineland, a territory that had been demilitarised and occupied by the Allies after the war.

In the country at large however, the plan had roused considerable anger because whatever the advantages of the arrangement, the reparations would continue until 1988. The Germans saw this as a millstone they would be passing on to their children and grandchildren and the Reichstag had come under considerable pressure to reject the Plan.

As the wrangling increased, Hitler began to play his cards. A National Committee was organised to repudiate the hated guilt clause and to fight against the payment of reparations that went with it. It consisted of certain Right Wing associations, the Stahlhelm, the Steel Helmet, a body of retired Army officers and war veterans, the anti-Republican German Nationalists and the Pan German League. When invited to join, Hitler, ever at the ready, seized the opportunity. This was his moment to get back into the limelight. As usual, he promptly began to manipulate the proceedings to his own ends.

The Committee did not succeed in its aims. Though bitterly fought, its onslaught failed to win the day and in November the Reichstag rejected its campaign. The one to have gained most from the affair was Adolph Hitler himself. It had given him a platform from which to broadcast his own policies and beliefs and the unimpressive performance of the other speakers had acted as a foil to show his dynamism to full effect. He appeared in the newspapers as a powerful figure and his alliance with the reputable Right Wing parties greatly increased his respectability, winning for him the trust of many in the middle classes.

The problems in America, caused by the Wall Street crash of late twenty-nine, were now having a serious knock-on effect and as nineteen-thirty got underway the reclamation of its loans was contributing to Germany's economic decline. Once again, there were battles resulting in bloodshed in the streets. As the slump worsened, Kurt, young, zealous and patriotic reasoned, surely to all of this, answers could be found.

Still basking in the accolades of his first class degree, he decided to redirect his studies and devote himself to the problems currently besetting his beloved homeland. Jettisoning his previous choice, he changed the subject of his dissertation to,

"The Economic Depression: Its Reasons and Remedies."

"Ah, biting off the big one are we? Well let's see what we can do," was his tutor's only comment.

Kurt was regarded as one of the university's leading lights. Certainly, he had a brilliant mind but as the Depression worsened, he felt he had made a mistake. No matter whom he talked to, nor what he read, his ideas were no more useful as signposts out of the economic morass, than Will o' the Wisps in a swamp. A worldwide slump and not even the best of brains knew what to do. The rising number of unemployed was swelling the Communists' ranks and it seemed that Germany was slipping back into the same dreadful state as had existed after the war's end.

He was reminded of that frightening time in 1919 when the Communist Spartacists had formed their own Soviets and Councils and tried to seize power and the Weimar government, needing the help of the Army, had signed an agreement with it. Aged thirteen, knowing little of politics, the fighting in the streets close by Kurt's home had scared him. The insurrections had continued and the situation came home that day in mid-January 1920, when thousands of workers and their families gathered outside the Reichstag, where The Factory Council Bill, was about to be put through.

Later, when the crowds refused to disperse, shots were fired. Further orders were issued and troops under General Luttwitz fired several rounds into the crowd, killing forty-two and wounding over a hundred. People panicked, screaming as they tried to drag the injured away. That was the day his father's friend, wounded and bleeding profusely, was carried into their house. Before he died, he had been able to tell them exactly what had happened. But the judiciary and civil service were still very much in the hands of the old brigade and those responsible were not called to account. It was then that Kurt began to take a serious interest in politics.

For the next four years or so after this event, there had been dreadful suffering in Germany and Kurt came to appreciate the huge difference wealth creates between rich and poor. It was not merely the obvious physical differences in living standards and leisure, but the immunity it afforded from much of the suffering inherent in the human condition. It granted power and freedom, freedom from dependency upon and subjection to, the will of others, differences far more precious than the mere dissimilarities between comfort and hardship, between leisured ease and hard, daily grind.

He came to realise that the world of the wealthy existed on a totally different plane. It was a world in which the pitfalls that await the poor could be circumvented, filled in or otherwise removed from one's path, a world in which unfortunate circumstances for which no allowance had been made, could still be accommodated and dealt with. It was a world in which one could follow one's destiny, call one's life one's own - a world inhabited by such families as Johanna's.

Yes, Kurt had been bemused by his father's advice.

Families like the von Cours had been able to shield themselves from the cruel brunt of those after-war years, by dealing in foreign exchange, long term real estate and by the manipulations of circumstance that those who can afford to ride out the storm, are able to apply.

In the first year of that awful inflation shortly after the war, Hans von Cours, astute banker that he was and sensing what was in the offing, had borrowed large amounts of capital which he had then invested. In the years that followed, as ruinous inflation wiped out the savings of the less fortunate, von Cours along with other bankers, entrepreneurs and industrialists who had done the same, watched their debts also dwindle. Such dealings were legal. It was simply a case of having the means and knowing the rules.

Now however, in the slump of this present Depression, the rules appeared not to be working and as Kurt saw much of what he was writing in his dissertation contradicted by what was happening around him, his faith in formulae was badly shaken. He came to believe his so-called work was nothing more than an academic exercise epitomising an unbridgeable gap between theoretical answer and effective remedy.

But if nobody came up with the answers, the threat of Communism would again become real. At times it seemed they were the only ones actually achieving anything. They were well organised now, getting their directives from the Party leadership in Russia, where the country's industries had been taken over by the workers, farms were being collectivised and private ownership of property abolished. A nightmare scenario indeed, thought Kurt.

Under the dictates of the Versailles Treaty, Germany's future was bleak. With reparations to be paid, the economy in recession, violence in the streets, political parties bickering and pulling different ways, Weimar's lack of strong leadership rendered it unable to clean up or get out of the mess. Seeing his degree as worthless and knowing no direction in which to turn, Kurt lost his incentive and became depressed.

It was while in this low state that a large poster, stuck in the centre of the notice board outside the university entrance, caught his eye. It boasted a portrait of Adolf Hitler. At first, Kurt paid little heed. A second glance at the poster however, tempted him to take a better look. The man was going to give a talk to the students in the forthcoming week. "He can't be any worse than the others," muttered Kurt and made a mental note of the time and date.

The appointed hour found him seated at the front. He was not expecting to be impressed, in fact, he considered the man little more than a big noise, but he would give him a hearing. When Hitler arrived, he did not at all match the image Kurt had formed of him. He had discarded his battle shirt in favour of a sober suit. Serious and quite slow in his opening statements, he addressed his audience without haranguing the Weimar Republic. Nor did he call its members the November Traitors and paint a gloomy picture of what the future held if the Republic remained in place.

Rather, he focussed on what was happening at present, concentrating on the immediate afflictions of hunger, homelessness and unemployment that were currently driving many into the Communist camp. Talking of the injustice of the reparation payments, the reduction of their armed forces and the degradation that had been visited on their homeland, he stated specifically what he intended to do to restore Germany's honour, plainly outlining what could be done and, most importantly, what could be done now.

Other than his voice, there was total silence in the hall. There was something unique in the combination of this man's scale of vision together with his obvious personal interest in his listeners. His ability to command attention, the passionate conviction thickening his voice, forced Kurt to believe Hitler was a man of strength and understanding, a man who actually could put an end to Germany's troubles. Here was a leader with whose aspirations and ideals he could identify and he became embarrassingly conscious of his inner emotion for this man who was lifting his depression from him.

When Hitler paused and allowed his gaze to roam slowly over those before him, Kurt glanced away, uncomfortably aware of the sudden ardour he was experiencing and when Hitler finished speaking, he hurriedly left the Hall. He did not go back to his rooms, nor did he want to meet his friends, for Hitler would be the topic of conversation and he was not ready to discuss with others the feelings this man aroused in him. He needed to be alone to define exactly what had so affected him.

In fact, Kurt was never to be ready to discuss with others the way Hitler affected him, although in times to come, he often noticed that being with those he sensed were similarly disposed, intensified it strongly.

Trying to settle his reactions he walked the city streets and did not turn his steps to home until the dawn had ushered in the day's first light.

Two days later, Kurt Krugenburg joined the Nazi Party.

CHAPTER THIRTY

Berlin, September 1930

*J*ohanna had spent the last hour browsing in one of the city's large bookstores. She had been selecting books for her second year at the University. Today was the start of the usual 'first-timers' week, but there would be other events and the chance to catch up with what was going on. She was waiting for Kurt, hoping he would not be late for he had said they could meet and he would walk there with her.

Moments later Kurt arrived. While on his way, he had been debating with himself whether to tell her about having joined the National Socialist Party, the Nazis. 'No, better not to mention it, not just yet,' he decided, 'I'd be wiser to wait until things quieten down a little.' With elections in the offing and the campaign in full swing, the National Socialists were certainly making their presence felt and Hitler's Brown Shirts, the Sturm Abteilung, (Storm Troops) S.A. for short, were everywhere so it seemed and not always making a good impression.

Hitler's recent rise to prominence on the political scene, far from making it easier for him to tell Johanna as he had expected, had caused tensions instead. Her latest appraisal of him was that he was a loud-mouthed opportunist and she had begun to refer to The Party as a whole, as 'a bunch of hoodlums and thugs'. He could see why. There had been a fair amount of brawling and fighting in the streets, sometimes with serious injuries but it was not all the fault of the Brown Shirts. They were being attacked as well, by the Communists and other rowdies. It was just election fever. It would calm down once the voting was over.

Given she had not attended any of the National Socialists' meetings and knew little about them, Kurt did think she was being unfair, but he was not going to risk entrenching her in her views by arguing against her. He was hoping that once she understood their aims, she would see them in a better light and would come to accept that the National Socialists were Germany's only realistic hope of a better future. Surely she knew that the terms contained in last year's Young Plan for the reparations payments which this government had accepted, meant that not only they themselves, but their children and their children's children would have to continue paying them until the late 1980's, working their days for the benefit of others, little better than slave labour. When Hitler came to power, he would scrap the reparations, no doubt about that.

Kurt had no intention of wrangling with her over politics. Everything about her was exactly what he wanted, her background, her family, her breeding and he knew her well enough to know she cared about him, regardless of his somewhat precarious financial state. Yes, he would put off telling her for a while. Heinrich Himmler, head of the S.S. since January last year, had said that certain elements within the S.A., were damaging the Party's reputation and that the S.S., the Schutz Staffel (Protection Squad) was to be a much more elite organisation. That was why he was making the standards for entry so strict. Kurt was confident that given the objectives Himmler had in mind, the Party image was bound to improve

"Kurt, we've walked all of five blocks and you've barely spoken one word to me." Johanna stopped walking and put her hand on his arm. She looked at him, appealingly.

While strolling along the boulevard, Kurt had been lost in thought.

"You're daydreaming. I don't think you even realise I'm here. Remember… me, Johanna, the girl you met at the book store, ten minutes ago."

Instantly apologetic and all gentleness Kurt turned to her, his expression softening into one of his disarming smiles.

"Oh, I remember…could any man forget?" He raised her slim fingers to his lips then, pressing them in his own strong hand, drew her arm through his. Careful to give her his full attention, he inclined towards her as they walked on. Johanna basked in the warm glow suffusing her body. She was happy. She was in love.

"So how's your life? What have you been doing with yourself?" she asked.

"My life's fine, fine," he replied promptly, hoping she would enquire no further. "How about you?" and he went on to ask about her mother whose anxiety over the forthcoming elections was causing disruption at home. It was an easy topic to broach. The campaign posters were everywhere.

"Oh please, don't even ask," Johanna grimaced. "I think I told you. Ever since Mama took it upon herself to plough all the way through that dreadful book Mein Kampf…and I mean all the way, from cover to cover, she believes all the terrible things Hitler's written in it and now won't listen to one word in his favour. Papa says she's being unreasonable, making a needless fuss and that the book's so badly written no-one else is reading it and Mama maintains that's the trouble. They should be then they'd learn what he's really like."

"Hitler wrote it in prison years ago," said Kurt. "He's matured since then. Your Papa's right. It's not worth your attention, whatever's in it."

But Johanna looked troubled and seemed not to hear.

"The rows at home," she said, "are because she's not keeping her opinion to herself when people are around and that's really upsetting Papa because he and some of his friends are starting to lean the other way. In fact, quite a few bankers and industrialists are beginning to say that with this terrible Depression putting people out of work and the Communists gaining strength again, if Adolf is able to sway the masses and turn the people against the Bolsheviks, perhaps he should be given a chance."

Kurt was pleased to hear it, but aimed to sound nonchalant.

"Your Papa and his friends could well be right. The talk in the department is on much the same lines."

"Right or wrong, Mama and Papa had another bad spat about it last night. They're poles apart over it at the moment, can't agree about Hitler at all, but I suppose that's because Papa's views are financial ones and Mummy's are humanitarian and she's very angry at Papa for what she calls his moral compromise and Papa's angry with her because, as his wife, she's not only disagreeing with him but worse still, she's letting people know."

They were crossing the road as she spoke. Gripping her elbow, Kurt deftly steered her through the traffic. Seeing the university entrance looming a little distance away, Johanna was suddenly annoyed with herself for wasting the last several precious minutes talking about her parents when she had wanted to use her time with Kurt to give him ideas about something else. It was the University Ball soon. She had been so hoping he would suggest taking her, but so far he had said nothing and she had hardly seen him the last few weeks. Tickets were rapidly running out. It was difficult because her parents were trying to pair her off with a partner of their choosing and if Kurt did not ask her soon and she refused the others, she may end up with no escort at all.

But more than that, the University Ball was a special occasion and she had come to feel that his asking her, or not, was the yardstick by which to measure where she stood with him. She cared about him desperately, had done for ages. He was affectionate towards her but had never shown whether, or how much he cared, in that way. He had been very preoccupied of late and she hoped he was not cooling off. It was worrying and she kept wondering what had been keeping him so busy recently.

They had reached their destination. Posters about the Ball were very much in evidence and she deliberately walked on until she was standing right by one. They were saying goodbye but still he had said nothing, nor had he suggested when they might meet again.

'No time now for a subtle raising of the subject,' she thought and took the plunge.

"Oh, by the way, I almost forgot...the Ball...?" she broke off, waiting for his reaction.

Kurt looked puzzled. "The Ball...oh yes...the Ball."

She waited, then, "Shall we go?" She spoke casually but was feeling very pushy. "Why yes...if you like."

They made their arrangements. Moments later, he was gone.

It was not the most wholehearted of invitations. In truth, she scolded herself it was no invitation at all. She had virtually asked to be taken. She tried not to mind, but her disappointment and the feeling it gave her, made her question whether she even wanted to go now. His lack of enthusiasm had spoiled the evening before it began.

Berating herself, she watched his retreating figure, dearly wishing she had not even mentioned the ball to him...pretty useless yardstick now with which to measure his feelings for her and why did she care so madly? She knew not...only that she did. Everything about him stirred something in her, his walk, the set of his shoulders. He had an air about him. Even with his back to her she could unerringly pick him out in any crowd.

When he finally vanished from view, she stood, thinking.

"Hello, anything wrong?" The voice sounded interested, concerned. Johanna spun round.

"Oh, Hello, No...I mean, thank you. Everything's fine." A little embarrassed, Johanna smiled. "Why do you ask?"

"Oh, just that," James grinned, "...well, there's a saying in Lancashire about, 'looking like you've found a ha'penny and lost a bob'."

"A bob?" she questioned.

"Yes, a bob. It's slang for a shilling. So, come on...what's wrong?"

Johanna looked up at her inquisitor. There's no fooling this man she thought and yet, as once before, was not disturbed that he could see through her. She did not feel caught out. On the contrary she was comforted by an instinctive feeling of trust, of being able to confide.

She laughed. "Yes, that just about sums up the situation, but it's nothing, just Kurt, being Kurt. But tell me, what are you doing here? I know you haven't come to learn to play the piano," she teased.

"In a way," he answered. "You know what they say. If you want to learn something, teach it and by your pupils you'll be taught. But no, I'm not teaching, just that I've been asked to assist with the Students' Musical Society. You know the usual, give talks, pass on a few tips, advise them how to avoid pitfalls and help when they're giving concerts."

"But won't that take up too much of your time?" Johanna was surprised at the interest James was showing.

"No. I'll enjoy it. The benefit's in their enthusiasm, the joy shared, or just listening to young people..." James trailed off. He did not usually talk about his feelings. "And you? How are you enjoying your studies, philosophy isn't it?"

Johanna nodded. "Yes, philosophy," she replied, "...but I'm not going to get buried in the dust of the past."

"Ah, sounds as though you've been plotting your path already." James was interested.

"I have," she answered. "I want my work to relate to the present. Of course, as expected, I'm having to study Kant, Plato, Schopenhauer and others on the unavoidable list, but what I really want to get on to is the effect certain philosophers have had, and are having, on European thought and consciousness here and now, especially the Germanic, explore the extent to which they've conditioned attitudes, influenced our thinking, and still are doing." She suddenly stopped speaking. "But I mustn't get carried away," she added.

"No, please do, I'm interested," James urged her.

"Well there's no doubt some philosophers have enriched men's lives enormously, but on the other hand, there are those whose ideas sound great at an intellectual level, but when put into practice have an opposite effect. I believe some of the ideas in circulation today are downright dangerous." she declared.

"Like Nietzsche, Gobineau, Housten Stewart Chamberlain?" asked James, mentioning a few of the names often quoted in recent racist publications.

"Sounds as though you've also been giving the matter some thought," Johanna countered. "Yes, those you've mentioned and those whose theories have been misinterpreted, or misunderstood and then fed to the public in distorted form," she replied.

"...or twisted to suit pet theories, then used to serve individual ends," added James.

"I wonder how many people," mused Johanna, "…know that Kant, Nietzsche, Housten Stewart Chamberlain and one or two other philosophers, became somewhat unstable, unbalanced and yet, once having been accepted, what they uttered still goes unchallenged."

James smiled at her. "Well, perhaps some were a bit too way-out all along, but they still opened fresh avenues of thought for scientists to test, for better or worse. You're right to question though and to let in fresh air if you can, but there may be some dyed in the wool professors in there, so be warned. Don't target the beliefs they've built their life's work on, not if you're aiming for a First or Honours…just a thought."

"Heavens and I thought philosophy was the search for truth at all costs," she answered.

They had just entered the students' main hall, when…

"What on earth…?" Johanna gasped and tried to dodge as a large banner swung across without warning and flapped her in the face. Bigger than a banqueting cloth, it continued its soaring flight until finally it was suspended tapestry-like from a high, inner wall. Raised up, it faced the hall like a gigantic altarpiece demanding veneration. It was bright, a very bright red with a gold edging and in its centre, a large, white orb. Displayed as it was, it was sacrilegiously reminiscent of the sacred, white host when presented for adoration in the monstrance, except that the Cross adulterating the 'white host' on the Nazi banner, was a crooked cross.

It was the stark, black sign of the Hakenkreuz, the Crooked Cross, The Swastica, the emblem the Nazis had adopted as their own.

Beneath it stood a long table loaded with Nazi propaganda, pamphlets and posters, books and flags, which were being distributed by several of the Brown Shirts helped by some students sporting swastika armbands. Others were festooning the hall with their emblems. The place was awash with their paraphernalia.

"Oh I refuse to believe this is all part of this year's course," Johanna looked around in disgust. "What is going on? Is this another of their fake, religious rituals…or a carnival?"

"If the band arrives, it's a carnival," said James.

"God forbid." Johanna muttered the words with feeling, dropped her books on a nearby bench and sat down. James took the seat beside her.

"It's due to the election. You know what the Nazis are like," he answered. "But I imagine we'll be looking at it until September 14th when the voting takes place."

"Oh, No," she wailed. "Surely, the university will order them to take it down and move everything. It looks awful and they've no right..." she broke off, looking at James for understanding. "But that's the trouble isn't it?" she added in an anxious tone. "The Nazis never reckon they need rights."

"That's about it," he agreed, "and that's why I doubt they will, the University I mean, order it all to be taken down. It will only invite trouble and the authorities aren't going to want the place broken up by the Brown Shirts especially just before the start of the semester, which is what may well happen if anyone interferes with their decorations."

"Tolerating their usual vulgar extravagance isn't the worst of it," said Johanna angrily. "The worst is the way in which every time it comes to dealing with the S.A., whatever the particular incident in question, we all just sidestep, excusing ourselves by pretending that it doesn't really matter, when it darn well does. Even when something does get to Court, they get let off and we all act like that's not important either. But it is and it's even more important when the real reason we're avoiding making an issue of it, as we are now, is because we know that if we do go against them, someone or something will get hurt or smashed.

"Just watch what happens," she told him forcefully. "We'll all pretend we don't care the place looks like a travelling circus until the Nazis decide, whenever that may be, to remove their trash, because we think it's better to have the place looking like this than to have it..." she hesitated, seeking the right word, "...wrecked. But if they keep getting away with it and aren't stopped it's going to get a lot more serious."

Seeing how upset she was, James wondered what more pressing anxiety had the Nazis behaviour triggered. She was not easily disturbed and he wanted to know why, but the clock on the wall showed after the hour and right now he had to go.

"Look, I have to dash. I'm late," he said. "But how about meeting for a coffee later, are you free, in about an hour shall we say?"

She forced a smile. "Thank you, I'd like that...in an hour."

The meeting of the Musical Society James had attended, ended earlier than planned. A rally was to be held in the city centre near the Lustgarten and some of the students wanted to go. This time it was not the Nazis. It was the Social Democrats. The Social Democratic Party had the largest number of seats in the Reichstag and had been in existence for decades. Given the way the Nazis were constantly claiming centre stage and throwing their weight about, one tended to forget just how minor a party the Nazi Party was, being the ninth in size, with only twelve seats in a Reichstag of around five hundred.

It was its bullyboy tactics in the streets and its loud, ubiquitous propaganda that made it effective. It reminded James of the saying, "If you can't be right, be wrong at the top of your voice."

He only hoped that none of the students would get hurt. He knew there was no chance of the rally ending without a fracas because the Nazis would have organised the S.A. to be there in force to disrupt it. Sprained fingers, or broken knuckles, could put paid to music practice for several weeks, if not permanently. Not injuring his own hands was something he himself always had to guard against.

Preventing the opposition from making itself heard was standard practice for the S.A. Indeed, it appeared that assaulting those who disagreed with them and physically disrupting the efforts of their adversaries were part of the purpose for which it had been formed. If the Communists turned out in strength as well, a fully pitched battle was inevitable. After any demonstration these days, the following morning's newspapers regularly printed accounts of the maimed and sometimes, the dead. Casualties were so commonplace many went unaccounted and it was impossible to know exactly how many had been wounded.

Whilst waiting for Johanna, James leaned on the stairwell balustrade, watching the comings and goings in the hall below. A group of the Nazi students were hanging around, looking decidedly cocky. Other students were just walking past as if not seeing, or not wanting to see what was going on. Despite the bustle, the atmosphere felt strained.

At the far end of the hall, a group of students entered. Johanna was amongst them and James made his way through the crowd to meet her. She hurried towards him.

"Sorry I'm late. It's such a big place. Leave the lift at the wrong floor and you get lost."

"I was beginning to think you had," he laughed. "Come on let's get out of here. Coffee...? I know a good place a couple of streets away."

On the pavements outside the university the Brown Shirts were strolling up and down. They looked innocuous enough and some were joking good-naturedly, with the students.

"Mood of the moment," commented James cynically. "Best not to hang around, they don't need much notice to undergo a personality change."

"They seem to be everywhere," Johanna complained as they entered the coffee shop and seated themselves at a table.

"Well, there are seventy thousand of them and that was only at the last tally, so there are probably more by now. The number's going up all the time."

"I'll be careful not to tell Mama that. She's become allergic to them," but immediately her smile faded. "No, I shouldn't joke. It's not funny, it's serious. She really hates them. If anyone as much as mentions Hitler, she either totally clams up or goes off at the deep end."

"Any special reason, I mean apart from the obvious, that many of us have?" asked James.

"Mmm," Johanna nodded, "...it's really about her uncle, her mother's sister's husband. He's been a father to her ever since her own father died when she was still a child and she adores him." Johanna glanced at her companion, a deep concern showing in her eyes. "You see, he's Jewish and has a sister in Austria and Mama's afraid. She's read Hitler's Mein Kampf, the entire book, no skipping the nasty bits, and she truly believes Hitler absolutely means what he says, that he will do it, he will kill the Jews if he gets the chance. Papa tells her she's being ridiculous. Have you read it?" she asked.

"Well, it's only just being translated into English. I found the German hard going, apart from it being so disgusting. I had to force myself to read it and then I wondered why I was doing."

"Yes," agreed Johanna, "most people just ignore it. But one of Papa's friends, Klaus someone or other, I don't remember his name but he's very big in the Ruhr coal industry, he was at dinner with us and he admitted, at the dinner table in front of all the other guests, that he agrees with Hitler. Of course, I'm sure he couldn't have meant about the Jews, probably just about the other things and getting rid of the Communists, but this Klaus went on to say that he'd made a contribution to Nazi funds. It was a huge figure. He said he knew he may be backing the wrong horse, but there were times when one had to take a chance and this was one."

"I could tell Mama was revolted and was about to say something. Papa could tell she was as well and he gave her a certain look that he has, a sort of 'don't you dare,' warning and so Mummy didn't speak, but from that moment on, she completely and very pointedly ignored Klaus and he left early.

"Papa was fuming and after the rest of the guests had gone, there was a most fearful quarrel. He took the high minded line that it was utterly inexcusable to be rude to any guest under one's roof, but I'm sure that what made him really furious was that this Klaus fellow had only been invited in the first place because Papa was hoping to sign a contract with him and he didn't get the chance."

James sympathised. "How's everything now?" he asked.

"Not great, Mama stuck fiercely to her guns, saying that the whole business was being made worse by the shoddy values people were exhibiting, allowing money to set their standards, when they already have more than enough to live well. That was when Papa told her to look at the standard of living she enjoys and to remember that she does not have to make the money to pay for it. At that, Mama flared up and hit back, telling him that their standard of living was set by him and if she did not 'keep up appearances,' and 'conform to the standards he felt appropriate,' he would pick another row with her for 'letting him down'."

From then on, the argument sank from bad to worse and got horribly out of hand until it seemed they were arguing about everything...truly awful. Mama's parting shot was a quote from Shakespeare, "King Lear".

"I," meaning Hitler of course, "...will do such things, what they are, yet I know not, but they shall be the terrors of the earth."

"Papa didn't answer. He doesn't read Shakespeare. Mama believes Hitler is dangerous and will create terrors on earth, that he is an opportunist who does not plan, but is driven by his will and reacts to events as they arise. He takes advantage of them and when one thing leads to another and gets out of control, he does not, will not, stop and Heaven alone knows what will happen then…how and when will it all end…and how and where will we all be when it does?"

"I agree," James responded thoughtfully. "Hitler is dangerous and when he's wound up he appears to come under forces from outside his control."

"James…you don't believe do you, that he will actually try? …I mean, about killing the Jews," Johanna asked, clearly worried by what her mother had said and seeking reassurance.

"I believe he's a total fanatic," said James, "...that's his strength, but it's also his weakness, because the danger with fanaticism is that sooner or later it loses touch with reality. Even so, in a civilised country like Germany, he would never be allowed."

Johanna relaxed. "Yes, of course. You're right. He would never be allowed."

CHAPTER THIRTY-ONE

Berlin. October 1930

*K*urt was in Munich. Having left his lodgings he strode across the street without changing his pace and continued steadily in the direction of the Brown House. He was on his way to keep an appointment there, in the offices of Reichsfuhrer S.S.Himmler. He had passed this way before without much noticing the place, but the Brown House looked very different now.

A palatial building, situated on one of Munich's prestigious streets, the Briennerstrasse, it had been purchased some months ago by Adolf Hitler for use as his National Socialist Headquarters in Munich. Those responsible for renovating it had done a lavish job. The Party could afford it now thanks to certain industrialists and others who had recently decided to lend their support. The election had certainly vindicated their judgement and, thought Kurt smiling with satisfaction, put the Party detractors in their place.

The National Socialist achievement was tremendous. The Party had increased its seats from a meagre twelve to an incredible one hundred and seven. No longer the ninth and one of the smallest political parties, it was now the second largest in the Reichstag. Mind you, thought Kurt smiling again, the Propaganda had been incredible, Goebbels at his best and the people had believed him. The extravaganza effects of the theatrical displays he had conceived and stage managed had been amazing too.

Their gains had caused great excitement. Though still in first position, the Social Democratic Party had lost some support. The Communists had gained and were lying third. The battle was now well and truly on with no holds barred. Within the Party itself, there was much jockeying for position with many newcomers flocking to join. Hitler had coined a name for them, 'The

Septemberlings,' and Kurt was pleased he had made his allegiance known some weeks ago.

He had been approached by one of the officials at a Party members' meeting after a Question and Answer session during which Kurt had made his presence evident, giving his opinion on a couple of currently vexing, economic issues. Nothing much had been mentioned at that first meeting, but he had been cross-examined later with a view to being called to Munich to be offered some sort of post. Waiting for confirmation, hoping he would not be overlooked, had proved an anxious time.

At last, a few days ago a summons had arrived for Kurt to present himself at the Party Headquarters in Munich, which was why he was here now. Reaching the steps that led to its entrance, Kurt curbed his urge to take them at a run. He wanted to arrive exactly on time, not early, not late, and was tempted to glance at his watch, but deliberately did not. He had no wish to appear overeager. It was not the impression he was aiming to create. The S.S. image was to be one of total self-assurance and one never knew what casual observer might be watching.

Heinrich Himmler had been in Hitler's entourage for some time. He was not an inspiring looking man. His closely cropped hair, nondescript face, tight-lipped little mouth and small humourless eyes peering forth from behind school-marmish spectacles, did nothing to impress. Judging by appearance, Kurt had presumed him to be one of Hitler's lesser minions. It was an assessment he had been quick to revise.

It was in January nineteen twenty-nine that Heinrich Himmler had been put in charge of the S.S., a company of around three hundred men. By the end of that year it had grown in size to around a thousand and despite the stringency of Himmler's selection process, it was expanding rapidly and now numbered over three thousand.

When charged to take over and build up the organisation Himmler knew exactly what Hitler wanted. The S.A. had grown to the extent of becoming top-heavy for the Party. In it were men with ambitions and agendas of their own, men who were wayward, whose loyalty was questionable and who could cause trouble. Hitler had come to realise that if the S.A. got out of hand, it could upset his plans.

From the beginning, the S.S., the Schutz Staffel, was a security force for the protection of the Fuhrer against rival factions. He intended it to consist of men who were to be Hitler's and Hitler's alone, men who would be loyal to him unto death, obey without question, carry out his every order and become for him, in every sense, an extension of his will and self. With that aim in mind and with utter single mindedness of purpose, Himmler determinedly set out to create a body of men who would, so he envisaged, be the finest, the most elite ever to have existed. It was certainly to become one of the most ruthless and formidable.

Calculating, meticulous and avidly attentive to detail, Reichsfuhrer-S.S. Himmler was proving himself to be worthy of the task. In giving the Fuhrer what he wanted, Himmler was also serving himself, for in making the S.S. his life's work, he had found a way of fulfilling his own aspirations, giving substance to his boyish fantasies.

Himmler keenly shared Hitler's interest in the folklore of Germanic myth. Charged with taking over the S.S. he worked on the idea of embodying it into a re-creation of the ancient Germanic order of Teutonic Knights. Sharing Hitler's visions of a pure-blood Aryan race, he was determined to forge the S.S. not merely into a replica of the ancient Germanic Knights, but into a much improved version. While retaining the glamour, the regalia and traditions of the Knights of Old, it would be further transformed by selective breeding and the wonders of modern science, into the blonde beasts of Friedrich Nietzsche's supermen, a breed the likes of which the world had not yet seen.

The men at the top of this organisation, the ones chosen to serve in Hitler's entourage must not only be fine specimens of Aryan manhood but suitable in many ways. Kurt Krugenburg seemed to be the sort of man required, a good economist, idealistic and young, young enough to have his idealism shaped. The notes on him revealed that his family was of no social standing, his father being nothing more than a small factory foreman who had lost his meagre savings in the disastrous inflation of the post war years. In the case of a man like the young Krugenburg, neediness was no bad thing. It could make him keen and ambitious, traits likely to blunt or at least take the fine edge off his principles, especially if he had his sights on the von Cours girl.

Further details on the file showed the girl's family to be way above his. That also could be helpful for through her he would form good connections socially, mix with potentially useful people whilst being free from the drag of fealty that comes from longstanding attachments. Furthermore, moving in such circles, he would want to be able to hold his own, thus making him even more susceptible to the lure of money. Yes, he looked like being a good choice.

For the post in question, Reichsfuhrer-S.S. Heinrich Himmler, was looking for a man capable of performing specific functions, one of which was to ferret out information and report to his chief everything it was in his interest to know, not least who could be trusted both inside and outside the Party. Himmler was fanatically tidy minded and had all the information he received carefully filed away.

Nothing succeeds like success and the electoral results were bringing considerable funds into the Party's coffers, but there was more where that came from, much more and Himmler intended to get to it. Adolf had his own financial advisors, but Himmler wanted to be in on everything, to know exactly where the money was coming from, what schemes were in the offing and how much was being paid, to whom, by whom and why and being an economist, young Krugenburg seemed just the man for the task.

Yes, knowledge is power and Himmler was resolved on becoming very powerful indeed.

The interview came to an end. It had gone well. Kurt had not been nervous, but as he left the Brown House he was glad it was over and was thoroughly relieved. Not only the money, but the position to which he had been appointed, exceeded anything he had expected and he was confident he could carry out what had been outlined to him. It fitted in with his personal plans and he had accepted straightaway.

Thank goodness, he had not mentioned any of this to Johanna, not even about his Party membership. It would have been unfortunate indeed given Himmler's requirement of total confidentiality. While working in economic and financial matters, always observing, eyes open, ears pricked, Kurt was to forage for information and report on all manner of people, on several aspects of their lives, their businesses, finances, political affiliations, even their affairs of heart, or as it had been phrased, their sexual activities. That was what being a V-Mann, a Verbindungsmann or Vertrauensmann, an intermediary or a trusted agent, was about, acting as a contact, keeping things secret, or as Himmler preferred to say, private. It would entail listening in on conversations not intended for his hearing. It would of course, prevent others from keeping their affairs private, but Kurt had no qualms because it was for the protection of the Party and as had been explained, the knowledge gleaned, being confidential, would be in safe hands.

His cover was to act as financial advisor to a Munich based industrial concern. He would be on its payroll and would put in a token amount of time for the firm in question, but the true purpose of this was to give Kurt a pretext to travel to Munich and report his findings. It suited Kurt perfectly. Disillusioned with his studies, he had taken a part time post in a large financial institution, but with no strings to pull, he was having to prove himself and was still on a low rung of their ladder. The money that was now being advanced to him was a fortune in comparison to his present pay and indications were that provided he gave satisfaction more benefits would follow.

He still had to provide further information about himself, details of his ancestry for three generations back, medical certificates and the like, all of which had to be checked and assessed prior to his appointment being formally confirmed, but Kurt was confident there would be no problem.

It had long been clear to him that if he wanted to get anywhere, he would need to make his own way. Given his intentions regarding Johanna, success in his professional life was a priority. The auspices now looked good. The S.S. was to be crucial to the creation of Hitler's Third Reich and to be in at the beginning was a decided advantage. He would have much preferred to be open with Johanna, but that must wait until the time was right. The position he had now been offered put any idea of telling her out of the question, but he need not be concerned. The strict secrecy demanded by the very nature of the work, guaranteed his privacy and, in any case, it was not necessary for her to know everything. The arrangements now in place gave him freedom of movement, plus a plausible explanation for any questions asked and Kurt decided to worry no more about it.

He had not seen much of Johanna during the last few weeks but he would make up for it now. Cushioned in its black velvet box in a nearby jeweller's window, was a large solitaire diamond ring. Kurt checked again the bulge of the wallet in his inner pocket, opened the shop door and strode in. He had no doubts about Johanna's acceptance of his proposal. Her parents had been making increasing difficulties for her lately. They had a different suitor and other plans lined up for their daughter. Johanna was having none of it. Her attitude was that she was certainly not going to be talked into marrying someone, "…nice enough and wealthy, but a wimp," which was how she described her parents' candidate. Not wanting to hear what she said, her parents were simply not listening.

"Well, they listen, but afterwards it's exactly as though I've never spoken," she complained. "They organise everything their way and when I don't go along with it, they blame me for creating what they call, socially embarrassing situations. It's ridiculous."

Kurt knew they were pressurising her. A proposal from him would strengthen her hand. They could object, of course. But they could not stop her saying yes to him and in a few months' time she would be twenty-one and have reached the age of consent. He would bide his time, taking care not to mention the Party and keep out of discussions if the topic arose.

Once they were married Johanna would, sooner or later, see things his way. Meanwhile, he told himself, he had better concentrate on seeing things Reichfuhrer S.S.Himmler's way.

James was uneasy. Although it was only a few blocks away from the fashionable Kurfurstendamm, the alley he had just entered looked littered and rundown. At its far end, a crowd had gathered probably waiting for the free meal van. Mostly they were just hanging around, but one could never be sure. Taking no chances he rerouted his steps. Disturbances erupted all too quickly these days. Unemployment figures were soaring again and the queues at the soup kitchens and charity hand-out shops had lengthened.

In the run up to the September elections, the brawls had been continuous. He had presumed they would stop once the voting was over, but not so, and demonstrations, protest marches and the growing numbers of S.A., forever on the prowl and practising their pugilistic skills, made one wary even to walk the streets.

The election results had taken everyone unawares. The Nazi success was staggering.

Sadly, it had surged to their heads, without satisfying their lust. For their opponents, it was a crushing blow. The violence of the S.A. was growing worse. The day the Reichstag reconvened there had been brawling both in and outside the building as Hitler and his cohorts, defying the ban on wearing uniforms, arrived to take their seats. Further destruction was wreaked, when a group of new Nazi deputies, presumably excited at the idea of taking their seats expressed their elation on their way down the Leipzigerstrasse, by smashing the windows of several shops they believed to be Jewish. Although this took place in broad daylight with shoppers going about their business as usual, not one of those present admitted to having seen it take place. No need to ask why, they feared to speak. As if afflicted by a contagion for which there was no cure, many city dwellers appeared to have become fatalistic about the Nazis' loutish ways, adopting an attitude, 'these things happen'. The victims were left to clean up as best they could.

It was shortly after lunchtime and James was none the happier for being late for his rehearsal. The tram in which he had been travelling had come to a sudden halt, not an uncommon occurrence these days. This time the trouble was due to nothing more threatening than damage to the tracks at one of the crossings, caused by the supporting wooden blocks having been pulled out for use as firewood. It was in its own way, the kind of incident that encouraged tolerance of the Brown Shirts, since they would act 'the good guys' and, any excuse for a fracas, would beat up the pillagers if they caught them at it.

People were sick of the ruined economy, of useless politicians, of reparations to foreigners, of the mess the country was in, of the jobless roaming the streets, of the crime and violence and Communist threat and, of having to climb down off trams and walk. Many would be glad for some strong man to get to the front, crack the hard whip and get things back in line and the sentiment that maybe Adolph Hitler should be given his chance, was being heard more often.

James reached the Concert Hall. As he made his way to the auditorium he heard the discord of instruments being tuned. The effect on him, as always, was instantaneous, sweeping him into a realm in which brawling in the streets, the Depression and the Nazi success it had helped to spawn, did not exist.

Despite the economic situation, there were still those with money to spend in the freedom of pleasures for which the capital was celebrated. The Weimar Constitution was known to be the most liberal in Europe. Nightlife thrived, cabarets and nightclubs continued to be crowded, concerts were played in packed halls and Berlin was still Berlin.

But some things were not the same. Two or three years ago, despite the all too obvious problems, the general atmosphere had been one of spontaneity, of easily changing moods reflecting genuine feeling, authentically expressing the ebb and flow of energies and life's response to what was going on around. It had now given way to one more guarded and contrived. James had noticed it on his return from Biarritz shortly before the mid-September election. Too much was happening too quickly to keep abreast of where it was leading and there was tension in the city. The political instability, unemployment, financial uncertainties, the ruin and unrest, each one another blow upon the bruises of Versailles could probably, each one on its own, have been dealt with.

Cumulatively, they were to prove a lethal brew.

James had known before leaving for the concert in London that the government was in trouble. The Social Democratic Chancellor Herman Muller had fallen from office in March. He had been regarded as weak and General Kurt Schleicher, an Army man, a powerful and manipulative string-puller, influential with old President Hindenburg, had decided to tumble him. The Army had its own candidate lined up and Schleicher went to work. He engineered the situation nicely and Muller 'resigned'. Heinrich Brunning, the Army's choice, then became Chancellor. He had shown great courage as a Commander during the war and had the support of President Hindenburg. Brunning's, 'stick to your guns, die on your feet' attitude was just what was needed...so the Army thought.

Brunning, an austere bachelor, was decisive by nature and unbending in his ways and his plans for the economy soon earned him the title of, 'The Hunger Chancellor'. Ingmar, still endeavouring to introduce a political flavour to her soirees, invited him one evening as her guest of honour. The occasion was not a success. Brunning's manner gave the impression of his not having known what he had let himself in for and he stayed "no time at all', so Ingmar later complained.

Ingmar was not the only one Brunning had disappointed. The Army's optimism that he would settle the political situation was short lived. During the summer, when his austerity measures had not been accepted, Brunning's unyielding rigidity was to prove disastrous. He refused to compromise or back down and when in July, the Reichstag obtained a majority vote against his policies, Brunning, still determined to get his own way invoked Article 48.

Article 48 of the Weimar Constitution allowed the Chancellor to call upon the President to sanction the dissolution of parliament and to implement his programme by Presidential Decree. Flying in the face of the Reichstag's majority vote against him, Brunning did exactly that, resulting in Parliament being dismissed and for fresh elections - the ones just held – to take place in September.

So it was that when returning from Biarritz, James had found the city in the throes of election fever. The campaigning had been violent, but expectations had been that once the votes were counted, the fighting and the shouting would die down and the cadence of daily life resumed once more. Sadly this was not to be. The increased power the Nazis had gained in the elections had made such hopes naive.

Article 48 was to become notorious for causing what it had been intended to prevent and Brunning's action was later to be seen as the first step on the road taking Germany into the trap of the Nazi Dictator and ultimate perdition.

His invocation of Article 48 undermined Democracy by allowing the decisions of government to be subject to the senilities of the old and failing one-time Field Marshall Hindenburg, now President Hindenburg, who was influenced by and prey to the persuasions of others who had agendas of their own.

It thus prepared the way for Adolph Hitler to seize power.

Marked by the beat of booted tread, rallied by the coarse discord of raucous marching songs, a monstrous force was now set forth, determined to destroy all in its way

CHAPTER THIRTY-TWO

Lancashire, December 1930

On reaching London after leaving Bude, Claire had tried to contact him but there had been no reply. When she tried again it was their caretaker who answered. No, the gentleman was not there. He thought he had gone away, but yes if he made contact he would pass on the Post Office box-number she had left.

Weeks passed and no word came. Claire assumed that freed from what he had called his difficulty, Bude was back in Rumania. The silence was a relief. She had no wish to see him. There was nothing to be gained.

Collecting her mail one day, she was surprised to find an official looking envelope awaiting her. It bore an impressive crest, with a motto in Rumanian. The embossed sheet of vellum it contained bore the black ink signature of Bude's father. He considered it incumbent upon him, so he wrote, to inform her of her situation and trusted the following facts would make her position clear.

Not having been granted the necessary dispensation permitting a Catholic to enter into marriage with a person of a faith other than his own, the ceremony in which his son had taken part was not recognised by the Catholic Church. It had therefore decreed no marriage existed.

Given also that no civil marriage had been entered into and, in the absence of legal impediment, the wedding of his son would have taken place by the time she received this letter.

Claire stared at the stiff leaf of parchment gripped in her hand. The sheer audacity of what she read beggared belief. Spurred by strong impulse she crossed the room, dropped the missive into the empty grate and reached for the matches. Abruptly she stopped, stooped, and retrieved it. To her mind the content of the letter was incredible but at least it spoke for itself, was proof enough that her marriage ceremony had taken place and having sealed and locked it away, she went to wash her hands. She wanted nothing further to do with him. Betrayed...cheated...deceived. Emotions hard to handle combined. "Marry me", his telegram had read. She believed she had...and had tried to make her marriage work.

Other than refusing to go through with the wedding when the registrar did not arrive on time, what could she have done? She tried to remember, but her recollections were as fragments of a dream she could not properly recall nor piece together. Not surprisingly, for shock can do strange things. A trace of irony touched her lips...a short, mirthless laugh escaped her...her marriage, the one that never was. Looking back upon what had occurred it was best regarded as a lesson learned.

She had known her love for James would never change. Despite her endeavours to put him from her mind her feelings for him had remained the same.

Gradually, week by week, her strength of character came to the fore. Pulling the threads of her life together, she obtained a post as buyer for the fashion section of a large department store and recommenced her studies in dress design, taking up where she had left off when Bude continued to object to her idea of starting a business of her own.

Maria, an older woman who now worked with her was French and since becoming a widow, had often toyed with the idea of returning to Paris. From the way Claire spoke about the city Maria could tell she had enjoyed living there and a few weeks ago had suggested Claire go back with her. As she had said, it offered more opportunities, better work experience and was the very heart of fashion.

Maria knew the city well and had relatives there. At first Claire was undecided, but influenced by Maria's confidence and enthusiasm, had seriously considered the idea. After all, Paris was not exactly a strange place to her. She had lived there with Bude, but might not therein lie the rub.

"Why miss this opportunity to find out?" Maria insisted.

So it was that Claire made enquiries and renewed a few of the contacts she already had. After past mishaps and mistakes she was doubly cautious and as replies filtered in, she and Maria vetted them carefully, paying more heed to possible drawbacks than to the benefits. For Claire, location was high on the list of priorities. It was early December before a promising offer arrived and she had until the end of January to make up her mind. Now that the move may actually take place, she decided to talk it over with Anna, for as experience had taught her, look before you leap.

Maria intended to spend Christmas with relatives in her home village close to Paris and Anna had pressed Claire to stay with her at Ardleagh. Not knowing where James would be Claire had hesitated. However, when Anna rang again saying James would be in Berlin over Christmas and, given that her rooms were far flung from the main house, Claire could keep her visit private, she had agreed.

Mid December and Claire boarded the train to take her to Lancashire. Sitting in a corner seat she listened to the steady drumming of the wheels, watching through half closed eyes, the landscape flashing by. The resolute stance she had taken regarding the breakup of her marriage had strengthened her and with perceptions now un-blinkered, her attitudes were different too. Nonetheless, the sheer suddenness with which all had taken place had shaken her and, Ardleagh, its unchanging peace and sense of timelessness, was once again tugging at her heart. Was returning a wise move? It was sure to resurrect images and emotions, best not recalled?

This once, just this once more, she promised herself. Soon Anna would be retired and pensioned and would probably come to live with her. When that happened, the shutters would close on all that Ardleagh had been for her, leaving only treasured images of its loveliness and James.

The train pulled to a halt at Crewe station. Doors opened and draughts of cold air swept through the carriage bearing specks of grit and soot and the acrid smell of ashes from the engine's smouldering coal. Whistles hooted, loud announcements blared making themselves heard above the clatter and the din, and vendors, their trolleys laden with sandwiches, mugs of steaming tea and newspapers, called loudly from the platforms.

Soon they were on their way again. Claire opened the newspaper she had just bought. It was not a large headline, only a minor one some way down a middle page, but it caught her eye immediately.

"Spain. Attempted coup. Uprising at Jaca. Rebels executed."

The report that followed stated,

"Captain Fermin Galan and Lieutenant Garcia Hernandez, self-confessed Republicans and conspirators in the plot of San Sebastian where the coup was hatched, have suffered the ultimate penalty. Galan and Hernandez, two young Army officers in the garrison of Jaca, a small town in the Pyrenees, rose prematurely on the twelfth of December ahead of the intended day of a national uprising involving several garrisons across the country, all of which had been organised to rise simultaneously three days later.

Details of the plot, hatched at San Sebastian have now been uncovered and investigations have revealed that its signatories planned to overthrow the Monarchy preparatory to setting up a provisional government and declaring Spain a Republic. Several of the rebels have been captured and are now in prison awaiting trial for treason. Their defence is that King Alphonse X111 contravened the Constitution when setting up the Military Dictatorship and the appointment of Primo de Rivera was illegal.

There is widespread sympathy in the Army and also from the public for the two young officers who within two days, were summarily tried and shot. The speed and ruthlessness of their execution, far from having put a stop to the rebellion, has poured fuel on its flames. The King is under further fire for not having exercised his prerogative of mercy for the executed men and there are riots, demonstrations and protests in their favour in Madrid and across the country. The situation remains extremely explosive."

The report went on to say, "Fearing a serious backlash the Army cooperated in making further arrests of those said to be involved. Tempers have heightened and demands for the release of those imprisoned continue to excite revolt. Across several sections of society, agitation for reform is gaining serious momentum and is likely to increase. It is now being questioned whether the Monarchy can survive."

Claire laid the newspaper aside. "A quiet Christmas," Anna had said. This would be no quiet Christmas. With so much trouble in Madrid, Amelia was sure to be arriving soon and she wondered if the news had reached the Hall. She glanced again at the paper lying on the seat. If Amelia came, would Leonora come also and if there were to be a family reunion, might it be that James would return as well?

In fact, at that moment all was quiet at Ardleagh. The inhabitants of the Hall were indeed oblivious of what was happening in Spain. Unless Amelia arrived, they were likely to remain so, for the Earl took pains to avoid all knowledge of unrest in that country. Uneasy that they may prelude his sister's return, he steered clear of matters concerning its troubles. As for Lady Margaret, she found most of what was in the newspapers depressing and had not bothered to read them at all of late.

In truth, she was taking scant interest in anything these days. She had not been well for the last few months. Frederick was no better than usual and no festivities had been planned for Christmas. The head gardener, as he always did, had made sure a large Christmas tree was standing in its usual place in the middle of the hall but it was not properly decorated and as Cook had said, "It looked more brave than cheerful."

Lady Margaret's doctor was sympathetic. He diagnosed her condition as 'dispirited'. Actually, her Ladyship was not so much dispirited as disgruntled. She had been hiding her resentment even from herself, for far too long. It was not a sentiment women of affluence were supposed to feel, let alone express. Its causes were not hard to find. Her husband's discontent, the unending boredom of her dull, daily round, the effort to keep smiling, at what? It had all become too much. She had been short changed. All that her upbringing had promised and primed her for, where was it now? It had vanished, faded from its one-time vibrancy to a pale, insipid nothing, like the colour in the drawing room's long, velvet curtains which she should have had replaced months ago. Her present lifestyle, if she could call it that, was a mere crumble of what it once had been.

It was not that she had not tried to do something about it, to devise other diversions in its stead. She had, Heaven knows. It was what the gathering to hear James' concert broadcast live from London, had been about. But the celebration had not been as she had planned. It had fallen flat, embarrassingly so, not at all as she had hoped. Her friends could not be described as music-lovers and the symphony he had played was one none of them had heard before. Its reception, in every sense, had been poor, but she could hardly turn it off.

There simply was no point in striving to match the elegance and gaiety of the Edwardian era, to live again the pleasures of The Season when the privileged of Society had descended upon London and laid claim to it as their own. Nonetheless, Margaret could not stop remembering that leisured age of time-honoured pursuits, when the plans they made for their delight-filled days had been as patterned and prescribed as the planets in the sky.

Needless to say, she had not dropped into this mental state overnight. Her mood had been brewing for some time, but the drop that had made her cup run o'er was her discovery that Frederick, without so much as a whisper to her, had put their Park Lane house on the market. Admittedly, they had scarcely used it in recent years, but that was part of the problem because they could have done. Even so, it had still been there like a beacon that beckoned, sustaining the hope they might do so again. Their continuing possession of it had been as a pledge to the future that things could still come right. Its sale would be a cruel admission that they never would.

"He really ought to have discussed it with me first," she muttered, but then again, perhaps she should have guessed from the way he had grumbled the last time they were in London. The jostle and the crowding, the streets choked with noisy horseless carriages, the nasty new buildings in Park Lane itself, cheek by jowl alongside the once gracious old homes, had upset him. He had even refused to go into the Park. No longer able to ride his horse there, he was damned if he would be wheeled around in it.

Despondently Margaret sat in her dressing gown, jaundicing her dejected mood still further with one miserable thought after another. She was also anxious about James living in Berlin. This dreadful economic Depression was causing further trouble in that German city and that man Hitler, fighting with the Communists, was stirring more unrest. Perhaps if she phoned James again, she could persuade him to come home for Christmas and then get him to stay.

Reading of the conflicts in the aftermath of the Jaca uprising, James was concerned. Whatever the measures taken in Spain, any restoration of calm in that country was never more than a remission from violence, reason being that the underlying cause of it, the existing injustice, remained potent as ever and always flared again.

"Plot of San Sebastian...Attempt to overthrow the Monarchy."

"So that's what the hustling in cliques had been about when they had been there 'on holiday' in the summer, Raimundo trying to uncover what was going on and who was involved...on holiday, my foot," exclaimed James.

Aware of Alva's over-weaning confidence in the Army and his insistence that his wife and daughter should stay put, James was apprehensive. Knowing that Amelia wanted to get out of Spain with Leonora but was now financially dependent on her husband, he decided to send her and Leonora a Christmas gift of tickets and travel expenses and invite them to Ardleagh. Better still, he also would go home for Christmas and as his mother wished, try to make peace with his father. His career had taken off well enough by now for him not to be afraid of turning down a request to play in case he was not asked again.

James was becoming jaundiced by events in Germany. The Nazis' success had certainly turned their heads. Their rough-neck behaviour, booing when he played a piece by Mendelssohn, a Jew, and hanging around in groups afterwards, waiting their chance to deliver a few punches, had left him thinking he had really had enough.

His mother had written again, asking him to visit and it would be good to get some life back into the old house, throw a few parties, arrange a Boxing Day meet for the hunt and invite a few old timers round for drinks and to foot follow. It would need a little organising, but if Amelia and Leonora came, they would help to get things back the way they used to be, but even as the thought occurred, James knew it could not be, not for him.

For him...things could never be, the way they used to be, not without Claire.

Until a year ago he had at least known from her appearance in the magazines, that she was safe and well, but there had been no sign of her for months, nor any mention of the photographer. Amelia still scoured the glossy magazines, but in vain and he had no idea where she was.

He had met up with one or two women down the years, but doing so had only further proved to him, there was no woman he wanted other than Claire and James vowed, no matter what, if ever he found her again, he would never let her go.

At last the train shunted into Manchester's Piccadilly station and Claire took a taxi for the remainder of her journey. From what she saw when passing though the outskirts of the towns, life for the Lancashire workers was as gruelling as ever. The rebellious, optimistic verve that had carried the workers forward in the year after the war had spent itself in the struggles since and was now wiped out by the Depression. In the harshness of that Lancashire winter of 1930 two million were out of work and the unemployed were again living hand to mouth, week in, week out as they so often had.

The miles slipped past and the landscape became familiar. Skirting the village, the taxi took the lane Claire knew so well, leading to the Hall. Yes, there it was, visible on the rise beyond. The car drew up beside the narrow gate. Reliable as ever, Anna had left it unlocked. For a little while after the taxi had driven away, Claire stood, the wind ruffling her dark hair, flurrying the velvet of her hat, tugging the folds of her coat. The years had only served to enhance her. She was older, more mature, the same, only more so, more womanly, more self-possessed.

She took the path that led to the river. All was exactly as in her dreams.

Her parting from Bude was final and in the months that had followed, she had found lying in the emptiness where her marriage had once been, the freedom to be herself. Freedom, that raises many questions, faces us with many choices. The life she had lived these past years, posing for the camera, pleasing the Image Maker, had been artificial and at times it seemed she had begun to metamorphose into the artificial also. Image, not Substance, and when the photos were developed and printed, she had looked at them and thought, 'That's me' and others had looked and said, "That's her." But that was not true. The photos were only a reflection of a persona that had little or nothing to do with whom she was. The clothes, the beautiful creations she had modelled, were no more than the wardrobe of an actress in some fictional stage-drama, acting out a character no longer existing once the curtain had come down. While married, she had tried to be the person her husband wanted and while he was reflecting her back upon herself, she had been. When that reflection was no longer, and the image was no more, had she known, the woman she had become.

Questions needing answers, uncertainties for which decisions must be made, she must think, make up her mind. As often in moments such as these, James' grand-father's quotation from the Bible, 'The Prophets', Amos, came to mind, "It is as when a man escapes the lion's mouth…"

"It's telling those who do not do as they should," he had explained, "…that when we run away from our problems, detour to avoid them or even veer off track, whichever way we choose to go, we will continue to find the same difficulties confronting us, in different situations and in different guise, until we learn to face and overcome them…for we are each on our own journey, each with our own purpose to fulfil, our own problems to resolve and in doing so, master the lessons we are here to learn."

And failure is not a wasted exercise, nor blameworthy of itself. It also brings its benefits.

"Experience always leaves behind a lantern, to light our forward path."

The Hall grounds were extensive. Following a little used byway, pictures from the past came back in vivid clarity. Recollections fresh as yesterday returned as if her efforts not to think had served to etch the memories more indelibly upon her mind, and she could no longer push away her longing, nor refuse it recognition. Thoughts and images, the ache and tenderness of all she had been trying to forget, had endured unaltered, untouched by time and the passing of the years.

It was late into the afternoon. She stood by the river where it bordered the wood, where its waters flowed still and deep. Beyond the old beech trees crowding the far bank, the setting sun of the December day hung poised before its last descent, a rose gold orb set in the darkening sky.

It was a profound happiness to be here in this calm and tranquil place, to listen to the silence save for the murmur of the river's flow, the flutter of a wing, to sense the stillness of its quiet, eternal beauty. A watching blackbird blinked an enquiring golden eye, then gliding low on jet black wings, was lost in the rustle of a rhododendron's shining leaves.

She turned, retracing her steps, savouring the pleasure of treading once again these ways and winding paths where in the shaded places, the hoar frost had stayed throughout the day, to crisp the ground and edge each blade and leaf with white and lacy trim.

Years ago, she had walked away from here, determined to make something more, something better, of herself and of her life. She had believed she could build a new life by abandoning the old. But as she now knew, our past remains a part of us forever and we build our future by holding to the riches it has bequeathed, letting go the parts that perhaps should not have been, secure in the knowledge that the lessons it has taught us are the ones that it was destined we should learn.

She was now able to embrace all that had shaped her life, the facts as they had been and lived on still, in the woman she had become, and deep inside she knew that if James came home, she would no longer avoid him or hide herself away.

Nearing the gateway in the boundary wall that marked the grounds from the gardens of the house, Claire looked back upon the years that she had been away, the years of striving, striving to become...what? To 'better herself', to make more of herself than she already was, to become...?

So, what had she? ...What was she to become? Strangely, as she reflected Claire no longer saw the word "Become" as one word, but as two, "Be" and "Come" and heard the voice of inner wisdom say,

"No, no more striving, only Be. Be still and allow to Come, what will."

Pushing open the gate Claire entered a realm of possibilities unknown...the uncertainties of what may be.

And wisdom's words remained unchanged, "Be still and allow to Come, what will."

★ ★ ★

List of Acknowledgements to the following Authors:

Fischer, Klaus P.: *Nazi Germany, A New History.*

Bullock, Alan: *Hitler, A Study in Tyranny*

Shirer, William L.: *The Rise and Fall of the Third Reich.*

Shirer, William L.: *A Berlin Diary.*

Padfield, Peter: *Himmler.*

Francois-Poncet, Andre: *The Fateful Years.*

Gilbert, Martin: *Kristallnacht, A Prelude to Destruction.*

Klemperer, Victor: *I Shall Bear Witness, the Diaries of Victor Klemperer 1933-1941.*

Klemperer, Victor: *To The Bitter End, the Diaries of Victor Klemperer 1942-45.*

Engelmann, Bernt: *In Hitler's Germany.*

Cornwell, John: *Hitler's Pope, The Secret History of Pius XII.*

Clay, Catrine and Leapman, Michael: *Master Race, The Lebensborn Experiment in Nazi Germany.*

Evans, Richard J.: *The Third Reich in Power.*

Thomas, Hugh: *The Spanish Civil War.*

Preston, Paul: *The Spanish Holocaust, Inquisition and Extermination in Twentieth-Century Spain.*

Preston, Paul: *The Coming of the Spanish Civil War.*

Preston, Paul: *The Spanish Civil War, Reaction, Revolution and Revenge*

Preston, Paul: *Revolution and War in Spain, 1931-1939. Edited by Paul Preston.*

Preston, Paul: *Franco.*

Carr, Raymond: *The Spanish Tragedy.*

Jackson, Gabriel: *A Concise History of the Spanish Civil War.*